A Long Time Coming

Lorna Brockway Lieske

Seven Sisters Publishing
Reading is heavenly...

No part of this publication may be reproduced in whole or in part, or stored in a retrieval system, or transmitted in any form or by any means, electronic, mechanical, photocopying, recording, or otherwise, without prior written permission of the publisher.

This is a work of fiction. Other than historical references, names, characters, places, and incidents either are the product of the author's imagination or are used fictitiously, and any resemblance to actual persons, business establishments, events, or locales is entirely coincidental.

A Long Time Coming
Copyright © 2014 Lorna Brockway Lieske
All rights reserved.
ISBN:0692334785
ISBN-13:9780692334782

FOR MY SISTER, CARLA.

SUMMER EVENINGS AMONG THE FIREFLIES,
WEAVING "STORY-COME-TRUE" ADVENTURES
FOR NEIGHBORHOOD PALS,
LINGER AS VIVID REMINDERS
OF THE HALCYON DAYS OF CHILDHOOD.

THANKS FOR SHARING MY LOVE OF STORYTELLING!

AND WITH SINCERE THANKS TO CATE,
WITHOUT WHOSE HELP AND ENCOURAGEMENT
THIS BOOK WOULD BE MOLDERING ON MY COMPUTER
AND LANGUISHING IN MY HEART!

CONTENTS

Chapter One	1
Chapter Two	14
Chapter Three	33
Chapter Four	49
Chapter Five	79
Chapter Six	98
Chapter Seven	122
Chapter Eight	146
Chapter Nine	163
Chapter Ten	176
Chapter Eleven	204
Chapter Twelve	225
Chapter Thirteen	248
Chapter Fourteen	277
Chapter Fifteen	304

Part One:
Emergence
Autumn, 1916

CHAPTER ONE

I.

The first time I saw Tully's Cove was through the soot-streaked window of a northbound train. Driven by a sense of anticipation I didn't entirely understand, I had anxiously followed our progress as the passenger car rocked and creaked like a ship adrift at sea in its unflagging journey over the tracks taking us to our new home. The terrain had grown rather nondescript as we advanced but I was transfixed nonetheless, using one of the lace-trimmed handkerchiefs given to me as a farewell gift to wipe away most of the interior grime that clouded my view and trying to ignore the face staring back at me that was as ordinary as the landscape on the other side of the murky glass through which I peered.

It had rained most of the trip – the cold, penetrating drizzle of autumn that makes the world smell of musky loam as it droops in dispirited surrender to the inevitability of winter. I love that smell but after being cooped up in a dank and musty train for three days I must admit I now have a rather claustrophobic reaction to it.

Rachel also was feeling the effects of our confinement. I could tell because although preening was second-nature to Rachel it had taken on an uncharacteristic nervous urgency as she struggled to maintain the smug dignity of a worldliness she was wearing just for the occasion of her first excursion by rail. It was a battle she waged valiantly against an enemy who attacked with equal vigor on two fronts; with dampness that wilted her tightly wound auburn curls and tedium that threatened to lull her to sleep and put even more wrinkles into the skirt she tried to keep neatly straightened beneath her. Determined to remain the epitome of what she perceived as ladylike, Rachel had spent the bulk of our journey tucking stray wisps of lank auburn hair under the lip of the secondhand hat she had successfully refurbished into something only slightly less than stylish and was at that moment trying for what seemed the hundredth time to urge life back into what had begun the day as a crisp, well-starched traveling ensemble.

Oblivious to the battle raging between Rachel and the elements, our father dozed noisily in his seat across the aisle from us. Striving for purchase in the unforgiving, narrow seat he kept shifting his rather bulky frame as he slept; long legs stretched out as far as possible under the seat in front of him, head tilted back at a precarious angle that made his unruly moustache even more reminiscent of a shaving brush and promised to give him a serious neck crick upon waking. Beside him sat our mother, the picture of tranquility, placidly watching the passing terrain and unobtrusively observing Rachel and me in the window's reflection with what can best be described as "cautious admiration." Mother was a slight, quiet woman who wore her advancing years gracefully and sought to engender in her daughters something akin her own quiet acquiescence to the realities of life. A kind and sensitive parent closely attuned to every nuance of her children's personalities, she was a person of strong character, deep-rooted beliefs, and unswerving common sense.

Sitting there watching my parents, I found myself once again marveling at the forces of nature that had drawn them together. As a child my father had frightened me. He was mercilessly disciplined and driven. As a result, he also was virtually unapproachable; a formidable obstacle to be surmounted only by way of the gentle woman who held his heart. As with most people, the years were having their way with him as he mellowed somewhat with age and yet he remained a mountainous, precipice-ridden presence. Dynamic, intelligent, and committed to his profession, he often came across as aloof and was – to the child I had been and the woman I had become – a person with whom conversation was difficult. The reality that two such dramatically different personalities shared a deep and abiding love for one another served to fortify my belief that there must surely be a God in strong command of the human drama and that such things were not left to mere chance or passing human fancy.

Once again reassured, I refocused my diligence as our journey drew to a close and the train bearing us on our way rumbled through rolling coastal acres dotted with farms and around the southern periphery of the city itself.

The town of Tully's Cove in reality was quite some distance inland of the cove from which it derived its name. Much of the local coastline and the cove itself were privately owned and shrouded in tales of questionable, if not outright illegal activity. But its colorful past served only to endear the region to me more and over the months that lay ahead I would become an eager listener when waylaid by one of the town's elder statesmen and regaled with legends of pirates, patriots, and related nineteenth century intrigue. It was to me a charming place; a town of nearly seven thousand, steeped in history and neatly arranged with the town square at its heart and streets radiating out from that point like the spokes of a wheel. I found the topography of the town creative and picturesque but Father was quick to point out what he perceived to be a major flaw in such a plan since only four streets ran directly north-south and east-west, with the rest being some combination thereof. What to me was charming was to my father totally illogical and, as a result, difficult to navigate.

The colorful tapestry of Tully's Cove had been enhanced over the years by the fact that an intriguing minority of the area's population consisted of what respectable folk called "Remittance Men." The term had been coined to describe young men from prominent families in Europe who had been forced from their homelands by some disgrace they had brought upon their kin and now lived quite fashionably in America – or farther north in Canada – by means of a periodic remittance from home. Henry Branson, the cove's most sedulous financial speculator, had been banished to the obscurity of New England by some youthful indiscretion, as had Nigel Pennington and Charles Morris who now invested themselves in nothing more productive than endless hours in the gentlemen's parlor at the Blue Heron Inn on the outskirts of town. Although Tully's Cove met the obscurity requirement of most remittance settlements, it was beyond dispute that its backwater quality failed to measure up to the social preferences of these fallen souls; the Cove's small contingent undoubtedly accepted it as the site of their banishment due to its proximity to Portland to the north and Boston to the south, both less than a day's journey by rail.

Over the months that followed we were to learn much more about these questionable gentlemen for, even in the infancy of a progressive new century, they often were the topic of conversation when ladies of quality gathered over their tea. But most of what was shared was pure hearsay and wild speculation as the majority of the so-called Remittance Men lived out their expatriation quietly and did not pursue their private vices more openly than anyone else in Tully's Cove. Regardless of that fact, however, in light of the war raging in Europe disdain and disapproval from the community festered and grew increasingly malignant for it was observed that honor – if they had any at all – should compel them to return to their homeland in this time of crisis and yet throughout the years of conflict ahead only one relinquished the safety of his New England exile.

II.

Rachel was first to alight from the train, hastily smoothing her crumpled skirt as she descended to the platform. Mother followed, and when I would have paused to allow Father to precede me he waved me forward with a persuasively curt gesture.

It was cold standing there beside the train as a brisk wind had risen off the coast to perform a bone-chilling duet with the penetrating autumn rain. Mother and Rachel quickly retreated to the shelter of the welcoming brick station house but I remained outside, filling my lungs with the cold, moist air, drawing refreshment from it after the stuffy confinement of the train. It was only late afternoon but lamps had been lit early due to the weather, flooding the station with light and spilling the inviting glow out onto the adjoining passenger platform. I stood there for a few moments after Father had followed our luggage inside, adrift in my own thoughts and watching the rain turn to quicksilver as it reflected the light from the lamps within.

Even at that early juncture I felt as if I were on the brink of some enormously significant discovery. Tully's Cove had intrigued me from the first time I had heard the name and located it on one of Father's maps as our imminent destination. It was as if here lay the threshold across which I must pass in order to uncover the ultimate pattern of my life. As a result of that persistent feeling of expectation, I had approached our move with eagerness and each facet of the transition had been a bona fide event. I felt neither sad nor apprehensive about being uprooted from the only place I had ever called home; change was beckoning me and I was eager to respond.

As I entered the station Father was being greeted by a rather portly gentleman in his late fifties whose somewhat threadbare suit coat and poorly executed bow tie had garnered the attention of a less than discretely disapproving

Rachel. Upon joining the group the man was introduced to me as Eli Thornton, caretaker of Tully's Cove's most impressive religious edifice, Christ Congregational Church, of which my father had been called to be Pastor and for which purpose we had come to New England.

Mr. Thornton had been extolling the virtues of a northern autumn when my appearance interrupted him but he continued nonplussed after cursory introductions had been made.

"Ah-yuh, we may be a bit soggy come September, but you'll find nothin' finer than a New England autumn, I can promise you that."

Mr. Thornton's ruddy complexion grew rosier as he spoke – whether from self-consciousness or his obvious love for his home state I couldn't tell – and he grasped his threadbare lapels as if in need of a home for his large workworn hands. His demeanor and the musical lilt of his New England accent were charming. As he spoke he transformed words like "September" and "finer" into "Septembuh" and "finuh," and the punctuation of his conversation with the characteristic New England "ah-yuh" was delightful. I was eager to hear more but Father was anxious to be moving along and adeptly turned the conversation to the business at hand.

"Martha, Mr. Thornton has been telling us that Christ Church lies on the northeast side of town overlooking the Cove. That should give us a lovely view come morning."

He turned his attention to the aging caretaker. "Speaking of which, Eli, we'd best be going if we're to arrive before dark."

Father's casual use of Mr. Thornton's Christian name obviously pleased the roughhewn gentlemen immensely and he backed away from us, bowing somewhat obsequiously, hat in hand.

We followed my father through the door Mr. Thornton held open, taking our places in the church's rather dilapidated carriage – a dash of ironic reality after the air of ceremonious diffidence with which Mr. Thornton treated us. It took him several minutes to successfully negotiate the carriage and team out from between two motorized conveyances designed by Mr. Ford, but soon we were on our way, our luggage having been sent ahead in the care of Mr. Thornton's assistant, a painfully shy, rather simple fellow by the name of Hannibal who had almost cowered in the dim periphery of the room until paroled by the task of transporting our bags.

Christ Congregational Church may well have been the Cove's center of piety but one never would have guessed such by the condition of the road leading to it. The church had been erected at a time when rapidly increasing population inspired optimistic expansion of the town's boundaries. Enthralled by expansionist fervor, some far-sighted soul had persuaded the church fathers that their new house of worship should be the vanguard of a growing community, and so they had built on the northeast corner of the town's property, just beyond – and above – existing brick streets. When the Cove's growth spurt tapered off within the year, plans to extend the city streets were abandoned by the Baptist majority on the City Council and the striking new church was left stranded and accessible only by means of an unpaved country road meandering northward from the last of the bricks. Over the years that followed parishioners had lost none of their devotion to the fine stone church, but the road had yet to be finished and on rainy days, such as the one that marked our arrival, it became a muddy quagmire and at certain points during the winter the church virtually was inaccessible. All this we learned while our guide sought to familiarize us with our new surroundings as the arduous journey toward the church and adjacent manse finally came to a successful conclusion.

The church did indeed overlook the cove and Atlantic Ocean some two miles to the southeast, standing at the crest of a hill and flanked on three sides by lush woodland boasting pine, birch, black walnut, sugar maple, and a host of indigenous brush, flowers, animals, and fowl. The flat horizon line of the ocean barely was discernible in the muted, misty light of the grey afternoon and I thought I could just hear the distant thunder of waves crashing against the rocky shoreline of the cove.

The congregation had built an impressive structure; massive fieldstone walls formed the body of the sanctuary, the symmetry of which was complimented by tall, narrow, twin stained glass windows arching gracefully under the eaves at ten foot intervals. There were three sets of two windows on each side for a total of twelve, with the masterfully executed art glass depicting significant Old Testament events such as Creation, the Flood, and the Exodus on the north side and the life and death of Christ on the south. From the outside the windows looked rather muddy and dull, but from within the least ray of sunlight would bring them to life and on sunny days the play of light and glass created a visual symphony rivaling any melody composed by Mozart or Bach.

The church itself was close to one hundred feet long and was crowned by a steeple which rose majestically from the sharply sloped slate roof, topped by a large bronze cross that was visible for miles. Within the church, centered at one end and directly below the steeple, stood the altar and off to the right the pulpit from which Father would speak. Finally, embedded in the wall behind and directly above the altar was another impressive stained glass window, round in shape, depicting Christ rising from the tomb and ascending to heaven; a beautiful and inspiring sight. According to local lore, that particular window was a small-scale reproduction of one somewhere in Europe and it was rumored that one of Tully's Cove's remittance men had arranged for its inclusion when the church was being planned.

Farther north, but within walking distance of the church, stood the manse, our new home, and a destination which seemed forever beyond our reach as the carriage wheels repeatedly bogged down in the muddy ruts of Church Street.

The manse, too, was a handsome stone structure, although far less ostentatious than its reverent counterpart. A large vaulted oak front door was its main source of ornamentation, opening into a roomy vestibule area with pew-like benches on opposing walls, presumably for callers waiting to see my father. There were large rooms to the right and left of the vestibule, both equipped with massive fireplaces and attractive bay windows; the room to the left serving as Father's study, the room to the right as the family's parlor. The study was a "wing" unto itself accessible only from the vestibule but pocket doors at the back of the parlor opened into the dining room behind it and from there doors led to the kitchen at the rear of the house. Directly ahead of the front door, beyond the vestibule, stood an open stairway leading to the bedrooms above, and a narrow hallway leading back to another kitchen entrance, passing a second door into the dining room on its way. The upper rooms basically were unremarkable except that the front bedroom shared the impressive fireplace which warmed the parlor beneath it and the upper hallway widened at the front of the house, directly above the vestibule, into what we came to refer to as the morning room. With almost ritualistic punctuality Mother and I would meet there to share the morning sun after breakfast was cleared away and Father and Rachel had been dispatched to their respective houses of learning. It was a quiet time – for me sometimes painfully so – a time for writing letters acknowledging calls and various hospitalities, and for gazing longingly out upon the descending forest, the rocky shoreline, and ultimately the ocean just visible across the horizon.

III.

Because it was well into the supper hour when we finally crossed the threshold of our new home, we were temporarily spared the inevitable host of well-wishers for which Mother tried to prepare us. Father had served only one parish since marrying so Rachel and I had no memory of the formalities of arrivals. Mother, however, had been raised in a minister's family and was well versed in what to expect. I sensed in her a feeling of relief that the "inspection" was to be postponed and, looking about us at the evidence of a household in upheaval, I shared her relief that an evening of organizing could precede compulsory visits from the well-meaning and the curious.

Our personal belongings – furniture, trunks, and the like – had arrived several days before and stood waiting like silent sentinels in various rooms throughout the house. As a result of Mother's meticulous labeling most had reached their appropriate destination, sparing us undue frustration as we set about the task of unpacking a few essentials after a hasty meal of fresh bread and cheese which had been procured before our assault on Church Street.

Mother, Rachel, and I spent that first evening primarily in the parlor, attempting to achieve at least a semblance of order for the following day's callers. Father, however, left us in the capable hands of Eli Thornton and immediately devoted himself to organizing his study (it was a given that he would do so, for only then could he be assured it would be done properly). Mr. Thornton and Hannibal stayed for quite some time, first helping us arrange the larger parlor items into a pleasing configuration and then moving on with Mother to survey conditions in the dining room – poor Hannibal pacing nervously much of the time like a deer about to bolt.

Once the trio had moved on and were safely out of earshot Rachel rose from where she had been kneeling – ostensibly to dust the legs of the upright piano – her lower lip protruding slightly in a quintessentially Rachelesque pout.

"What's troubling Mother," she asked in a wounded whisper. "I've never seen her so on edge before."

"You've never seen her preparing for an onslaught of the curious before." I was unpacking the small crate cradling Mother's few porcelain treasures and Rachel's insensitivity to the cause of her anxiety grated on my nerves. "It's not an easy thing for a minister's wife to move to a new parish, Rachel. They may hire the man, but there are a great many unspoken expectations placed upon his wife."

Rachel's expression was quizzical and utterly feminine.

"I don't understand..." she began vaguely, plopping down on the settee with an exaggerated sigh.

"My dear little sister," I replied, sounding more like the stereotypical schoolmarm than I care to admit, "surely you realize that many of tomorrow's callers won't be coming solely to pay their respects to the new preacher but to take a good, long look at his wife and his household."

"That's not fair," she replied, her voice full of petulance and self-pity. "I can't possibly do all this work and still be ready to meet people in the morning!"

She sank deeper into the settee's cushions in melodramatic disdain.

"*You* can't possibly do all this work?" I sputtered in exasperation. "You've hardly done anything..."

I was tired and edgy and her self-sympathy proved to be the proverbial straw on the camel's back. I was contemplating pulling her to her feet by her pouty lower lip when Mother came back on the scene.

"Well, ladies," she began as she surveyed the room, "I think it's time to concede to the clock. I believe we've done all that can be done tonight. Frankly, I think Mr. Thornton would have stayed all night but he clearly was tired after working all day and Hannibal obviously needed to escape – the poor dear bolted out the kitchen door the minute I insisted we call it a day."

She sat down rather stiffly next to Rachel and put her arm around the shoulders of her younger daughter. Rachel accepted our mother's embrace while tossing something resembling a sneer in my direction.

"I think it's time you girls bolted as well," Mother continued. "Up stairs and into bed, that is."

Rachel eagerly complied with Mother's dismissal to a warm bed, her eyelids drooping almost flirtatiously in exaggerated sleepiness as she extricated herself from Mother's affectionate embrace with a long and graceful stretch.

Although I felt bone weary I stayed behind as Rachel disappeared into the shadows of the vestibule – her steps on the stairs sounding surprisingly energetic for someone on the verge of exhaustion. Sharing a few quiet moments with our mother and offering some moral support for the potential "ordeal-by-visitation" that lay ahead appealed to me more right then than the lure of a warm bed.

Not surprisingly, when she finally broke the comfortable silence that settled between us her thoughts were not of herself.

"Your father is convinced that this move will be a very positive one," she began, gazing affectionately into the slowly dying fire. "It is a larger town and a larger congregation, but I must admit to some apprehension when it comes to you girls.

Her kind eyes turned their full attention on me.

"I only hope we haven't uprooted you too abruptly..."

Surprised by her concern, I crossed the room to join her on the settee, offering what I thought had been patently obvious from the beginning. "You needn't worry about

Rachel and me. Rachel is eager to meet new friends and enjoy the benefits of living in a bigger town; and me? Well, suffice it to say that I've been intrigued by Tully's Cove since the day Father told us we were moving. There's nothing to worry about. We'll both be fine."

She seemed slightly less than reassured and I slipped my arm across her shoulders as she had done with Rachel.

"Yes, you're undoubtedly right," she sighed. "Rachel will do well."

There was a pause as she leaned forward to prod the smoldering embers of the fire. "I only hope that we all can be happy here..."

I wondered at the uncharacteristic tone of skepticism that had entered her voice and her slight emphasis on the word "all," but she had risen and was walking toward the vestibule doorway indicating an end to our brief sabbatical.

We parted for the evening at the foot of the stairs, she to the study to be with Father and me upstairs to bed.

Sleep came easily that first night despite the pervasive feeling of anticipation which, for me, had colored every facet of our move. I took a few moments to move several crates and my trunk, but putting fresh linens on the beds in my parents' and my room was the extent of my gesture at settling in.

I crawled gratefully under the covers with the intention of unwinding to the gentle harmony of wind and rain, but within minutes was sound asleep.

CHAPTER TWO

I.

I was roused from sleep the following morning by Father calling to me from the foot of the stairs; it was more his tone than the content of his brief edict which told me I had stayed in bed long enough. Hurriedly tying my woolen robe around me, I paused just long enough to run a comb through my hair and pull back the curtains for a look outside.

Due to an unexpected drop in temperatures overnight I was greeted by a brilliant morning that took my breath away. Moisture from the previous day's rain had frozen and now clung to every leaf, limb, and blade of grass making them look as if they were encased in glass. The pristine beauty of it made my heart ache and I longed to linger and savor this fantasy world before the autumn sunshine returned us to reality, but Father's voice rang in my ears and I hurriedly turned from the window, receiving a jolt from the real world as I stubbed my toe on a crate in my haste to get downstairs.

My hobbled entrance into the kitchen caused Mother to turn from the stove where she was preparing hotcakes. She greeted me with a cheerful smile while indicating a stack of clean dishes with which I could set the table.

Father had already assumed his customary seat at the head of the rectangular oak table and glanced up from his reading as I entered the room. "Good morning, Martha, I trust you slept well. What scripture shall we share this morning?"

It wasn't a rebuke exactly, but there was in his tone what I perceived to be disapproval and I felt my face flushing with embarrassment. Whether intended or not, his words often had the effect of making me feel as if I wasn't pulling my share of the load and I longed to compensate. Within moments I had finished setting the table and stood ready to help mother at the stove. By the time the aroma of breakfast had snaked its way up the back stairs and lured a drowsy-eyed Rachel down to join us Mother was piling hotcakes on a platter and I had just poured hot syrup into the crockery pitcher we never used for anything else.

"Mmmmmm," Rachel purred as she took her seat on Father's right. "The hotcakes smell wonderful, Mother. Why didn't anyone call me to help?"

"Never mind, dear," Mother interjected, quickly preempting the retort she seemed to instinctively know was on the tip of my tongue. "You can help me clear things away."

Breakfast passed pleasantly enough, with Rachel winning a smile or two from Father, and Mother and I joining their banter from time to time. Watching Rachel in a rather surreptitious manner, I once again was struck by how surprisingly intuitive our parents had been when selecting our Biblical names. My lovely and somewhat shallow little sister seemed to me the very incarnation of Rachel, the Old Testament beauty for whose hand Jacob toiled fourteen years, and I certainly was type-cast in my role as Martha, the New Testament follower of Christ who was preoccupied with duty and responsibility. I could imagine that, like my namesake I, too, might well miss the opportunity to learn at the feet of the Lord because of feeling duty-bound to finish the household chores. Such dilemmas would never trouble Rachel. Rachel's world was simply and logically defined by what Rachel needed and wanted. She was sweet, captivating, and unapologetically manipulative and self-serving. The reality made me smile humorlessly at my proclivity for over-compensating while trying to win approval that never would be given; and wince inwardly at the dreary image it produced.

When Father excused himself and headed over to the church to begin exploring and organizing his new domain, Rachel followed his lead and scurried upstairs to continue her morning ablutions – leaving the mealtime detritus to Mother and me in spite of her earlier pledge to assist.

II.

A somewhat more than middle-aged woman who introduced herself as Emma Secord peered nearsightedly at my mother as she opened the front door to greet our first guest. Obviously accustomed to free access to the manse, she brushed past Mother's outstretched hand and hurried into the parlor, leaving us in a wake of incessant, sing-songy chatter.

"...My, my, my, it's a cold morning, I hope to tell ya... surely we'll be sufferin' a bitter winter, yes indeed..."

She dropped her generous weight heavily into the overstuffed chair adjacent the fireplace and continued talking while warming her hands and taking in her surroundings like a fox surveying the chicken coop.

"Well, now, Mrs. Pendleton, looks to me as if you're nearly settled in already..." Mrs. Secord said with an odd clicking of her tongue that sent spittle flying. "No reason to put things off as I see it. It's right proper to drop anchor and put down roots quick-like, I hope to tell ya."

Mother smiled at the older woman – whether merely a display of good manners or at Mrs. Secord's mixture of metaphors I wasn't sure – handing her a cup of tea and gently nudging her way into the conversation as she poured tea for me as well.

"I'm glad you stopped by, Mrs. Secord. My daughters and I have been looking forward to receiving guests today."

I smiled into my cup trusting the Lord to forgive her for stretching the truth.

Mrs. Secord turned her watery blue eyes toward Rachel and me, acknowledging our presence for the first time.

"Ah, fine looking girls – the preacher hasn't any sons to follow in his footsteps?" She placed an emphasis on the word "sons" that gave me the impression she expected some sort of apology from us for disrupting the universe in such an uppity manner but, waiting for no answer, responded to her own question with that annoying clicking of her tongue and something about the importance of sons and arrows in one's quiver – she hoped to tell us – and then lapsed into more aimless chatter.

Polite to a fault, Mother was nonetheless visibly relieved when another knock at the front door signaled the arrival of more callers, but it was Rachel who nearly overturned the tea service in her haste to escape Mrs. Secord's detailed report on the various maladies afflicting the members of Father's new flock.

Mother and I rose as Eli Thornton was ushered into the parlor accompanied by a female version of himself who I knew immediately must be his widowed sister, Augusta, of whom he had spoken with warmth and respect the previous evening.

"Mrs. Pendleton, girls, I'd like you to meet my sister, Augusta Wilkes," Eli offered, obviously proud to handle the introductions.

Augusta came forward, a warm and genuinely friendly smile on her face, and took Mother's hand in both of hers.

"Mrs. Pendleton," she said somewhat reverently, "I truly am pleased to meet you and hope you and your family will be as happy here as we are to have you."

Her smile reached out to embrace Rachel and me but faltered slightly as her eyes fell on Mrs. Secord helping herself to more tea and a generous third portion of the sugar cookies Mother had baked that morning.

"Emma Secord," she scolded, "I dare say you'll be first in line come Judgment Day!"

"Ah-yuh; nuthin' wrong with being where you aim to go, I hope to tell ya."

The gentle rebuke was lost on Mrs. Secord who settled back into her chair watching intently as Augusta shared with us the homemade delicacies she had brought along so we could "taste" her welcome.

Our next visitors were the Choate sisters; wizened spinsters who brought to mind a pair of magpies with lined, papery skin stretched across narrow faces and beady eyes that openly stared at us from above identical pince-nez eyewear perched precariously on thin, beaklike noses. One could tell both from their appearance and their demeanor that the Choates were women of means and influence. They made that influence immediately felt with rather pointed remarks about the quality of the house that was now our home; obviously intending to put Mother on notice that she should be grateful and take care of what was not hers.

Mother took the Choate sisters in stride, responding to their comments with a warmth and graciousness I found admirable. I fought back the urge to parry verbally with them a bit in defense of my victimized mother and Rachel went so far as to stick her tongue out at them and mimic them behind their backs – earning a subtle swat from Mother as she diverted the spinsters' attention lest they catch Rachel's pantomime in their peripheral vision. Once duly constrained, we sat dutifully next to one another on the settee, hands clasped tightly in our laps as we strove to mirror our mother and acquiesce to good manners.

Augusta hovered somewhat protectively around my mother as the Choates' discourse continued but Mrs. Secord departed, having said her goodbyes rather hastily shortly after the Choates arrived. The magpies had regarded Mrs. Secord with undisguised distaste that successfully penetrated the thick-skinned veneer which was her defining characteristic and intimidated an otherwise socially-oblivious soul.

By the time a lull in the flow of visitors occurred around the dinner hour we had welcomed numerous other callers: Grace Whitley, a heavily pregnant young matron with huge, sad eyes and a simple elegance I found compelling; Mabel Newcomb and her daughters Clara and Hope – the eldest of eight girls – with whom Rachel struck up an immediate friendship; the widows Starkey and Wentworth, matrons of the congregation – and rivals of the Choates in the charm department – the latter of whom spoke not a syllable but punctuated virtually everything Widow Starkey said by bobbing her head in sycophantic affirmation; and others whose names escaped me almost immediately upon being introduced. The conversation was cordial and all very much the same: they were happy to meet us; they hoped we had had a pleasant journey; they hoped we'd be happy in Tully's Cove; they looked forward to Father's first sermon on Sunday.

It wasn't until mid-afternoon that the passing parade took an interesting turn, making me glad I had resisted the urge to slip away and giving me my first glimpse of the more colorful side of Tully's Cove as well as introducing those who would play significant roles in the drama ahead.

Five ladies still lingered over their tea and Mother had just introduced me to a gaunt-faced woman named Helen who identified herself as the church organist and shook my hand so vigorously I thought it would fall off, when the hum of chatter died away and our focus was drawn to an arrival that had captured the attention of our guests.

"Look at this," cooed an elderly woman sitting directly across from the large bay window, "it's Jocelyn Collier come calling."

"Who's that with her," asked a ruddy complexioned woman named Garnet, distracted from the mantle where she had been displaying an inordinate amount of interest in Mother's porcelain.

"Why, that's her cousin Jacob himself," observed a third in hushed tones.

"Land's sake," chimed in a buxom matron whose named I had missed, "don't believe I've seen him more than twice in the three years they've been here."

She moved to the window, pushing aside the lace curtain for a better look.

"Why haven't you seen him more," asked Rachel, her curiosity piqued and the child within peeking through her façade of maturity. "Does he hide away because he's disfigured?"

"Rachel!" Mother admonished, as much with her eyes as with her voice.

"Hardly, child," smiled the elderly woman.

"He's a 'Remittance Man,'" broke in the church organist in a conspiratorial whisper.

"A what," I asked, finding the undercurrent of excitement contagious and wanting to hear more.

"A Remittance Man," the elderly woman stated, taking control of the conversation. "You'll find them scattered about this part of the country and up yonder in Canada. Mostly English they be; living here because of some disgrace they've brought upon the family name in Europe."

"What did he do?" Rachel's eyes widened as she leaned forward in her chair, coaxing the story on.

"Ladies, please," Mother interrupted. "Miss Collier is almost to the door. We mustn't take pleasure in the misfortune of others. Surely she has suffered because of her cousin."

"Ah-yuh," Augusta agreed, coming to Mother's side. "That she has, Mrs. Pendleton. Why Jocelyn Collier is down-right saintly. Leaving home and family to join her cousin and care for him in his exile. She's a fine, Christian lady, and that's a fact."

The other ladies concurred and as Mother went to the door to admit our latest guest the conversation was deliberately turned to a less indelicate subject.

A tall and stately woman entered the parlor at Mother's side a moment later, somewhere between twenty-five and thirty years old, somewhere between pretty and plain. She carried her broad shouldered frame with a distance and dignity that bordered on aloof; sandy brown hair pulled back in a conservative chignon, cool hazel eyes never shirking your gaze. I was struck by the firmness of her confident handshake and felt I had met my first friend in Tully's Cove.

After introductions had been made all around – for Miss Collier, like her cousin, was apparently something of a recluse and therefore not well acquainted with her neighbors – polite conversation resumed, although it was clear that the Remittance Man's cousin was to be the focus of attention.

"How are things at the Manor, Miss Collier?"

The question came from the elderly woman who had heralded Jocelyn's arrival, and who obviously could avoid the subject no longer.

Jocelyn had taken an empty seat next to me and I thought I felt her stiffen, although her voice remained as placid as a pond at dawn.

"Everything is running quite smoothly, thank you…"

"How is that cousin of yours," broke in the organist, "We'd surely love to bid him welcome come Sunday morning."

"Jacob is well, thank you, but not one to attend public worship, I'm afraid."

Her face was slightly flushed under the light of their sudden scrutiny and I longed to ease her discomfort. Unfortunately, in an effort to turn the subject and hopefully lead to more general insights into the lives of the town's citizens, I blundered into the very topic I sought to avoid.

"What line of work is your cousin in," I asked. "Do you own one of the picturesque farms we saw as we approached town?"

Jocelyn shifted uncomfortably and I realized that an almost breathless silence had fallen over the room.

"We do have a small acreage under cultivation," she said, choosing her words carefully, "but our major income is derived from... from investments in England."

I deeply appreciated the graciousness of her reply for, having belatedly realized the impertinence of my question, I felt a more curt response would have served me right. But Jocelyn recovered quickly and with Mother's adept handling of the conversation there were no further references to her cousin's status in the community – either unintentional or deliberate.

As the afternoon progressed I became less embarrassed by my faux pas, and more comfortable with our elegant neighbor. It also became amusingly apparent that there was strong reluctance to leave on the part of the other ladies lest they miss some interesting tidbit about the man I came to realize was the Cove's most mysterious resident. They were intrigued – and I must admit that I, too, had fallen prey to that baser characteristic of human nature that finds scandal so fascinating.

In the end it was Jocelyn's departure, not surprisingly, which finally triggered the exodus from our parlor. Hearing the approach of her cousin's automobile, she hastily gathered her things and offered a general glance of farewell to her neighbors that some in the room might have taken as condescending. Mother and I walked her to the door; Rachel having vanished once realizing there would be no further discussion of Remittance Men. I took an almost perverse pleasure in the fact that she was missing an opportunity to glimpse the man again.

Within minutes of Jocelyn's exit the parlor was empty.

An unexpected result of the day's festivities was Jocelyn's offer to tutor Rachel in French on a weekly basis. Mother at first had firmly declined Miss Collier's generosity but finally gave in to Rachel's pleading (inspired more by curiosity than a love of learning) and Jocelyn's assurances that it certainly was no imposition and would, in fact, be a pleasure as well as aid her in maintaining her second language. Mother also undoubtedly empathized with Miss Collier's tenuous status within the community and acquiesced as a gesture of friendship.

And so it was arranged that Rachel and I would visit Jocelyn on Saturday and Rachel would have her first taste of a continental education; news of which undoubtedly made the rounds quickly once our guests returned home and tribal drums relayed the message from gossip to gossip.

III.

Saturday dawned bright and sunny, with a brisk chill in the air that was something more than invigorating. Every tree and bush adorning the rolling terrain outside my bedroom window was dressed in its most colorful finery – reds, oranges, and yellows of every hue waited to celebrate autumn with anyone willing to take notice.

Invigorated by the beauty of a New England autumn, I dressed with a light heart and energized enthusiasm marked my trek toward the stairs, passing my sleeping sister's room on the way. I have to admit that my step became even more energized and enthusiastic when I noticed her door was slightly ajar, and there was more than a dollop of satisfaction in disturbing her "Princess-and-the-Pea" constitution by hitting all the squeaky spots in numerous stair treads on my way down. As a result, I entered the kitchen with something of a flourish, feeling quite pleased with myself – after all, Rachel had an uncanny ability to stay in bed longer than anyone – only to find she was an uncharacteristically early-riser that particular morning and even had usurped my job of setting the table! I stopped short, utterly deflated, taking stock of an event not likely to be repeated any time soon.

Rachel beamed happily at me. Although we weren't scheduled to go to the Manor until early afternoon she appeared ready to leave, dressed in a slim, midnight blue plaid skirt and white shirtwaist accented by delicate lace trim with a midnight blue ribbon at her throat. She looked fresh and lovely and made me feel quite dowdy despite the fact that I, too, had dressed with some care for the occasion of a visit with our wealthy English neighbor.

"What do you think their house will be like," Rachel asked after Mother left the kitchen to call Father for breakfast.

With some success, I attempted to feign indifference. "Oh, I don't know, probably cold and austere."

"Oh Martha, you're no fun," she pouted, lower lip extended slightly. "Clara Newcomb told me Miss Collier and her cousin live in the grandest house in the Cove!"

We had known Clara Newcomb for less than a week but already had encountered her tendency toward exaggeration. I told Rachel as much and she fell into a sullen silence.

Breakfast conversation centered on Father's preparation for church the following morning and the delicious maple syrup and assorted breads and preserves brought by various well-wishers throughout the week. It probably was inevitable, however, that the subject of Rachel's French lessons would surface and as Father cleared his throat – often a portent of something unpleasant coming – I braced myself for a repeat performance of his thoughts on the subject.

"I want you to know I am not pleased with this latest venture of yours," Father began, addressing Mother solemnly as he spread a spoonful of raspberry preserves on a corn muffin. "Those so-called 'Remittance Men' are an embarrassment to this community as much as they are to the families that have banished them. If not outright criminals they are, at the very least, corrupt and as a result cast the pall of moral degradation in their wake." Warming to his subject, and obviously pleased with his eloquence, he wagged a finger in Mother's direction. "That man's very presence here is an indictment of his character. I find it difficult to believe you want your daughters associating with such people."

Mother's response was gentle and yet very firm.

"The girls won't be 'associating' with a Remittance Man, Phillip. And 'that man,' as you call him, has a name." She gave in to an exasperated sigh. "Jacob Collier isn't the one who invited the girls to their home, offering to give Rachel something special she can't get in school. His cousin Jocelyn has..."

She rose from the table and began clearing things away. "... and Jocelyn Collier's presence in Tully's Cove is a testimony not an indictment; a testimony to her kindness and charity. She certainly didn't have to leave her home and all that was familiar and precious to her. She chose to come here; chose to come here so her cousin wouldn't be alone and entirely cut off from his family. In my opinion, Jocelyn Collier should be the topic of this conversation, not her cousin. Miss Collier is a wonderful example of self-sacrifice and Christian charity. And I find her offer to tutor Rachel extremely generous. Quite frankly, I think we all would do well to take a lesson from her. And if you could have seen the way the upright ladies of Tully's Cove treated her – with morbid curiosity and something just short of disdain – I think you also would agree that it is our Christian duty to see that she is ostracized from the good people of Tully's Cove as little as possible."

I literally was taken aback by Mother's vigorous defense of Miss Collier. It made me wonder if perhaps she identified with the young woman's status as an outsider more closely than one would expect for rarely did she speak so forcefully on ground occupied without Father's blessing. I was proud of her. I could see that my father also was impressed – if not actually convinced – for the furrowed brow he invariably knit when upset or challenged began to relax.

"Well now," he said, slowly stirring his black coffee, "maybe there's the final word on the subject."

He took a long, cautious drink.

"They probably won't encounter Mr. Collier anyway."

Rachel's face betrayed the fact that she strongly hoped he was wrong... and, if I'm totally honest, I must admit I hoped so, too.

IV.

The acreage acquired for the Colliers when they moved to Maine three years earlier included a landmark overlooking the cove known as Patriot's Point. The name dated back to the War of 1812 when the caves located in the rocks leading up from the cove had been used to store supplies for the fledgling American military. Of course, Maine was still part of Massachusetts during that war, not becoming a state in its own right until 1820, but the coves and rocky inlets at the southern end of the state were well-suited as a transfer point and had served the Americans well – and given Mainers something to boast about ever since. Due to America's use of privateers during our second armed conflict with England – many of which, it must be admitted, walked a fine line between legitimate military action and sheer piracy – the British of the day had called the overlook "Pirate's Point" but in light of the outcome of the war the name "patriot" had won out and had stood the test of time.

It was a beautiful spot. There was no land in the area that stood at a higher elevation or commanded a more majestic view of the cove and the ocean beyond. Although the house the Colliers occupied had been built a safe distance from the overlook precipice, there was a walkway leading to the cliffs from the well-manicured gardens which wandered dangerously near the edge and made one grateful for the four-foot-high retaining wall that had been added after a previous resident had fallen to their death.

The house was very English in style which, as I would learn later from Jocelyn, was the deciding factor for her and her cousin when first considering their options for living accommodations in Tully's Cove. I appreciated the beauty of the house immediately but it wasn't until much later that I learned the history behind its architectural styles. Built at the turn of the last century, its owner had sought to capture the spirit of his English heritage. Beginning as a Tudor manor house – complete with wide oak timbers crisscrossing its whitewashed outer walls, and numerous bay windows and dormers sporting glass panels secured in decorative lattice frames – the structure had grown to include a wing typifying features of the more conservative Cotswold architecture, including sturdy stone walls with over-sized corner stones from foundation to eaves and heavy stone trim along the edges of the roofline. The stone may have been quarried in New England but the soul of the structure was pure Britain. Unifying the two architectural styles was a slate roof that appeared to drape itself over the house as if to shield those within from more than just the elements.

I had to admit Clara Newcomb had not exaggerated in saying that the Collier home was the nicest in the Cove. In truth, I never had seen anything like it.

Rachel and I were brought to the Manor at the appointed hour and ushered into a small parlor overlooking the gardens. The small, cozy room felt far removed from the large, ornate entrance gallery through which we had passed wide-eyed. This definitely was a woman's room. The furnishings were all very delicate, the chairs and settee upholstered in demure rose-colored chintz, the hue of which was picked up by fine lace curtains at the windows; even the smallest accent piece reflected the femininity and elegant taste of the room's occupant.

Jocelyn was waiting for us and rose as we entered.

"Welcome," she said, wrapping her warm fingers around my cold, clammy hand. "I'm so glad you've come. I was concerned that something might make you change your minds."

I read in her words a reference to her tenuous status within the community and sought to reassure her.

"I don't think anything short of the Second Coming would have kept Rachel away and I was only too glad to accompany her – thank you for including me, by the way."

We had taken our place on the settee she indicated and as I finished speaking a mousy, simple appearing woman came in bearing a tray with tea service and a plate of assorted sweet breads and small cakes.

"I thought we might begin by sharing some tea," Jocelyn stated, dismissing the housemaid with a scowl and an abrupt wave of her hand. "I hope you don't mind."

We assured her we didn't and complimented not only the bountiful tea she was spreading but their lovely home as well.

"I suppose it is beautiful," she replied, "but I think I would prefer something smaller and less ostentatious."

Her expression had become veiled; she seemed suddenly distracted and for a moment it was as if she no longer saw us there. Within seconds she had recovered herself, however, and chatted amiably about gardens, fashion, and other general small talk.

When we had finished our tea and it was time for Rachel's lesson to begin, Jocelyn suggested that I might enjoy a stroll through their garden. I found the prospect appealing but was hesitant to leave the "safety" of her secluded parlor and thought it prudent to respect Father's wishes that our visits be devoid of contact with Jocelyn's miscreant cousin.

She seemed to read my thoughts and added with deliberate casualness, "I always find the garden to be the perfect place to enjoy some solitude and since I'm alone in the house today you surely would be uninterrupted."

I felt embarrassed to be so transparent and yet appreciated knowing her cousin wasn't home. Accepting her offer of a solitary walk, I left them to their study of the lingua franca.

One didn't notice it immediately but part of the garden's charm was that it was a horticultural map of the city of Tully's Cove, whose wagon wheel design one could see and appreciate to perfection when looking down across the town from this elevated vantage point. At the garden's center, or "hub," was a small gazebo representing the city's covered bandstand at the heart of the town square. From that focal point numerous "avenues" radiated outward, each representing one of the city's main spoke-like streets, and lined with different flowers, bushes, and small flowering trees. Of course, nothing was in bloom now but even with my limited knowledge of such things I realized that this was something quite unique and explored each avenue in its turn imagining it at the peak of the growing season.

As I neared the end of the garden's easternmost avenue I came upon a heavy, ornate wrought iron gate. I assumed that this marked the end of the walled garden and would have turned to retrace my steps had I not noticed a cobblestone path leading from the gate to an obviously less-tended portion of the estate. My hand hesitated above the rusty handle for my hostess's invitation had specified a walk in the garden, not an investigation of the rest of the grounds. Expecting to find the gate firmly secured, however, I impulsively gave in to the urge to grasp the handle. There was resistance from the latch but it turned relatively easily and after pushing forward on the gate, whose rust-encrusted hinges loudly protested the intrusion, I found myself walking along the uneven cobblestones and consciously resisting the rigidly sensible part of me who said to turn back.

The path meandered through what had at one time undoubtedly been an extension of the garden behind me. As I carefully picked my way through overgrown bushes choked by weeds and equally troublesome low-hanging branches, the sound of the ocean grew increasingly near. I had just about convinced myself that the sea was farther away than it sounded and it was time to turn back when the cobblestone path widened suddenly and broke free of the foliage into a curved fanlike patio ringed along the far side by a wall about four feet high. The sound of the ocean was very clear now and I hurried across to look over the wall.

The view that greeted me was spectacular. Almost directly below I could see distinctly the rocky cove from which the town derived its name and beyond it the vast expanse of the Atlantic Ocean. The view and the smell of the thundering surf were intoxicating and I was quickly oblivious to everything else until a voice shattered my reverie.

"Excuse me, miss."

The unexpected words caused my heart to leap and I felt I must have jumped at least a foot. "Oh, I'm so sorry..." I stammered, turning from the lookout as I spoke, expecting a reprimand from the gardener. My repentant stammering broke off in midsentence, however, for the gentleman who stood before me wore neither the dress nor the demeanor of a gardener and I knew instantly that I had inadvertently come face to face with Jacob Collier.

The owner of Patriot's Point stood tall and broad-shouldered before me. He wore his dark, wavy hair slightly longer than was the fashion, his face was angular, his eyes large but very cold; a strong face – not conventionally handsome but not unappealing either.

"I apologize for startling you," he began, "but that wall is unsafe in places and I felt I should caution you."

His voice was deep and resonant but rather flat and definitely lacking warmth. My face flushed hotly and I felt mortified both for such an immature reaction and for being caught where I had no right to go in the first place.

"You must be Miss Pendleton," he continued since I obviously was unable to give an account of myself.

"Yes..." I managed to squeak out, slowly gathering my wits about me as my heart slipped down my throat back to its proper location.

"I apologize again for starling you and interrupting your solitude but, as I said, that wall is unsafe."

"No, please, I should be the one to apologize. I'm afraid I wandered farther than intended but the sound of the sea was mesmerizing and I'm grateful for the exquisite view I came upon."

My heart was beating at its normal pace now and I found it easier to converse, although I still felt like a child caught with a hand in the cookie jar.

He walked across the patio and joined me, looking out across the ocean.

"This must have been a very lovely spot at one time," I said, indicating the patio and surrounding woods.

"It has an interesting history," he replied with a vacant, unreadable look on his face.

"I find your entire estate fascinating... and appreciate your cousin's generosity in inviting me to come along when my sister has her French lessons..."

I felt the need to fill the silence for he made me feel vaguely uncomfortable. I had never spoken with anyone of dubious character before and suddenly was anxious for the conversation to end.

"You have a lovely home," I concluded lamely.

"I suppose it is beautiful," he replied, "but I would rather have something less... formidable."

It struck me that that was almost exactly what Jocelyn had said and I wondered why he chose to imply that living here was her idea. I smiled slightly, deciding he must feel deriding it was manly.

Our eyes met and just for a moment his expression no longer was veiled and he appraised me as if seeing me for the first time.

"I had best start back to the house," I said quietly. "I didn't intend to be gone so long."

I started to cross the patio but audibly caught my breath as he crossed in front of me.

"Just clearing the way for you," he stated flatly in reply to my gasp.

His face returned to stone as he turned and silently preceded me up the congested path, pausing just long enough to hold up a low-hanging branch or push aside the encroaching underbrush as we walked back toward the house.

When we reached the gate to the garden Mr. Collier stood aside for me to enter and gave the slightest of bows. "I'm pleased to have met you, Miss Pendleton," he said coolly and formally, holding the gate open until I passed through, "but would suggest that you not mention the incident to my cousin."

His request was curious but I agreed to say nothing, assuming he preferred Jocelyn believe him to be absent from the estate. That assumption was affirmed as I heard the sound of a key grating in the gate's lock as I walked away.

Returning to the house as quickly as possible, I wondered whether perhaps I *should* tell Jocelyn I had encountered her cousin. I finally decided against it for fear of causing her undue concern – as well as being embarrassed to admit that I had explored beyond the garden.

CHAPTER THREE

I.

We had been in Tully's Cove for nearly three weeks as September drew to a close. The days were growing shorter, the temperature colder, and the colorful autumn foliage was slowly losing its brilliance as the yearly cycle neared completion and the ground became increasingly littered with brittle, brown leaves.

In an attempt to savor the fleeting glory of my favorite season, I began taking long walks through the wooded area around the church and sometimes down into the tree-lined streets of the town itself. Life had settled into a quiet routine of letter writing and household accounting in the morning room after breakfast and then assorted housekeeping chores over the course of each day. Within that pattern there was little room for deviation, but a secondary routine also developed which added callers to receive and calls to return, my long solitary walks, and of course at week's end there was the standing appointment for Rachel's lessons at Patriot's Point. We had been there twice since my unexpected meeting with Jacob Collier but, although I had visited the garden each time, there had been no further encounters with the Remittance Man.

One particularly clear and crisp October day I hurried through the morning's chores afraid the tone of the day would change before I could follow Mother's suggestion and take some bread and soup to a church member recovering from child birth. It was early afternoon before I was finally able to don my sturdiest pair of shoes and a thickly quilted tartan cape to begin the trek into town. The basket containing a loaf of my own oatmeal bread and a large crock of Mother's hearty vegetable soup weighed heavily on my arm, making me decide to go straight into town and save the casual part of my walk for the unencumbered return trip.

We had had only one light snow thus far which quickly melted as it was sandwiched between the sun's rays and the still-warm earth so the ruts of Church Street were fairly solid and easy to travel. Nonetheless, I stayed to the shoulder of the road for most of my walk lest I misjudge and end up sinking a shoe into unseen muck as had happened on a previous trip. I smiled to myself recalling what surely must have been a humorous sight for I literally had walked out of my shoe and then hopped awkwardly on one foot trying to keep my balance and dislodge the errant shoe with the increasingly muddied toe of my unshod foot. Although there had been little humor apparent at the time, it was one of those incidents which in retrospect can be appreciated for the laughable moment they are.

As I reached the brick roadway leading into town my pace quickened. There was something invigorating about the bustle of Tully's Cove on a work day and I was glad that my errand would take me near the center of town rather than along the quiet side streets.

Grace Whitley had been one of the women who came calling the day after our arrival and I looked forward to visiting with her again and meeting her newborn son. One was immediately struck by her beauty – even in an advanced state of pregnancy – and also by the sorrow reflected in her huge grey eyes. I had warmed to Grace instinctively, partly because I had received the impression that first day that some of the other ladies thought her rather common. No one had said anything against her but their distaste was almost palpable. Perhaps it was because she broke with tradition and didn't hide away until the birth of her child, or perhaps it was due to their discomfort with her husband's line of work for he was employed as assistant to the undertaker – not an occupation likely to garner many invitations to dinner. Regardless of the cause, I felt Grace was a lonely young woman and, as with Jocelyn, felt drawn to her.

The Whitleys occupied rooms above the funeral parlor and I must admit to a moment's hesitation before crossing the street and approaching the storefront whose window was draped in black crepe and which bore the inscription "Eternal Rest Funeral Home" in large, gothic letters.

By the time I had climbed the outdoor staircase leading to their apartment, Grace was waiting at the front door, smiling sweetly, an index finger to her lips indicating the need for hushed tones.

"I just got the baby to sleep," she whispered, stepping aside for me to enter.

The window shades were drawn and as my eyes grew accustomed to the semi-darkness I saw that we were in a small parlor off from which were two other rooms, one I could see to be a kitchen and the other I presumed to be the bedroom.

"I hope it's all right that I stopped by," I began, taking my place in the wing chair she indicated. "I've been anxious to see your baby but decided to wait as I'm sure you've been swamped with callers."

She gave me a rather wan smile and her hand trembled nervously as she brushed a stray wisp of hair from her tired face.

"Actually," she replied candidly, "I've had only two other visitors."

My face undoubtedly registered surprise for I found that not only curious in light of the seemingly obsessive desire of most women to ogle babies (and share horror stories about giving birth) but almost rude and I wondered why her neighbors would snub her.

"They'll probably all come at once," I suggested, consciously injecting my comment with a jovial tone I hoped would cover my incredulity.

"Perhaps," she replied quietly, but words she left unspoken contradicted her polite optimism.

The awkwardness of our initial exchange didn't last and we were soon chatting aimlessly about babies and related subjects until finally interrupted by an infant's demand for attention from the adjoining room. Grace had relaxed considerably as our conversation progressed and brightened noticeably when the baby's cries beckoned her.

She smiled broadly, rising to her feet. "Oh good, now you can meet Winston."

I could hear her cooing gentle endearments as she prepared her son to receive his newest admirer and when she emerged, cradling the baby in her arms, the joy on her face made my heart ache. She came over to where I sat, placing the baby in my arms and pulling up a small upholstered stool so she could sit near us and admire the infant with me.

He was a handsome baby with the creamy, flawless complexion of his mother and dark hair and eyes of his father. His tiny fingers wrapped themselves around my index finger and I was touched by the perfection of his miniature features; perfect down to the minute crescents at the base of his tiny fingernails.

"Oh Grace," I observed in a reverent whisper, "he's beautiful."

Her smile was unabashedly proud as she observed her son. "Thank you," she breathed, "he's the most important thing in the world to me, this child."

Winston had turned his head toward my body instinctively nuzzling my breast and we shared an unselfconscious laugh at the futility of his quest. Grace took the child from me, settled into the rocking chair, and began to nurse.

"He looks so much like your husband," I offered, as much a compliment as an observation.

She was instantly subdued and the pleasure left her face. "Do you really think so?"

I assured her that I did, to which she responded flatly, "I wish David would see the resemblance."

I realized anew that throughout the course of our conversation Grace had seemed sad or distant whenever her husband was mentioned. I knew, of course, what Mr. Whitley did for a living and had seen them in church, but Grace had shared little about him other than the fact that they had married seven years ago after being sweethearts since childhood. Not every man welcomed the interruption and responsibility represented by the arrival of children and it seemed clear that David Whitley must not share his wife's excitement over the birth of their son.

Once again I was full of sorrow for the young woman before me.

When Winston had eaten his fill and drifted off into the deep and tranquil sleep reserved for a treasured child, I attempted to draw Grace out of the silence that had settled between us by inquiring about an upcoming community celebration about which Rachel had excitedly – and almost unintelligibly – informed me the previous day.

"It's an annual event that's been going on as long as I can remember," Grace explained quietly as she shifted the sleeping infant and stretched her cramped arm. "There are few things that Tully's Cove really goes all out for but the Harvest Festival definitely is one. I'm not familiar with this year's schedule but traditionally there's a brief service at your father's church – since it's the biggest in town – and then the whole county turns out down at Bailey's Orchard where there are booths, displays, games, contests – lots of good food – a horse race, and then a community dance at the armory in the evening to bring things to a close."

"That sounds like great fun," I stated. "I can see why girls like Clara Newcomb and my sister are so excited."

Grace had a way with words and seemed to enjoy painting a picture of the event for me. Her descriptions of the savory foods and lively activities, the brightly colored decorations and strings of paper lanterns swaying beneath a full moon were so vivid I could almost taste the homemade delicacies and hear the happy participants dancing under the stars.

"I don't know many people yet," I ventured, "so I hope you and your husband will be there."

Grace's smile was kind and full of feeling. "We may attend some of the earlier festivities but I know we won't be at the dance."

"Your husband doesn't like to dance?"

Grace looked lovingly down at the sleeping infant in her arms and brushed his forehead gently with her lips before answering. "No, that's not it. David used to love to dance but... well, we don't dance anymore."

Her voice had fallen to a whisper and her eyes no longer met mine.

"I guess it's very different now that there's a baby in the house," I suggested lamely, feeling I had stumbled into a personal problem and should help Grace avoid divulging more than she intended.

"I'm sure you and your sister will have a wonderful time," she said, reaching across and laying a delicate hand on my arm. "It will be the perfect opportunity for you to get acquainted with other young people."

I suddenly felt very young indeed and very inexperienced and knew that even though there were only a few years between us I was incapable of understanding whatever burdened the young matron before me and was equally incapable of helping her.

II.

Walking home after leaving Grace I found myself preoccupied by contradictory thoughts – anticipation of the gaiety associated with the upcoming Harvest Festival and concern about the sadness which seemed to pervade a young woman I felt certain would be flourishing were it not for the man to whom she was married. Even though I had met David Whitley only in passing, I began to dislike him intensely as my sympathy for Grace painted an increasingly dismal portrait of her spouse.

I realized rather abruptly that as a result of my preoccupation I had strayed considerably from my intended route home and had wandered into an unfamiliar section of the wooded terrain surrounding the Cove. The area seemed wild and unkempt so I felt certain that I was in the undeveloped area between town and the church and that a continued northern route would soon return me to the area of the woods with which I was familiar.

There were no sounds apart from the crunching of brittle leaves underfoot as I walked and the occasional call of a bird or rustling of an unseen rabbit or squirrel. The unspoiled beauty of my surroundings served to embolden me. There was a sense of freedom found in exploring the Cove on my own and I particularly appreciated the solitude my walks provided as well as the opportunity to think through problems such as the plight of Grace Whitley, or at least what I perceived as her plight.

The path I followed – if it could be called a path – narrowed considerably as I entered a stand of birch trees reaching heavenward in an almost pleading gesture from the tangle of brush growing up around them. Rachel would have been quick to point out that trees are incapable of "pleading" as my tendency to give inanimate objects human emotions and attributes was a source of irritation to her. But to me they truly did appear to be reaching upward from the undergrowth with which they competed in a manner reminiscent of the troubled swimmer we had seen one summer who urgently thrust his arms from the churning water to grasp the hands of his rescuer. It reminded me again of Grace Whitley and as I sat on an adjacent log in an effort to get my bearings my mind once again was filled with thoughts of the sad young woman I longed to befriend.

I don't know just how long I sat there but was eventually jarred from my preoccupation by the sound of approaching horses. I stood, listening closely; more than one rider was coming toward me rapidly but before I could pinpoint the direction so to be well out of their way they had come crashing through the overgrown bushes and might well have run me down had the lead rider not caught sight of my plaid cape and forcefully reigned in his mount. The horse reared angrily and came to a stop so close to me that I could feel the warmth of its breath as it snorted and stomped.

Stumbling backward in fright, I fell over the log on which I had been sitting and came down hard on the ground behind it with my legs draped over the log in a most unladylike fashion, my cape askew over one shoulder, and the rim of my hat resting on the bridge of my nose.

One of the riders was laughing heartily at my predicament and as I pushed the hat back, eager to confront their carelessness, I found myself looking up into the unsmiling face of Jacob Collier.

"Are you all right," he demanded over the guffaws of his companion.

"Yes, no thanks to the two of you!" I was angry and made no effort at masking my emotions. "Your carelessness could have tragic consequences," I continued, rising to my feet and glaring his laughing friend into silence.

"Quite so," Mr. Collier replied, "but we hardly expected to encounter a pedestrian in this isolated portion of my property."

"*Your* property," I stammered, feeling my face growing hot with the flush of embarrassment.

"Yes. Where did you think you were?"

"I was on my way home from making a call in town," I began to explain, feebly gesturing in what I had assumed to be a northerly direction. "I realized the area was unfamiliar but had no idea how far I had strayed..."

Anger and fear were receding and only my embarrassment remained. "...I assure you I never meant to trespass."

"No, of course not," he agreed, dismissing my meager apology with a wave of his hand. "But the direction you've chosen has taken you some distance east of your destination."

I glanced at both men, my eyes coming to rest on his companion, sitting astride his horse silently regarding our exchange with a rakish smile. Mr. Collier followed my gaze and after tersely apologizing for his lack of manners introduced the rider to me as Gavin Marshall, a business associate – which probably meant he was another Remittance Man.

Both men were fashionably attired in attractive riding garb and made a striking impression astride their fine mounts, but Gavin Marshall was undeniably the most handsome man I had ever seen and I felt plain and dowdy under his open scrutiny. His hair was the color of wheat before harvest, lying thick and unmussed despite their hard riding. His features were absolutely perfect, his build strong and masculine, but most striking were his eyes – large and deep blue, they were arrestingly accented by dark lashes and brows. There also was an arrogance about him which, for me, detracted from his handsome appearance. I was sure he was a man accustomed to having whatever he wanted and wasn't averse to using his looks to get his way. In a flash of unkindness to my sibling, I realized he reminded me of Rachel.

Mr. Marshall was smiling benignly down at me as Jacob Collier identified me as the new preacher's daughter but there was a smirk in his eyes that made me feel as if I were being assessed without the benefit of clothing as he acknowledged the introduction.

"Miss Pendleton," he said, "I would have been in church long ago had I realized the accoutrements were so appealing."

"The church is impressive," I replied, choosing to ignore his hollow compliment, "but I trust aesthetics will not be your sole inspiration should you deign to join us for worship."

Now it was Mr. Collier who laughed, reaching across and slapping his friend good-naturedly on the shoulder. The sternness ebbed away as he relaxed and he seemed more affable than my initial impression of him. I also was struck by the realization that he was much more attractive than I had thought the first time we met.

"You cut me to the quick, Miss Pendleton," Gavin Marshall said, raising a hand to his heart in mock injury. "How could my motivation be anything but the desire to hear your father expound upon the Good Book?"

His smile was disarming and I felt my resolve to dislike him wavering slightly. There was something about him that was almost automatically endearing. Despite the fact that he looked at a woman in a flagrantly lustful way, his manner was courtly and when he spoke he made one feel as if she were the most important and interesting person he had ever encountered; a charming and dangerous combination.

"Jake, old man," he proclaimed, "we must see Miss Pendleton safely to her destination!"

"Indeed we shall," Jacob replied pleasantly, swinging down from the saddle.

He was standing very close to me and the smell of leather and shaving soap was new and appealing. He looked directly into my eyes and for a moment longer he was friendly and his face held none of the aloofness which I had found so disconcerting when we met in his garden. Whether it was something I said or simply because, as I was to discover, his mood was subject to sudden change, the friendly openness quickly passed as I tried to dissuade them from seeing me home.

"I assure you, gentlemen, that I am quite capable of finding my way home. I am in no need of an escort."

Gavin leaned forward and rested his folded arms across the horn of his saddle, flicking the ends of his reins in my direction. "One never knows what peril might lurk about just waiting for an unsuspecting damsel to pass by. I think you should reconsider."

The reproach was on my lips that it was likely he would be the only peril a damsel might encounter, but I remained silent.

"More to the point, Miss Pendleton," Jacob broke in coolly, "is the fact that you already have wandered astray once and since you are on my property I feel it is my responsibility, as well as my prerogative, to see you safely home. Will you join me on my horse, or shall I put you there?"

I was about to protest but there was a stubbornness to the set of his jaw and a cool determination in his eyes that made me decide it was best to acquiesce. Besides, Gavin Marshall was looking on with such undisguised pleasure that I was determined not to give him the satisfaction of seeing Jacob Collier put me on the horse if he should choose to follow through with his threat.

Mr. Collier held the spirited animal steady for me as I mounted but I experienced some difficulty nonetheless in trying to maintain a semblance of propriety sitting astride a horse without the benefit of proper riding clothes. I noted with satisfaction, however, that should he care to indulge all Gavin Marshall would see was a bit of plain petticoat trim, a snatch of heavy woolen stockings, and a pair of extremely sensible shoes. I was not at all the type of woman likely to hold his attention for long; a reality which brought me a sense of gratification – as well as making me feel hopelessly unattractive.

Jacob swung up effortlessly. He sat behind me on the horse's rump and when he reached around me to take the reins I once again was aware of the pleasing smell of shaving soap. Quite frankly, I never had sat so close to a man who wasn't a member of my family and the experience seemed to alert all my senses. The realization that, apparently, I was as impressionable as the vacuous heroines of popular novels of the day – of whom I always made fun when Rachel shared one with me – was humiliating to say the least.

I made a conscious effort to concentrate on the horse.

III.

When we had emerged from the woods and were ascending Church Street I found myself growing increasingly aware of the awkwardness of my situation. I quite literally was in the arms of the community's most notorious gentleman – a person my father had made abundantly clear was not acceptable company and should be assiduously avoided. I far from relished being brought home in such fashion by a man of questionable character but was at a loss as to how to extricate myself without seeming extremely rude and ungrateful. Mr. Collier had treated me with the utmost respect – albeit a bit scornfully – and I hardly felt threatened by him, nor did I wish to insult him.

Jacob seemed to have read my thoughts for he drew up his horse and paused just before coming into full view of the house. He and Mr. Marshall had talked around me most of the way home and Gavin stopped in mid-sentence as Jacob reined his horse over to the side of the road.

"What is it, Jake? Why are you stopping here?"

Before Jacob could answer, Gavin heaved an exasperated sigh.

"Oh come now, Miss Pendleton's virtue is hardly in jeopardy merely because we have escorted her home!" He directed his attention to me. "Surely your reputation isn't that pristine – or is it that ours is so reprehensible?"

I began to reply but he impulsively spurred his horse on and made any further consideration of the situation moot.

After murmuring a quiet "Sorry," Jacob followed in Mr. Marshall's wake and as unfortunate coincidence – or fate – would have it, Mother was just seeing the Widows Starkey and Wentworth to their carriage as we pulled up in front of the house!

The widowed matrons – renowned for their overworked tongues – looked from me to my two companions and back to me openly aghast. Mrs. Starkey's hand flew to cover her heart in blatant dismay and Mrs. Wentworth's perfumed handkerchief dabbed daintily at her nose as if an unpleasant odor had suddenly permeated the atmosphere. I didn't know whether to laugh at the caricature of prudishness they presented or cry over the helpless irony of the situation.

Mr. Collier vaulted down from the back of the horse to help me dismount as I rather breathlessly introduced my escorts and explained to the dumfounded trio before us that I had become lost in the woods and how my companions had found me and insisted on seeing me safely home. Gavin Marshall obviously enjoyed horrifying the two older ladies but I felt that Mr. Collier would have preferred to spare me – or himself – the awkwardness of the moment.

When I had finished speaking there was just the slightest hesitation before my mother broke the silence and reached out a slender hand to my rescuer.

"Mr. Collier," she began, "I am indeed grateful to you for seeing Martha home. I have been concerned that something like this might happen as we are all still quite unfamiliar with the area." Without skipping a beat she added warmly, "Would you and Mr. Marshall like a cup of tea? I'm sure my husband also would want to thank you."

I have no doubt that Gavin Marshall would have liked nothing better than to further pique the widows by accepting Mother's offer but Mr. Collier was in full command of the moment and declined her invitation before Gavin could speak. Jacob obviously was surprised and impressed by Mother's graciousness. He still held her hand in his right and covering it with his left, he spoke in a tone of voice I had yet to hear him use. Mother flushed slightly as he then raised her hand to his lips and, in an archaic gesture of respect, kissed it lightly before releasing her and remounting his horse. To me he had nothing further to say but gave a faint smile and a slight nod before turning to the two older women and wishing them a good day.

Mr. Marshall, unable to resist a parting shot, called back gaily as they trotted away that he looked forward to seeing *more* of me.

Mrs. Starkey, who had been uncharacteristically silent during the brief exchange, regarded me with a look of speculation which made me feel – and undoubtedly look – as if I were guilty of less than ladylike behavior.

"My dear Martha," she began, opening wide her heavily lidded eyes and shaking her head slowly, "what could you have been thinking, accepting a ride from the likes of them?"

Mrs. Wentworth's head bobbed in agreement and she murmured her characteristic "ah-yuh" of agreement as she put her arm around me as one would when seeking to console the victim of some tragedy.

"Heaven only knows what might have happened," Mrs. Starkey continued, "...alone in the woods with Jacob Collier!"

Mrs. Wentworth bobbed and shuddered dramatically at the unmentionable fate Mrs. Starkey's words implied.

"But I wasn't alone with Mr. Collier," I was quick to point out, "Mr. Marshall was there as well."

"Gavin Marshall," she intoned as one would the name of some dreaded disease. "Why, that's even worse!"

The magnitude of the situation was underscored when Mrs. Wentworth startled both my mother and me by punctuating her habitually bobbing head with an almost ethereal "Even worse!"

I believe Mrs. Starkey would have given us a recitation of the aggregate sins of the Misters Collier and Marshall there on the spot but my mother wedged her way into the conversation by observing that I was undoubtedly tired and in need of something warm to drink. We started for the door in hopes that our guests would recognize the gesture as closure of the matter. They fell into step beside us, however, and proceeded to usher us into our parlor where Mrs. Starkey continued undaunted.

"I feel it my duty to tell you, Mrs. Pendleton, that Martha may very well have just narrowly escaped disaster!"

"I appreciate your concern, ladies, and I know that Mr. Collier is one of your 'Remittance Men,' but given the circumstances I can't see that my daughter's actions were inappropriate."

"You don't understand, Mrs. Pendleton. Jacob Collier isn't just a scoundrel like those banished from the Continent for muddying the family name."

She glanced furtively over her shoulder while Mrs. Wentworth bobbed approval of her assessment.

"Jacob Collier is a murderer!"

"Ladies, really..." Mother began in startled opposition to Mrs. Starkey's unexpected proclamation.

"You'd do well to hear me out," Mrs. Starkey interrupted.

She drew herself up in self-righteous indignation, looking even more prudish as she continued.

"Ask anyone; it's a well known fact that Martha's friend was sent here to avoid being charged in connection with the sudden death of a young lady he was courting. Died under most suspicious circumstances, she did, and then your Mr. Collier is whisked away to America before the poor girl is even cold! There may be no proving it, but even a blind man can see where the guilt surely lies."

She looked straight at me before delivering her final pronouncement.

"Jacob Collier killed her!"

CHAPTER FOUR

I.

It was five days before the Harvest Festival but in light of what the widows Starkey and Wentworth had told us after I was escorted home by the Cove's two most notorious residents, the upcoming festivities had received little of my attention. After being given a slightly edited account of my "misadventure" (we omitted the widows' diatribe, particularly Mrs. Starkey's indictment of Jacob Collier as a murderer) Father had insisted that I curtail my walks – and I freely admit that I was inclined to do so even without such an injunction. The entire experience had rattled me.

Was it possible? Could someone use family position and influence literally to get away with murder? The question haunted me not only on moral grounds but because I found it difficult to believe that Jacob Collier could be capable of doing such a thing. Granted, I knew him superficially at best but there was something about him – a look in his eyes that I had seen at the cliff overlook and again in the woods and the tone of his voice when he spoke to my mother. I admit I might have been slightly infatuated; he was dark and dangerous yet respectful toward me and my mother – the appeal was almost too cliché. But regardless of my possible distraction, I just found the accusation difficult to swallow. Women like Bertha Starkey and Sarah Wentworth suffered from a malignancy of spirit caused by a lethal longing for significance and an abysmally narrow world view. Surely they were mistaken; willing links in the poisonous chain of unsubstantiated gossip.

Jacob Collier just couldn't – mustn't – be guilty of murder.

Rachel and I were scheduled to spend Monday afternoon at church working on decorations to dress up the sanctuary for the worship service signaling the start of the Festival. I knew that Augusta Wilkes would be there and hoped for an opportunity to speak with her about Mr. Collier. If anyone could put things in perspective it would be Augusta. She was a lifelong resident of the Cove and patently level-headed; surely she would know facts from speculation and hearsay. I felt if only I could speak to Augusta perhaps I could learn the truth about Jacob Collier's exile.

My heart was such a jumble of emotions. I kept telling myself that my interest in the matter was due to my blossoming friendship with Jocelyn and a sense of moral indignation that the "landed gentry" should be able to use their wealth and status to live above the law. But, again, I also had to admit that there was something compelling about the man himself. I truly believed it was the aura of mystery surrounding him that attracted me. Whatever the cause, the dispassionately objective side of me hoped that Augusta could dispel some of the mystery – and likewise the allure.

Augusta was in a workroom in the church cellar when Rachel and I went over to the church after dinner at noon. She and several other ladies were making ornaments for the pews from brightly colored leaves and corn husks tied into bunches with copper colored ribbon. We took our places at the long table and, after brief instructions on the art of tying leaves and corn husks together, tried to make ourselves useful.

News of my escapade in the woods had spread rapidly as Mrs. Starkey and Mrs. Wentworth made the rounds and there was more than one curious glance in my direction while we worked. I could tell that Mrs. Raney, a woman I recalled from our first day as having displayed an inappropriate interest in Mother's meager collection of porcelain figurines, was dying to ask me about the incident. Doubtless all would have had insights to share. But perhaps there are some benefits to being a minister's child for, although they undoubtedly spoke of it among themselves, no one broached the subject with me.

My mind definitely was not on my work and, after being mildly reprimanded for having put together the wrong combination of leaves and husks, Augusta asked me to help her with some other work upstairs. My disgruntled co-workers probably were relieved to see me go but instead of wanting to win their approval and prove myself adept at leaf-tying, I was glad to be given the chance to speak with Augusta privately.

As we climbed the stairs, Augusta explained that she needed assistance taking some measurements around the chancel.

As we worked I gathered my courage and plunged in.

"I suppose you heard about my adventure in the woods," I began tentatively.

"Ah-yuh, but don't you worry yourself over what the widows are saying. You're the innocent in their story and they the sages who enlighten you and your mother. And anyways, most folks know to take what they say and divide it in two."

She smiled warmly and patted my arm in reassurance.

"Oh, I don't care so much what the widows may say about me," I replied hastily, "but I would like to ask you about some of the things they told us."

"Surely; I'd be glad to help if I can."

We sat down in the front pew and I told her the entire story – including my impression of the two men and what the widows had said about Jacob Collier.

"I just need to know if it's true, Augusta. Do you know why Jocelyn and her cousin are here?"

Augusta assessed me quietly and glanced around the empty church before speaking.

"Before I answer your question, let me ask one of you."

"All right."

"Why the interest in Jacob Collier? He's not the kind of man a body wants to see a child like you take up with."

There was deep concern in her voice and I felt my face growing hot under her scrutiny.

"I'm not 'interested' in Mr. Collier," I stammered, eager to correct her misperception, "and I'm certainly not 'taking up' with him. It's just that I care about his cousin and Rachel goes to his home for French lessons. I've talked to him before and I don't think he... I can't believe someone could use their money to get away with murder! This is 1916 America, for goodness sake, not medieval Europe!"

Augusta's face still registered concern and told me she wasn't completely satisfied with my explanation.

Avoiding her eyes I looked down at my hands.

"I guess I do find him attractive..." I confessed. "But can't you see, if I know the truth then he won't be such a mystery – and won't be so intriguing."

She smiled at my honesty and seemed relieved.

"Martha, you're a smart girl with a good head on your shoulders. I know you'll be all right."

There was a pregnant silence as she gathered her thoughts.

"When the Colliers first came here they hired Wilson Edwards – the lawyer, have you met him? They needed some legal work done in relation to buying Patriot's Point and Wilson's the best there is when it comes to such things. Anyway, in the course of doin' that work with them, Miss Collier let slip some of the details of why they'd come to the Cove – can't imagine how it happened as she's usually real stand-offish and doesn't say much more than 'howdy-do,' but the mistake was made. Well, unfortunately Wilson confided in his wife – one of the Cove's biggest talkers, ah-yuh – and the rest, as they say, is history. The story spread like wildfire, with all sorts of embellishments along the way, I'm sure, and Jacob Collier suddenly was more tainted than a leper. Now, I don't go judgin' whether he's guilty or clean – will be leavin' that to the Lord – but apparently it's true that a young lady he was courting up and died and shortly afterward his family sent him here. Some around town say she took poison, others say she threw herself from a balcony; could be one or the other, could be neither. Whatever the cause of her death, seems it never was fixed to anyone's satisfaction whether she took her own life or whether someone took it from her."

She paused for a moment to let her words register before continuing. "Best as I can tell, the Collier clan must be highly regarded in their part of the world. Guess the publicity and ugly speculation rocked the family to its foundation so they decided to try to silence the scandal-mongers by scootin' Mr. Jacob out of the picture. They be not the first – or the last, I reckon – to take the easy road rather than face a problem full on."

She stood and brushed unseen dust from her hands.

"That's all I can tell you, Martha; 'cept that we'd all be wise to leave him alone. If he's guilty then chances are he's also dangerous, and if he's innocent... well, we'd still best leave him set as he appears to be festering in bitterness and that can't bring nobody no good. I'm sure Miss Collier rues the day she made that slip of the tongue. It changed her cousin from social pariah like the other Remittance Men into a suspected murderer – someone even more mistrusted and avoided by the good people of Tully's Cove."

In a gesture of benediction, Augusta patted the hands that lay clenched tensely in my lap and walked slowly down the long center aisle toward the narthex and the closet staircase leading to the cellar. The sound of her footsteps echoed in my ears as did her words.

So it was true. The widows had embellished the story only in declaring Jacob positively guilty. And I had to admit that little of what Augusta knew weighed on the side of innocence. A young woman had died under questionable circumstances – I could imagine the furor it caused as people speculated as to what actually had happened. It would rattle the bones of an influential family like the Colliers. So in the end it was decided that the best way to handle the situation was to remove the person whose presence – and undoubtedly whose demeanor – fueled the fire. And as a result, Jacob Collier found himself quietly banished to the obscurity of a small New England city, his only connection with home being the presence and ministrations of his long-suffering cousin.

I had found out what I wanted to know. And it did help dispel some of the aura of mystery surrounding Mr. Collier – time would tell if it also would dispel the allure.

I rose and walked slowly down the center aisle of the church immune to the cascade of reflected stained glass glory all around me. Instead of returning to the volunteers in the cellar, however, I pushed open the heavy arched double doors, stepped out of the church and sat down on the wide top step.

The crisp autumn air was a tonic and I found myself thinking that Augusta's advice was sound. One could pity a person like Jacob Collier and befriend an innocent bystander like his cousin, but it was wisest under the circumstances to leave it at that.

"What are you doing out here," the petulant voice of my sister interrupted my contemplation, reminding me of my duty. "I'm not going to do all that work by myself!"

Satisfied with the chastisement of her prodigal sister, Rachel turned with a flourish and flounced back into the church.

I stood, brushed a smattering of autumn debris from my backside, and followed Rachel back downstairs feeling moderately energized by a new sense of resolve to leave Mr. Jacob Collier at Patriot's Point and get on with the business at hand.

II.

The extent of Augusta's concern about my "taking up" with Jacob Collier was made abundantly clear over the next few days as she demonstrated an undaunted determination to introduce me to every eligible bachelor in the county. It was both humorous and somewhat mortifying to be the target of her matchmaking zeal as she sought my assistance on errands related to the Festival that took us to businesses where we "coincidentally" encountered gentlemen she obviously considered appropriate for the preacher's daughter.

At first I was as unsuspecting as a lamb going to slaughter and was pleased to be sought out to accompany her. As pleasant as time with Augusta always was, my suspicions eventually were aroused, however, and after a second afternoon of errands which took us to the mill, the bank, and the county newspaper – each stop garnering introductions to unmarried men – I felt certain my assessment of Augusta's intentions was correct. Her enthusiastic marketing campaign made me feel rather like an undesirable relative teetering on the brink of spinsterhood, and yet I also was deeply touched as I knew her motives were sterling. Giving credit where due, however, it nonetheless was imperative that I dissuade her from this incommodiously noble pursuit and convince her that I was not in the market for a husband – Jacob Collier or otherwise.

It was Thursday afternoon – just two days before the Harvest Festival – and sitting beside Augusta on the squeaky, unyielding seat of her carriage I found myself wondering which unsuspecting bachelors she had selected for today's rounds.

"Where are we off to," I asked with deliberate nonchalance.

"Well, I need to pick up new bunting from the Emporium for the D.A.R. booth, then there's a bushel of apples from the Dunbar farm that needs to be brought into town for the pies the Ladies' Auxiliary is puttin' up..."

"How did all these errands come to fall on you, Augusta? It seems to me you do much more than anyone else."

"Oh no, not really. Besides I don't mind – 'specially when someone comes along to help."

She smiled warmly at me and I felt most ungrateful in seeking to thwart her plans.

"I'm more than happy to come along," I began, determined to take advantage of the opening she had provided, "but please Augusta... no more introductions to unmarried men."

She started ever so slightly.

"Say what?"

She looked innocent enough but an undisguised twinkle in her eye gave her away and told me she wasn't altogether disappointed to have been found out.

"Oh come now, Augusta. Every stop we've made over the last two days has included at least one introduction to an eligible bachelor. There was Mr. Riley at the bank, Mr. Carlton at *The Sentinel*, Mr. Browne and Mr. McFarland at the Courthouse – need I go on?"

I reached over and took her gloved hand in mine before continuing. "I appreciate what you're trying to do, and understand you're only trying to protect me from... from what you perceive to be my interest in Mr. Collier, but there's truly no need to worry. I'm not looking for a husband and if I were I certainly wouldn't consider Jacob Collier a likely candidate – why, Father wouldn't even let him in the door!"

"Well now," she replied with a defensive sniff, "seems to me a young lady like you ought to be meetin' some of the Cove's finest – and not just comin' out of church on Sunday morning."

Her seriousness made me chuckle and it took little cajoling before she, too, began to see the humor in our husband-hunting and she had readily added her wheezy laugh to my own.

"Please Augusta," I reiterated, "promise me you'll stop trying to play matchmaker. Promise me?"

She was silent for a moment but in the end gave me her word that she would abandon her crusade to find a suitable match for me.

We already had ridden some distance west toward the prosperous Dunbar acreage – and their overweight, underage son – but Augusta reined in her dapple mare and without comment turned the buggy around on the wide shoulder of the unpaved road. My face must have expressed my question for before I could ask she explained our about-face tersely and without additional comment.

"Eli brung those apples into town yesterday."

III.

It seemed as if the entire town turned out for Saturday morning's worship service. Virtually every pew was filled to capacity and benches had been added in the back and up in the choir loft to accommodate the overflow. The bunches of leaves and husks with their copper colored ribbon looked very attractive where they had been fastened to the ends of the pews facing each other across the center aisle. In addition, an arrangement of pumpkins, hay bales, corn stalks and brightly colored leaves had been placed on the floor just in front of the altar, adding a beautiful splash of autumn color to the chancel and heightening the festive atmosphere in the church.

It was an idyllic autumn morning; sunlight pouring through the stained glass windows brought to life every facet of the intricately worked art glass and rained brilliant colors down upon the assembled congregation. I was seated between Rachel and my mother in the pew we had inherited from the former pastor's family. We each had chosen our clothing with particular care that day and made rather a handsome trio, I thought. Mother had chosen a beautiful russet colored wool skirt with matching waistcoat set off by an emerald green pin-striped blouse with a high, lace-trimmed collar; an outfit she had been reserving for Christmas but which seemed too perfect for the day to leave in the clothespress. Seated to my left on the aisle Rachel was the picture of serene femininity. She was clad in a forest green skirt and a creamy ivory shirtwaist, the front of which boasted a cascade of ruffles. She had topped it all off with a muted forest green plaid vest that contrasted nicely with the ruffles at her throat. It was my favorite of her outfits; a castoff from a wealthy parishioner at Father's last church but on Rachel it could never look second hand or out of style. Virtually everyone had dressed for the occasion and the church was filled with bright autumn colors, stiff starched collars, and meticulously ironed pleats and creases. My own outfit was a bit more tailored and, in light of the festive colors I saw all around me, definitely too dark. I realized that once again I unwittingly had cast myself in the role of the dowdy spinster. Why such realizations never come to one while standing in front of the clothespress I never will know. Shifting rather self-consciously, I intentionally turned my attention to the hymnal clutched like a life preserver by my glove-clad hands.

As Father stepped from the sacristy into the chancel I felt myself relax and a tingle of pride rippled down my spine. He looked so strong and handsome in his somber black cassock and there was a sense of dignity and poise in his manner which instantly held one's attention. I knew he had labored tirelessly over his message as it was one of the few opportunities afforded a minister to speak to a broader spectrum of the community than the portion represented by his flock. Father could be aloof and rather abrupt but he had a soft spot in his heart when it came to preaching the Gospel and a sense of urgency for those on the road to perdition. He was in his element.

Father's message that morning was based on scripture which reflected the harvest theme. He had chosen a passage from II Corinthians in the New Testament:

"Now He who supplied seed to the sower and bread for food will also increase the harvest of your righteousness so that you can be generous on every occasion, and your generosity will result in thanksgiving to God. Because of the service by which you have proven yourselves, men will praise God for the obedience that accompanies your confession of the gospel of Christ..."

Father spoke with passion and deep personal conviction, drawing a parallel between the material harvest we celebrated and the spiritual harvest ripening all around us. How could we help but respond to the mercy shown to us in the death and resurrection of Christ, he demanded, except by sharing our material blessings with those less fortunate and our spiritual blessings with those groping in the dark? His words elicited several "amen's" from the Baptist quarter, and the fervor with which he spoke was challenging and inspiring.

From where I was sitting I could see that beads of perspiration had appeared on his brow and by the time he had drawn his message to a close the exertion had given him a mildly disheveled appearance. No worse for wear, however, he led the congregation in a rousing rendition of the traditional Thanksgiving hymn "Now Thank We All Our God" and closed the service with prayers of gratitude for a bountiful harvest, petitions for a spiritual revival, and –

being a rabid isolationist – an admonition to the government to keep us out of the war currently raging in Europe.

As we wormed our way toward the narthex and the doors where Father was greeting departing worshippers, I noticed Jocelyn Collier sitting by herself near the back of the church. She looked lovely in grey merino, but also appeared a little forlorn. I tried to reach out to her with a welcoming smile but she seemed to look right through me and I couldn't get her attention. It was obvious that, as usual, she had come unaccompanied. I made a mental note to invite her to sit with us in the future.

Grace Whitley and her unsmiling husband, David, also were in attendance, as were the Choate sisters (looking more like magpies than ever in their apparently identical black suits), the widows Starkey and Wentworth (carefully inspecting the passing parade), a host of familiar and unfamiliar faces, and, of course, Eli Thornton and his sister, Augusta Wilkes.

Mother had gone off with Augusta to attend to some details pertaining to the church's booth at the Festival, and Rachel and I were almost to the narthex when a voice called to me from behind.

"Miss Pendleton; how nice to see you again!"

It was Gavin Marshall, smiling broadly and speaking at a volume obviously intended to draw the attention of others. He needn't have worried, however, for if a woman had a heartbeat her eyes were inevitably drawn to him. He looked even more handsome than usual that morning in grey pinstriped trousers complimented by a charcoal grey coat and vest with a burgundy-red cravat at his throat.

"Good morning, Mr. Marshall," I replied stiffly, fighting valiantly against the color that threatened to flood my face as speculative glances were cast our way.

He was next to us in a moment, taking my gloved hand in his and acting as if we were old and dear friends.

Rachel was enthralled instantly and I determined that Mr. Marshall should not have the opportunity to work his magic on my impressionable little sister. Explaining rather curtly that we were expected elsewhere, I attempted to shepherd Rachel past him but he was equally determined to prolong our conversation and bodily blocked my retreat.

"Aren't you going to introduce me to your lovely companion," he asked rather flippantly, almost drooling over the pretty girl at my side.

"This is my little sister, Mr. Marshall," I stated matter-of-factly, avoiding use of her Christian name and emphasizing the word *little*. "Mr. Marshall is an acquaintance of the Colliers," I informed Rachel in hopes that she would thus realize he was not someone of whom Father would approve.

The warning was lost on her, however, and she smiled sweetly, looking up at him through thick, dark lashes.

"I'm very pleased to meet you, Mr. Marshall. I'm Rachel Pendleton."

Gavin smiled charmingly and, turning once again to me, referred vaguely to our conversation in the woods.

"You see, it was high time that I put in an appearance among the devout."

"Were you here for the entire service, Mr. Marshall," I asked, making no attempt to disguise my skepticism.

"From opening hymn through the last 'amen.'"

He turned his attention to Rachel. "You see, Miss Rachel, your sister is of the opinion that there is no hope for this lonely old reprobate. I hope you will not share that assessment."

"Oh, Martha and I rarely ever agree," she replied coyly. "She doesn't like anybody."

"There are few people who truly are hopeless, Mr. Marshall," I interjected, "but unfortunately most scoffers do eventually join their ranks."

"Once again you cut me to the quick, Miss Pendleton. I had hoped that your father's admonition to share your blessings with those groping in the dark would extend to the likes of me."

He smiled good-naturedly and I found my dislike wavering.

"Did you also take note of his admonition to repentance and revival?"

"Touché', Miss Pendleton, touché'! I think it's time to change the subject... May I hope to see you ladies at the dance this evening?"

"Oh yes," Rachel replied enthusiastically, "we'll look forward to it."

His smile was disarming.

"Alas, I'm afraid you can't speak for your elder sister. But if half the Pendleton delegation deigns to acknowledge me I shall consider it an evening well spent. Good day, ladies."

As he walked away from us I physically turned Rachel back toward the front of the church determined to leave by another exit. In doing so I made eye contact with Grace Whitley standing next to her husband who was engrossed in conversation with a man I didn't recognize. She looked almost frightened but glanced away quickly when our eyes met. I decided to seek her out at some point during the day's activities.

IV.

Hope and Clara Newcomb, with whom Rachel had grown close over the past weeks, were to be our companions and guides for the day. They arrived at the manse only moments after we returned from church and waited impatiently while we changed into clothing better suited for the county fair atmosphere the Harvest Festival was sure to provide. It was obvious from their excitement that this was a much-anticipated event for residents of the region and I began to share their enthusiasm the more exuberantly they spoke.

As a result of their contagious excitement we decided not to wait for my parents, who were being picked up by Eli Thornton a bit later, but chose instead to walk the few miles that lay between the church and Bailey's Orchard, the traditional location of the Festival. It was a perfect day for such an outing. Indian Summer was evident in every nuance; the almost painfully blue sky, the glorious colors all around us, and the unseasonably mild wind which sent the colorful autumn leaves swimming down from denuded limbs to join the ocean of yellow and orange that swirled around us and crunched underfoot as we walked.

I enjoyed listening to the carefree chatter of my three companions as their conversation flitted from school work to boys, from boys to innocuous gossip concerning their peers, and ultimately came to rest on clothing – specifically what they would be wearing to the dance that evening.

Listening to their schoolgirl prattle I felt infinitely older than they – a difference belying the four or five years that lay between us and reminding me of how my last conversation with Grace Whitley had had the opposite effect. Then I had felt incredibly young and naïve, despite the fact that Grace was but a few years my senior.

As we completed the last mile of our trek, I came to the conclusion that the feelings of limbo I was experiencing must be due to the fact that my life was in a period of transition. I no longer could be placed in the same category as Rachel and her friends but likewise fell short of the realities and responsibilities of life encountered by young matrons like Grace. Such thoughts were mildly alarming for I felt that I should by now be doing something more than merely continuing to be my parents' child. I had completed high school and even taken the equivalent of two years' coursework at a small women's collegiate academy but didn't really feel equipped to do anything. A vague concern about the future had been nagging at me for some time and slowly was crystallizing into a conviction that the time had come to make some decisions about the direction my life should take. It was 1916 after all, and lots of modern women were looking out for themselves and moving beyond the confines of home and family. Why, in larger cities women working in factories and offices were commonplace – and if we became involved in the war as many predicted would happen, their numbers, by necessity, would grow exponentially. I didn't know what I might be able to contribute but shrugged aside the fleeting thought that perhaps I shouldn't have been so quick to dissuade Augusta from her short-lived crusade to find me a spouse. No; active husband-hunting could have disastrous results and, anyway, I definitely wasn't ready for marriage – or was it, as Rachel liked to imply, that I was too late?

Bailey's Orchard was a long-defunct apple orchard deeded to the city of Tully's Cove during Reconstruction – Matthew Bailey having been inspired by the creation of Yellowstone National Park in 1872. It consisted of approximately seven acres of land from which most of the old trees had been cleared over the years. Where it fronted the main road leading out from town, rough-hewn split rail fencing marked the approach to a main gate pronouncing it a gift to the people of Tully's Cove. It was a logical site for events like the Harvest Festival and was a regular stop on the Chautauqua circuit as well.

Both sides of the road approaching the entrance were crowded with carriages of every description and flatbed wagons covered with straw and quilts on which groups had traveled from outlying areas. There were even a few automobiles wedged in among the more traditional conveyances; a source of much curiosity for many of the men folk in attendance that afternoon. As a result of all the traffic it was much easier to be on foot rather than responsible for a wagon and team and we congratulated ourselves on our collective wisdom in coming ahead of my parents.

Directly beyond the main entrance an avenue of brightly decorated booths had been set up where virtually every church and civic organization filled their allotted space with baked goods and homemade items – "fripperies" Eli called them – for sale to support their work or ministry. To the right of the booths was an area set aside for competitive recreation, the schedule including everything from three-legged races and bobbing for apples to pie eating contests and a turkey shoot. Directly across from the game field, and to the left of the booths, a large tent had been erected sheltering rows of long, improvised trestle tables for patrons of the volunteer fire department's pig roast and the D.A.R.'s pie sale. Beyond the tent, in an area peppered with ancient, gnarled trees, a section had been designated for picnickers, and adjacent that was an area where local artisans and craftsmen demonstrated their skills and displayed their wares. The mingling of delightful odors and the cacophony of sound was wonderful and I soon was absorbed in people-watching and a devotee of this annual event.

Rachel and her friends – eager to go directly to the game field where most of the fellows their age were equally eager to demonstrate their prowess in sport – vowed that they would go no farther if permitted to move on unaccompanied. Feeling that a chaperone was superfluous in such a public environment, I agreed that they could go on without me and that we would rendezvous in an hour's time.

I began to work my way slowly down the avenue of booths, exploring the various items offered and enjoying the shouts and chatter as each booth's volunteers good-naturedly hawked their wares. Virtually every display included a tempting array of homemade delicacies and I strolled casually among them, savoring the mixture of tantalizing aromas and trying to decide what I wanted to buy. There were rhubarb tarts and applesauce cake at the Knight's of Columbus's booth, the Baptists were in the midst of a loud and boisterous taffy-pull, Johnny cake with raspberry sauce was offered by the Women's Temperance League – the list was long and everything was almost equally enticing.

After pausing for a few moments to listen to a man distributing leaflets advertising the "Horrors of the Hun" and enumerating the reasons the U.S. must intervene in the war in Europe, I finally selected a wedge of chocolate fudge from the Methodists and retreated to a bench beside a gnarled old tree to devour my prize and watch the people go by. As I sat, a second man came by distributing leaflets and shouting to passersby his equally strident rhetoric regarding the necessity and logic of U.S. isolationism.

I shook my head in confusion. How would we ever be able to decide what was best when there were such ardent voices on both sides of the war debate? I certainly didn't envy President Wilson; I could see no way he could come out of this politically unscathed. Unwrapping my chocolate, I mentally wrapped up my concern about the war debate, and deliberately turned my thoughts back to the Festival.

Deeply engrossed in my appreciation of chocolate and conducting an impromptu survey of family life in Tully's Cove, I was oblivious to the fact that I was no longer alone on the bench until a slightly raspy male voice interrupted my thoughts.

"Quite entertaining, isn't it, this cross-section of New England humanity?"

It was Andrew Carlton, assistant editor of *The Sentinel* – and one of the targets of Augusta's ill-advised matchmaking efforts – who had joined me. Tall to the point of awkwardness, he was nice looking and had a matter-of-fact frankness that was both refreshing and rather disconcerting. His ginger-colored hair and eyes might have made him appear pale and colorless had it not been for the dark-rimmed spectacles he wore and the fact that there was a keen alertness about him that added dimension both to his appearance and his personality. We had hit if off well when introduced by Augusta and I was pleased to see him again.

"Yes, it is entertaining. There's so much to learn from those around us if we'd just take the time to pay attention."

"Ah, a philosopher," he replied.

"Not really, just an observer; and what about you? I would think that in your line of work you would have observation down to a science."

"Ideally, yes. But with me observation is purely vocation. I'm afraid there's no room for the philosopher in newspaper work."

"Nonsense," I said impulsively. "I've read your column and editorials. Your insights into the issues of the day – particularly the war – are compelling. You may not like to admit it, but you are very much the philosopher."

"You flatter me, Miss Pendleton," he replied. "But I'm afraid foisting my opinions on the masses by means of a totally biased vehicle like the editorial page hardly qualifies me as a free and original thinker. No, I'm afraid I am just the simple newspaperman, an observer of the passing parade." He gestured toward the jostling crowd with an almost paternalistic look on his face.

I followed his gesture and was struck by the thought that he really was quite fortunate to be doing something he obviously valued – this observing of the passing parade – and actually making a living in its pursuit. Before the impropriety of such an observation could restrain me I told him as much, adding somewhat wistfully that I wished I could be paid for my people-watching.

It was during the silence which followed that I realized my blunder, but his quiet regarding of me showed no sign of offense and when at length he spoke his voice was edged with the excitement of a dawning idea.

"Why not, Miss Pendleton," he asked with all the fervor of a reporter after a scoop. "Why shouldn't you be paid for 'people-watching' as you put it?"

His question struck me as a bit ridiculous, and incredulity colored my response. "And just who would be interested in purchasing such a valuable commodity?"

"I would," he replied enthusiastically, "me, that is, *The Sentinel* would! Look here, Miss Pendleton, ever since Joe Maitland retired in June I've been wearing his hat as well as my own."

"Joe Maitland?"

"Sorry, forgot he was before your time. Joe Maitland was an old codger who covered the society news for us."

"'Society' news – here in Tully's Cove?" I couldn't keep the sarcasm from my voice, nor control the raising of an incredulous eyebrow.

"...the soft stuff: civic groups, church news, weddings – things like that. I've been after my boss for months to hire someone... Don't know why I never thought of it before. A woman would be perfect!"

He was talking very rapidly as the idea took shape in his mind and I was having trouble keeping up.

"Just what are you suggesting; perfect for what?"

"To take Joe Maitland's place!"

He seemed surprised that I failed to share the clarity of his vision and made an obvious effort to slow down.

"But Mr. Carlton, I have no journalism experience – you don't even know if I can put two sentences together in a coherent manner."

"Don't I recall Mrs. Wilkes mentioning that you'd gone to college?"

"Yes, but only for two years. That hardly qualifies me to..."

"That's two years longer than most people around here."

"But Mr. Carlton... I'm a *girl*!"

I instantly regretted the provincialism of my observation as well as the involuntary deprecatory gesture that my self-consciousness evoked.

"So what," Andrew sputtered in response. "This is 1916, for goodness sakes! Isn't there the soul of a suffragette lurking beneath that placid exterior?"

He laughed pleasantly but there was an edge of challenge to his voice and I could see that he was completely serious.

"Well, to tell you the truth, I had been thinking about my future. I would like to be able to look after myself..."

"There, you see? It's the ideal solution!"

"...but I had rather pictured myself doing millinery work or teaching school – and just how can you be so certain your editor would hire me?"

"Miss Pendleton, I can assure you that the idea will appeal to him for at least three reasons. Number one, it will get me off his back. Number two, he's a bit of a radical at heart and should be quite smitten with the idea of giving the preacher's daughter a job. And lastly," he smiled rather sardonically at me, "he won't have to pay you as much as a man!"

"With all that in my favor, how can I lose?"

He laughed at my friendly sarcasm, ending in a satisfied sigh when I admitted the idea at least was interesting.

A silence settled between us as he nodded his head in thoughtful affirmation of a mental reassessment of what he was suggesting and adjusted the glasses that had slipped down his nose. When his eyes met mine again they were serious and his manner very businesslike.

"Why don't you stop by *The Sentinel* on Monday afternoon? In the meantime I'll speak to Layton – Mr.

Carmichael – and then the three of us can talk things over. How does that sound?"

"Wonderful – I guess – and a little hard to believe. I can just imagine my father's reaction!"

"Then don't tell him until you know what the job would entail and have had a chance to make up your mind."

He pulled a small notebook from his pocket, made a few hasty entries, adjusted his glasses again and rose to his feet.

"I better get busy covering this thing. I've enjoyed talking with you and hope you'll take the things I've said seriously."

We shook hands rather formally and then he disappeared into the crowd, leaving me to sort through our conversation.

I had long since finished my fudge but was still sitting on the bench considering my unexpected prospect for employment when I noticed that David Whitley was taking his turn at the spit tending the fire department's slowly roasting pig. I took advantage of my anonymous vantage point to observe him for a few moments and came to the conclusion that my original assessment of the man surely was accurate. He wasn't unpleasant in appearance, but so grim and unsmiling – even in so festive a setting – that my heart was stabbed by pity for his devoted young wife.

Grace was watching her husband from a blanket that had been spread in the sunshine adjacent the tent-enclosed eating area and so, abandoning my bench to a tired-looking woman with four children in tow, I went over to speak with her.

"Martha, how good to see you," she said in response to my greeting. "Won't you join me?"

I explained that I must soon be off to track down my young charges but would gladly share her patch of warm sunshine for a few moments.

Winston lay in a large wicker basket at her side heavily bundled as a precaution against the fickle nature of Indian Summer. He was busying himself with an intense inspection of his fingers and seemed unaware of the commotion around him. It was enjoyable to watch him and for a few moments neither of us spoke.

"I want to thank you once again for your visit," Grace said at length. "It not only lifted my spirits but made me realize I'm not the only woman my age in Tully's Cove."

I bit back the polite protest that surely she had many friends for it was obvious she did not, and once again I wondered at this sweet, lovely woman being shunned by the townswomen. Instead, I assured her that the visit had been my pleasure and that I had been looking forward to our next meeting ever since.

"In fact," I added. "I saw you in church this morning and hoped to talk with you but I guess you didn't see me."

"I'm sorry," she replied. "I did see you, but you were speaking with a – gentleman – and I didn't want to interrupt."

"Gavin Marshall," I volunteered. "And it probably was the first time he has crossed the threshold of a church in a very long while."

She looked away from me, her voice dropping to just above a whisper. "Gavin Marshall is a very dangerous man. He's not the type of person you want to befriend, Martha."

"Yes, so I've been told by several concerned parties. Well, you needn't worry," I assured her lightly. "I'd hardly describe what has transpired between Mr. Marshall and me as an overture of friendship."

"No, seriously, Martha, stay away from Gavin Marshall."

Her voice was intense and she touched my arm firmly as she continued. "One... hears things. He has sullied the reputation of many women in his day, and surely wouldn't hesitate to ruin the good name of the preacher's daughter – would probably take satisfaction in doing so."

After a pause she added, "I don't think he really likes women very much."

"I'd say he likes them *too* much. But please, Grace, don't worry about me. I'm not only the preacher's daughter, I'm a person with convictions of my own and a fairly strong backbone to hang them on. And trust me, I don't intend to have anything other than casual, public encounters with Gavin Marshall."

She didn't seem particularly relieved by my reassurances, and I thought there was more she wanted to say but we were interrupted by an eruption of protest from Winston who had grown weary of studying his fingers and the ribbon which held a knit cap snugly about his head. It also was past time that I met Rachel and her comrades, so we were forced to end our conversation somewhat abruptly as she tried to quiet the baby and I set off to find my sister.

As I walked hurriedly toward the game field I found myself wondering why Grace thought it necessary to warn me about Gavin Marshall. She didn't strike me as the type to indulge in idle gossip so I could imagine that what she said about Mr. Marshall was probably based in fact but still was puzzled at the intensity of her words. The citizens of Tully's Cove certainly seemed preoccupied with distrust for the Remittance Men in their midst and apparently Grace Whitley was no exception. I agreed that there was good reason to be cautious where those gentlemen were concerned but hoped I never would share the Cove's paranoia about them.

When I finally got the game field I wasn't surprised to find that Rachel and her companions were nowhere in sight. Feeling more exasperated than concerned, I began searching the sea of faces for the errant trio but they were not to be found among the spectators who rimmed the playing field.

As I broadened the scope of my search I finally found someone who had seen them walking in the direction of the picnic area.

My pace quickened as I mentally prepared the lecture I intended to deliver but my tirade was jolted from me for, when I finally caught sight of them, they were the enrapt audience of none other than Gavin Marshall himself!

"Ladies," I barked, interrupting the flamboyant Mr. Marshall and sounding like the embittered spinster I'm sure he perceived me to be. "I thought it was agreed that we would meet at the game field. This hardly qualifies as a minor deviation from that agreement! You have just shown that you are not to be trusted with any degree of liberty! Get your things together and come along."

Mr. Marshall was restraining himself visibly from once again laughing at my expense. Luckily for me he chose not to indulge for at that moment I could just as easily have slapped him as look at him and laughter probably would have pushed me over the edge.

I whirled abruptly to begin walking away but he caught my arm as I turned and I found myself powerless to go on.

"Miss Pendleton," he said in a tone of voice that should have been reserved for the simple-minded, "please forgive the infraction. We simply began walking as we talked and ended up here without realizing how far afield we had wandered. So, I'm afraid I'm to blame for the truancy of these ladies."

I replied slowly, my voice as calm and icy as I could make it. "Mr. Marshall, these girls are old enough to distinguish appropriate from inappropriate behavior..."

"And I suppose being with me definitely is inappropriate behavior," he interrupted, returning to an apparently favorite theme.

"I hate to disappoint you," I countered, a withering look emphasizing my words, "but wandering off with you is no more inappropriate than wandering off with any other grown man would be. I'm sure you can find friends closer to your own age who would be more interesting – and appropriate – companions."

"Well, now that *you're* here," he began, turning up the charm and smiling roguishly. He didn't bother to finish his flirtatious comment, however, for he could see that I would not be mellowing this time.

After a moment's silence he spoke again and there was almost a note of sincerity in his voice. "Miss Pendleton, please rest assured that the incident was entirely innocent and your message clearly received."

There was no mocking in his smile now and, even though I tried to see through the apparent sincerity to the rascal I knew him to be, my anger began to subside.

To Rachel and the Newcomb girls he added, "Miss Rachel, ladies, I hope the consequences of a few moments spent with this outcast will not be too severe."

"I'm sorry, Mr. Marshall," Rachel replied, looking rather desperate as well as thoroughly smitten by his charm and the attention he paid her.

As he walked away Rachel turned to me and said simply, "Martha, you are horrible and I shall never speak to you again."

V.

Our idyllic, unseasonably warm day quickly gave way to a cold autumn evening as a biting wind rose off the coast causing temperatures to drop nearly twenty degrees by nightfall. As a result, the open-air dance floor which had been set up outside the Armory stood lonely and forlorn for most of the evening, its strings of unlit paper lanterns whipped back and forth by a wind that signaled an end to our brief encounter with Indian Summer.

Thus far true to her word, Rachel had uttered not one syllable to me since the moment Mr. Marshall had walked away from us at the Festival. We had met Mother and

Father at the appointed time and even with them Rachel had been subdued and of few words. Whether our parents noticed it and thought more of it than to attribute the phenomenon to fatigue I can't say, but I was becoming increasingly annoyed. By the time we had eaten a hasty supper, changed for the dance, and ridden over to the Armory I was waiting anxiously for her resolve to weaken, as I was sure it would.

Knowing full well that a New England autumn is a fickle commodity, the interior of the Armory had been decorated as well as the outdoor dance floor so it was no imposition to hold the festivities entirely indoors when temperatures plummeted. Patriotic red, white, and blue bunting was draped around the walls of the Armory's main room, and there were arrangements of cornstalks, bales of hay, pumpkins, and the like in each of the four corners. Along three of the four walls, between each cornstalk arrangement, long benches had been placed for those waiting to dance or resting between songs. Along the fourth wall was a refreshment table, and right above that was a fairly large balcony where the band was ensconced and where a gallery of sorts had been set up so those less inclined to dance could sit to visit and enjoy the music.

Mother and Father retreated to the balcony almost immediately upon arriving for, even though they didn't think dancing was sinful, they weren't ready to display their prowess on the dance floor to the community at large. Rachel, on the other hand, was a flurry of lavender taffeta as she swished past me in her eagerness to join the group of young people who beckoned her. My enthusiasm was somewhere between Rachel's and my parents' and I followed her with deliberate nonchalance, taking a seat in a seemingly discrete spot adjacent a corner cornstalk arrangement.

A broad cross section of the area's population was in attendance that evening, and although they didn't completely blend it still set a friendly tone for the event to see country folks and city dwellers dancing the night away and rubbing elbows whether intentionally or not. Visible was everything from freshly starched dungarees to carefully creased gabardine, from country calicos to taffeta and lace. It was a pleasant enough distraction just to sit and watch the procession of young and old, rich and poor as they danced through my field of vision but there also was an urge to be part of the fun. After all, I wasn't being paid for "people-watching" – not yet, anyway.

I had just finished dancing with Gilbert Riley, a rather dour young man who worked as a teller at the bank and had been one of the first "eligibles" to whom Augusta had introduced me, when I caught sight of Andrew Carlton sitting by himself and went over to keep him company.

"You aren't dancing, Mr. Carlton," I observed, taking note of the fact that he was about the only person in the room who didn't appear slightly damp around the edges.

"I'm afraid my height makes me a rather cumbersome partner," he responded frankly, once again adjusting his glasses, "and I think I prefer to observe rather than participate in this particular societal ritual anyway. Besides," he added pointedly, "someone has to cover this event for *The Sentinel*."

"Don't worry," I assured him, "I haven't forgotten our conversation. And I've decided to take you up on your invitation to come down to the newspaper and discuss things with your editor. How's that for a tribute to your skills in salesmanship?"

"Salesmanship has nothing to do with it, it's just a very good idea, one that solves both your dilemma regarding employment and ours regarding a serious lack of personnel."

We spoke a while longer about the possibility of my employment and then he excused himself as he needed to speak with those running the dance, leaving me once again to my thoughts and the colorful cavalcade before me.

After spending a few minutes doing a seated version of the lively two-step the band was playing, I went upstairs to check in with my parents but soon found myself back on the dance floor in the capable arms – and victim of the somewhat less capable feet – of another of Augusta's protégés.

I already was uncomfortably warm for the temperature in the crowded hall had risen significantly as the evening progressed, but after almost ten minutes of dodging the thunderous steps of my partner I had passed from uncomfortable to dangerously close to feeling faint – the last thing I intended to do in front of our new neighbors. Hastily excusing myself from the cluster of young people he had ushered me over to at the end of our dance, I headed for the nearest exit in order to get some fresh air and elbow room.

The air outside was refreshingly cold and I drank it in until my lungs felt brittle. I began to walk around the building intending to reenter the hall through the main entrance adjacent the outdoor dance floor. It had grown very cold and by the time I rounded the far side of the Armory, approaching the bushes skirting the decorated outdoor area, my teeth were chattering and I definitely was ready to go back inside.

As my steps brought me to the temporary platform intended for starlight dancing, I found myself the unintentional observer of one lone couple who had braved the cold for a few moments solitude dancing with the moon. Clouds momentarily obscured the moon's light and the couple took on hues of pure enchantment as they waltzed around the floor to the faint strains of Strauss coming from within the closed building.

Even though I was chilled to the bone I couldn't tear myself away from the beauty of their dance as they swirled around the floor. As they passed the skirt of her grey dress brushed dangerously close to where I stood in the shadows and I drew back quickly lest my presence break the spell.

In a moment they stopped at the center of the floor; her partner gently lifting her chin, their mouths meeting in a long and increasingly passionate kiss.

I stood transfixed in the chilly gloom.

Slowly his hands caressed the perfect symmetry of her shoulders, arms and waist, finally coming to rest on her hips and pulling her tightly into his embrace. As his hands continued their quest and she leaned into the ardor of his kisses on her neck, the moon broke free from its captors and showered the couple with its milky-white glow.

Like stage lighting strategically illuminating the key scene in a play, the moonlight seemed to focus only on the entwined couple at the center of the dance floor.

The clouds continued to drift away, moonlight slowly revealing that the woman who had her back to me was wearing lavender rather than grey.

Turning to leave, I suddenly stood immobilized, enchantment transmogrified into utter disbelief as the moonlight imparted its final revelation; the man was none other than Gavin Marshall – and the recipient of his ardor was my little sister!

CHAPTER FIVE

I.

Six days had passed since the Harvest Festival and still Rachel hadn't spoken to me. After what I had observed in the moonlight that evening I joined her conversational moratorium and so a deep and almost painful silence was erecting a wall between us. Rachel had skipped church the next morning, citing an aching head and upset stomach as reason for staying in bed, so I had been spared the necessity of facing her so soon after the shock of seeing her in Gavin Marshall's embrace. I never would have thought it possible but silence slowly was becoming the norm between us and we were growing adept at avoiding one another; a necessary strategy if knowledge of our impasse was to remain ours alone.

    I was glad my anonymity that night had been preserved for it meant that at least for the moment I was at an advantage and had time to figure out how best to handle the situation. I knew I didn't want to rush right in and tell our parents what I had witnessed fearing my father's reaction might do more harm than good. On the other hand, I didn't want to let the matter rest, either; as much as she drove me to distraction at times, I loved my little sister and didn't want to see her hurt or used by a man of low character like Gavin Marshall! I don't know what Rachel would have done had she suspected that my silence was due to what I had seen. And until I was ready to confront her I thought it best to let her think she simply was being true to her resolve never to speak to me again.

The task of avoiding Rachel and of keeping my mind otherwise occupied was made somewhat easier due to the fact that I had followed through on my promise to Andrew Carlton and had gone to *The Sentinel* on Monday after the festival to discuss the possibility of employment. That meeting led to my reluctant acceptance of a trial assignment covering the week's church news, which meant sitting in on various committee meetings around town. Since I had decided not to mention the project to my parents, it took a little conniving in order to be a relatively inconspicuous visitor at meetings held in churches other than my father's. But in each case a variation on the basic theme of wanting to get acquainted garnered a welcome for me and I don't think anyone suspected I was taking notes to include in a summary for the church page of Sunday's newspaper. I visited the Baptists on Tuesday, the ladies of the Methodist Missionary League on Wednesday, both the Catholics and the Lutherans on Thursday and finished up the week sitting in on three meetings of our own congregation. I was pleased, and a bit surprised, by the level of service the activities of our local churches represented. Even though it was a tedious job, I began to feel that the information I was compiling had merit and actually deserved to be reported in the local paper. As a result, my small role in the process took on a sense of importance and I found myself taking the job quite seriously.

The last meeting I covered that week was a gathering of our congregation's Women for World Relief, an organization whose "world" relief efforts consisted of sending used clothing, books, and the like only as far as a mission school in Appalachia. My mother also was in attendance which made taking notes more difficult since she expected me to sit with her. She cast several curious glances my way during the meeting but never came right out and questioned my surreptitious note-taking.

When the meeting was over and the ladies were milling around visiting I decided the time had come to make my escape and go home to begin transcribing my notes. It wasn't difficult to slip away from Mother for several ladies seemed eager to speak with her about various aspects of their work. The only impediment to my escape was a brief pang of guilt as a glance back revealed the Choate sisters descending upon her, talons glistening. But there was no time for regrets – after all, I was a reporter facing a deadline. Absolving myself on those grounds, I left Mother to her own devices and went off to finish my work.

II.

It was a tradition in our house that on Sundays no one touched the newspaper until Father had had an opportunity to read it from cover to cover after church; a small indulgence which never had been questioned. For the first time in my life I stepped over the line of mere temptation where that unspoken rule was concerned and stole away to my room as soon as the paper arrived in order to see the fruit of my maiden voyage as a journalist.

Still in my heavy flannel nightgown, I crawled back under the bedclothes and nestled into the plumped pillow I had propped against the headboard in anticipation of my return. Normally I carefully contemplated and digested every morsel of news relating to national and world events before turning to the local scene, but not even front page headlines reporting the ongoing slaughter at the battle of the Somme in France could distract me from my quest that morning. Immediately turning to the last page of the first section, I sought out the "Around the Town" heading, under which would be my reports.

They were all there. Every word I had written was faithfully reproduced. I felt like a proud parent, a feeling of satisfaction unlike anything I had experienced before. I literally hugged the tome and am certain an uncharacteristic giggle slipped past my unguarded lips.

It wasn't until I had read and reread my article several times that my eyes drifted upward and focused on the headline once again. My heart skipped a beat and my mouth fell open in disbelief as I read the words "Reported by Martha Pendleton" neatly printed below and to one side of the "Around the Town" banner!

My feeling of pride turned to panic.

What had possessed Mr. Carmichael to do such a thing? This was just a trial run. I hadn't accepted a post with the newspaper but there it was for the world to see – including my parents!

I felt winded and more than just a little betrayed.

Was this his idea of a joke? I supposed that the radical side of his nature had won out and he couldn't resist the shock value (or the extra sales it might generate) to break the "story" of the preacher's daughter working for the newspaper in such a stark and insalubrious manner.

For more than just a moment I thought I was going to be physically ill, but slowly the panic began to subside and my more rational side took charge. After all, why should I feel guilt-ridden and embarrassed? I had done nothing illegal or morally wrong. I merely had tried my hand at an honest vocation, something many young women my age were doing nowadays. On top of that, the fact remained that the articles really were quite good. After all, they had printed them word-for-word. And finally – and most convincing to the fear rising and abating within me like a tide – few people were likely to have made it that far through the newspaper before church so I undoubtedly still had time to break the news to my father in my own way.

I freely admit to dressing with an even greater degree of care and modesty than usual that morning. I was particularly conservative in my choice of attire and when finished looked unimpeachably well bred if not down-right matronly. There was a corner of my heart that longed to shout my good fortune to the world and go to church dressed in the garb of a working reporter, with printer's visor and black sleeve garters plainly visible, but such bravado was fleeting at best and the "schoolmarm" in me definitely had the upper hand. By the time I was ready to go downstairs and walk over to church with Mother and Rachel the reporter had put away her pencil, the fearful child had withdrawn her hand from the cookie jar, and the spinster was ready to greet the world.

Being an avowed atheist, Mr. Carmichael wouldn't be darkening the door of any house of worship that morning but I hoped to run into Andrew Carlton in order to secure his silence. From our discussions I knew Andrew was an intermittent churchgoer but thought perhaps he would make the effort that morning since he was sure to realize the implications of the unexpected by-line and what its affect on me likely would be.

Throughout the service I found it difficult to keep my mind on what was being said and repeatedly was caught unprepared for the congregational responses or hymns until my mother's gentle nudge brought me back to the activities at hand.

Whenever possible I would steal a glimpse around the crowded sanctuary in hopes of catching sight of my mentor. Each time, however, my mission was thwarted by the persistent feeling that everyone who returned my glance did so disapprovingly, and that every conversational aside behind gloved hands included a quiet indictment of the preacher's daughter. My eyes would quickly fall to avert their gaze and the end of the service came with my being no closer to knowing whether or not Andrew Carlton was in attendance.

As we began weaving our way down the center aisle my mother slipped her hand into the crook of my arm and looked into my eyes searchingly.

"Are you feeling all right this morning," she asked quietly while brushing the hair back from my forehead feeling for warmth on my brow.

My assurances did little to ease the look of concern on her face and I undoubtedly increased that concern by almost immediately slipping away upon catching sight of Andrew resting his lanky frame against one of the pillar supports along the side aisle. I know she wondered at my hasty departure but for the moment I was willing she think my behavior was inspired by the young man I was so eager to see.

Andrew opened his mouth to speak but before he could utter a sound I began a hushed tirade.

"Do you have any idea the awkward position that by-line has put me in? Not only am I not yet employed by *The Sentinel* but I haven't even begun to broach the subject with my parents! And here the entire town is let in on my secret! I can't imagine what got into Mr. Carmichael's head. How could he be so callous and totally inconsiderate regarding the potential awkwardness of my situation? Good Lord, Andrew, I thought I made it abundantly clear that taking a job wouldn't go over well with my family. It may not be such a big thing to the two of you but to me this is really serious. You don't know my father. He's the type of man who still believes that other than motherhood the only acceptable occupation for a woman is teaching school, and then only until she finds someone who will marry her..."

I continued along the same lines with pauses for breath or distracted greetings to passersby until Andrew finally raised a hand in protest and silenced me after I had said essentially the same thing about three different ways.

"I'm sorry, Martha, and I agree with you that Layton should have waited until you were officially on board before using your name."

His tone was kind but his voice was firm and commanding. "I haven't talked with him so I really don't know why he decided to give you a by-line. To tell you the truth, I'm afraid it may well have been an effort to capitalize a bit on who you are – 'Around the Town' usually doesn't carry one. But you have to admit I did warn you that he's the type of person who likes to stir things up."

He pushed his glasses up from their perch at the middle of his nose and smiled rather sheepishly before continuing. "I'm sorry if this makes it more difficult for you to deal with your father but please don't let it keep you from accepting the job. I still feel you're the right person to take over. You really did a fine job – you're a natural – and I'm not just saying that because I don't want to do it anymore."

I heaved a short, cathartic sigh as Andrew finished speaking.

Having gotten the anger and embarrassment out of my system, I knew in my heart I wasn't going to let this unexpected turn of events prevent me from considering the job for I kept coming back to the feeling of satisfaction experienced upon seeing my work in print. I think even at that early point I was hooked. I had enjoyed covering the various meetings – tedious as they may have been – and now knew the thrill of producing a marketable product. It may have been just a small, relatively insignificant report in a small local newspaper but it had served to give me a sense of purpose. And I had to admit that, despite being angry and embarrassed, deep down it was thrilling to have seen my name in print as well as my words – and even deeper down I also had to admit that perhaps, like Mr. Carmichael, I took some measure of satisfaction in thwarting the status quo.

Without meaning to I had conquered my own objections and misgivings about accepting the job. Now the only remaining hurdle was to break the news to my family... to my *father*.

III.

"Martha, will you please tell your father that dinner is ready?"

Mother was leaning into the oven extracting the roast lamb so couldn't see the look of horror that crossed my face upon hearing her request. Dinner might have been ready but I wasn't ready yet. I had gone over at least ten different scenarios for breaking the news to my father, discarding much, if not all, of each one. Why did time pass so quickly when you needed to think something through?

"Martha?"

She still hadn't looked at me but I could tell from her voice that she once again was wondering just where my mind was.

"I'll go get him," Rachel interceded tersely, putting down the basket of rolls she carried and throwing an icy glare my way.

A moment or two later Father and Rachel came from the hallway arm-in-arm and I was relieved to see that he appeared relaxed and in a good mood. He even went so far as to go around the table seating each of us in turn before sitting down at the head of the table and serving us on the plates stacked in front of him. I added a silent postscript to our table prayer thanking God for Father's good humor and asking for an extra portion of fortitude to go with my lamb and sweet potatoes.

In spite of my nervous fidgeting and lack of appetite, the meal passed very pleasantly. Father's good mood even extended to some lively banter and uncharacteristic teasing of my mother and, even though I hated to break the spell, I knew that there could be no moment remotely more likely to elicit a positive response to my news.

The time had come – but I put off the inevitable until Father was ready to excuse himself and return to his study.

"Father," I began haltingly, "before you leave, there's something I need to talk with you about."

He smiled warmly as he settled back into his chair and regarded me almost affectionately.

"I appreciate your concern, and your embarrassment is very touching, but let me relieve your mind. I already know what you want to talk with me about and you needn't worry, you have my permission."

I couldn't believe my ears! Was this the same man who once devoted an entire sermon to a chastisement of women becoming involved with the suffragette movement?

"You already know?" I stammered.

"Yes, dear," Mother interjected, laying a cool hand on my arm. "I hope you'll forgive me but once I figured out what was going on I couldn't resist the urge to tell your father."

"Mr. Carlton isn't much of a churchgoer," Father continued, "but that can change and I have a great deal of respect for the young man. So, if he wants to come calling, it's all right with me."

"If he wants to come calling?"

My voice was filled with confusion and incredulity. "You think he's interested in... Oh, no!"

In an instant the reality of the situation became mortifyingly clear to me.

Mother had interpreted the events of the past few days exactly as I had allowed her to and, having drawn that conclusion, decided to make the way easier for me by sharing her insights with my father. Now I understood his jovial mood. He thought a young man was finally interested in his aging daughter without her objection. This was going to make matters even more difficult.

"I'm afraid you don't understand," I began tentatively. "I don't quite know how to tell you this. Mr. Carlton has no desire to come calling..."

"Oh, Martha..." Mother broke in, her voice full of sympathy.

"No, Mother, wait. You really don't understand."

They were silent and expectant, and I was aware of a satisfied, almost sly half-smile playing at the corner of Rachel's mouth as she lapped up my growing discomfort.

"I'm sorry for the confusion, but Mr. Carlton and I are not interested in one another. I'm afraid I allowed you to get that impression, Mother, and I apologize for that... Maybe the best way to explain things is just to show you."

I excused myself from the table and went to retrieve the paper from where I had placed it next to Father's reading chair by the fireplace in his study.

I don't think they spoke a word in my absence and when I returned three pairs of eyes were fixed on me. Having handed the paper to my father, I returned to my chair, took a deep breath, and plunged in.

"If you'll turn to the last page of the first section you'll see what this is all about."

"I don't understand, Martha," my mother said. "Is there a story about you in *The Sentinel*?"

"Not exactly..."

I said no more, waiting for my father's reaction.

Even before he spoke I could see the storm clouds gathering between his eyebrows. He passed the paper over to my mother, pushed his plate toward the center of the table, and regarded me stonily.

"I can see now that by your actions this morning you already know my opinion on this matter."

His statement was simple, to the point, and left little room for discussion.

"Yes, you're right; I do know how you must feel about me getting a job. But there's something you need to understand..."

I don't think I ever really had crossed my father before but I was just beginning to realize how much he influenced my personality for, even though there was a lump in my throat the size of an egg, I was determined that he hear me out.

"Father, I'm twenty years old – it's time I began to look out for myself. It's time I began to do something with my life."

"And just what do you mean by that," he demanded. "Who's been filling your head with this rubbish? If you mean to say that a woman should look outside the home for fulfillment I'm afraid you have some very harsh lessons to learn. Raising a family and making a good home is the highest, most noble goal to which any woman can aspire."

His fist came down with a resounding thud on the oak table. "Do you mean to tell me you don't see value in raising children and being a good wife?"

My mother started to protest but he silenced her with a curt wave of his hand. "I don't know what's gone wrong with young people today – a woman work as an equal in a man's world? Ridiculous! It can't be done! You're too emotional, too weak to function that way. Next thing you know, you'll be wearing trousers and brandishing a cigar!"

He ran a hand through his unruly hair but barely paused for breath before continuing. "Look at your sister. You don't hear her espousing any of this nonsense. Rachel will make some man a fine wife!"

He looked at me scornfully. "Why can't you be more like your sister?"

I had anticipated his disapproval but his last words burned as badly as if he had struck me. I was terribly hurt and surprisingly angry. So angry, in fact, that it was all I could do to keep from striking back by informing him of his beloved younger daughter's recent escapade. At that moment I would have loved to see his face when told that Rachel not only danced with Gavin Marshall but allowed herself to be caressed and kissed by the man.

The words were on my lips but just in time I caught myself. That wasn't the way I wanted to win this argument. I wanted my father to see me for who I was – and to respect me. And I truly didn't feel that what I was doing broke any moral or Biblical code of conduct.

"Martha, dear," my mother said, trying to intercede, "you don't need to worry about your future. You're a member of this household and will be until you marry. Isn't that enough?"

"No, Mother, I'm afraid it isn't. We don't know for sure that I'll ever get married, and it would be wrong of me to rely on you and Father for the rest of my life."

I hoped my father was listening but his glazed expression revealed nothing. "All across the country girls my age are taking on jobs," I continued. "It's not that unusual. And it's only part time. And it's not as if I'll be tramping all over town spending time at the police station and the courthouse. They just want me to write reports on churches, weddings, teas, and the like. It's completely respectable..."

At that point my father muttered something unintelligible, pushed his chair away from the table with a painful scratching noise, and stalked out of the room.

I turned and looked pleadingly at my mother.

"Martha," she said calmly, "you simply cannot do this."

"Mother," I replied with more confidence than I felt, "I already have."

IV.

I took a long walk that afternoon. I needed to get out of the house for a while and walking in the cold autumn air served both to revive me and clear my head. I headed east toward the western boundary of the Collier's property. Jocelyn had told me that other than an occasional ride through that part of their land no one ever went there. It offered just the type of solitude I needed right then, and I took the risk that this time I wouldn't be overtaken by any careless riders.

It is an ironic twist of the human journey that family is both the greatest source of joy and nurturing a person can experience as well as a potential source of intense pain and suffering. I had known anger and disappointment within my family before, and never had felt that I quite measured up where my father was concerned, but this was the first time that the chasm of a rift in our relationship yawned dangerously before us.

I hoped that Father would mellow in time and see that what I was doing in no way reflected upon his role as father nor upon his responsibility as a spiritual leader within the community. I hoped that he would come to see that times were changing and many young women were choosing to look outside the home for their security. I hoped these things but didn't feel very optimistic that they ever would come to pass. Father was a deeply traditional man and refused to consider, let along tolerate, what he perceived as radical opinions or behavior. And he definitely had the courage of his convictions; he didn't just talk the talk, he walked the walk as well – one of the things I always had admired about him.

Ever since I could remember, we had been the captive audience of Father's quite loquacious discourses on the issue of social equality and voting rights for women. He saw little difference between the nonviolent strategies of the homegrown National American Woman Suffrage Association and more radical tactics employed by suffragettes in Europe. Reports that a protest by England's arm of the movement – the Women's Social and Political Union led by Emmeline Pankhurst – involved breaking windows of government buildings and even throwing stones at the Prime Minister's home fueled countless paternal tirades on the subject. And I thought we never would hear the end of it when Alice Paul returned to America after studying in London and subsequently organized an elaborate NAWSA parade the day before Woodrow Wilson's inauguration in

March 1913. Approximately eight thousand women from virtually every strata of society had marched in formation down Pennsylvania Avenue that day, accompanied by suffrage-themed floats and led by a Joan of Arc figure clad in flowing white robes sitting astride a white horse to symbolize their righteous fight for a moral cause. Reports that the crowd of onlookers – mostly male – spat upon and physically assaulted participants were met by the stoic observation of men like my father that such responses were to be expected when women chose to challenge the natural order of things and engage in radical activities.

The root difference here was that I didn't feel like a radical. Although I would have liked to vote I had no intention of running out and joining a suffragette rally. I simply wanted to take care of myself and do something productive – an ambition I felt my father could relate to and, quite frankly, should respect.

But then I reminded myself, I was a daughter, not a son.

I remembered reading an account by Elizabeth Cady Stanton of a seminal event from her childhood. Her only brother, Eleazar, had just died and the household was in deep mourning. Eleven-year-old Elizabeth, overwhelmed by the loss, crawled onto her father's lap seeking comfort. In a moment etched forever into her heart and mind, Elizabeth's grieving father had put his arms around her and sighed, "Oh, my daughter, I wish you were a boy!" When telling the story, Mrs. Stanton always emphasized it was at that moment she vowed to do everything she could to prove to her father that she was as bright, capable, and valuable as any son could ever be.

I freely admit to admiring women like Elizabeth Cady Stanton – and definitely could relate to her feelings regarding her father – but I wasn't modeling myself after them nor did I see myself in such a public, "radical" role. What had Andrew called it – the "society news?" That's all I wanted to do; cover weddings teas, and church activities. What was so unladylike about that?

I must have wandered aimlessly for more than an hour, going over the same territory in my mind again and again, becoming increasingly frustrated and feeling increasingly alienated. There was no visible solution other than not working for *The Sentinel* and I already had decided that that was not an acceptable compromise.

At the beginning of my walk I had blazed my own trail through the Collier's woods but had come upon the thread of a path and without even thinking about it began to follow its lead.

Although very narrow, the path was well-worn and before long I could hear the unmistakable sound of water and soon found myself walking beside a tumbling brook full of stones and fallen branches over which the water danced and played on its way to the sea. I always have loved the sound of moving water and it had a calming effect on me.

Somewhere just ahead there surely was a small drop-off for I heard the distinct sound of falling water and as the sound became louder the path widened until revealing a small clearing next to an impressive little waterfall. Across the clearing stood an old, unkempt gazebo, and next to a gigantic Frazier fir stood a small marble bench littered with tree and bird droppings where one could see and hear the waterfall to best advantage. It was an enchanting little oasis and, after cleaning it off with my handkerchief, I sat on the bench to lose myself in the serenity of the spot.

After only a few moments, however, my solitude was interrupted by rustling noises in the underbrush around the perimeter of the clearing. It sounded too large to be a rabbit or squirrel and I found myself hoping fervently that it wasn't a skunk or some equally unwelcome intruder.

Just as I prepared to dash off down the path my visitor bounded through the bushes and I was relieved to welcome a friendly spaniel who came running over to me wiggling from end to end in gleeful introduction. The exuberant beast obviously was female for she definitely was soon to deliver a litter; her distended belly a burden of which she seemed oblivious. Unable to resist her overture of friendship, I squatted down beside her to rumple her fur and murmur the words of endearment animals always evoked from me.

Without warning she lunged forward to give me a slobbery caress and I found myself thrown off balance and just as suddenly plopped down on my backside in a most ungraceful pose.

"This is strangely reminiscent of our last meeting," a voice from behind me observed, and I knew without looking that once again I had stumbled – quite literally – upon the owner of Patriot's Point.

"You have the uncanny knack of discovering my places of refuge," he added vacantly as I struggled to my feet.

"And I find myself apologizing once again for intruding" I began, trying to be more articulate than the last time we spoke. "This time, however, I do have permission for Jocelyn has told me I am welcome to walk here whenever I wish."

"Jocelyn is extremely generous with my possessions," he replied rather bitterly, "but then she has no way of knowing that I find it more than a bit annoying."

He shifted an impressive rifle from his left to his right shoulder and I noticed an exquisite ring-necked pheasant and several quail tied together and suspended from a strap attached to the belt of his trousers. "Molly and I have been hunting, Miss Pendleton," he volunteered in response to my assessment of his appearance. "Do you enjoy the sport?"

"I've never been," I replied quietly.

"Ah yes, you are a walker, aren't you? A passerby; the harmless intruder, isn't that right?"

"I see no reason for sarcasm, Mr. Collier."

In my current state of mind it wouldn't have taken much to make me cry, and I turned to walk away without further comment.

A voluminous silence stretched between us, taut and uncomfortable.

It was Mr. Collier who finally spoke, heaving a long sigh. "You are quite right, Miss Pendleton, and I ask your forgiveness."

The apology was unexpected; I made no reply but didn't move on.

In a moment he continued. "This is a beautiful spot, isn't it?"

"Yes, it is," I said, taking a few steps back into the clearing.

Now it was his turn to squat down beside the dog; the affection in his eyes as he rumpled her ears helping to ease the tension between us.

"You like dogs, Miss Pendleton?"

"Yes, very much so, although it's been quite some time since I've had a pet of my own."

"That's too bad. In my opinion everyone should have a four-legged confidant."

The dog had flopped awkwardly onto its side; he scratched her distended belly and chuckled softly when her back leg began kicking reflexively. "I'll tell you what," he said, "I'll let you know when Molly has her pups and you can come out and see whether one appeals to you."

Both he and the dog looked up at me expectantly.

"They're very good listeners, Miss Pendleton."

Now it was my turn to be defensive. "And what makes you think I'm in need of a good listener?"

"Aren't we all," he replied simply.

He rose to his feet before continuing and regarded me with a look bordering on sympathetic. "I've always been good at deduction, Miss Pendleton. I read the newspaper and, since I haven't seen any woman's name in print before,

I deduce that you've earned the distinction of becoming the first female to be employed by *The Sentinel*. This obviously is a significant achievement, therefore I further deduce that you should be extremely pleased with yourself, if not actually down-right gloating, but instead I find you wandering around my property looking for all the world as if you've just lost your dearest friend. This brings me to a final deduction. Being familiar with the attitudes of men like your father – quite frankly, having been raised by one – I deduce that the good reverend isn't pleased with your new-found vocation and probably has made his displeasure known in no uncertain terms."

Seeking shelter from his disturbingly accurate insights I entered the gazebo and gazed up into its cobweb-laced rafters before responding.

"And I'm sure you can relate..."

His voice instantly was cold. "Was that an attempt at pay-back for my sarcasm? Let me assure you, such things are not lost on me even in my advanced state of degradation."

His words snapped me back to reality and I had to stop for a moment to recall just what I had said. "I'm sorry, Mr. Collier," I stammered, "I didn't mean to offend you. I only meant..."

"...that a 'Remittance Man' surely could relate to the situation you find yourself in with your own family right now. Am I correct?"

He had crossed the clearing to where I stood in the gazebo's entryway and I backed away from him until impeded by the opposite railing.

"I'm sorry, Mr. Collier, truly I am. I wasn't thinking..."

"And I'm the worst of all of them, aren't I," he demanded bitterly. "I know what they say about me in town. I know what you all think." Anger and something like hopelessness flashed in his eyes and I truly was sorry for the man even as fear of him rose like bile within me. "You know nothing about it!"

He turned and stalked across the clearing with long, angry strides. I took advantage of the moment to slip from the gazebo and dash into the woods. Molly ran along with me for a while, bounding merrily in and out of the tall brush until a distant gunshot called her to her master.

CHAPTER SIX

I.

Over the next few weeks I busied myself with activities related to the newest facet of my life and had minimal contact with my family. Although there undoubtedly were tongues wagging around town as more and more people became aware of my venture, very few remarks were directed my way and many of those that were actually were favorable. Several younger women registered their encouragement – especially those who associated with the suffragette movement or were emboldened by my actions to admit their inclinations – and even a few of the community's older matrons went so far as to compliment my work. There actually was a certain amount of celebrity in what I was doing and I must admit that the attention was no small consolation for the accompanying tensions at home.

The relationship between my father and me did not improve with the passage of time. As I became more confident in my role with *The Sentinel* I also became more confident in the conviction that I was doing nothing wrong, which did little to redress the "sin" he perceived me to be committing. For the most part we stayed out of each other's way and at meal time a rather stony silence or stilted casualness pervaded, with Mother and Rachel carrying on the bulk of the conversation. I was not immune to my father's anger and disappointment and would have done almost anything to mend the rift between us but the time had come to stand on my own two feet and I guess, in so doing, I was growing into an acceptance of my father's disapproval.

Working for *The Sentinel* definitely was a learning experience. Even though my role was peripheral – I covered my teas and church meetings and went into the office only once a week – I couldn't help but pick up tidbits here and there and add a unique lexicon to my vocabulary as words such as "beat" and "copy" took on new meanings in light of their journalistic usages.

Mr. Carmichael was unabashedly thrilled with his accomplishment. I believe he felt he had pulled off a coup of sorts in hiring the preacher's daughter and continued to advertise the feat by including a by-line above my work long after the novelty surely had passed.

He was an intriguing person; short and stocky with sparse graying hair, an elfin nose, and rapidly expanding middle he was more the image of St. Nick than the William Randolph Hearst he fancied himself. Mr. Hearst may have had his journalistic empire and influence in the Spanish-American War, but Mr. Carmichael had his beloved Sentinel and his current denouement in the war against convention. He rarely spoke to me but I knew that I was a welcome addition to his small staff if for no other reason than the pleasure it gave him to thumb his nose at the status quo.

Andrew Carlton was a different story. In Andrew I had found a true comrade and the friendship that blossomed between us meant a great deal to me. At first I felt that his overtures were motivated purely by his relief to be free from the tedium of the stories I now covered. As we became better acquainted, however, I began to realize that he actually perceived me as something of an equal and even sought my opinions on many issues of the day.

I hadn't been raised entirely in a Victorian vacuum but it still was refreshing to be treated as if my brain was good for something besides homemaking and child care. Not that I looked upon those pursuits with the contempt of which my father accused me; far from it. I had every hope that I would soon met and marry that special someone and make a home together. But, in the meantime, I was convinced that the path I had chosen was an appropriate one, and it was stimulating and flattering to be accepted even marginally in what my father called a "man's" world.

It was my habit to deliver my stories to *The Sentinel* office on Wednesday afternoon for publication in the following Sunday's edition. On the Wednesday before Thanksgiving I started out for town shortly after lunch and would have made the trip at my usual brisk pace had it not been for two things.

It had begun to snow that morning, bringing with it a stillness that made my solitary descent like walking through a world in which I was the only living being. The slushy snow itself dictated a slower pace but it was something in the stillness that distracted me and further hampered my progress.

I was completely comfortable walking alone around the Cove, having done so ever since our arrival, and always basked in the uninterrupted solitude those walks provided. But that particular day the falling snow served to muffle normal sound and I had the uncanny feeling that I was not alone. I tried reassuring myself that it was just because the snow had silenced the woodland sounds to which I had grown accustomed but my mind wouldn't be consoled. As I walked I became convinced that there was another sound; not the rustling of leaves or the sound of a scurrying animal but the slow, steady step of another pair of feet walking slowly and deliberately through the snow.

I was sure of it.

I slowed my pace even more and it seemed to me that there was a corresponding slowing of the steps I heard behind me. Several times I stopped completely, standing perfectly still with every fiber of my being straining to locate and identify what it was that I was hearing. But each time I stopped to listen I would hear nothing except the almost imperceptible sound of the wet snow as it settled onto that which already had fallen.

Even as I told myself I was being ridiculous, a cold chill ran down my spine; I instinctively quickened my pace only to perceive a quickened footfall behind me.

"Hello," I called out, stopping again and straining to hear. "Hannibal, is that you?"

Eli Thornton's shy, simple-minded assistant had absorbed Eli's and Augusta's paternalistic interest in Rachel and me and so was the likely candidate to be shadowing my journey.

"You don't need to hide, Hannibal. Come out and walk with me."

There was no reply.

"Hannibal?"

My words echoed back thinly.

I tried again. "Is someone there?"

There was still no response; no sound at all apart from my own breathing which had become more rapid and shallow as I began to give in to the fear that tugged at my sleeve.

Part of me said to ignore the sound. Who cared if Hannibal – or someone else for that matter – was walking in the woods and chose to remain anonymous? There were plenty of times when I would have wanted to do so myself. But an equally convincing part of me pointed out that if such was the case shouldn't he or she change course so as to avoid the undesired meeting and the obvious discomfiture they were causing me?

Although wanting to listen to the first of my inner voices, there in the moment –feeling drenched rather than invigorated by the solitude – I was inclined to listen more closely to the second and once again quickened my steps. Relief finally calmed my sense of urgency when a few moments later I emerged from the woods within yards of the main road leading into Tully's Cove.

A normal amount of mid-week activity greeted me as I continued on toward *The Sentinel* office. I was grateful for the companionship of pedestrians and vehicles and was able to conclude my journey with a revived sense of security – and only a few furtive glances behind me.

Neither Andrew nor Mr. Carmichael heard me enter the office for just as I closed the door behind me Mr. Carmichael pounded his desk with a gnarled fist.

"Nonsense," he barked at Andrew. "It most certainly is not our concern. We have no right to go interfering in the affairs of other sovereign nations – especially when it would jeopardize the lives of American citizens! And for what, I ask you? Why should we involve ourselves in a territorial squabble thousands of miles away? Throughout history rival tyrants have turned Europe into a battleground and this is nothing different!"

Mr. Carmichael was seated at his desk and Andrew, towering above him, leaned forward to rest both palms on the flat surface and look directly at his employer.

"How can you call this a territorial squabble," he asked in disbelief. "Germany is threatening much more than the integrity of her neighbors' borders. How can we stand idly by and do nothing when hundreds of thousands are dying at the Somme alone?"

A vein in Mr. Carmichael's forehead bulged with conviction and he obviously had more to say on the subject but had caught sight of me and with deliberate restraint said only, "We'll talk later," and stalked off toward the back of the large open room where the printing press stood waiting.

Andrew hesitated a moment, head sagging forward a bit, his hands still flat on Mr. Carmichael's desk, before heaving a frustrated sigh and turning to acknowledge my presence as I hung my coat and scarf over a hook on the chipped wainscoting.

"Good afternoon, Martha. I'm sorry you had to witness that exchange."

"I only caught the tail end of it," I assured him. "Arguing about the war again?"

"What else? Layton is about as rabid an isolationist as they come."

"Well, that's at least one thing he and my father would agree on."

He smiled good-naturedly, indicating the chair next to his adjacent desk. "You look a bit rattled, Martha. Are you all right? Don't let our disagreements get to you."

I tried to assure him that I was fine but finally gave in to his probing and told him about my experience on the way to town and my suspicions about being followed.

He listened attentively, pushing his glasses up his nose with the absent-minded reflex I had come to recognize as a gesture of concentration as much as self-consciousness.

"If it wasn't Hannibal –and it very well could have been – what you probably heard," he suggested, "was the sound of your own footsteps echoing back to you in the stillness. That would account for the fact that the sound sped up and slowed down with you. Snow can act as a baffle of sorts that creates an almost cave-like effect."

Eager for reassurance, I latched onto his explanation with vigor. His suggestion was so simple – and acceptably logical – that it was like walking from a darkened room into the light.

"Of course," I replied, my voice saturated with relief. "That must have been it. You must think me rather foolish to have been frightened by my own footsteps!"

"Not at all," he stated matter-of-factly. "No one is immune to that sort of thing, especially in that setting." Taking the notebook from me he added, "Let's see what the ladies have been up to this week."

He went over the material I had written, making comments and notations here and there as he read. In less than fifteen minutes we were finished and as I rose to leave he presented me with an off-hand compliment.

"You really write quite well, Martha. Perhaps you could do some other fill-in work for us one day."

"Thank you, Andrew, I'd like that," I replied as casually as possible for his words, although stated with the enthusiasm one usually reserves for discussing the weather, made my heart skip a beat. I had been fancying myself taking on other responsibilities with *The Sentinel* – having the actual possibility dangled before me was almost too good to be true.

Andrew's simple explanation of my experience in the woods, his casual compliment, and his suggestion that my writing assignments might be expanded sent me on my way in a nearly euphoric state. It had stopped snowing, I no longer was apprehensive about walking home alone, and all seemed right with the world as I set out to conquer the hill that stood between me and warm, dry feet.

Where the main road curved toward Church Street, exposing the opening to my shortcut up the hill, I hesitated a moment before committing myself to another solitary trek through the woods. Residual euphoria from the possibility of an expanded role at the newspaper carried me forward, however, and soon I was retracing my steps, walking the opposite direction in the footprints I had left in the snow.

When I came upon the last spot where I had paused on my way down the hill to listen to the sounds behind me, I automatically stopped once again and listened to the silence.

As I did so my eyes fell upon something I hadn't seen before.

There in the snow, off to one side of the path but clearly visible, was another set of footprints!

I hadn't noticed anything closer to the main road due to the fact that the path grew narrower as it continued down the slope on its way into town and my "companion" either left me at that point or must have taken to walking among the trees.

I felt a lump of consternation rising in my throat as I took a few steps forward, examining the adjacent footprints as I walked. They were substantially larger than those left by my boots but the distance between them was quite small, suggesting their owner had indeed been walking cautiously and in step with me. And I knew there had been no other footprints when walking toward town; these were as fresh in the new snow as my own.

So I had been right all along. Just as Andrew's explanation of the muffling effect of falling snow had initially quelled my fears, this discovery reawakened those fears with a vengeance. I usually wasn't frightened easily but could think of no other logical interpretation. At the very least someone had desired anonymity so much that they were unwilling to identify themselves even when I called out to them. At the very worst someone actually had been following me!

The first possibility was mildly disturbing, the second more menacing.

And since I was inclined to err on the side of caution, I took my wool scarf from around my neck, wrapped it over my head and ears and, with it snuggly tied under my chin – and with more than one furtive look around – began trotting up the hill at the quickest pace I could manage.

This was more than disconcerting; I felt spied upon and vaguely threatened. Whose purpose would it serve to follow someone in the woods and not acknowledge a request to show himself? My fear took on an edge of anger as my question led me to Gavin Marshall and Jacob Collier. I could imagine the former of those gentlemen getting quite a chuckle out of causing me such alarm. Mr. Collier didn't seem the type but Mr. Marshall struck me as a man who might enjoy having the upper hand in such a manner, especially in light of my reactions to him thus far.

By the time the manse came into view I had been forced to slow to a walk as the cold air and steep incline had caused a sharp pain in my side that made it impossible to maintain the urgent pace my discovery inspired. It was almost dinner time and darkness had long since shrouded the trees in sinister shadows which added to my feeling of foreboding.

The lights of home had never seemed more inviting and a wave of relief surged over me as the shadows were defeated by their assurance of refuge.

I'm embarrassed to admit that my hand trembled slightly as my fingers wrapped around the door knob.

II.

The relationship between sisters is a unique and intriguing one. Rachel and I definitely had had our ups and downs over the years and were dissimilar in many significant ways. Her resolve never to speak to me again following the Gavin Marshall incident at the Harvest Festival had lasted the longest of any similar proclamation, but after my disagreement with our father Rachel slowly had begun to soften toward me. Although our previous intimacy was far from completely restored, we were on much better terms. Rachel may have been rather shallow and self-centered during those early adult years but she had a gentle heart and found it difficult to stay angry very long. Something had happened that changed her attitude toward me – perhaps as a direct result of the tension between our father and me pity had oozed its way in and familial love had taken things from there.

I likewise had had a change of heart regarding her. Initially it had been my intention to speak to my parents about what I had witnessed between Rachel and Mr.

Marshall at the Harvest Festival dance. Having put it off, however, I found it impossible to broach the subject after the confrontations surrounding my employment. Because I had been tempted to use Rachel's indiscretion to mitigate Father's anger over my taking a job and expunge his idealistic view of her, common sense told me that to bring it up now would smack of retaliation and make the incident virtually unbelievable should she choose to deny it, which she undoubtedly would. Consequently, I had decided that the best course of action was to handle things myself and make sure Rachel and Mr. Marshall saw each other as little as possible and never were alone again.

So Rachel and I had, in a manner of speaking, met one another half way. Her anger had abated and been replaced by a sense of pity for her prodigal sister, and my fear for her had changed to a wary watchfulness – shaky common ground but common ground nonetheless.

As a result of our recovering relationship, it was Rachel's company I sought once the shadows, suspicions, and fears of the day had been closed out by the door I leaned against heavily. When my heartbeat and breathing resumed their normal rate and I could untie my scarf and take off my boots without being thwarted by trembling fingers, I crossed the vestibule area and headed down the darkened hallway toward the inviting light and comforting murmur of voices coming from the kitchen at the rear of the house.

Mother was just putting the finishing touches on our supper, a large bibbed apron protecting her dress and making her the picture of contented domesticity. After the uncertainty that had dogged my path that day, the warmth of the room and the atmosphere she provided were as refreshing as a cool drink on a hot afternoon and I stood in the doorway for a moment just drinking it in.

At first I thought Mother was alone in the room and must have been talking to herself when I heard voices earlier, but as I entered I caught sight of Rachel sitting on the floor in the opposite corner next to the heavy cast iron Franklin stove. She was playing with an adorable spaniel puppy sporting a bright red ribbon about its neck tied in a lavish bow that was almost as big as the puppy's head. Rachel looked up as I entered and greeted me with a delighted grin.

"Oh Martha, look what came for you today!"

"For me?"

"Yes," she replied, impatient with my lack of immediate enthusiasm. "From Patriot's Point! There's a note. Open it!"

Mother had turned from her labors, smiled warmly at Rachel's cryptic imperative, and indicated a sealed envelope on the kitchen table with my name written across the front in small, neat letters. I picked it up but even before breaking the seal guessed its contents.

Mr. Collier's message was polite, to the point, and only mildly conciliatory:

"*Dear Miss Pendleton:*

Molly's pups are now ready to leave her. I have taken the liberty of selecting the runt of the litter for you. It was my father's belief that the runt is always the best dog. I hope you will accept this token of my esteem. I have called the pup 'Gazebo.'

Respectfully, Jacob Collier"

"What does it say," Rachel demanded, curiosity having driven her to her feet and drawn her to my shoulder.

I handed the note to her, smiling down at the puppy who had followed her to me and now was sniffing and nibbling my thick woolen stockings.

She was a precious little thing. The first thing one noticed was her ears; covered with silky, milk-colored hair, they were over-long and definitely something she would have to grow into. When she shook her head, as she did now in her battle with my stockings, they flopped across her face, covering her muzzle and causing her huge brown eyes to blink in surprise at the unexplainable intrusion. Her smooth coat was a mixture of milky fur and splotches of varying shades of liver and brown. Her face was the same milky color but her right eye was encircled by a dark brown splotch and when I held her face still between my hands and looked into her eyes I noticed that the eyelashes of the encircled eye were a contrasting pale gold while those on the opposite eye were a ruddy brown. It was a most appealing canine face and I was instantly smitten.

"What an odd name," Rachel observed as she finished reading Mr. Collier's note to our mother.

"Is there some significance to it," Mother asked while spooning mashed potatoes into a large serving bowl.

"I suppose you could say that."

I replied as casually as possible, explaining the circumstances surrounding my acquaintance with Molly and sharing selected portions of my conversation with Mr. Collier. I had no intention of alarming her and so the abridged version made no mention of the less pleasant moments of my third encounter with the Cove's most notorious Remittance Man.

Supper that evening was the most pleasant we had had since that fateful Sunday two months ago. Although my father disapproved of the source of the puppy he couldn't resist her appealing nature any more than I, for he was the source of our love of animals. The pup won him over with hardly any effort and when she stayed contentedly in her basket on the kitchen side of the doorway while we ate, she sealed her position as a member of the family.

In the past my father had been adamant that one's bedroom was not the place for a dog and we never had challenged him, however tempted we might have been. When we retired that evening we reluctantly agreed that the kitchen would be the best place for the puppy since her basket could be kept in close proximity to the warm Franklin stove. Father seemed immovable on the point so neither pleading nor tears appeared plausible strategies. After a lengthy farewell, Rachel and I went to our rooms, empathizing with one another that Gazebo was sure to suffer irreparable trauma as a result of being abandoned on her first night with us.

In the wee hours of the morning, while listening to the whimpered protestations of the kitchen's lonely occupant, I heard my father's heavy footfall as he made his way downstairs.

Straining to hear, the unintelligible low rumble of Father's voice rose from the kitchen. I was afraid Gazebo soon would find herself banished to the back shed if incapable of better self-control and fought the urge to hurry downstairs to intercede on her behalf.

I listened to his returned, wondering what had happened to the poor little pup, and was utterly amazed to suddenly feel the wet nose of an intruder nuzzling my hand as it lay draped over the edge of the bed.

Father quietly closed my bedroom door and went on his way.

I lifted the dog up to my bed by the scruff of her neck and she nestled into the curve of my body. Within minutes we were sound asleep.

III.

It didn't take long to push to the back of my mind the unsettling events of the day Gazebo – now called simply 'Bo' – came into our lives. The snow that had fallen that day had signaled the beginning of truly wintry weather and I no longer took my shortcut into town nor walked very far into the surrounding woods.

Because of the change in weather I began making two trips into town each day using the manse's sled and team to take Rachel to and from school. Bo was my constant companion and would accompany me on these excursions perched beside me on the front seat, her snout aloft and nostrils pulsating as she eagerly explored the world through her sense of smell. I felt confident handling the sled and team, and with Bo at my side there was nothing sinister in the shadows for I no longer was alone.

As a result of going into town on a daily basis I began going to the newspaper office more frequently as well. There really was no reason for me to do so but since I had to pass near the building on my way I found it impossible to resist the urge to stop in and see what was going on.

Andrew wasn't always there when I stopped, nor was Mr. Carmichael, but Jeremiah Quigley, a wizened old gentleman whose name complimented his 'Legend of Sleepy Hollow' appearance to perfection, seemed never to leave the place and could be counted on for an update on who was doing what in the world of journalism. Once he grew accustomed to the idea of having a woman around the office Mr. Quigley took it upon himself to attempt to educate me about the inner workings of the printing industry. I'm sure he thought me dull and slow-witted when I failed to thrill to or excel at learning the intricacies of setting type or running a press. It wasn't that I wasn't interested, it was just that the process was so slow and laborious – and messy – that I found my mind wandering and symptoms of serious boredom setting in when he would lead me back to the massive oily machine while passing the time of day and soon set off into an impromptu lecture and object lesson.

It was during one of those spontaneous lessons, when neither Andrew nor Mr. Carmichael was in the office, that the incessant ringing of the telephone rescued me from the brink of a hands-on demonstration. Mr. Quigley would have ignored the interruption in order to proceed with his instruction but I seized upon its persistence as a means of extrication just moments before finding myself wrist-deep in ink and oil.

Mr. Carmichael's urgent voice sputtered at the other end of the line. "Quigley? Who is this? To whom am I speaking?"

"This is Martha Pendleton, Mr. Carmichael. I'm sorry but Mr. Quigley and I are the only ones here right now."

"Damnation," he exclaimed, frustration mounting in his voice. "Do you have any idea where Carlton is?"

I explained to him that I did not and then turned the earpiece over to Mr. Quigley who took my place at the wall-mounted phone box and proceeded to inform his employer that Andrew hadn't yet returned from a nearby community where he was interviewing the mayor regarding an upcoming building project.

I could hear Mr. Carmichael's voice grumbling and barking through the wire as Mr. Quigley held the earpiece away from his head to compensate for the volume of the other man's pronouncements.

Mr. Quigley added little to the conversation except for an occasional "Yes sir," "No sir," and "I see," so I was startled when the earpiece abruptly was thrust back into my hand with no explanation as he turned and walked away.

I held it for a moment without speaking before stepping up to the phone box and addressing myself to the mouthpiece once again. "This is Martha, Mr. Carmichael. Is there something more you need?"

His voice was surprisingly calm and controlled after the frustrated deluge of words I had overhead from Mr. Quigley's end of the one-sided conversation just concluded.

"Martha," he began, calling me by name for the first time. "I'm afraid I'm going to have to ask you to do a little extra work for the paper today."

My heart skipped a beat and my throat constricted in anticipation.

"There's a story breaking over at the courthouse and neither Andrew nor I are available to cover it. I need you to go over there and collect the facts for me."

He paused but I had nothing to say into the silence.

"Now, there's really not that much to it. All I want you to do is sit in on Judge Proctor's afternoon session and find out what they're charging Hector Nash with. Hector Nash, got that? You won't even need to speak. Just make sure you get the basics – what do they say he did, when did it happen, who accuses him, where did it happen, when will he come to trial? Got it; nothing different from what you do every week at church meetings really. Just make sure you get it down exactly. We'll take it from there. Can you do that for me?"

Although my voice quavered slightly, I assured him that I could do as he asked.

He rang off with an enthusiastic "Good girl!" and I sat down to contemplate the magnitude of what I had just agreed to do.

Logistically it wasn't a problem. Rachel would be in school until three o'clock. That gave me the rest of the morning to calm down, find out what time to be at the courthouse, collect what I would need, and attend Judge Proctor's afternoon session. I swallowed hard and reassured myself that it would be easy. All I had to do was sit there and take notes, just as I did every week at the various church and civic meetings around town, as Mr. Carmichael had reminded me.

Utilizing my deepest, most mature voice, I called the courthouse and was informed that the afternoon session would begin at one o'clock. That gave me nearly three hours to wait. I called home to let Mother know I wouldn't be home for lunch, gathered up a few issues of *The Sentinel* in order to familiarize myself with the type of information normally reported, took out my notebook and jotted down a few reminders of what Mr. Carmichael wanted to know, and settled in at Andrew's desk to wait out the clock with Bo at my feet.

The Courthouse stood on the east side of the town square on the corner of one of the two streets that ran directly east-west from that center "hub." It was a dignified old building; a three story red brick affair trimmed in white, with four Doric columns supporting the front entrance's extended roofline and capped off by an elaborate widow's walk from which one could just catch a glimpse of the ocean farther east across the rooftops.

I had never been there before and as I stood looking up at the impressive façade from the bottom of the steps the realization struck me that very few women would have seen the inside of this particular building for only men were called to serve on juries and there were no females involved in any aspect of the local government housed within. Women were allowed in, of course, for the building's basement level held the town jail – accessible from the back – and women did go there to visit and were, occasionally, among the incarcerated. I doubted whether more than a handful of women had ever crossed the threshold of the main part of the building, however, and realized I wouldn't have been much more conspicuous had I been wearing trousers and smoking a cigar. What would Alice Paul do in such a situation, I asked myself, looking to one of America's best known suffragettes for inspiration. The answer set my feet in motion for I saw the determined set of her jaw as she took stogie in hand and marched ahead of me into the building.

I had timed my arrival for thirty minutes before the appointed hour so to be able to find my way without undue haste and frustration once inside. It turned out to be the wisest decision I would make that day for the clerk assigned to the first floor anteroom, although pleasant enough, was at first convinced that I was mistaken as to my destination and then determined to dissuade me from going farther.

"Ma'am," he repeated when I had firmly stated my purpose for the third time, "surely you don't want to spend a lovely afternoon cooped up inside this old place listening to a lot of confusing legal talk. This just ain't no place for a lady like you."

When I assured him that this was, indeed, where I wanted to spend the afternoon and that listening to a lot of legal talk might be confusing but that I could handle it, he added in a slightly less pleasant, rather condescending tone, "Does your father know where you are?"

"I can assure you, sir," I replied with a brusque confidence that was only slightly less than skin deep, "that my *employer* knows where I am and even that is more than you have any need or right to require from me."

He was somewhat taken aback by my abrupt manner – as was I – and I took advantage of the moment to brush by him and through the anteroom into the open courtroom beyond. My hands were trembling a bit, my palms were sweaty, and my heart was thudding in my chest, but I had overcome the first hurdle and even that small victory was encouraging; I was beginning to like this new version of me.

By the time Judge Proctor entered his courtroom I had taken what I considered to be an inconspicuous seat near the back of the room behind a smattering of other spectators present for the afternoon arraignments. Mostly family members, they sat in hushed clusters, concern for loved ones etched in the contours of their faces and the droop of their shoulders. This was a world to which I never had been exposed and I had to fight back an emotional reaction to the sorrow and broken lives before me. In a town the size of Tully's Cove the amount of crime was nominal but however small the percentage might be the impact on individual lives was not diminished. I was beginning to understand why my father often looked drawn and weary after visiting the jail for not only did he seek to mend the hard hearts of those confined but consoling loved ones often left without security surely was a drain on his spiritual reserves.

I had no idea who among the four men sitting with their backs to me in front of the sheriff was Hector Nash but I didn't have long to wait for after Judge Proctor dispatched the first case Mr. Nash was called forward.

He was a young man of no more than thirty-five dressed in neatly mended overalls and a clean work shirt. His hair had been carefully combed and slicked back from his face with pomade and I caught sight of an expression on his face as he glanced back at his wife that told me this setting was new to him, too.

"Mr. Nash," Judge Proctor began, "you are accused of stealing from your employer. Do you understand the charges against you?"

"Yes sir," was the quiet response. "I been told they say I didn't hold up my end of the bargain."

"That is correct."

The Judge put on a pair of spectacles and began shuffling through an assortment of papers on the desk before him, separating the one on which he wished to focus. "You have been under contract to work the 50-acre parcel of land located north and west of Whimsy Creek in return for a distribution of the proceeds from whatever yield you receive in a 60-40 proportion, is that correct?"

Mr. Nash looked up at the judge with a rather bewildered expression.

Judge Proctor cleared his throat before reiterating. "You are to get 40% of the crop and the landlord is to receive 60%, is that correct?"

"That's what they say, sir, but I never..."

I was hastily scribbling down notes, fearful that I would miss something important, so didn't notice when a tall, well dressed man entered the room and walked directly down the center aisle toward the railing separating the gallery from the proceedings area.

As had been the case thus far, it wasn't until I heard his voice that I realized Jacob Collier had come on the scene.

"Your Honor," his confident voice cut through Mr. Nash's halting protestations, "please excuse this unorthodox interruption of the matter at hand but I have just returned from New York and so am newly aware of these proceedings."

"Mr. Collier, this is merely an initial hearing on the matter. Your opportunity to give testimony will come in open court at a later date."

The judge was smiling benignly but his eyes held an edge of contempt for the elegant man before him.

"I understand that, Your Honor. But it is my intention that this matter not proceed to trial. As I mentioned, I have been out of state and was unaware of the problem that had arisen between Mr. Nash and my family. Mr. Nash is entirely correct. He never agreed to a 60-40 division of his yield. In all of our discussions we spoke only of an even 50-50 distribution."

"Then I don't understand, Mr. Collier; why has this matter been brought before my court?"

"I'm not exactly clear on that myself, sir. I can only say that it is a mistake and I apologize for taking any of your valuable time."

Judge Proctor's benign expression had changed to open disapproval of the gentleman before him and my concern for Mr. Nash was transferring itself to Mr. Collier with every word the judge uttered.

"I can hold you in contempt, sir, for trifling with this court."

"Yes, sir; you would be totally within your rights to do so. I can only say that this mistake was not made with malice and I ask that you release Mr. Nash and allow us to settle the matter between ourselves. I can assure the Court that it will not be burdened with any further misunderstandings of this nature."

Judge Proctor paused before responding; turning first to the humble man before the bench and then back to Jacob Collier. "Mr. Nash, go home and consider this matter closed. Mr. Collier, don't let me see you in my courtroom again, is that clear?"

"Very clear sir. Thank you."

Out of deference to the judge's authority Jacob backed away from the railing a few steps before turning to walk up the aisle and out of the room. As he turned our eyes met and a look of exasperation passed over his face.

If I could have avoided him I would have but he was, essentially, my assignment so I followed him and Mr. Nash into the anteroom.

"I'm sorry, Nash," Mr. Collier was saying as I approached the two men. "I don't know what got into her. Don't worry about anything. Just go home and try to forget this ugly business."

A short, thin woman brushed past me and was swept up into Mr. Nash's arms. As Jacob turned to avert his eyes from the emotional scene he caught sight of me standing off to one side and regarded me blankly for a moment before turning to leave.

"Mr. Collier," I called out after swallowing hard.

He stopped and visibly heaved a sigh before turning back to me.

"Sorry to bother you but I'm covering Mr. Nash's court appearance for *The Sentinel* and would like to ask you a few questions."

He ran a hand through his hair in a gesture of exasperation. "Miss Pendleton, I hardly think what has just transpired qualifies as a court appearance. Nash has been dismissed. Isn't that sufficient evidence that there is no story here?"

"I'm afraid I'll have to let my editor be the judge of that."

I could see his point but felt duty-bound to take back to Mr. Carmichael all the information possible. "I really appreciate what you just did for Mr. Nash and I suspect Mr. Carmichael will think our readers will, too."

"Miss Pendleton, I intervened on Nash's behalf because it was the right thing to do. I'm no one's knight errant. I am just a man trying to live a quiet life with as little interference from outsiders as possible. I would like to be left alone. I hope your editor will respect that."

"Like it or not, you're a person of interest to this community, Mr. Collier," I replied, my courage fortified by the knowledge that covering this story definitely was a pivotal moment for me and I dare not let Mr. Carmichael down. "As such, I'm afraid something as public as a court appearance won't be seen as 'interference from outsiders,' as you put it."

He lingered and I felt emboldened as a result. "Your tenuous status can't be ignored and so I say again, what you did for Mr. Nash is probably quite newsworthy. Frankly, I think you should let people see this side of you more often. Your reputation might wear itself out if you did."

"That's where you're wrong, Miss Pendleton. I'm afraid I've earned that reputation. Candid moments can be deceiving; there are no reprieves for the likes of me. Good day, miss."

He held out his hand and I freely surrendered to his firm grasp. He paused with my hand in his for just a moment before raising it to his lips. It was the same old fashioned, gallant gesture he had shown my mother that long ago day when he and Gavin Marshall had escorted me home from my wanderings on his property.

"Thank you," he said, his voice barely above a whisper, and then he was gone.

IV.

When Mr. Carmichael returned to the office he found me putting the finishing touches on my first attempt at a hard news story. After returning from the courthouse I had had just enough time left to transcribe my notes into what I felt was a reasonably presentable first draft. I knew it was taking liberties but I couldn't resist taking advantage of the opportunity.

The Sentinel's owner read the copy twice before directing his full attention to me.

"Martha," he began gruffly, "this isn't the story I sent you to cover."

He indicated the pages he had just tossed to his desk. "It's not bad but when I give a reporter an assignment that's the information I expect to receive."

"I understand, Mr. Carmichael," I responded cautiously, "but Mr. Nash was dismissed, so instead of wasting your time I decided to wait around and see what else of interest might be on the docket. I realize I overstepped my bounds but I didn't want to come back empty handed."

He digested my words for a moment and then looked again at the neatly penned pages I had brought him.

"Well, this will have to be reworked," he growled, "but we may be able to use some of it."

I took that as a dismissal – and a triumph! – and turned to leave the office.

"By the way," he asked, almost as an afterthought, "why was Nash's case dismissed?"

"I can't say," I replied, choosing my words carefully so as not to come right out and lie. "There apparently was some kind of mix-up and the judge just told him to go home."

It wasn't Mr. Nash's privacy or feelings I was attempting to protect by steering Mr. Carmichael away from the facts of his case. It clearly was Jacob Collier who was at the heart of my decision. The idea of staying and covering another case had come to me as I watched his tall, elegant frame leave the courthouse and I never once questioned the ethics of such a decision. The remainder of my actions had flowed from that point without effort or qualm.

CHAPTER SEVEN

I.

Even at the height of our verbal embargo I had continued to accompany Rachel to Patriot's Point for her weekly French lesson with Jocelyn Collier. She undoubtedly would have preferred to go without me but acquiesced without debate rather than involve our mother who became increasingly concerned about the anger she saw festering between her daughters.

Rachel had a keen mind when inspired and took to her second language with an enthusiasm she rarely bestowed on academic pursuits; if I hadn't known better I would have thought she had an ulterior motive like planning a trip to the continent. Whatever the source of her inspiration, it was enjoyable to observe her progress – even when our wordless war was at its peak – and it had been well worth the embarrassment of sitting in Jocelyn's cheery parlor with Rachel and me making conversation around each other. Once we had entered the post-prodigal phase of our relationship, however, and pity for my ouster from the inner sanctum of our family circle had replaced her stony silence our weekly excursions to Jocelyn's home became more comfortable and almost companionable once again.

We normally began with tea and then I would either walk in the garden or, once winter arrived, explore the Collier's extensive library while Rachel had her lesson. Upon its conclusion the three of us usually would visit for a while longer either in the parlor or in the library. As she became more comfortable and confident around Jocelyn and her home, Rachel had a habit of disappearing at that point as she exhibited little interest in or patience for domestic chit-chat. To be honest, I wasn't very interested in it either but, understandably, there were limits to a friendship with Jocelyn and conversation didn't stray very far afield.

The Saturday after Mr. Nash's story was absent from the newspaper, Rachel and I arrived at Patriot's Point at the appointed hour and were ushered into Jocelyn's parlor as usual. She was waiting for us there, looking fresh and lovely in an emerald brocade jacket and matching slim wool skirt, her eyes looking more green than hazel as they took on the highlights of her outfit and accessories. She accepted our compliments with some humor, the way friends are apt to do, denigrating what she perceived to be her large hands and feet.

My admiration for the young woman hadn't diminished as we became better acquainted but had been tempered along the way by what can best be described as a rather patrician attitude when it came to speaking about and dealing with those she regarded as somehow beneath her, like her household staff. It was an unattractive characteristic that I found embarrassing and it made me feel more than mildly uncomfortable.

"I'm so glad to see the two of you today," Jocelyn said rising from her chair to greet us. Her voice was warm and friendly even while her gesture toward the maid who had just brought in fresh scones and honey was abrupt, if not actually rude. "I've been pitifully lonely this week; sometimes I think I'll go mad living in this mausoleum."

She turned her attention to the maid who was pouring boiling water into the tea server. "All right, Cora," she said, scowling quite fiercely as she took her seat, "you may go now."

The middle-aged woman she called Cora was the same woman I remembered having seen on other occasions when we had arrived before tea was quite ready. A mousy and simple-looking person, Jocelyn regarded her with such open disdain that I wondered why she kept her on staff.

Cora placed the tea service before Jocelyn and left the room hurriedly, bumping into a three-legged table next to the door and causing an ominous tinkling of glass knick-knacks in her haste to oblige her employer's obvious desire that she be seen as little as possible.

"It is virtually impossible to get competent help," Jocelyn observed while pouring tea into delicate porcelain cups. "That's one thing I definitely miss about England; there servants at least know their job – and their place."

Her words reminded me of a less-than-flattering article I had read about the lifestyles of successful industrialists like J.P. Morgan and Andrew Carnegie; men to whom the appellation "robber baron" had – fairly or unfairly – been affixed. Focusing on the opulence of these Horatio Algers, the article reported that the William Vanderbilts – whose lavish New York City home covered half a city block – insisted that all housework be completed by nine o'clock each morning so that they need never gaze on a member of the servant class. Now, the Colliers were by no means in the same league as the Vanderbilts and Morgans but Jocelyn's demeanor around the hired help suggested she might well share their attitude toward those who found themselves in domestic service. It wasn't an attractive characteristic but I wasn't bold enough to challenge her on it. After all, I was hardly her equal. Rachel and I were her guests due solely to her largess and the status enjoyed by clergy and their families which brought them into circles from which a dramatic disparity in income normally would have found them excluded. I suppose that inclusion was due to the elevated opinion of the clergy arising from their heightened level of education and their perceived proximity to God. Whatever the cause, I probably was more acutely aware of my "place" than the servants Jocelyn disparaged, and definitely didn't know her well enough yet to openly challenge her values.

Thanksgiving had just passed and with its departure went every hope for further respite from the cold that now permeated everything and seemed bent on settling in our bones. Snow was becoming an apparently permanent part of the landscape and I no longer was even tempted to forage about the grounds of Patriot's Point during our visits. When the two scholars began their work I went into the library, intending to indulge in foraging of a different nature.

The heavily paneled, richly appointed room was dimly lit and chilly but a fire had been laid in the massive stone fireplace as if my destination had been anticipated and I appreciated Jocelyn's thoughtfulness.

There was no need to do much browsing among the leather-bound tomes that lined the walls for I was in the mood for poetry and knew that the collected works of Emily Dickinson were among the titles sheltered in that room. I quickly found what I was looking for and soon was curled up in one of the wing chairs adjacent the fireplace with the rich-smelling volume propped against my knees.

As I read, Dickinson's intensely personal style and the dim solitude of the room drew me into deep, relaxed introspection and I soon was dozing in the flickering firelight.

I probably would have slept until time to go home if not for a rush of adrenaline as my slumbering grasp slackened and the book I held slid to the floor with a muffled thud on the thick area rug. I woke with a start and, as my eyes grew accustomed to the semi-dark, was surprised to discover someone kneeling before the fireplace, their identity obscured by the contrast cast by the light of the fire before them.

Our reclusive host turned from the fire, his high cheekbones and aristocratic nose highlighted by the play of light and shadow dancing about the room. "Sorry. Did I wake you?"

"No," I stammered, still slightly disoriented and not exactly sure just what had startled me from my dozing.

"I didn't want to disturb you but the fire needed tending."

His words were offered more as an observation than as an explanation of his presence.

I leaned down to retrieve the book that had slipped from my grasp, altering my position as I did so from comfortable house cat to something I perceived as being a bit more ladylike.

When he finished stoking the fire I thought he would go but instead he shifted from kneeling to a relaxed position sitting on the raised stone dais which served to separate the expansive fireplace from the thick oriental carpet covering that portion of the beautiful hardwood floor.

Neither of us spoke. Silence stretched tautly over a moment that felt more like an eternity for the silence was hardly what one would call companionable. I found myself wishing he would leave since I had nowhere else to go and he had the luxury of unlimited access to the house.

Mr. Collier finally broke the silence, leaning forward and resting his crossed forearms on his knees as he spoke.

"Actually," he began, "I should be honest with you and admit that I had hoped to find you here this afternoon. You usually end up in this room, so I kept the fire going..."

"You kept the fire going?"

"Yes... You see, I wanted to speak with you – to thank you for not writing a story about Hector Nash."

"You hardly need to thank me," I assured him. "As you said at the time, there simply was no story worth writing."

A skeptical smile crossed his face as he exhaled pointedly. "Miss Pendleton, let's be frank with one another. Anything involving me is newsworthy in the eyes of the Cove."

I started to object but it was useless to dispute the point with him for he was right. If Mr. Carmichael had known that Nash's legal trouble involved Jacob Collier he would have given it front page status regardless of the fact that Mr. Nash had been dismissed.

"Yes," I conceded, my voice barely a whisper.

"So, I want you to know," he continued, "that I appreciate the decency of your gesture. Nash has had enough trouble lately; having his name dragged through the mud by the press would have been like rubbing salt in a wound."

"I agree with you, Mr. Collier, that a story on Mr. Nash would have been pointless and perhaps even cruel..."

Indignation unexpectedly welled up within me.

"But I must take exception to your disparaging of the press. Mr. Nash's name would hardly have been 'dragged through the mud' as you put it. It's the press's responsibility to share information with the people it serves. In a free society journalism is vital to an informed public."

"You're learning the rhetoric well, Miss Pendleton," he broke in, his voice sharply edged. "You say it's the press's responsibility to keep the public informed? I would shift your emphasis slightly to say that *responsible* journalism is vital to an informed public, to a democracy, but responsible journalism has hardly been my experience when dealing with men like Carlton and Carmichael."

I bridled at his words. "Now wait a minute. Do you really think *The Sentinel* is irresponsible? You obviously don't know those men at all. Mr. Carmichael may be something of a hothead, but he never would print something that wasn't true and, for your information, Andrew Carlton is one of the finest, most ethical people I have ever known!"

Conviction had given me confidence and I no longer was particularly conscious of or concerned about my "place."

He looked down at his hands and smiled somewhat ruefully. "I apologize," he said quietly, shaking his head. "I didn't mean to offend you. I set out to thank you."

He rose and looked back into the fire before speaking again. "It appears that you and I are destined to misunderstand one another. There seems to be no end of gazebos in my life. Perhaps it's my fate."

I didn't catch the meaning of his reference to Bo but the veiled reference to his past focused my attention. My confidence bolstered, I found myself sailing rather boldly into unchartered waters.

"Mr. Collier, may I speak frankly?"

He said nothing to stop me, so I continued.

"I know little about you so-called 'Remittance Men' other than what one hears from certain quarters..."

"From the likes of Mrs. Starkey and Mrs. Wentworth," he interjected. "Yes, I can imagine."

I saw no need to contradict this characterization; there was no denying that the widows Starkey and Wentworth were the Cove's busiest busy-bodies.

"Couldn't you put that part of your life behind you and make a fresh start here? If you became more a part of the community – let people get to know you – surely things would improve for you and Jocelyn."

He walked slowly across the carpet and stood for a moment behind the chair in which I was seated before responding.

"Miss Pendleton..." He paused before starting again. "Martha, you are very kind, but you are also extremely naïve."

I was surprised both by his use of my first name and by his voice which was actually quite tender.

He said nothing further but moved to the side of my chair and reached down with a strong hand, turning my face toward his with such utter tenderness I thought I would melt at his touch. There was a heart-wrenchingly sad smile on his lips as he bent down and lightly kissed my forehead.

He crossed to the French doors adjacent the fireplace and left the house.

It had been a gesture totally lacking in passion, the type of tenderness bestowed on a child, but I was moved deeply and felt the warmth of his touch long afterward. I, too, crossed to the French doors and watched through the glass as he walked toward the stables a short distance to the west. I was not one to be easily swept away by emotion but the sight of him walking through the gently falling snow into the gathering shadows of early evening was the most utterly romantic image I had ever witnessed. If he had turned to look back I think my heart would have burst but he walked on and, in just a moment, had become one with the dark.

As I stood before the doors a moment longer, my eyes were drawn to a dark figure emerging from the shadows encroaching upon the adjacent carriage house. I watched as the figure took shape and was startled by the realization that it was Rachel heading back to the main house through the snow. I had assumed she was still with Jocelyn and realized that it must be later than I thought.

I turned to leave the room and nearly walked into our hostess who had come up behind me without making a sound. I stepped back abruptly with a startled gasp.

"I thought I heard voices in here," she said. "Were you talking with someone?"

I was puzzled by the accusing tone in her voice but readily admitted that I had had a brief conversation with her cousin when he came in to stoke the fire.

"How considerate of him," she said rather icily. "I didn't realize he was here."

She turned and walked ahead of me toward the opposite door. "I apologize for my cousin's intrusion on your reading."

"It wasn't an intrusion; really."

I tried to reassure her for the tone in her voice troubled me and I didn't want her alarmed by what had turned out to be an interesting – even pleasant – exchange.

"You don't need to apologize for him; your cousin really is quite nice."

She gave me a look that can only be described as withering and I was determined to alleviate an increasingly awkward situation. I tried a change of subject.

"Did you and Rachel have a nice visit after her lesson?"

"Briefly, but I was called away by a problem in the kitchen and she was gone when I got back. That was about half an hour ago. I thought we must have gotten our signals crossed and that the two of you had left so came to investigate when I heard voices."

We had left the library and were standing in the large entrance gallery. Rachel joined us at that point, breathless, flushed, and slightly disheveled from hurrying through the snow.

"Ah, here you are," Jocelyn observed, a shallow smile softening her clouded face. "We had begun to think you had decided to walk home."

Rachel's smile was lavish.

"I'm sorry. I've been in the carriage house admiring your new roadster."

"My cousin's latest acquisition," Jocelyn explained dryly. "I'm afraid I have little interest in automobiles."

I was about to comment that I found Rachel's interest surprising but at that moment the grandfather clock behind us began its solemn proclamation that we were approaching the dinner hour; Rachel and I bid our hostess a hasty and somewhat awkward farewell.

The thought struck me as we climbed into the Collier's enclosed carriage that at least two of us seemed relieved that our weekly gathering had come to an end.

II.

Rachel turned 17 on December 24th of that year. Ever since she was a little girl Rachel had expressed the opinion that being born on Christmas Eve was a distinct disadvantage for she believed her birth definitely was overshadowed by the universally significant birth celebrated the next day. One had to admit that she had a point and so over the years we all had attempted to compensate for her "misfortune" by making the 24th as much her day as possible.

As was our tradition, we began the day with a special family breakfast featuring as many of her favorite foods as possible as well as the presentation of the small gifts we exchanged on such occasions. Every family member was somewhat coddled on his or her birthday; treated to a "choreless" day in which the others took care of all incidental matters while the celebrant read or sewed or pursued some other interest at their leisure. Rachel's day was always further enhanced by the privilege of selecting the family's Christmas tree and reading the Christmas story from the Gospel of Matthew later in the evening when we gathered around the decorated tree to share its magic and a glass or two of eggnog. This year was to be no different, except for the addition of a caroling outing for Rachel with a group of young people from church.

To his credit, my father recognized the importance of Christmas – and birthdays – in the life of a child and had always set aside a good part of Christmas Eve to spend with his family. As a result, he hitched up the sled and team shortly after lunch and drove his quartet of females (for Bo had to come along) to the farm of a member who owned a large stand of evergreens and had graciously offered us our choice from among them.

"How about this one," Father called out to Rachel, shaking the snow from the boughs of a medium-sized Frazier fir.

"Too small," she decreed unequivocally.

As always, she defused his attempts to limit the size of the trunk through which she obliged him to chop.

Mother and I exchanged knowing smiles as we watched the annual ritual unfolding before us. Father could be expected to suggest two or three other modest candidates before ultimately accepting Rachel's impressive choice and growing unseasonably warm as he labored to secure his little girl's ideal Christmas tree.

It was an endearing scene; part of our family's Christmas tradition without which the season would have seemed somehow lacking. I knew my mother loved it and probably stored these outings among her cherished memories. I, on the other hand, had always felt a bit like the outsider as year after year I watched Rachel and our father sharing this adventure. This year that feeling was even more pronounced since my father and I were still at odds with one another.

Once Rachel's selection had been downed and securely tied to the back of the sleigh we began the long ride home. As we traveled Mother led us in appropriate songs of the season, Father's rich baritone lending harmony and depth to the trio of sopranos he accompanied. I sat beside Mother in the second row of the sleigh's bench seats, cuddling Bo for warmth and happily joining the sing-along.

We had just begun a slightly off-key rendition of "Silent Night" as the manse came into view, reaching the final phrase just as we drew up to the front door. Father dragged the final note out for dramatic effect, jumping down from the sleigh as he did so and eliciting an exuberant response from Bo who threw back her puppy head and howled. We all broke out laughing, the mood easy and open. I hugged the dog tightly and kissed her on top of her snout. It was the happiest family time we had shared since I had fallen from grace and I was glad my father and I could put aside our differences so that Rachel's birthday would be pleasant.

Mother and Rachel went into the house ahead of my father and me in order to make room in the parlor for the tree and brew some hot chocolate to warm us. I remained outside and steadied the tree while Father released the ropes that held it to the sleigh.

"It's a beautiful tree," I observed as he took it from me and tamped the trunk firmly against the ground to release the boughs and shake free the remaining snow and any loose needles.

"Yes, it is," he responded tersely.

"Are you going to help decorate it before going back to church?"

"No. I'm afraid I'll have to leave that task to you ladies."

His tone was pleasant enough but, as I had noticed often since our initial flare-up over my employment, he didn't look at me as we talked, kept his responses brief, and seemed eager to get away.

Father no longer openly confronted me with his disapproval over my taking a job. Instead he kept me at arm's length and treated me almost like a stranger; a form of disapproval initially as painful as constant arguing would have been. I'm sure it was all part of his strategy to cow me into submission and get me to comply with his wishes. But I was growing calloused. I still wanted and needed my parents' love and approval but was now willing to sacrifice the latter for something I felt to be worthy of their scorn. And, if I was brutally honest with myself, my father and I really had always been strangers.

Shoulders squared, I followed him into the house.

For the first time in her life, Rachel seemed eager to hurry the festivities commemorating her birth. She surprised us all be forsaking the "choreless" day tradition and actually helped out more than on an ordinary day. She not only changed her bed linens and helped with the laundry in order to hasten our departure to get a tree but also pitched in to help put supper on the table and then cleared things away – almost constantly clock-watching during the meal and subsequent decorating of the Christmas tree.

When it came time to gather around the glittering tree to read the Christmas story and toast one another's health with eggnog sipped from great-grandmother's crystal, Rachel's pace did not abate. She read St. Matthew's account of the advent of the Christ Child in a clipped and hurried fashion and was only mildly successful in hiding her delight when Mother's playing of "The First Noel" was interrupted by the arrival of the group of carolers with whom she was to spend the remainder of the evening. Almost falling over herself in her haste, Rachel pulled on a heavy woolen sweater, donned her coat, and finished her winter wrappings off with the matching scarf and mittens I had given her for her birthday. Ready in record-breaking time, she didn't even spare us a glance as she bounded out the door.

As the young people departed, Mother observed stoically that it appeared her little girl had been replaced by a young woman whose sense of social satisfaction had shifted from family to friends her own age. She stood at the window and watched them go, crowded happily onto two large flatbed sleighs pulled by draft horses whose jingling harness bells added festive punctuation to the jumble of singing.

It was a bittersweet moment for my parents and, although he wasn't the birthday celebrant, I thought my father looked just a bit older when he excused himself to retire for the night.

III.

Christmas morning dawned cold, cloudless, and utterly still. There was a brilliant, pristine beauty both without and within as the morning sun reflected off the dazzling snow outside and the brightly colored glass ornaments adorning our tree by the parlor window. Specks of red, green, and blue refracted light danced gaily on the walls and ceiling, delighting the unsuspecting passerby with a shower of color.

We all fell victim to a festive sense of urgency that morning. For Father that urgency translated into anticipation of the heavily-attended worship service to come. It drove him from his bed, downstairs to a solitary breakfast, and through the snow over to church before the rest of us were even awake. Mother, Rachel, and I felt the urgency too, but for us it was more an anticipation of activities peripheral to the worship service that drove us rather than the logistics of worship itself.

"I can't find my stockings," Rachel shrilled, her proclamation defying the laws of physics as it traveled efficiently down to the kitchen from under the bed where her head was thrust as she groped in vain for the missing garments.

"Look under your bed," Mother suggested in a loud, calm voice as she slid a well-tailored turkey into the oven's enveloping heat.

"That's where I am!"

Rachel's voice was now a shriek and Mother turned to me with a pleading smile.

"Go help your sister, will you please Martha?"

I had been fidgeting nervously for the past fifteen minutes in eager anticipation of our departure and was more than just a little irked with Rachel for slowing the process down even more. With Bo at my heels I hurried to my sister's rescue, hiking my skirt up and taking the stairs two at a time.

"Here," I said coolly, dangling a pair of stockings tantalizingly over the bed frame blocking me from her view. "You can borrow a pair of mine."

She extracted her head with no small degree of caution, looked up at me from her perch on the floor, and smiled bewitchingly.

"Thank-you sister, dear. What would we do without each other?"

"I'd have more clothes of my own," I observed dryly, "you'd go around half dressed!"

"Well, ladies, are we almost ready to go?"

Mother's voice from the doorway interrupted before Rachel could compose an appropriate retort.

"Almost," Rachel chirped, pulling on my stockings and straightening her skirt as she rose from the floor.

Mother smiled warmly at us. "Do you think we have time for one last distraction?"

Her question was rhetorical for as surely as we had turkey for Christmas dinner we also shared this time-honored ritual before leaving for church.

She held out two small, delicately wrapped packages.

For our family Christmas was a lavish holiday only in terms of the sacred sentiment of the day – and a traditional over-indulgence in good food. Other than the modest offerings my newfound income afforded, there were no gifts tucked under the tree on Christmas morning for Father had neither the resources nor the inclination to shower his children with material possessions. Mother, however, always managed to secure some small extravagance for each of us and, as a result, our Christmas attire was subtly enhanced; making us feel almost as finely arrayed as the wealthy among the congregation.

"Oh Mother, thank you," Rachel breathed in genuine appreciation of the intricately carved cameo brooch that lay in the palm of her hand.

"You are most welcome, darling. It seems a young woman has replaced my little girl and I thought she might like a woman's piece of jewelry. I hope you will enjoy it for many years to come."

She patted Rachel's cheek affectionately and cradled her face in both hands for a moment before turning to me.

"And what about you, Martha, aren't you going to open your gift?"

"Yes, thank you," I stammered awkwardly as I untied the ribbon securing the gilt edged paper.

Inside the box was a beautiful lavaliere watch.

"It's lovely..."

"I thought it an appropriate gift for *The Sentinel*'s star reporter."

She smiled tenderly at me and her words were warm and genuine, conveying at last acceptance of my decision to work at the newspaper.

No material gift would ever mean more.

"Thank you, Mother. You don't know how much this means to me."

"Oh yes, sweetheart," she said quietly, "I believe I do."

IV.

The church was as resplendent as the brilliant morning that greeted us. Evergreen roping had been draped from sill to sill below the beautiful stained glass windows, a lighted candle surrounded by greenery and red ribbon serving as accent where the roping was drawn up and secured to each sill. Small evergreen wreaths decorated with holly berries had been attached to the pew ends facing the center aisle, larger versions of which greeted worshipers on the double doors leading into the sanctuary. The altar also was draped with evergreen rope secured with red ribbon but was further adorned with candles, additional greenery, and a large, delicately crafted nativity scene serving as centerpiece. The effect was wonderful, but the crowning touch was the huge Christmas tree standing behind and to the left of the altar. It was a magnificent specimen of evergreen perfection tastefully decorated with simple white bows, white beaded roping, and candles. As had been the case at the time of the Harvest Festival, we were struck by the level of devotion demonstrated by the parishioners of this quiet backwater community and the worshipful atmosphere their efforts created.

Also as on that other occasion, the sanctuary was filled nearly beyond capacity as the Christmas-and-Easter-Christians turned out to see and be seen in their holiday finery. We threaded our way through the crowds of chatting people, exchanging traditional yuletide greetings and small talk en route to our pew near the front of the church.

Rachel seemed unusually distracted that morning, barely acknowledging the presence of those around her and craning her neck to survey the milling crowd. After nearly stepping on her for the third time as she stopped short in front of me, I was struck by the thought that perhaps she was on the look-out for Gavin Marshall, hoping to impress him with her newly acquired 17-year-old maturity. The thought made my stomach constrict and I, too, began to examine the sea of faces hoping to intercept or prevent an encounter.

Thoughts of Gavin Marshall expanded as I observed the ebb and flow around me. As is true of any group of humans, they were an imperfect lot to say the least, with gossip being the most obvious of their failings and the "seven deadlies" an unavoidable undercurrent. But even though greed, pride, and envy may have colored the motives of some that morning (with lust and wrath dogging the heels of others) most managed their vices successfully and, in so doing, presented at least a façade of civility to the rest of the world – especially at Christmas. And lest I be accused of letting myself off the hook, I admit to struggles with pride and envy and, in anticipation of the savory meal awaiting us at home, an unhealthy dose of gluttony from time to time.

As we reached the opening to our pew, Rachel obviously caught sight of her quarry for she brightened noticeably and stood aside for me to enter. Instantly my guard was up and I stood rooted to the spot as she, on tiptoe tried to see over my shoulder.

"Rachel!"

An enthusiastic young voice came from behind me and I turned with surprise and relief to find that she had apparently been watching for Byron Mayfield, the son of one of the church's deacons.

"Byron," she said pertly, her lovely face wreathed in smiles, "now my Christmas is complete!"

Byron went crimson with pleasure.

"Merry Christmas Mrs. Pendleton, Miss Martha," he said, acknowledging that Rachel was not alone. "May I... May I sit with you, Rachel?"

His consternation was touching and I was pleased when Mother quickly interjected that we would be happy to have him join us. Rachel followed us primly into the pew with an extremely feminine rustling of skirt that was undoubtedly not lost upon her young admirer.

As the choir began to sing an opening anthem, Mother turned to me and whispered in a voice flooded with relief, "I hate to admit it but I was afraid it might be Mr. Marshall for whom Rachel was so carefully grooming this morning!"

I was taken aback by her perceptiveness. I had never uttered a word about what I had witnessed at the Harvest Festival so was under the impression that I shouldered anxiety for Rachel unassisted where Gavin Marshall was concerned. Although I had no intention of bringing it up after all this time, there was comfort in the realization that Mother had noticed the attention Mr. Marshall had paid her younger daughter on previous occasions. And she obviously recognized the latent threat men like Gavin posed to young women like Rachel; I wondered exactly how much she knew and squeezed her hand in conspiratorial acknowledgement of her confession.

As the choir's anthem drew to a close, Father rose from his seat behind the pulpit and knelt for a moment's prayer at the knee-high railing in front of the altar. Upon rising he turned to the congregation and addressed us in a somber, booming voice.

"Cast all joy from your heart this morning! This is indeed the saddest of all days!"

A startled hush fell over the sanctuary.

"The birth we gather to celebrate today is pointless," he continued. "The infant of Bethlehem – perfect mixture of God and man – was born, lived, suffered, died, and rose from the dead for *nothing*. Look around you. Can't you see that this is true?"

He was walking up the pulpit steps as he spoke and every eye in the church was riveted to his face.

I settled comfortably against the wooden pew in satisfied – and slightly smug – anticipation for I knew instinctively where he led. We may have had our differences but in the pulpit I read my father like a book.

If he hadn't heeded the calling of God the stage ultimately should have captured my father as his flare for sermonic drama gave vent to the actor buried deep within his soul. Nowhere else was he able to express himself so vividly. On his own he was rigid and opinionated, in the pulpit he was Demosthenes reborn. If I could have communicated with this person I'm certain we would have been closer. But unfortunately I seemed to be like him only in that regard; I was becoming best able to express myself from the "pulpit" of the printed page.

Once he had shocked the people from their holiday complacency, Father went on to weave the threads of his message into a rich tapestry depicting the purpose of the Messiah's coming. He took us from the edge of the manger which cradled the newborn King to the foot of the cross where the suffering deity cried out in anguish from the weight of the world's sin, and ultimately had us standing in triumph before the gaping maw of the empty tomb where the culmination of God's plan of salvation was evident in the scraps of burial cloth left behind by the resurrected Christ.

His words truly were inspired and, judging by the expressions on the faces around me, it was apparent that I was not the only one who felt they now understood Christmas like never before.

Rachel and her companion, unfortunately, were obviously not among those touched by Father's message. Throughout the service they had played a flirtatious kind of cat and mouse as hands accidentally brushed while sharing a hymnal and feet bumped as they shifted position. It was difficult not to notice and I think it must have been only her relief that Rachel's ardor was aimed at someone her own age that kept Mother from intervening and insisting that their attention be properly directed toward the front of the church.

When the service was over, Mother excused herself to join Father where he stood greeting parishioners and visitors at the narthex doors. As she walked away she gave me a look that left no doubt that I had been appointed chaperone over Rachel and Byron. With resignation I trailed behind them as we retraced our steps down the center aisle, once again exchanging Christmas greetings as we went.

As we passed the family pew of one of Rachel's schoolmates the girl called out to Rachel over the shoulder of her mother.

"Feeling better, Rachel? So sorry you missed the party after caroling last night."

"What did she mean by that," I asked as we walked on. "You weren't home until well after eleven. Where were you if you didn't go to the party?"

"Oh, Martha, don't listen to a word Lucy Stimson says. She's as empty-headed as Hannibal, and about as reliable. Just because I mentioned having an upset stomach she assumes I went home early. She doesn't know that she's talking about."

She turned her full attention and charm on Byron.

"I was at the party the entire time, wasn't I Byron?"

"Uh… yes, of course," Byron stammered. "Lucy's a ninny."

I believed Byron to be an honest person but somehow his response seemed to skirt Rachel's actual question and didn't ring true. He also was blushing and seemed extremely uncomfortable. Rachel, on the other hand, looked blank, innocent, and perfectly composed. She either had nothing to hide or was becoming alarmingly adept at prevarication.

"Miss Martha," Byron continued, the pitch of his voice cracking embarrassingly, "may I escort you and Rachel home?"

"Certainly Byron," I replied. "That would be very nice."

I turned my head so he wouldn't see the smile playing at the corners of my mouth and in doing so noticed Gavin Marshall standing a few rows down from us as if waiting for someone. His posture was strikingly irreverent as he leaned against a pillar with his foot on the seat of an adjacent pew. I would have avoided him if I could but decided that perhaps it was best that he see Rachel directing her attention toward a boy her own age. Surely the advances I had witnessed on the night of the Harvest Festival had been a meaningless dalliance on his part but, if not, nothing would serve to better reinforce Rachel's youth than the sight of her current suitor.

As we approached he turned on the charm, smiling broadly.

"Well, Merry Christmas, ladies!" What a vision the two of you are this morning."

"Thank you, Mr. Marshall," I responded primly. "Merry Christmas."

His smile was transforming itself into a rakish grin and, in hopes of controlling the moment, I turned my attention to Byron.

"Byron, have you met Mr. Marshall?"

"No ma'am," Gavin interjected without missing a beat. "I've never had the pleasure of meeting this dashing young man."

My primness was becoming increasingly frosty.

"Mr. Marshall, this is Byron Mayfield, a friend of my little sister."

Gavin directed his attention to Rachel for the first time.

"Well, Miss Rachel, any friend of yours is certainly a friend of mine."

For just a moment I thought I saw a potent look pass between the two of them but Rachel's posture toward the gentleman was stiffly polite so I dismissed it as something fabricated out of my anticipation of something between them. She seemed utterly disinterested in him and I couldn't suppress a relieved and satisfied smile. It was the first time I ever appreciate her fickle nature!

My smile wasn't lost on Mr. Marshall who couldn't let it pass without comment.

"Can it be that your holiday cheer extends to the likes of me, Miss Pendleton? You're quite lovely when you smile, you know. Such loveliness truly is a gift to those with whom it is shared."

"You may take it as one, Mr. Marshall," I replied politely, my face growing warm under his scrutiny even though I felt I still had the upper hand. "The Gift we celebrate today surely extends to all God's creatures."

He smiled sardonically at my attempt to inject a religious note into our conversation but refrained from interjecting the irreverent comeback that surely was on the tip of his tongue.

His smile was disarming.

As always when one came into contact with Gavin Marshall there was no ignoring the raw magnetism of the man. He was blessed – or cursed – with an aura that attracted women like moths to a flame. It was obvious for, even as crowded as the church was that morning, the eyes of virtually every woman capable of drawing breath eventually were drawn to him. Although I was repelled and even mildly disgusted by the type of person I perceived him to be, I was not immune to his charm and only with effort maintained my dislike of the man.

Byron was attempting to lead Rachel away from the hopeless distraction presented by his sophisticated, handsome counterpart but there really was no place to go and Mr. Marshall once again directed his attention to the young man.

"Byron," he said, clapping the youth on the shoulder and adopting the familiar tone one would use among friends. "Allow me to compliment you on your taste in women. There are few ladies in Tully's Cove who compare favorably to the Pendleton sisters."

In an effort to rescue the embarrassed young man beside me, I interrupted Gavin's meaningless flattery.

"It's our taste you should be complimenting, Mr. Marshall. Byron is a perfect example of the qualities every young woman looks for in a gentleman. We're privileged to have him escort us this morning."

The conversation was growing increasingly stilted and artificial as we parried but Gavin seemed to be enjoying himself, smiling broadly once again while putting on his overcoat.

"Ah, the rogue and the gentleman," he observed smugly. "One wonders just which you actually prefer."

Without further comment he turned and walked away.

"What did he mean by that?"

"Quite frankly, Byron, I would imagine he was referring to the image he has of himself as God's gift to women; certainly not an admirable characteristic. Let's go, shall we?"

Rachel slipped her hand into the crook of Byron's arm, her simple, "Yes, let's" instantly dispelling the young man's confusion and concern. He once again was the proud escort of the prettiest girl in school and nothing else mattered.

But as we walked out of church and through the snow toward home, Gavin Marshall's words echoed in my mind and I wondered just what he did mean. On the surface my explanation seemed accurate – he obviously saw himself as every woman's ideal. But his words had seemed more pointed than that and I began to worry that perhaps he sensed my reluctant attraction to Jacob Collier. The possibility embarrassed me to distraction.

I cringed inwardly at the smug satisfaction he would take in knowing that I found the Cove's most notorious "Remittance Man" so intriguing and sympathetic a character.

CHAPTER EIGHT

I.

The winter of 1917 passed slowly. Once the holidays were behind us and we had officially embarked upon the new year it began to feel as if the bitterly cold, snow covered days had curled contentedly before the inviting fireplaces that defined every New Englander's winter existence and decided to tarry with us as long as possible.

At first the enforced isolation had been refreshing. Social commitments had dwindled to almost nonexistent and the time spent together as a family was personally enriching. Rachel and I were getting along better than ever and the relationship between my father and me was taking its first wobbly steps toward normalcy – probably because the weather temporarily prevented my writing for *The Sentinel*. The days were filled with comfortably mundane household tasks, excursions into the white wilderness with Bo, and evenings before the fire playing cards with Mother, Rachel and, on occasion, my father.

The pervasive quietude of that white shroud would always be a special sanctuary for me. I loved to listen to it, observe it, and stand in its midst. But after three consecutive weeks of almost constantly falling snow – two of which keeping us virtually stranded at the top of the hill – I began to experience the restlessness and irritability that Mother calmly attributed to "cabin fever" and accurately predicted would pass once the weather broke; which it finally did the second week in February.

If anyone had told me that I could experience pure childlike glee at the sight of a sled and work crew clearing a snow covered road I would have questioned their grip on reality. Nevertheless, such was precisely the case when the five heavily bundled figures trudging determinedly up the hill came into my peripheral vision one morning as I toyed with a fictitious news story while sitting at the desk before the window in the upstairs morning room.

"Mother... Rachel," I shouted down the stairs, taking them two at a time. "Here comes the road crew!"

Mother was in the kitchen brewing a pot of fresh coffee.

"Yes, I know, I've been watching their progress for some time now."

Her voice held a trace of laughter. "They'll be in need of warmth and refreshment by the time they make it all the way up here. Go stoke the fire in the parlor while I get some sandwiches ready, would you please?"

I was only too happy to comply, almost tripping over Bo in my haste.

The parlor was dark and chilly but when I drew the curtains back from the window the winter sun brought instant cheerfulness to the room. The banked embers in the fireplace waited patiently, eagerly receiving the fuel I fed them, crackling and popping cheerfully as the flames grew. I smiled and heaved a relieved sigh into the flickering warmth, sitting cross-legged on the floor with my arm around Bo. Civilization was once again within our reach.

Rachel found us there a few moments later, squatting down beside me on the hearthrug and scratching Bo behind the ears as the dog wriggled all over in delight.

"Didn't you hear me," I asked, surprised by her calm. "The road crew is clearing Church Street."

"I heard you," she replied. "So what?"

"So what? So we'll be able to go into town again, that's what!"

"Just in time for winter term to begin on schedule," she observed drily. "Somehow I don't quite share your excitement at the prospect."

I looked at her like a cow looking at a new gate.

"Rachel, you never cease to amaze me. Is this the same girl who claimed last winter she would die if she had to stay cooped up away from her school friends during a three day storm? It's been almost two weeks. Aren't you eager to see your friends? Aren't you dying to see Byron?"

She looked at me as if I were the younger sister.

"I'm not a child, Martha," she replied simply, her voice cool and composed, "and I don't want to talk about Byron."

"That's a first," I teased. "Since when don't you want to talk about boys?"

Rachel nudged Bo back toward me as she rose to her feet.

"You sound just like Mother. Why can't you all just accept the fact that I'm grown up?"

There was in her voice a trace of the pouting little girl I knew so well but I had to admit she did seem different lately. After a moment's reflection I decided it must be a phase she was going through – when covering church meetings I constantly heard women talking about "phases" in relation to their children. Yes, Rachel must be going through a phase. After a few days back at school with the Newcomb sisters I imagined we would see the return of the giggly young girl. Anyway I hoped so for, as much as she annoyed me, I found myself missing that girl most acutely as of late.

It took another fifteen to twenty minutes before the road crew finally reached the church and with dogged determination began to forge a path over Father's footprints between there and the house. By the time they reached us they were red-faced, puffing, and physically spent.

"In...vigorating," was Eli Thornton's breathless assessment when Mother observed that they must be exhausted from all their toil.

Without much coaxing, the five men gratefully shed their boots and several layers of protective clothing and gathered around the fireplace in the parlor. Their apologies for the intrusion and thanks for the coffee and sandwiches were profuse.

"Ah-yuh," Eli intoned as he gratefully accepted a second sandwich, "the good Lord done over-blessed us with this storm, I'm afraid."

The others chimed in their agreement with a weary but enthusiastic chorus of "Ah-yuh's."

"But we'll appreciate it come spring planting," added a burly man I didn't recognize.

Hannibal looked confused and observed soberly, "It'll be gone by then, won't it Eli?"

Two of the men started to chuckle, but Eli's straightforward explanation about replenishing the soil's moisture cut them off. I, too, had smiled at Hannibal's simple thought processes and was proud of Eli for defending and enlightening him so deftly. He put us all in our place.

Everyone in town knew Hannibal and most accepted him without a second thought. He was ubiquitous to the Cove; a permanent fixture devoted to Eli and Augusta and sharing devotion to whatever and whomever they embraced. He was always showing up around the church or manse to watch and "help" Eli in his work. But even though he was often around, I hadn't spoken more than a few words to him. He was extremely shy around women and seemed to avoid feminine encounters. In fact, I had only seen him a few times after our arrival the previous fall when he helped transport our luggage up the hill. His was a presence you sensed more than realized. I recalled that he had been a shadowy observer at the Harvest Festival activities and remembered Augusta mentioning that he slipped into and out of church on Sunday mornings virtually unnoticed. I once again was certain that it must have been he who shadowed my footsteps into town the day I was followed. That frightening experience was almost forgotten, especially since I no longer walked alone now that Bo was part of my life but I still took comfort in concluding anew that Hannibal's shy, socially awkward ways was the logical explanation.

I smiled at Hannibal and offered him the plate of sandwiches which was making its third trip around the room. He averted his eyes and fumbled to pass the plate on to the fellow sitting next to him without spilling his coffee in the process.

II.

Two weeks away from *The Sentinel* made me feel almost like a stranger again. In spite of my minor successes in the world of journalism I still was a rank amateur and my lengthy absence made me once again feel like a gawky interloper.

I stood before the door, gloved hand frozen in hesitation above the knob. After all, what business did I have thinking I could write for a newspaper anyway? I wasn't highly educated, nor was I exceptionally intelligent, and I knew virtually nothing of the world beyond my ken. I was the daughter of a small town pastor. Period. End of story. And yet there was this persistent feeling that life should hold something more than a small town ending for me.

Was that presumptuous?

Probably so.

Wasn't I supposed to find the right man, settle down in the right house, have the right number of children, and live my life in the right way?

Probably so.

I had virtually talked myself out of going any farther and would have turned and slunk away if Bo hadn't risen up on her hind legs to look in the window. The movement caught Andrew's eye as he came to his desk from the printing press in the back room. He gestured for me to enter and smiled broadly as Bo bounded over to renew their acquaintance.

"Well, Bo," he said, rumpling her fur and playfully pushing her back and forth between his large hands, "it's about time you brought your owner in to visit us again."

His smile of welcome extended itself to me. "I see you survived your first New England blizzard."

"Yes, although I must admit there were moments when I doubted it could be done. I don't remember ever being so restless before. I couldn't stand not knowing what was going on; nearly drove me crazy."

"Ah," he observed sagely, his gingery eyes twinkling behind his glasses and his eyebrow darting upward in uncharacteristic mirth, "the ink is beginning to seep into your veins." He smiled teasingly. "You'll never be the same once it does. It's as addicting as any narcotic... but infinitely more satisfying."

The momentary departure from his customarily calm and businesslike manner helped put me at ease and I returned his smile.

He, too, seemed to realize his lapse and punctuated his final observation with the self-conscious habit of pushing his glasses up his nose, even though they were fine as they were. I sat down in the chair he indicated and Bo trotted over to the front door to wait on an adjacent rug.

Once we were settled in our chairs Andrew continued. "Layton and I were talking about you just yesterday."

His tone was as mellow as always but I sensed an undercurrent beneath his words that piqued my interest.

He adjusted his glasses once again before speaking. "We both feel that you should be helping us out from time to time with more than just the social news. How would you feel about that?"

My face must clearly have betrayed the feelings of shyness and inadequacy that had overwhelmed me just a few moments earlier, for his registered surprise and then concern in quick succession and he broke in before I could answer.

"You're not thinking about quitting, are you?"

I felt I could be honest with Andrew so began to explain my feelings while standing outside the door and my inclination to flee.

"Martha, I can't begin to tell you what a mistake I feel that would be. I'm not one to exaggerate, so you know I mean it when I say you have a real gift for writing and shouldn't put it back on the shelf."

His glasses had slipped down the bridge of his delicate nose but he left them untouched, hand raised to halt the protest forming on my lips. "And I know what you're going to say. The fact that you're a woman should have absolutely nothing to do with your decision to work with us."

He paused fleetingly, giving emphasis to his words. "Martha, we talk about it quite a bit and neither Layton nor I see women's suffrage as only a passing fancy. It's an issue that's been festering below the surface for generations. And there's a growing number of people who feel you women should have the vote. It's a battle worth waging, and women like you are needed to keep the fight going."

"I've never really thought of myself as a suffragette, Andrew. And anyway, what good will my working for the newspaper do?"

"Working for the paper will make you a visible reminder to everyone who reads it that women have abilities beyond rocking the cradle."

He looked mildly disappointed and shook his head somewhat sadly. "I shouldn't have to tell you that. Open your eyes, Martha; the world around us is changing."

"Even if I agree with much of what the suffragettes espouse," I explained quietly, "it's very difficult to do something when important people in your life oppose it so strongly."

The specter of my father's angry disapproval hovered accusingly before me.

"Few worthwhile things come easily, Martha," he said kindly. "Please don't leave us. I really enjoy working with you and would like to teach you more about all this."

He spoke softly, reaching across the desk and patting my arm reassuringly and continuing in a sweeping gesture indicating the glamorous extent of 'all this.'

He made me smile.

His words and his tenderness also made up my mind for me.

What Andrew said was true and there was no going back. The world was changing – I was changing.

I heaved a heavy, cathartic sigh realizing that I had, indeed, missed *The Sentinel* during the blizzard's isolation; missed it quite dreadfully if I was totally honest with myself. It was an admission that brought a degree of clarity with it.

Andrew was right. The ink was seeping into my blood. And that addiction was dictating a course that continued to distance me from the traditional role my father envisioned for a young woman; especially a young woman who also happened to be his daughter.

When Bo and I left the office I had my first official news story to cover for the next edition. I also had a replenished sense of self and a certain amount of renewed confidence. Not much, but it was a beginning. And as we walked away I experienced an echo of the feelings that had colored my initial anticipation of our move to Tully's Cove. Perhaps this was the threshold I had come to equate with the move and perceived myself destined to cross. Perhaps *The Sentinel* held the key to my future.

III.

I didn't feel like going straight home on that first afternoon of post-blizzard freedom so decided to drop in on Grace Whitley before turning the sleigh north toward Church Street.

During those introspective days of snow-induced confinement I had come to the realization that I hadn't seen Grace for several weeks. I had revisited every church service and social function attended during Christmas and New Years and couldn't recall seeing Grace or her husband at any of them. Not even the service on Christmas Day; although I had been rather preoccupied that day, first with concern about Rachel and Gavin Marshall and then with juggling Bryon Mayfield's feelings and Mr. Marshall's attempts at humor. Nevertheless, Grace was missing from every holiday scene I could bring to mind and grew increasingly conspicuous by that absence. She wasn't an intermittent church-goer so even if she hadn't attended the various social functions leading up to Christmas, I would have – should have – seen her at church activities. I had grown convinced that something had happened to prevent her from attending and as a result every time I thought of Grace it was with an increased sense of concern and an urgency to speak with her. From the day of our first meeting there had been a natural rapport between us and I was more than mildly concerned for my friend. I knew her marriage was unhappy. I also knew that if her "disappearance" was due to illness we would have heard since Father regularly called on the sick and homebound of the congregation. The combination of those two facts led me to a renewed focus on her unhappiness.

As I climbed the stairs to their apartment, with Bo loping awkwardly from step to step behind me, I scolded myself for letting so much time pass before following up on my concerns. I should have acted on this before Christmas yielded to New Years and New Years yielded to the blizzard.

I prayed that things weren't worse for Grace and her little family.

At first there was no response to my knock. The curtains were tightly drawn across the two windows visible from the stairs and I heard no trace of sound from within. I was about to give up when at last there was the smallest movement at the parlor window and then Grace opened the door.

"Why Martha," she said, "what a nice surprise! I was napping and just heard you knocking a moment ago. Have you been out here long?"

I apologized for waking her and assured her that we had just arrived.

"Please come in," she invited, opening the door wider and stepping aside for us to enter.

The interior gloominess was a sharp contrast to the brilliance of the snow-covered day outside and it took a moment or two for my eyes to adjust.

Grace was wrapped in a bulky woolen dressing gown, but otherwise there was no evidence of illness about the place. A general lack of tidiness, however, renewed my concern for I knew Grace to be a fastidious housekeeper. The appearance of the room contradicted the cheerful façade she extended to me in greeting.

"This is the first time I've been able to get into town since the big storm," I began, taking my place in the wing chair I had occupied on my first visit. "I had some business to take care of at the newspaper but wasn't quite ready to go home yet after being cooped up for so long. I hope you don't mind our coming by unannounced."

"You are more than welcome," Grace replied, "and I know what you mean about the blizzard. As much as I love my home, the walls do begin to close in after a while."

"Yes, and you've been confined even longer, haven't you," I suggested hesitantly, taking advantage of the opening she provided. "It seems like forever since I've seen you around town."

Bo wandered away from me as I spoke and took up residence at our hostess's feet.

"Oh really?" Grace replied slowly and quietly. "No, I've been around. I guess our paths just haven't been crossing much lately."

Her words seemed evasive and carefully chosen. I felt she was stretching the truth. My review of the holiday season made me confident that she had been absent from virtually every holiday event. After all, Grace was the type of woman who stood out in a crowd whether she wanted to or not. No, I knew she most certainly had not been "around" as she put it.

She didn't look at me as she spoke and continued to evade my eyes when I failed to respond. Instead she absently reached out a long, slender arm and began scratching Bo behind the ears.

As she reached down her arm extended beyond the cuff of her dressing gown exposing four evenly spaced yellowish-blue splotches on the top of her arm just above the wrist. In the silence that had fallen between us those marks held my attention and when she turned slightly to accommodate Bo, who had rolled over to have her belly scratched, I caught sight of a fifth splotch on the inside of her arm.

It slowly dawned on me that I was staring at the remnants of bruises. Almost simultaneously came the realization that the pattern of those bruises looked like the distinctive imprint left by fingers. My mind began to race and I couldn't take my eyes from her arm. Anger and revulsion gripped me as my imagination reconstructed the scenario those marks implied. Only an uncompromising grip could have left such pronounced bruises on her alabaster skin.

My eyes rose to her face just as hers registered where my gaze had been resting on her arm. She shrank away from the dog and yanked the sleeve of the dressing gown down past her wrist.

I was filled with fear for her.

"Grace..." I stammered awkwardly.

"Oh Martha, it's not what you think," she cried at my unfinished indictment of her husband. Before she could go further the tears welling up in her eyes spilled over and cascaded down her lovely, tragic face. "Well, not exactly anyway."

She put her hands over her face, no longer attempting to hide her bruised forearm, revealing bruises on the other arm as well.

We both were silent for what felt like a very long time.

"Grace," I said finally, "if you and Winston aren't safe here you've got to leave."

"Oh Martha, we're not in any real danger," she replied with a half-hearted smile, wiping away her tears as she spoke. "And besides, there's no place to go. I have no family, no money, no property... and there's really no reason to leave."

The look on my face undoubtedly articulated my fear, concern, and confusion, as well as the revulsion I was feeling toward her husband but I said nothing.

Grace looked away from me and silence fell between us once again.

"Martha," she began at last with steely determination in her voice, "there's something I've got to explain to you."

"You don't owe me any explanation," I assured her quietly.

"No, you're wrong. In a very real sense I do. You've been very kind to me and I've repaid your friendship with denial and evasiveness."

She smiled again; a tragic and rather hopeless smile that nearly broke my heart. "Everyone else in town already thinks they know," she continued, "but I want you to know the truth."

I was increasingly uneasy and not entirely sure I wanted to hear what she was about to divulge. Previous conversations between us darted through my mind; conversations during which I had felt Grace wavered on the verge of telling me something quite personal. She and Jocelyn Collier were the only friends I had in Tully's Cove but between Grace and me there seemed to be a deeper level of trust developing than I believed would ever be possible with Jocelyn. Both struck me as quietly courageous women who shouldered burdens I could barely comprehend and so, out of respect – and gratitude for the gift of intimacy she was offering – I said nothing further to dissuade Grace from saying what was on her mind.

"Please Martha, stop looking at me as if I were some kind of paragon," she began, her voice breaking with emotion. "I'm not worthy of that status."

I wanted to say something to comfort and reassure her but she continued before I could speak.

"I don't know exactly where to begin," she mused with a heavy sigh.

There was another lengthy silence before she spoke again. "David and I have been married for almost six years now. We're not from Tully's Cove originally; we grew up near a little crossroads up north called Pettigrew. Neither of us come from privileged backgrounds. My parents died when I was young and I was raised by an elderly aunt. David is the oldest of nine children. His father is a farmer so David worked very hard from an early age."

She fidgeted nervously with the fringed tassel on the sash of her dressing gown and again silence fell between us. "David hated farming so when Mr. Carter took him on two years ago as an apprentice and then let us live up here as part of the arrangement, we were about as happy as two people can be."

She smiled faintly at the recollection. "David literally threw himself into his work. He was determined not to disappoint Mr. Carter and equally determined to learn the business as quickly and as well as he possibly could. As a result, he started being gone longer and longer hours and I found myself spending more and more time alone. It wasn't that I resented how hard he worked – I really was very proud of him – but I was growing more and more lonely and we were spending less and less time together. When we first got married we used to love to go places together – picnics, church socials, dances – but it got to the point where we had very little even to say to one another let alone go out and do something special."

She paused for a moment or two, biting her lower lip in a gesture of concentration, and inclining her head in the direction of the room in which Winston slept, listening for sounds of him stirring.

"It's probably coming from such a small town that made me so gullible," she continued bitterly, "and looking back on it I can see just how big a fool I was."

She smiled ruefully into the past. "Like I said, David was spending long hours with Mr. Carter. Well, I started spending some of that time taking walks all over the countryside. I didn't know many of the women in town and being kind of shy around others it was the natural way for me to compensate for the lack of companionship."

She shifted uneasily. "On one of those walks I met a man I had never seen before. He was handsome and charming and had the knack of saying exactly what I needed to hear. We met by accident several times when I was out walking – although looking back I realize he probably had begun watching for me."

A faraway look had come over Grace's face and her voice had dropped to little more than a whisper. "During one of those meetings, early last spring, his flowery words were accompanied by subtle but persistent advances..."

"Please Grace," I interrupted. "Please don't go on."

"No. You need to know what happened to me. I was so lonely, Martha, and so smitten with him that I... I let myself be swept up into his embrace and into his kiss."

I looked away, embarrassed for my friend.

"Nothing more than that ever happened, Martha – *nothing*! – even though we saw each other several more times before I came to my senses and realized how superficial and *specific* his intentions were. But you see, Martha, someone had seen us! It only takes one moment of indiscretion to ruin your life, and I had succumbed to many more than just one. I can only guess who saw us but the story soon was spreading like wildfire among the fine women of Tully's Cove that the wife of the mortician's apprentice was being unfaithful. And of course it finally got back to David... And right about then I discovered that I was going to have a baby. A baby! I couldn't believe it. After all those childless years, the thing I had hoped for more than anything in the world became in David's eyes the crowning evidence of my infidelity."

She paused again, the clock on the mantle ticking loudly into the silence.

"I admitted to him – and now to you – that I was not totally innocent. I told him everything, how lonely I had been and what a fool I was to be taken in by what I then recognized as an obvious attempt at seduction. David and I have known each other all our lives, Martha – he knows me – but he was too hurt and too angry to hear me. No matter what I say, he is convinced that Winston isn't his child."

Her eyes pleaded with me for understanding and absolution. "I may be many things, Martha – fool chief among them – but I am not an adultress... and Winston is not Gavin Marshall's son!"

Although I undoubtedly flinched when she said it, the name of the man responsible for Grace's plight came as no surprise to me. Even before she revealed his identity only one man's image assumed the role of Grace's seducer as she told her story. As far as I was concerned there was only one man in the Cove who fit the picture she painted.

I had known instinctively that it was right to distrust Gavin Marshall but had had no idea just how vile he really was. And in my mind – although undoubtedly colored by inexperience and naïvete – it indeed was vile of a man to use charm and flattery as a prelude to improper advances. I may have been woefully inexperienced when it came to the game of intimacy but I held strong convictions nonetheless. There could be no excuse for Gavin Marshall's behavior. And on top of everything, Grace was a married woman. Of course I realized that such things happened – even in Tully's Cove – but, unfortunately, was totally incapable of articulating anything that might absolve the tragic young woman baring her soul to me.

Grace broke into my reverie. "Now can you see why I had to tell you," she asked quietly, her voice full of shame. "I've seen you with him several times, Martha... Don't trust him! Don't let Gavin Marshall ruin your life like he's ruined mine!"

Her words startled me and for a moment I didn't know what she meant. Then it became crystal clear. She had misinterpreted the exchanges she had witnessed between Gavin Marshall and me as an indication that I was his latest targeted conquest. I might have laughed had it not been for the knot in my stomach as I thought of how Mr. Marshall had been plying my innocent little sister with flattery and subtle advances.

"Oh Grace," I said. "I haven't been the object of Mr. Marshall's attention..."

"But I've seen you," she protested.

"Yes, you've seen us together, but it was never for the purpose you suppose. I'm not the type of woman who would interest Gavin Marshall. There's nothing but hostility between the two of us."

Now it was my turn to pause as I wasn't sure I wanted to divulge anything more. "Grace, up until Christmas Mr. Marshall was half-heartedly pursuing my sister Rachel."

"*What?*" she sputtered in disbelief. "Why, she's only a child!"

Grace's voice was angry; an emotion with which I could easily identify when Gavin Marshall was the topic of conversation.

"Don't worry," I assured her, "that's all in the past now. For a while I'm sure Rachel was totally smitten with him but she's wonderfully fickle – thank God – and has turned her attention toward a boy at school. The novelty undoubtedly wore off – it always does with Rachel – and I did my best to prevent any meetings so nothing was able to develop and Rachel became distracted by someone she sees all the time. So whatever Mr. Marshall's intentions – and after what you've told me, I can only assume the worst! – time and her own fickle nature may have saved Rachel from disaster!"

Grace reiterated her concern and her anger but in time I was able to convince her that Rachel's inability to stick with anything for very long had won the day and pushed Gavin Marshall out of the picture. After all, she hadn't mentioned him or attempted to see him since around Thanksgiving. I was almost certain that was the end of it.

Almost.

CHAPTER NINE

I.

I spent the winter of 1917 learning more about the newspaper business than I would have thought possible. Andrew was an excellent and determined teacher and spent many hours tutoring me on the fine points of writing concise, readable news stories as well as teaching me the intricacies of the printing process. I loved the former and tolerated the latter.

In addition to my ongoing responsibilities covering the society news I now was spending several days a week at *The Sentinel* office either bent over a typewriter or up to my elbows in grease and ink as Andrew and Mr. Quigley taught me how to nurse and cajole the printing press into producing just one more edition of the newspaper. Andrew was of the opinion that any newspaperman worth his salt was one who could also hold his own in the production-end of the process – and there were to be no exceptions merely on the basis of gender. Mr. Quigley was delighted for he now had a willing – if somewhat reluctant – student as I could no longer escape the impromptu lessons he had tried to give me and which I had become so adept at avoiding.

By March I had become reasonably competent in both aspects of newspaper work and Andrew was unabashedly pleased with both of us.

When I made the decision to commit myself to learning more about newspaper work and spend more of my time in its pursuit, I did so with the realization that there undoubtedly would be repercussions at home for my father's disapproval was a given. I put off sharing that decision with my family for several weeks but at last it became necessary to explain my increasingly frequent and prolonged absences. As anticipated, a renewed sense of anger and disappointment erupted from my father almost before the words were out of my mouth.

"This folly has gone on about long enough!"

We were once again at Sunday dinner and Father once again was pushing his plate away from him in exasperation over the news I shared.

"How can it be folly, Father, to do something that God obviously has given you the ability to do?"

I stood my ground – albeit from the relative safety of my seat at the opposite end of the table – and kept my eyes on his. "How can it be folly to want to make your life count for something? How can it be folly to want to take care of yourself?"

"I don't see any reason to have this discussion again," he seethed quietly. "You know my opinion on the matter. A woman's place is in the home, not running around town at all hours, coming into contact with God only knows what, and working with God only knows who."

"Working with God only knows who?" I asked incredulously. "Mr. Carmichael and Andrew both are well-educated men, Father, and if you'll recall, Andrew was perfectly acceptable to you when you thought he wanted to court me!"

"You're twisting my words," he retorted hotly. "There's a difference between knowing someone socially and following them somewhere you have no business going."

"I'm sorry, Father, but I don't see the distinction. If they're acceptable in one context, then they're acceptable in another!"

He didn't reply immediately but looked down at his plate with a mixture of frustration and something akin resignation on his face. If silence has ever been deafening it was at that moment. No one made a sound. No one moved a muscle.

Finally, Mother reached over and tenderly patted his hand. He looked at her with tired, kind eyes and for just a moment I thought perhaps he was going to relent. The eyes he turned to me were far less kind.

"I'm not going to argue with you, Martha," he said with solemn resolution in his voice. "I will state my position one time and one time only."

He paused again and when he spoke it was with confident conviction. "What you are doing is simply not acceptable. And if you insist on continuing with this so-called 'job' of yours you will no longer be welcome in my home."

Rachel gasped and Mother's hand flinched noticeably where it lay atop his. "Now wait a minute, both of you," she interjected, her voice full of urgency and alarm. "Please... please don't say things you're going to regret later!"

"I think that's already been done," I replied, blinking back the tears that stung my eyes before continuing. "I'm so sorry you feel that way, Father. I'm also sorry that I can't agree with you. I wish I could, but I just don't."

I rose from my seat, pushed my chair in as noiselessly as possible, and turned to leave the room. "And if you want," I added from the doorway, "I'll find another place to live."

There was no response and no one tried to stop me as I left the dining room. The only sound to be heard was Father's knife grating against china as he slowly sliced through the meat on his plate.

I put on my coat and boots and left the house, oblivious to the cold and the gathering shadows of late afternoon. Bo slipped out behind me as I closed the door and together we began to walk away.

At the crest of the hill, where Church Street began, I stopped and looked back at the house. I don't know what I expected to see, some trace of the warmth and security home should represent I suppose. But no lamps were lit in the front rooms of the house and it already had receded into the shadows and dusk of twilight.

I turned and walked on.

II.

To a certain extent I was prepared to handle my father's negative reaction to my expanded role at the newspaper. Despite the feelings of inadequacy I had experienced after the confinement of the blizzard, I simply was not the same person who had moved to Tully's Cove the previous autumn. Perhaps it was inevitable that during the intervening months – while living under the pall of my father's disapproval – I had grown more independent and had discovered a limited amount of self-sufficiency born from insulating myself against the sting of his rejection. That didn't mean I needed and revered my family any less but things definitely were different.

Frankly, I just thought my father was wrong. That never had happened before. Although I loved and respected him immensely, there was a certain sense of liberation in seeing him through what were undoubtedly more mature, objective eyes. I was becoming accustomed to his disapproval; I certainly was no longer crippled by it.

After leaving the house that Sunday, Bo and I walked for a long time without direction. It was a crystal clear night and a brilliantly full moon had risen so as long as we stayed out of the denser parts of the woods we were able to see clearly.

I hadn't been back to the Collier's gazebo since the uncomfortable autumn encounter with Jocelyn's cousin that had precipitated Bo's coming into my life. Suddenly I felt compelled to go there, to think things through in the moonlit solitude of the clearing that sheltered that Victorian structure. It was only a five or ten minute walk from where we were, and only about twenty minutes from the manse. The more I thought about the gazebo the more it held out to me the respite I needed.

I had always loved gazebos and even though I avoided this particular one – and even though it stood on someone else's property – I had felt a sense of ownership toward it ever since the first time my wanderings had led to its discovery. Standing there in the moonlight, with Bo looking up at me expectantly, there was no place I would rather be.

We walked on.

The clearing was flooded with moonlight and looked as enchanted in reality as it had in my mind's eye. There was no sound other than that made by the two of us for the stream was deeply frozen and the scant winter foliage lay silent in the still night air.

I stood for a long time in the middle of the clearing, drinking in the quiet and letting the cold wash over me.

There indeed was comfort to be found in solitude; a relatively new discovery for me. Since moving to Tully's Cove I had found that I could enjoy being alone, that I actually enjoyed being in my own company. Over the months I had made the related discovery – although at times denied – that I was a person of independent thought and opinion, someone to whom I actually should listen. I had ideas of my own about the world around me. I had opinions about things that happened in our community. I could attend something like the court hearing for Hector Nash and understand what I heard and draw my own conclusions and inferences from what was presented. I was moderately informed about the war in Europe and had ideas about those events; ideas that weren't mere reflections of the attitudes and opinions of others but were the result of my own processing of the information. It was a rather startling revelation – and one that tasted good once I allowed myself to savor its discovery.

I found myself wondering how many others like me there were out there; women who read books and newspapers and knew things about the world around them; women who had developed opinions of their own and were able to think for themselves; women who were growing restive standing in the shadows of fathers and husbands. It was a gratifying – albeit potentially volatile – thought.

Unfortunately, for too many women that discovery might never be made. Attitudes like those espoused by my father perpetuated a very narrow view of their feminine counterparts – labeling those who dared challenge tradition obstreperous at best and sinful at worst. And even though there were rumblings from certain quarters that life could and should hold something more, substantive changes seemed a long time coming. Suffragettes had been rocking the boat literally for decades trying to secure the right to vote but for most of them rocking the boat eventually gave way to rocking the cradle. And for most women ultimate fulfillment would include family and motherhood. But surely it was possible that there was more dimension to life than that. After all, God gave the ability to reason not only to Adam.

Such were my thoughts as I stood in the moonlight.

When I retreated to the shadows of the gazebo's interior I continued to go over the same territory, all of which eventually led back to the conflict between my father and me. I felt as if I were at a crossroads and yet at the same time like I stood before a most formidable brick wall.

I pulled my coat and scarf more snugly around my neck, stuffed my hands into my pockets somewhat disconsolately, and sat down to brood.

It's difficult to say just how long I sat there in the gazebo, adrift in my thoughts while the blue-black shadows of night shifted and changed with the course of the moon. It was quiet, it was comforting, but it did nothing to soften my resolve.

My father was wrong. There was nothing ungodly or antisocial about a woman working outside the home. I might never marry and have children, but I did have a contribution to make. I could write; I enjoyed writing; I needed to write.

I heaved a long, cathartic sigh, wiped my eyes and blew my nose. I could go back to the manse, still shaken but at peace with myself and ready to deal with the next chapter of my life – the chapter I was writing for myself.

Bo came bounding into the gazebo and leaped up onto the bench beside me before I could rise. She was dusted with snow, tongue lolling out one side of her mouth in playful glee as she lunged forward at full speed. Lurching away in an effort to avoid her wet, slobbery enthusiasm, my hand instinctively darted backward in order to brace myself and encountered what felt like damp, crumpled paper in the shadows. I immediately dismissed the discovery as just a leaf snagged in its autumnal descent by a sliver of wood, but my eyes darted downward automatically and in so doing found a damp, yellowed envelope beneath my fingers. I picked it up and was surprised to find that it was unopened. Holding it out into the moonlight and turning it over for further inspection I was even more surprised to find my name neatly printed on the front!

I knew without a moment's hesitation that the handwriting was Jacob Collier's. I had long since committed to memory the note accompanying Bo when he sent her to me. That note now lay tucked away behind a loose flap of fabric in my jewelry box and I knew the penmanship as well as I remembered the contents.

I opened the envelope and read the note with hands that quivered from much more than just the cold.

"*Dear Miss Pendleton,*" he had written. "*It seems I continually find myself encountering you at the oddest times and in the most unexpected places. I apologize for any* concern I may have caused you as a result of any of those meetings."

The next sentences were smeared and difficult to read. "To say that you have added an unique dimension to my existence here in America would be an understatement; you and your family have shown me more kindness than I have experienced in a long, long time, and much more than I deserve. I feel compelled to return that kindness and so would like to make a gift of this gazebo. I cannot physically move it into proximity of your home but you have my assurance that after today I shall never return here and shall never intrude upon your privacy in this place. I know how important solitude can be and so I make it my gift to you.
With sincere regard, Jacob Collier"

The note was dated a day or two after our last encounter when he found me sleeping in front of the library fire while Rachel had her French lesson. He had said then that we seemed destined to misunderstand each other and that there seemed to be no end of "gazebos" in his life. At the time the meaning of the statement had been lost on me, but now, in view of his "gift," I understood what he had meant.

Every time we had spoken – at the overlook at Patriot's Point, in the woods on his property, in the courthouse, and at the gazebo – I had been someplace unexpected and our exchanges were indeed peppered with misunderstandings. But, actually, it seemed more appropriate for me to be making a gift of my absence to him rather than the other way around for every time we met I had somehow managed to invade his privacy.

My mind began composing a reply to his note.

He was such an intriguing person.

III.

An icy chill had descended upon the manse; a chill that had nothing at all to do with the weather. Everything seemed strained. My father spoke in monosyllables whenever I was around. My mother looked worried and drawn and eventually stopped trying to convince me to go back to the way things had been. Even Rachel was increasingly distant and aloof.

In order to avoid the strain and discomfort of the house I began spending more and more time in town. I even went so far as to inquire about rates at one of the more modest rooming houses but wasn't quite ready to make a permanent break with what, in my heart, was still my main source of shelter and security.

The more time I spent away from the manse the more I spent at *The Sentinel*. I had become a fixture around the place and gradually was becoming the same around the town itself as I went about my work. It actually was getting to the point where very few eyebrows were raised when a woman appeared on the scene to represent the newspaper and my by-line was now commonplace and only mildly shocking to area residents. Many people undoubtedly shared my father's sentiments when it came to a woman's "place," but the majority of them kept their opinions to themselves – at least in my presence.

I still was relegated to features and the less "worldly" news stories but even so Andrew and Mr. Carmichael kept me busy and seemed increasingly confident of my abilities. Both men apparently felt somewhat to blame for the rift between my family and me. Mr. Carmichael never actually came right out and said anything on the subject but he was extremely tolerant of my ineptitude as I continued to learn the ins and outs of the newspaper world and was in many ways more mentor than employer.

And then there was Andrew.

It seemed as if for every act of distancing that took place within my family there was a corresponding increase in attentiveness and proximity on the part of Andrew. I didn't even have to say anything, he seemed to know instinctively when some comment or action on the part of my father – or even my mother – had caused me pain. He was supportive and encouraging. He never pried but always seemed to say the right thing – or said nothing at all if that's what the moment required. He listened without judging. He gave advice without preaching. He quickly was becoming the best friend I had ever had.

I arrived at the newspaper one morning late in March to find Andrew and Mr. Carmichael once again in a heated debate about the war in Europe – this time as to the underlying causes. Andrew was pointing to the assassination of Archduke Francis Ferdinand by a Serbian nationalist as the precipitating event. Mr. Carmichael espoused a less event-specific cause.

"All you have to do is look at the background of the region, man! Are you a reporter? Do your research!"

Mr. Carmichael was in his element. His voice had risen about an octave, his eyes were round with intensity, his complexion growing slightly purple from the exertion. "Everyone over there has just been waiting for an excuse to take their own misfortune out on their neighbor. It's a tribal war, nothing more. You can't expect such hot-blooded people to live in close proximity with anyone different from themselves. They've all been blaming failures and hardships on the other side for generations. Why, even President Wilson says it was caused by nothing in particular! The Archduke is a minor player, nothing more."

Andrew was equally dogmatic, if somewhat less strident in his delivery. "I *have* done my research, Layton," he replied in response to Mr. Carmichael's implication of shallow thinking on his part. "Quite frankly, I think you're the one oversimplifying the matter. I'm not denying the toll taken by years of strife in the region. I'm with you on that point. But I just don't think anything but minor skirmishes would be the outcome – as has been the case in the past – if that zealot hadn't crossed the line and killed Ferdinand."

He turned his attention toward me.

"What do you think, Martha?"

Both men's eyes were on me. They had no way of knowing the monumental nature of the question and how it momentarily staggered me. It goes without saying that my father never discussed world events with me or asked my opinion on anything. Even with Andrew and Mr. Carmichael I had been judiciously circumspect; up to that point I had been a peripheral participant in their conversations and debates, listening to and learning from them but not actively joining in.

"It's difficult to say," I began hesitantly, terrified of sounding stupid. "I suppose all those years of small scale clashes could boil over into full scale warfare on their own..."

"Ah-hah!" Layton crowed triumphantly.

"...but I think it's more likely that you're both right. The Archduke's assassination probably was the straw that broke the camel's back and pushed them over the edge."

Andrew smiled and said I was a born diplomat, and even though he sullenly accused my position of being "damnably wishy-washy," Mr. Carmichael declined to take the offensive further and went off toward the back of the office muttering to no one in particular that none of us really knew anything about what was going on over there.

"You know, he's right," Andrew commented as he cleared off a chair for me to sit on and gathered up some papers scattered across his desk.

"About what? About the Archduke being a 'minor player' as he put it?"

"No. No, I still don't agree with him on that score but he's right about none of us really knowing what's going on over there."

He pushed his glasses up his nose before continuing. "I've been thinking about that a lot lately. No one over here can really know what those people are going through. We just can't understand what they're fighting about."

He adjusted his glasses again. "Layton talks about an old friend who works for a wire service in Paris."

His left hand touched his glasses.

"You know, Martha, I'd like to go over there and see things firsthand; see for myself what's going on and try my hand at reporting for a wire service. As I see it it's only a question of time before we're in this thing ourselves anyway. Ever since Germany disavowed the Sussex Pledge and started expanding their submarine activity we've been walking a very thin line."

He leaned forward to emphasize what he was saying. "Now that President Wilson has severed diplomatic relations with Germany and Congress is arming our merchant ships it's just a matter of time before we come into active contact with them and get sucked into this war full scale."

For a moment I was dumbfounded. I barely registered his comments about our becoming involved in the war for the suggestion of his going to Europe came as a total surprise and the possibility of his leaving was patently unpleasant.

"What do you think," he asked, leaning even further forward in his chair and once again adjusting his glasses.

"I think it's a terrible idea," I replied truthfully. "You can't leave! What would I do without you?"

He seemed mildly taken aback by my frankness and sat up straight. "What a nice thing to say," he began slowly, a smile spreading across his face. "I didn't think my leaving would affect anyone."

"How could it not affect anyone," I demanded incredulously. "You're the best reporter this town has! And," I confessed, "you're the best friend I have."

"Thank you, Martha. You pay me a very great compliment." He smiled shyly. "Perhaps I do have a contribution to make right here in Tully's Cove."

"Of course you do," I assured him. "Why, we couldn't get along without you – I couldn't get along without you."

He looked as if he were about to object so I impulsively took his slender hand between my gloved fingers to give emphasis to my words. "I mean that. You've been such a good friend to me over the past few months. You got me this job..."

"...and promptly got you ostracized from your family," he interjected with a sardonic laugh.

"Well, there is that," I admitted with a smirk. "But seriously, you've taught me everything I know about reporting and printing, you've encouraged me to stand on my own two feet – you've helped me more than you'll ever know."

His smile was shy and tender. "No, Martha, in all truthfulness, you've been the one who's helped me."

CHAPTER TEN

I.

I had written a brief note to Jacob Collier acknowledging his "gift" of the gazebo. It had been my intention to leave it for him the next time Rachel and I visited Jocelyn but out of the blue Rachel announced at dinner one evening that she no longer was interested in studying French and would no longer be going to Patriot's Point.

Mother's attempts to discover the reasons behind what seemed a hasty decision were met with vague and evasive responses that really told us nothing at all. Every point in favor of continuing fell on deaf ears. Rachel very obviously had made up her mind and, as my father pointed out, one could hardly be forced to learn anything.

"It's just as well," he added with a note of triumph in his voice. "I never did like the idea of Rachel spending time with that young woman."

I took note of the fact that he failed to include me in the scope of his concern and when Mother countered patiently with her argument that Jocelyn deserved neither ostracism nor suspicion I stopped listening.

It was disappointing that there would no longer be any reason for us to visit Patriot's Point on a regular basis. Jocelyn had always been the consummate hostess even if our friendship had never progressed beyond a certain point. I enjoyed her company and believed she enjoyed mine. I would miss her.

In addition, spending each Saturday afternoon adrift in the rather surreal world of the wealthy had been a pleasant diversion. While Jocelyn tutored Rachel I had had occasion to observe and experience a way of life that was totally foreign to me – and had stumbled into encounters with one of the most fascinating and intriguing people one could hope to meet. I wasn't ready for things to change. I had assumed that I would have the opportunity to deliver my note to Jacob. I had hoped to learn more about both Colliers and perhaps help them leave the past behind. I had looked forward to seeing their unique "street-map" gardens in full bloom... I just hadn't expected the relationship to be severed so prematurely; and since Jocelyn rarely dipped her toe into the mainstream of Tully's Cove society "severed" was the only word that seemed to apply for I could envision no other setting than our visits to their home through which we would have any substantive contact with them.

That night I rewrote my note to Jacob Collier for the fourth time and wrote a note directed to Jocelyn thanking her for all her kindnesses to us and expressing my regret that our weekly get-togethers had come to an end. The note was open-ended but somehow I didn't expect her to go out of her way to invite me into her home on a purely social basis.

II.

In the morning I decided to seek out Eli Thornton who was sure to be working around the church. If routine held true to form, Hannibal would be with Eli and I would ask him to take the notes up to Patriot's Point.

As expected, Eli and Hannibal were at the church bright and early. From my room I could see them cleaning out the flower beds around the main entrance in preparation for spring planting. I dressed hurriedly and, with Bo at my heels, went down to speak with them.

Acknowledging our approach, Eli rose from where he had been working manure into the damp earth. Hannibal copied Eli's gesture of respect for a lady, rising awkwardly to his feet but stepping back and away from me as I came closer. As Eli and I exchanged pleasantries Hannibal remained silent and kept his eyes on the toes of his worn boots or watched Bo as she ran around the church yard.

"Won't it be nice to see flowers once again," I asked rhetorically. "You two always keep the grounds looking so nice."

"Thank you, Miss Martha," Eli replied, wiping his grimy hands on his overalls and surveying his handiwork. "Ah-yuh, it's surely a pleasure to get my hands into God's good earth each spring."

I directed my attention to his companion. "How about you, Hannibal, do you enjoy taking care of the church?"

Hannibal shifted uncomfortably, swallowed hard, but said nothing.

"Speak up, Hannibal," Eli prompted, nudging the other man with his elbow. "Miss Pendleton asked you a question."

"Yes 'um," he responded meekly. "I like workin' with Eli."

"Well, you do a wonderful job, Hannibal, and we all appreciate it."

He almost made eye contact with me then, smiling shyly and blushing crimson from the neckline of his jacket to the hairline just visible under the brim of his hat.

I had tried being friendly to Hannibal many times but his shyness always got in the way. This time apparently was going to be no different and I wondered whether I'd be able to communicate clearly what I wanted and actually be able to convince him to help me.

Bo came to the rescue, bounding up to Hannibal in an exuberant demand for attention. Visibly relieved, he stooped down to pet her.

"I was wondering, Eli," I began, changing the subject to the purpose of my visit, "would it be all right if I borrowed

Hannibal for a little while? I have some work he could help me with – but only if it wouldn't inconvenience you."

"Hannibal comes and goes as he pleases," Eli replied matter-of-factly. "Go along with Miss Pendleton, Hannibal. We're almost finished here now anyway."

Hannibal's face drained of color. I was certain he would rather have a tooth extracted than go anywhere with me and for a moment I thought he might bolt into the woods. If only he weren't so terribly shy around women! I was beginning to doubt whether he would be able to help me and was about to give up when Bo once again intervened, dancing excitedly around him and giving him something neutral on which to focus his attention. With a few backward glances toward the security of Eli and the church, Hannibal joined me as I walked away.

"I really appreciate your help, Hannibal," I began slowly. "It won't take very long and then you can go back to see what Eli's working on, okay?"

"Oh-Kay," he parroted and then lapsed into silence.

I knew Hannibal couldn't read so had used my best stationery to designate the note to Jocelyn and regular white paper for the note to her cousin. As we walked down the church's sloping drive, I showed him the envelopes and carefully explained what I wanted him to do.

He stopped short when I said the name "Collier" and seemed reluctant to go on.

"You don't wanna go up there, Miss Martha."

There was concern and almost fear in his voice.

"It's all right, Hannibal," I explained. "Miss Collier is a friend of mine. These are just thank-you notes for some nice things they've done for me and my family."

"It's not good up there, Miss Martha," he continued, unconvinced by my explanation. "They're bad."

I never had known Hannibal to have so much to say. Despite the fact that he seemed oblivious to much of the world around him, his childlike mind was obviously astute enough to absorb the Cove's prejudice against the Remittance Men in their midst – particularly the one residing at Patriot's Point.

"Hannibal, they're not bad people. Miss Collier is a friend. She's been teaching Miss Rachel, and you know my father wouldn't let anything bad happen to Miss Rachel. Anyway, you don't have to stay up there very long, just long enough to give the white envelope to Mr. Collier and the ivory colored one to Miss Jocelyn. You can take Bo with you if you'd like, to keep you company. Please do this favor for me, Hannibal. Okay?"

"Oh-Kay," he replied haltingly.

The promise of Bo's companionship seemed to do the trick for Hannibal obviously was reassured only slightly by my words; his face continuing to register a mixture of concern and fear that once again gave me second thoughts about asking for his help at all. But in spite of his sincere reluctance and painful shyness I could tell that he wanted to be of help to the preacher's family. He was a kind and generous person.

Taking the envelopes from me Hannibal walked off down the road reiterating his misgivings to Bo as she danced happily around him.

III.

After finishing the few household chores that still fell under my jurisdiction I left the house and wandered back over to the church. On days when I had no responsibilities at the newspaper it was difficult to occupy my time. Staying around the manse was simply too uncomfortable to be a viable option and as a result I did a lot of wandering. At one time Rachel would have been a source of solace for me but she was at school for the better part of each weekday and even after school she rarely was a source of companionship anymore. At times it seemed like she avoided the house as much as I did.

We were all drifting apart. The burden of responsibility for the tension between us lay heavily on me. I vacillated between being indignant at their narrow-mindedness and being cowed into giving it all up and running home for safety and absolution. As a result, lingering around the manse was not the pleasant occupation it once had been for nothing was the same. Conversation between my mother and me was a bit stilted even though I knew she still loved me dearly and wanted things to be right again. Unfortunately, even though she partially understood my decisions and found some measure of pride in my accomplishments, her definition of "right" was limited to going back to the way things were, not any change on the part of my father. And so I found myself playing the role of dutiful daughter – helping with meals and other household tasks without really investing myself in any of it any more.

I was sitting on the church steps, once again going over the many facets of my situation and waiting for it to be time to help mother get things around for the noon meal when Bo's distant bark heralded her return. As she came into view I could see that Hannibal was still with her. I hadn't expected him to check back with me – frankly, I thought he'd avoid me like the plague for a while – but he walked toward me with purpose so I knew he must have something to say. I stood as they came to the crest of the approach to the church, brushing off the back of my skirt as they came up the walk.

Bo ran ahead of Hannibal, bounding up to me with exuberance more appropriate to a separation of weeks rather than little more than an hour.

Hannibal came to a stop a few yards away.

"Hello there. I didn't expect to see you again today. Were you able to deliver the notes for me?"

"Yes 'um, I done what you asked. But you said I wouldn't have to stay there – that man made me stay there..."

"What are you saying, Hannibal? What man made you stay?"

"The man what lives there. He made me stay 'til he wrote this..."

He reached deep into the pocket of his jacket. My heart skipped a beat as he extracted what had undoubtedly begun the return trip as a crisp, clean envelope but now was crumpled and soiled.

"Is that for me, Hannibal? Did Mr. Collier ask you to bring that to me?"

He seemed reluctant to give me the note but said nothing. After a moment he held it out.

I took it and put it into the pocket of my skirt. "Hannibal, you said Mr. Collier made you stay – he wasn't mean to you, was he?"

He shook his head vigorously. A look of childlike wonder crossed his face and he tilted his head to one side as he spoke. "He talked to me. Showed me his auto-mo-beel – let me sit in it when he wrote the letter."

"Well," I replied, relief flooding my voice, "that doesn't sound so bad. You see, Hannibal, he's not such a bad person."

"No ma'am." He paused and then added shyly, "He's my friend."

His abrupt turn-about and the innocence of his statement made me smile. "That's nice, Hannibal. We all need friends."

He turned to go but then seemed to think better of it and looked back at me. "Are we friends, Miss Martha?"

Before I could reply he continued. "I ain't got friends 'cuz I'm dumb – 'cept Eli an' Miss Augusta, they're my friends, but most folks don't like bein' round me 'cuz I'm dumb."

It was an observation, a straight-forward relating of fact with no sadness or self-pity.

A lump of emotion rose in my throat and I couldn't help feeling sorry for him even though I knew he didn't want or need my pity. It undoubtedly was true that even though everyone tolerated Hannibal and accepted him as part of the backdrop of their lives it was unlikely that any of them sought out his company. He was backward. And people are uncomfortable around the simple-minded, the feeble, the elderly; anyone who reminds us of our own frailty and fleetingness.

Hannibal's simple dignity and overture of friendship made my situation somehow less important. More than anything I wanted to assure him of my acceptance. "Of course we're friends, Hannibal – and anyone who doesn't like being with you just isn't very smart. Why you know lots of things. You haven't been to school but that doesn't mean you're dumb. Look at all the things you can help people with – Eli wouldn't be able to do half of what he does around here if it weren't for you!"

His smile was radiant and he looked me right in the eyes before turning abruptly and walking down the hill.

"Goodbye, Hannibal," I called after him. "Thank you!"

I watched him walk away before taking Jacob's note from my pocket, more than mildly amazed by the conversation we had just shared.

The note was succinct, obtuse, and utterly perplexing:
"I am in receipt of your acknowledgement of my gift. After much soul-searching, however, I must go back on my pledge. Please meet me at 9 o'clock this evening. It is a matter of great importance or I never would impose upon you. With regards, J"
It never crossed my mind not to meet him.

IV.

I couldn't wait for dinner to be over that evening and don't think I said more than two words the entire time. My silence probably went unnoticed, however, for I didn't talk much at all anymore and luckily Rachel was her old chatty self that evening, chirping merrily about nothing in particular. For once I welcomed her superficial prattle. Rachel seemed to be the one most deeply affected by the undercurrent of tension that had darkened our family life since I started working and I suffered severe pangs of guilt over it. She swung back and forth between the lighthearted, silly girl we knew and loved and a secretive, reclusive young woman who was almost unrecognizable. The return of the schoolgirl was welcome, however fleeting it might be, for it gave an allusion of normalcy to what had become a cold and formal nightly ritual. As long as we stayed away from the source of my father's displeasure we were pleasant and polite. But we slowly were becoming a family of strangers.

After helping my mother clear the table and clean up the kitchen I excused myself, called Bo, and left the house without explanation. Alert to the sense of purpose behind our excursion, she trotted along next to me without making any demands for attention as we walked into the woods.

It was almost completely dark by the time we reached the gazebo. I hadn't been back since the night Bo and I discovered Jacob's note gifting me with the solitude of the place. Somehow I felt even more like an interloper now that he had pledged never to return there. I loved the spot, loved the gazebo nestled in its heart, but felt almost guilty because Jacob had surrendered it to me. I was glad he wanted to meet me there.

Jacob was already in the clearing when we emerged from the woods into the open area surrounding the gazebo. He was sitting on the bench near the little waterfall, apparently reluctant to trespass into the structure he had impulsively given to me.

He rose as we approached.

"Good evening, Martha," he began, bending down to offer Bo his upturned palm; a non-threatening gesture most canines recognize. She sniffed his hand and the cuffs of his trousers carefully before deciding he was acceptable and removing herself from the unyielding position she had taken between us.

He looked up at me and smiled. "I'm glad to see she keeps an eye on you," he said, coming to an upright stance. "I'm also glad you came."

"Your note was compellingly vague," I told him. "I couldn't not come."

He smiled again, apologetically. "Sorry for the intrigue. I needed to talk with you and when you unwittingly supplied the messenger I decided to take advantage of it."

He stooped down to scratch Bo behind the ears. "Your friend seemed reluctant to stay very long so I'm afraid the note was unavoidably cryptic; and it probably was best that way."

"Hannibal is so shy I'm surprised he stayed at all," I replied. "Thank you, by the way, for being kind to him. Sitting in your roadster really impressed him."

"He seemed like a nice enough fellow. And I figured if you trusted him I could, too."

"Oh, Hannibal is completely trustworthy," I assured him. "He just doesn't understand exactly what's going on all the time."

Jacob nodded understandingly.

There was a long moment of silence.

"Mr. Collier," I asked finally, "why did you want to see me?"

Jacob heaved a sigh and sat down on the bench. "Martha, please come and sit down."

I did so, sitting at an angle at the opposite end so to see his face in the moonlight. Bo settled in at my feet.

"I can't believe I'm doing this," he told the night, shaking his head in disbelief and smiling somewhat ruefully. "I can't believe I'm getting involved."

"Getting involved in what; what's this all about?"

He took a deep breath. "Martha, I have to tell you something about Gavin Marshall. There's something you've just got to know…"

I winced inwardly.

"Not you, too," I moaned in embarrassed frustration. "Jacob, you don't need to worry. I know all about Mr. Marshall. And despite what the entire Cove apparently thinks," I sputtered defensively, "I am not interested in him, nor he in me!"

Jacob looked mildly astonished. "Martha, no, wait, I'm sorry but that's not what I'm talking about. I'm not concerned about you and Gavin."

Sensing my embarrassment, he reached across the bench and patted my hand. "Let me start again," he suggested. "Gavin and I have known each other for quite some time now. He was the first person I met in the States who didn't treat me like I had the plague once they discovered my situation…"

"Wait a minute," I interrupted. "You mean he's not a 'Remittance Man'?"

Jacob scowled slightly at the segue my question presented. "No, he's an American; not a particularly honorable one, I suppose, but not an exiled Brit either." Returning to topic, he continued. "I won't go into details but we've seen and done a lot together. Gavin has always been a bit of a rogue where women are concerned and when your family came on the scene I have to admit I found his flirtations and banter with you and your sister rather amusing."

He removed his hand from mine.

"I'm afraid I've done something extremely harmful," he explained. "It's just that in the beginning I simply didn't care. I thought it was funny; thought it would pass..."

Now I really was confused. "Thought what was funny; thought what would pass?"

He sighed in frustration. "This is going nowhere. I better just come to the point."

He paused as if gathering his thoughts. Looking both determined and resigned he forged ahead. "Let me put it this way – over the past few months you and your sister have been coming to my home for more than just French lessons."

"What are you saying," I asked. "I don't understand..."

"Martha, Gavin has been at the Point almost every Saturday since you and Rachel first accepted my cousin's invitation." He took my hand again as if to steady me. "Gavin has been seeing your sister..."

I yanked my hand away from him in disbelief.

"That's impossible! I don't believe you!"

Reacting to the vehemence of my response, Bo was instantly alert – reconsidering Jacob Collier's status as friend or foe.

"Martha, I know it sounds unbelievable to you," he began, reaching down once again to assure Bo he meant no harm, "but you've got to believe me because it's the truth. And we've got to do something about it. I should have intervened long ago but, as I said, I found it amusing at first and thought it would pass."

"How could they possibly meet," I insisted. "Rachel came to the Point for French lessons and then we visited with Jocelyn. That's all."

"I know that was the initial purpose but think back. For a long time now, hasn't Rachel made excuses to wander off at some point virtually every week you've been there?"

I made no response.

"Well, hasn't she?"

"Y-yes," I conceded, "but just for a few minutes. She was never gone very long."

"I'm willing to bet that on average she was gone at least twenty minutes, sometimes much longer. If you'll think back you'll have to admit that I'm right. I'm sorry to be blunt, but twenty minutes is plenty of time for a fleeting assignation."

"Just what are you suggesting? No," I added emphatically, "it's just not possible. I refuse to believe it. Where could they meet? I would have seen him!"

"Martha," Jacob observed patiently, "Patriot's Point is a big place. If you don't want to be seen it's an easy thing to accomplish, trust me."

He sighed again before continuing. "For the most part they met in the quarters above the carriage house."

I stared at him in open disbelief.

"It's adjacent the main house, Martha," he stressed, "coming and going was very easy for them."

I couldn't believe what I was hearing. And I didn't like what I was thinking. My mind leapt back to the Saturday Jacob and I had talked in the library when I awoke to find him tending the fire. He had left the room through French doors which happen to face the carriage house. While watching him walk away I had seen Rachel leaving that smaller structure by way of a side entrance. She had been breathless and flushed when she joined Jocelyn and me in the main hall a moment later claiming to have been examining Jacob's new roadster. At the time I thought it odd since she had never seemed interested in automobiles before but placed no real significance on it; now the significance virtually shouted at me.

I stood and walked into the gazebo, gripping the far railing for support.

"I just can't believe this," I whispered into the dark.

"I'm sorry," Jacob said simply. "I can imagine how this makes you feel. Rachel is very young and, frankly, Gavin isn't the kind of man with whom you would want her to associate at any age. I understand, Martha, believe me, I do. That's why I decided I had to tell you. And I apologize for letting it go on so long, for facilitating their relationship by allowing Gavin to use the carriage house."

I made no reply and so he continued.

"Gavin really isn't an evil person, Martha. In his own way I think he actually cares for Rachel quite deeply..."

I turned and glared him into silence.

"Cares for her quite deeply," I scoffed. "Men like Gavin Marshall are incapable of caring for anyone deeply or truly! I'm sure he's ruined lives everywhere he's been – just as he's done right here in Tully's Cove!"

I was thinking of Grace Whitley and dying a bit inwardly to realize that my own sister might now fall into the same category as that tragic young woman.

"Yes, I'm afraid he has," Jacob admitted quietly.

There was another long silence between us before he spoke again.

"What are you going to do?"

"I don't know," I replied dismally. "This will destroy my father. Rachel means the world to him."

Jacob came to me then, standing behind me and putting his hands on my shoulders. "Perhaps he doesn't need to know. Perhaps we can work it out together."

He spoke quietly, his lips close to my ear. Even as distraught as I was over what he had told me his nearness made my heart beat faster.

"Perhaps," I replied meekly. "Dear God, I really don't know what to do."

He turned me to face him and drew me into a loose embrace. "I'm so sorry. It seems I make nothing but bad decisions. And those decisions always seem to impact the innocent."

One of his hands moved up to cradle my head against his chest. His last words were spoken into my hair.

I started to cry.

The tears were not because of what I had learned that evening nor because it added weight to the burden already on my family and the responsibility I felt for it. Incredible as it seems, I began to cry because it felt so good to be in Jacob's arms. There was a sense of shelter there I had been craving. I felt a release of my burdens. My arms, which had been hanging slack at my side, moved up to encircle him and return his embrace.

His arms tightened around me.

We stood there for a moment tightly wrapped in one another's arms, my body tense from a mournful longing for this man I barely knew.

Jacob seemed to suddenly become aware of our embrace, moving his hands once again to my shoulders and stepping back until I was at arm's length.

"Please don't cry, Martha," he said kindly, releasing me. "We'll figure this thing out. I'll talk to Gavin and you watch Rachel. Between the two of us we ought to be able to defuse their relationship. If you know what you're looking for you should be able to keep Rachel from seeing him. And maybe I can convince Gavin that things have gone far enough. Perhaps we could go to New York; Gavin loves New York."

I nodded drearily, wiping my eyes with the back of my hand.

"Come on," he continued. "I'll walk you home."

We walked through the woods in silence, Bo shadowing our steps. There was nothing more to say. I kept going over what Jacob had told me but soon realized I was spending just as much time going back over how it had felt to be in his arms. I could empathize with Rachel's fascination with Gavin Marshall for Jacob Collier held the same allure for me.

But these were dangerous men.

And these were dangerous feelings.

When we came to the country road that marked the boundary of Jacob's property and eventually led to the manse I assured him that Bo and I could go the rest of the way without an escort and that I could use the time alone to think things through.

He said he understood. Acknowledging the value of solitude, he apologized again for not intervening sooner and said good night.

Glancing over my shoulder as Bo and I walked away I could see that he remained where he was, watching as we disappeared into the shadows.

We walked on.

Before we had gone very far Bo began acting strangely. She stopped abruptly with ears alert, peered into the darkness and growled softly under her breath.

I stopped, too, listened carefully but heard nothing.

"Come on, Bo," I said impatiently. "There's nothing out there."

She took a few steps forward with me but then stopped again, head tilted to one side and again growled under her breath.

"Bo!" I said sternly, snapping my fingers. "Come. It's just a squirrel or something. Let's go."

This time she stood her ground.

At first I was just overcome by annoyance with the bad timing of her "mighty hunter" routine. But as I stood there waiting for her to react to my command I was struck by the realization that I really did hear nothing. Nothing. I don't know what Bo heard but even at that time of year I should have been hearing all sorts of night sounds. And I heard nothing at all. The unexpected presence of something foreign to the woods had spooked and quieted its residents. It might have been just us but Bo's reaction made me think otherwise.

"Jacob?" I called quietly into the dark. "Jacob, is that you?"

There was no answer.

There was no sound.

I swallowed hard. The manse was only a short distance away. I refused to be spooked by something I didn't hear.

"Come on, Bo," I demanded, tugging on her collar. "Let's go."

She started to move on with me but we had only gone a few more steps when we both heard movement in the woods behind us.

She barked menacingly into the night.

If Bo had smelled a rabbit or a squirrel she would have been after it in a heartbeat but instead she stayed by my side. So what had caused the noise? I stood still and strained to hear any further movement. It was foolish to be afraid of the dark, especially with Bo along, but she was doing little to reassure me and I was becoming jittery.

"Jacob?" I called again, rather feebly.

Again my question was answered by silence.

If there was someone out there and it wasn't Jacob who could it be?

Fear turned to relieved amusement as I realized that it must be Hannibal trailing along behind us to make sure we got back to the house all right.

"Hannibal?" I called out in relief. "Hannibal, is that you? It's all right Hannibal. Come and walk with Bo and me, we could use the company."

There was a rustling in the woods and I smiled in anticipation of Hannibal's emergence from the darkness. No one came forward, however, and in response Bo took a defensive position between me and the direction from which the sound had come and growled threateningly.

It seemed as if the sound was receding and suddenly Bo bolted into the woods, barking with authority.

"Bo!" I called after her. "Bo, come back!"

My voice echoed back to me but Bo did not obey. I could hear her barking in the distance.

"It was probably nothing," I said aloud. "We probably just scared the life out of a deer."

I shook my head and smiled as the barking stopped. "Silly dog!"

The night sounds returned and I walked on.

V.

I had absolutely no idea what I was going to do about Rachel. I lay in bed as long as possible the next morning going over the events of the previous evening and trying different strategies on for size as I mulled things over.

How could I have been so blind not to see what was going on? They had managed their subterfuge extremely well but still I should have known. I could see Gavin Marshall smirking at me in smug satisfaction and would have welcomed the opportunity to wipe that roguish smile right off his handsome face.

How could Rachel be such a fool? Even as I asked myself that question I knew the answer. She was young, she was boy-crazy, and Gavin Marshall was an extremely handsome and sophisticated man. She was just the type of young woman to whom a man like that would be drawn – pretty, flirtatious, and woefully naïve. I was simultaneously angry with her and frightened for her. Something had to be done and it was obvious that I was the one who had to take action. I swung my legs over the edge of the bed and slid into my house shoes with resolve and something akin confidence. Rachel would be at school all day. That gave me several hours to decide how to approach the problem.

Once downstairs I went through the motions as we moved through our morning routine. I helped Mother clear away the breakfast dishes, put some food out for Bo, dusted and swept the downstairs rooms while Mother did some baking and then rode into town with her since she had some calls to make. She dropped me off at the newspaper with seemingly sincere wishes for a good day.

Andrew smiled broadly when he saw me come in.

"Morning, Martha. I've got a couple of assignments for you that I think you'll find interesting."

"Andrew, you're a lifesaver," I observed, taking the chair he had drawn up beside his desk.

"Glad to be of service, but just what do your life need saving from?"

"You don't want to know," I replied with a half-smile.

Now there was genuine concern in his voice. "More trouble with your father?"

"No, believe it or not; although it certainly affects him. It affects the whole family."

"Can I help?"

The question was simple and his intentions sincere but I didn't want anyone, not even Andrew, to know about Rachel and Gavin Marshall. He accepted my polite refusal of his offer and went on to explain my assignments. But when he was certain that I knew exactly what each entailed he broached the subject of "life saving" once again. Andrew was the most genuine person I had ever known and although I felt embarrassed and even a little ashamed, I soon found myself reluctantly trusting him with the details of what I had learned about Rachel the night before.

As I quietly shared what Jacob Collier had told me I felt increasingly at ease. It was a relief to unburden myself to someone objective, nonjudgmental, and totally trustworthy. It was a relief to unburden myself to Andrew.

"You've got to talk to her, Martha," he said when I had finished. "It's as simple as that. You've got to know just how far this relationship has progressed and do whatever must be done to protect Rachel's future from being destroyed by this man. I understand your reluctance to involve your parents but you can't just keep an eye on her and hope for the best. You've got to talk things out, make her see what kind of man Gavin Marshall is and get her away from him."

"I know you're right," I admitted freely. "Every solution I think of leads me back to that conclusion. It's just that we're not on very good terms anymore and I'm not sure she'll listen to me."

"You've got to try, Martha. She's only seventeen years old. No seventeen-year-old is capable of being objective in a situation like this. Forgive me for being indelicate but she's being manipulated by a really experienced player. Gavin Marshall's been around. No seventeen-year-old is going to be his equal – and let's not kid ourselves about where this is heading."

He stood up to file some papers he had been sorting before I came in. "Tell you what," he continued, "I'll go along with you if you'd like me to. We could catch her right after school and go some place to talk."

I agreed with him that meeting her after school was a good idea but decided it would be best to go alone.

"It's going to be difficult enough to get her to talk to me," I explained. "I'm afraid it might be impossible if someone else were along. I'll get started on these articles and then go up to school to meet her."

He walked with me to the door and took my hand as we said goodbye.

"I know you can do this, Martha," he assured me. "I have such confidence in your abilities; your love and concern for her will do the rest."

I wasn't sure I shared his optimism, but felt better now that I had decided what to do. At least after talking with Rachel I would have a better idea of where things stood and what could and should be done next.

I dove into my assignments and tried to forget about Rachel but clocks all over town seemed to have conspired against me that afternoon in their refusal to approach the hour of three o'clock. I did the background work on both feature stories Andrew had given me and still had nearly an hour and a half before classes would be dismissed at the high school. Walking there would take about ten minutes but that would leave more than an hour yet to pass. I knew trying to keep my mind on anything else was probably hopeless so decided to walk slowly, let myself be distracted by anything and everything that crossed my path, and then spend any extra time going over the conversation I already was rehearsing in my head.

The school which served the children of Tully's Cove was a two-story red brick structure similar to the courthouse in design and appearance. The lower level served the elementary grades and the upper floor was officially christened "Tully's Cove Central High School" as if there were a competitor somewhere else in town. The school lacked the courthouse's impressive columns across the front but sported a twin of the widow's walk cupola crowning its sloping roofline. A large bell that had summoned the Cove's children for generations was housed within the cupola and an American flag flapped proudly in the wind from a pole perched atop the cupola's highest point.

I found a patch of warm sunshine on the low brick wall surrounding the school and sat down to wait for Rachel to appear.

At the appointed hour the bell began to clang commandingly and children of all shapes, sizes, and ages poured from the building in a frantic rush to freedom. Many of the older students assumed more of a saunter than a rush as they left the school and so I wasn't surprised at first when Rachel failed to appear. After waiting what felt like an eternity, however, I walked past the few loitering students who remained and went into the building to track down my errant sister.

For a few minutes I wandered around the interior of the building hoping that our paths would cross but Rachel was nowhere to be seen. I was about ready to start going door to door when Mr. Tucker, the gentleman who taught English to all upper grade students and who occasionally contributed poetry to the newspaper, emerged from the main office.

When he saw me he smiled in recognition. "Miss Pendleton, how nice to see you. I imagine you're here inquiring after your sister?"

"Yes sir, as a matter of fact I am," I replied, taking the outstretched hand he offered and shaking it firmly.

"Well, they should have her make-up work gathered in the office," he informed me. "You can pick it up there."

He released my hand and began to walk away.

"I trust she's feeling better," he called back over his shoulder. "Please tell her to hurry back to us. She should finish reading 'Moby Dick' this week if possible."

I was glad he moved on quickly for I had been caught utterly off guard by what he had just said and needed a moment to collect my thoughts.

He apparently thought that Rachel was ill.

That meant Rachel hadn't been going to school.

That meant Rachel was truant.

And there was only one thing *that* could mean.

Rachel must be spending her days with Gavin Marshall!

Things were worse than I had imagined. Much worse!

VI.

The long walk back to the manse was a troubled one. I couldn't believe that Rachel was involved in such deceit. Obviously she must be deeply involved with Mr. Marshall if she were willing to construct such a web of deception in order to spend time with the man. I kept going back over various incidents and events of the last few months which had seemed unusual but innocuous at the time: Rachel's explanation of the time spent in the carriage house at Patriot's Point; her sudden affection for Byron Mayfield; her eagerness to spend time with friends but never at the manse; an unexpected interest in her studies which required time spent at the library in town. Even her increased attention to chores around the house had probably been part of a ploy. And I had thought her behavior was caused by the tumult I had brought into the family. That was why I had been blind to what was really going on; I was too busy taking responsibility for the change in her just as I had been taking responsibility for every other negative thing that happened at home.

I was growing to actually hate Gavin Marshall with every step I took for I knew that Rachel would never have become involved in such a convoluted series of lies if she hadn't fallen under the influence of this deceiver. Well, things had gone far enough and I was going to do something about it.

Rachel was home by the time I got back to the house. She was pretty and perky and jabbering away to Mother as the two of them got dinner around.

"Hello, dear," Mother said in welcome. "Dinner's almost ready."

Her greeting was an indictment in its innocence.

I washed my hands at the sink and watched Rachel surreptitiously as she went from kitchen to dining room with plates and food. There was little left to do and in just a few minutes we were all seated at the dining table.

"How did school go today," I asked Rachel nonchalantly.

Her response was understandably vague. "Oh, all right, I suppose."

I couldn't resist baiting her a bit. "I ran into Mr. Tucker in town. How's that big English assignment coming along?"

I could see by the look on her face that she was unprepared to respond to further questioning but realized she had to say something.

"Oh, fine, I guess."

"What assignment is that, dear," Mother asked with doe-like innocence.

"We have to write a paper..." she replied, groping for details about which she knew nothing.

"Oh really," I said feigning confusion. "I thought you were reading 'Moby Dick.'"

Rachel flushed with embarrassment but no one seemed to notice other than me.

"Well..." she stammered, "we have to write a paper after we read the book."

She hurried to change the subject and after that I had little to add to the mealtime conversation.

When dinner had been cleared away and the dishes washed and stored back in the cabinets, Father went off to his study and Mother excused herself to do some mending upstairs.

I knew the time had come for me to confront Rachel.

She seemed determined to get away from me, trying numerous ploys to extricate herself from my company but I was equally determined to stay with her and defused her every ruse. She tried to elude me by leaving the house under the guise of checking on the chickens but I tagged along, refusing to be shaken off.

After ascertaining that all was secure in the chicken coop – and before she could think of another diversionary tactic – I gathered my courage, linked arms with her, told her we had to talk, and led her off toward the church which I knew would be deserted at that time of day. She came along willingly enough, suspicious perhaps but still not realizing my intent.

We went into the sanctuary and sat down in a front pew where we would be sure to see and easily hear if anyone came into the building.

Dusk was one of my favorite times of day in the church for the stained glass windows were still clearly enhanced by the fading light but their intensity was muted, creating a quiet, meditative atmosphere.

I took a deep breath and plunged in.

"You didn't go to school today, did you?"

"What," she sputtered in surprise. "Of course I did!"

"Rachel, I didn't just see Mr. Tucker in town, I saw him at your school. I stopped by to walk home with you. He said you were absent..."

"You didn't tell him the truth, did you," she interjected almost frantically.

"No, I didn't. It caught me a little off guard and I didn't know just what to say."

"Oh, thank God," she sighed.

With wide eyes and fluttering, fearful gestures she plunged into an aimless explanation. "I'm sorry, Martha, please don't tell Mother and Father. I'll never play hooky again, I promise! It's just that some of the kids wanted to..."

Now it was my turn to interrupt.

"Rachel," I began, "don't dig yourself in deeper. I know you weren't off with any of your classmates."

"What do you mean," she asked, her eyes growing wary and her posture defensive.

"I mean I know you didn't play hooky to be with your friends."

I reached over and took her hands in mine. "Rachel, I know you've been seeing Gavin Marshall."

"What?" she cried in genuine shock, snatching her hands away from me as if scalded. "That's ridiculous!"

"Rachel, there's no use denying it. I know. I know it's been going on for a long time. And I know you must have been lying about being ill so to spend time with him. Am I right?"

She said nothing.

"I know I'm right, Rachel."

"So?" she retorted angrily. "So what if you are right! If you weren't all so mean to him and so against him we wouldn't have to sneak around behind everybody's back."

I took another deep breath. "Rachel, do you know how old Mr. Marshall is?"

"He's twenty-eight. What difference does that make?"

"That's eleven years older than you, Rachel – eleven years. Think about it. I don't want to hurt your feelings, honey, and I don't mean to be vulgar, but what can a grown man like Gavin Marshall want from a schoolgirl of seventeen?"

"He doesn't want anything!" she said defensively. "We're in love. Gavin loves me."

I had to bite my tongue to keep from snapping that a man like Gavin Marshall was incapable of loving anyone other than himself. I realized that such a comment would only sever communications and so kept praying for calm and self control.

"Rachel, honey, you may think you're in love but at your age these feelings don't last. Look at all the times over the last couple of years that you've thought you were completely, eternally in love."

"That was different," she insisted. "I am in love with Gavin and he's in love with me... and we're going to be married."

Now it was my turn to sputter in surprise. "Rachel, that's impossible. There's no way Gavin Marshall is going to marry you! No matter what he's said to you it's been just that – words. He's just not the marrying kind."

"How would you know?" She almost spat the words at me. "You don't know Gavin at all. You don't know anything!"

It was getting increasingly difficult to remain calm and not say unkind things about her lack of discernment. "Rachel, you're right. I don't know the man personally. But in a way I do know him because I know how he's treated grown women, women right here in Tully's Cove. You're just a baby, you can't possibly understand men like him."

"You're just jealous!" she countered hotly. "You're saying these bad things because you're jealous. You're jealous because I have someone strong and handsome like Gavin and you have no one!"

That arrow hit its mark and I was quiet for a moment.

"Rachel, I'm saying these things because they're true and because I love you and don't want to see you hurt."

She backed down a little. There was less venom in her words but she was still defensive and almost condescending when she continued.

"Martha, I'm sorry, but you just don't understand. You've never given Gavin a chance." She looked away dreamy-eyed. "He's the most wonderful, exciting man. And he loves me. You'll see. You'll all see. Gavin loves me and he's going to marry me."

"Rachel, how can you be sure that he's going to marry you? Has he come right out and proposed? I don't see a ring on your finger. Has he talked to Father about this marriage you're so sure of?"

"Of course he hasn't talked to Father. Can you imagine what a scene Father would make? Father will just have to get used to the idea..."

She looked at me and smiled meekly. "He'll just have to get used to the idea."

"Oh, Rachel, I don't know what more to say. I just don't trust this man."

"You can trust him, Martha," she stated sweetly. "He said so..."

She looked down for a moment before adding softly, "He said so. You see, I'm going to have a baby."

There was no tragedy in her voice, it was just a sweet, calm statement of fact. I, on the other hand, felt like my heart and stomach had just exchanged places.

"Oh God, Rachel, no! Please tell me that's not true!"

"It *is* true, Martha. I love Gavin and I'm going to have his baby. And we're going to go away. He has it all planned."

I wasn't prepared for this deviation from the scenario I had been rehearsing all day. "He has it all planned," I repeated incredulously. "He may be planning to leave, Rachel, but I would bet money it's to get away from his responsibility not to take you with him."

I had gone too far.

"Martha, I refuse to talk with you further about this."

Her voice was cool and very adult. "There's nothing you can do to stop me."

"I can tell Father," I observed simply.

Her face drained of color but she said nothing.

I was eager to seize upon what I perceived to be a momentary advantage and so forged ahead. "Rachel, I'll make a bargain with you."

"I'm listening," she said softly.

"I won't tell Father if you promise not to do anything foolish before you and I have had a chance to think this through and sit down together and talk with Mr. Marshall. Promise?"

"Yes, Martha," she said in quiet acquiescence. "I promise."

CHAPTER ELEVEN

I.

By morning Rachel was gone.

I knew it instinctively. I didn't need to check. I think in my heart I knew she was leaving even as she promised not to do anything until we had had an opportunity to talk further. Perhaps their departure always had been planned for that evening. Perhaps confrontation pushed talk into action. Whichever was the case, by the time I surfaced from a night of turbulent, leaden sleep Rachel had made what I always would feel was the second worse decision of her life; the first being getting involved with Gavin Marshall at all.

I was standing at my window looking out across the church grounds and trying to find some measure of alertness in my dull, aching head when I heard my mother come up the stairs. She rapped first at my door to ascertain that I was awake and then went on down the hall to Rachel's room.

Every muscle of my body tensed in anticipation.

In just a moment she was calling to me, her voice edged with panic. "Martha!"

I rushed to Rachel's door and found Mother slumped on the floor, a crumpled piece of paper clutched in her hand, her face as white as the sheets on Rachel's unmussed bed.

"Martha," she said again, her voice full of stunned sorrow and disbelief. "Rachel has run away."

I crossed the room and knelt beside her.

"She says she's going to marry Gavin Marshall," she continued incredulously, holding the note out for me to take. "I don't understand. How can that possibly be?"

Her eyes were wide with shock as she struggled to comprehend this totally unexpected act on the part of her younger daughter.

"Oh Mother," I began gently, skimming Rachel's note as I spoke. "I'm so sorry. Apparently she and Mr. Marshall have been seeing one another secretly for quite some time."

The eyes she turned toward me were wounded. "You knew about this?"

"Only for a day or so," I assured her. "Rachel and I talked about it last night. She promised not to do anything rash."

"Dear God, I'd call this something rash!" Her face paled as a new thought occurred. "We'll have to notify the police. They'll have to bring her back."

Her face became even paler as another, perhaps even harsher, reality dawned. "Dear God, what am I going to tell your father?"

I ignored the question as I reread Rachel's note. "Mother, there's something else you need to know. Rachel doesn't say everything in the note..."

"What? What doesn't she say, Martha?"

I was silent, shaking my head sardonically. I *would* have to be the one to tell them that Rachel was going to have a child. How typical of her to leave that choice little tidbit to me. The thought crossed my mind that my father probably would find some way to hold me responsible for that as well as everything else that went wrong in our family.

"Mother, I really don't want to be the one to have to tell you this but last night when we were talking Rachel told me... she said..."

It was difficult to say the words for I knew they were going to devastate her.

"Yes, Martha," she prompted. "What did Rachel tell you? Do you know where they are?"

"No. I wish I did. No, Mother, I'm afraid it's something else."

"Well, what is it?" There was an edge of exasperation to her voice. "How could it be any worse than it already is?"

She stopped abruptly. "Oh God, no," she murmured in quiet horror.

I closed my eyes and said what she could not. "She's going to have a baby."

I had hoped that once it was said I would feel a sense of release but there was to be no easing of this burden. "At least that's what she told me," I added lamely.

Mother was silent for a time, collecting her thoughts. Although her eyes were brimming with tears, when she spoke she was almost eerily calm.

"She doesn't say so in the note," she observed, rising from the floor to sit at the edge of Rachel's bed. "Perhaps she just said it to you for effect. You know how melodramatic Rachel is."

Her words were edged with hope but lacked conviction. "Oh Martha," she said sadly, "if you knew what was going on why didn't you say something to us right away?"

"I don't know, Mother," I admitted, joining her on the bed. "Communication hasn't been this family's strong suit lately. And Rachel promised not to do anything before we had talked things over again. I shouldn't have trusted her, but I did."

She reached across and patted my hand. Kindness and control returned to her voice. "I'm not blaming you, honey. It's not your fault."

She heaved a long, sad sigh. "I blame myself. How could she have gone around seeing this man without raising my suspicions?"

She wiped away the tears that had begun to flow again. I had never seen her look so sad.

"Rachel obviously was very determined," I pointed out. "Think about it. She's gone out of her way to make it appear that she was involved in school, interested in boys her own age, and long ago forgotten her flirtation with Gavin Marshall."

I almost added that she also had been stunningly duplicitous and manipulative but realized in time that Mother undoubtedly wasn't in a state of mind to face the reality of those rather stark character flaws.

"Please don't blame yourself, Mother," I said instead. "It's not your fault either."

"But it is," she said sadly. "It is. How could I let something like this happen? My poor baby. My poor little lamb..."

She rose slowly and left the room.

Yes, her poor little lamb. That was Rachel. I shook my head and heaved a sigh. Just what would Rachel have to do to fall from grace, I wondered. It wasn't that I didn't fear for her and long to ease my mother's pain. It wasn't that I wouldn't rescue Rachel if I could. But where was Rachel's responsibility in all of this? Would she never be held accountable for her actions and decisions?

I listened to Mother's receding footsteps as she went back downstairs. She would finish preparing breakfast and then she would tell Father when he came over from church to eat. I stayed where I was. I had no appetite anyway and absolutely no intention of being in the room when my father was told. This was something for the two of them to face together.

Before going back to my own room, I looked around to see what Rachel had taken with her. Maybe I could tell how serious she was by what she had taken along. Nothing was in disarray, but everything of value was gone as were most of her clothes, a few family pictures, and the Bible she kept by her bed. Well, at least she had taken that along, too. I was sure she was going to need it.

II.

I waited a long time up in my room before going down to the kitchen. I wanted to be sure no one was around before venturing away from the relative anonymity of my bedroom.

The house was uncannily quiet. To my utter amazement there had been no blow up; no explosion when my father learned that his little girl had committed what in his eyes had always been the cardinal sin.

I did feel terrible for Rachel and was frightened for her, too. I also was deeply sorry for my parents. But at the same time I had to acknowledge feeling somewhat vindicated. In light of Rachel's transgressions my working for the paper surely would pale to insignificance. Such a selfish silver lining made me feel somewhat sullied but the thoughts persisted. Certainly Father now would finally see that what I was doing merely challenged tradition, not morality.

By the time I went downstairs I was sure the house was empty. They obviously had left in haste for dishes and food were still on the table. They undoubtedly had gone off to report Rachel's absence to the local authorities so she could be brought back as inconspicuously as possible. I put everything away, cleaned up the dishes, and took the scraps out to Bo's food dish on the back porch.

I stopped short. Last night's food was still in the dish. In fact, all of the previous day's food was still there. It was unusual but not exactly alarming. From time to time Bo would be missing for a day or two when swept away by the urge to hunt and herd the unsuspecting animals inhabiting the woods around the Cove. Even in the face of family tragedy Bo brought a smile to my face. She was a character, that dog. I knew she could take care of herself so tried not to worry. If she wasn't home by evening I would go out looking for her.

I whistled and called her name as loudly as I could in hopes of discovering she was, in fact, nearby. There was no response so I sat down on the back steps to sort things through and decide what to do next.

One thing was perfectly clear. I had to see Jacob Collier. If anyone was going to know where Gavin Marshall might take my sister, it would be Jacob. I would have to call him. I was reluctant to trust the nature of our conversation to the Cove's party lines but there was no time to track down Hannibal and use him as our go-between again. Time was of the essence. If we could find Gavin and Rachel before the police did we could save them a lot of trouble and hopefully spare my parents further embarrassment and concern. We had to find them. And so I had to talk to Jacob.

I went back into the house, took the receiver from its hook and waited for the operator's greeting. There was interest in her voice when I asked to be connected with the Manor House at Patriot's Point but she dutifully put me through.

Knowing that the operator could easily listen in, I decided ahead of time to phrase my request in such a way as to imply to any eavesdropper that I was asking to speak with Jacob on behalf of the newspaper. I trusted that Jacob would understand and follow my lead.

My request to speak to him was met with hesitation from the servant's voice at the other end of the line. The voice was cold and clipped as she asked who was calling before informing me that Mr. Collier wasn't available.

"Could you take a message, please," I asked. "Tell Mr. Collier that Miss Pendleton called and asked him to return my call at *The Sentinel* office. Got that? Have him call Miss Pendleton at *The Sentinel*."

"Yes miss," the disembodied voice mumbled, hanging up almost simultaneously.

III.

Andrew was in the back room of the newspaper office when I arrived. He and Mr. Quigley were laying out that day's edition and were turned away from me, bent over the slanted layout table. Initially neither heard nor sensed my presence and I stood behind them, watching them work, until Mr. Quigley turned and discovered me standing almost at his elbow.

"Good Lord, Miss Pendleton," he exclaimed. "You nearly startled the life out of me! Don't sneak up on a body that way!"

He bustled off toward the press, fussing to himself about ill-mannered young people.

Andrew was more pleased to see me, but no more complimentary. "Martha, you look awful. What's happened?"

I sat on the stool Mr. Quigley had just vacated and managed to croak out the morning's events around the lump of consternation growing in my throat.

He sighed deeply and took my hand. "Martha, I'm so sorry. Didn't you have a chance to talk with her?"

"Yes, we talked," I replied glumly, "last night."

I relayed to him all that had transpired after we had parted the day before – my conversation with Mr. Tucker, Rachel's vague answers to my questions at dinner, and the details of our conversation when I confronted her later in the church.

He listened thoughtfully, interrupting once or twice to ask for clarification. "Martha, I know it's just words but I truly am sorry," he said, trying to console me. He still held my hand in his and covered it protectively with his other hand as he spoke. "If there's anything I can do – anything – all you have to do is ask."

"Thank you, Andrew, but I don't think there's anything anyone can do right now. Just please don't tell anybody what's going on, all right?"

He knew the request was rhetorical but assured me that whatever I told him would be kept in strictest confidence.

I turned back to the layout he and Mr. Quigley had been working on, noticing the day's date as I did so. It was April 1, 1917.

The irony struck me as rather funny.

"Some April Fool's joke, huh," I asked with a weak laugh.

"I wish it were an April Fool's joke... Say, you don't suppose it could be, do you?"

"No, I'm afraid not. Although I wouldn't put it past Gavin Marshall to think up such an elaborate prank and find it incredibly amusing. No, there's nothing funny about this, and I'm afraid it's only too real."

The telephone rang as I spoke. Andrew squeezed my hand and went off to answer it. When he returned he looked even more concerned. "It's for you. It's Jacob Collier."

I thanked him, told him I'd explain in a minute, and hurried off to take the call. "Mr. Collier," I began brightly, striking the verbal pose of the reporter. "Martha Pendleton here. Thank you for returning my call."

I went on before he could speak. "I was wondering if you would be available sometime today for a few more questions pertaining to the story we discussed the day before yesterday."

"Why yes, Miss Pendleton," he replied, matching my formality tone for tone. "I think it would be a good idea for us to talk again. Shall we say in an hour at the same place?"

"Thank you, Mr. Collier; that will be fine."

He rang off promptly but I lingered for a moment longer and heard the tell tale click of another telephone somewhere along the line. As foolish as I felt, it had been wise to play the role of the reporter after a story. Suspicion would be aroused regardless of the nature of our conversation so, at least on the surface, it appeared business-oriented.

Andrew was waiting for me at his desk, trying – and failing – to look nonchalant.

"I've got to talk to Mr. Collier," I explained in response to the question he didn't ask. "If anyone around here knows Gavin Marshall it's he. So if anyone will have an idea where to find Rachel I believe he will."

"I'll come with you."

The statement was made soberly and seriously – but it was the last thing in the world I wanted.

"Andrew, I appreciate your concern but I don't need protecting from Mr. Collier. It'll be a five minute conversation at best. Five minutes. Please believe me; I don't have anything to fear from Jacob Collier. None of us do."

He looked unconvinced but didn't argue with me. "Where are you meeting him?"

"At the..." I caught myself in midsentence. "No, now wait a minute. I don't want you to follow me, either. I've had enough of being followed lately. Hannibal does it all the time. I don't want you to start, too."

He smiled and adjusted his glasses. "Hannibal follows you?"

"I'm sure of it. So you see I already have one guardian angel, I don't need another."

"All right," he relented. "I won't argue with you... and I won't follow you, either. But please be careful, Martha. You say you don't have anything to fear from Jacob Collier and maybe you're right. But just remember, your sister undoubtedly would say the same thing about Gavin Marshall."

IV.

I went directly from the newspaper's office to the gazebo. It was a beautiful afternoon brimming with the promise of spring but, due to my preoccupation with the events of the past two days, I hardly noticed the sunshine and warmth. I could have been slugging my way through three feet of snow or a downpour of rain and wouldn't have thought much about it. I had to talk to Jacob. I had to have some clue – anything – that might help put the pieces together and find Rachel before things went much further. Nothing else mattered. Nothing else registered.

I left the sunshine-drenched open road for a path that led into thickly budded woods and significantly cooler temperatures. By the time the gazebo came into view I was shivering.

Jacob was waiting for me on the bench. He stood as I approached. "Martha, what is it? What's happened?"

"She's gone," I blurted out. "She's run away... Rachel ran off with Gavin Marshall!"

I went inside the gazebo hoping its latticework would shield me a bit from the breeze and the emotions that dogged my heels. Jacob stood in the entranceway but came no farther.

"Damn," he exclaimed angrily. "Gavin assured me they would do nothing rash!"

"The exact line Rachel fed me!"

"Do you know when they left?"

"Sometime during the night; she was gone by the time we got up this morning but no one heard anything unusual beforehand."

Jacob doubled his fist and pounded it against the gazebo's framework. "I never should have trusted him..."

"Nor I her," I agreed. "But we did and the damage is done. What I want to know is if you have any idea where he might take her."

He thought for a moment and then shook his head. "Not right off hand, no."

"How about New York; the other day you mentioned taking Gavin there to get him away from Rachel. Do you think that's where he'd go?"

"He might, I suppose. He does love the nightlife there. But I don't know, Martha. If Gavin has taken Rachel with him, I think he's more likely to go somewhere less flashy."

"I think that's just where he'd take her," I insisted angrily. "Someplace where he can show off his latest acquisition and impress her with the nightlife of the big city – until he tires of her, that is."

"If that were his intention I might agree with you," Jacob said firmly, "but it's not. Martha, when I talked to Gavin he said he was going to marry her!"

"I don't believe that for a minute!" I nearly spat out the words and turned away from him in disgust.

He crossed the distance between us, turning me around by the shoulders and shaking me gently. "Martha, don't be so bitter! Why can't you believe that Gavin may actually have honest feelings for your sister?"

I looked him square in the eyes as I spoke. "Because I know all about Grace Whitley, that's why!"

"Grace Whitley," he asked in a confused tone, shaking his head. "What do you mean, you know all about Grace Whitley?"

"I know that Gavin Marshall tried to seduce her," I replied angrily. "And I know her husband believes that he succeeded."

"Martha, if you know all about Grace Whitley then you also know that Gavin is not the father of her child."

"I do know that," I replied hotly. "And I believe her. But he could have been – probably would have been if she hadn't seen through him and ended the relationship. He befriended a lonely woman only to take advantage of her. And he had only one thing on his mind. He may not be the father of her child but he might as well be – he ruined her reputation as well as her marriage... And now he's seduced my little sister!"

My last words were a choked sob. Feeling angry and utterly helpless, I wrenched free from the loose grasp he maintained on my shoulders, doubled my fists and slammed them down against the railing.

As I raised them for another frustrated blow, Jacob grabbed my wrists and held them firmly until I was quiet. "Martha, I'm sorry," he said softly, pulling me to him, my clenched fists pinned between us. "I can see that you're hurting and I understand why. But I have to tell you that after talking with Gavin I'm not so sure about him anymore. Maybe he really does love your sister."

He heaved a sigh. "I don't know... I definitely believe he wouldn't intentionally do anything to harm her. I know it sounds cliché but maybe Rachel is just what he needs to find purpose and direction for his life... Maybe they'll be all right."

There was weariness in his voice and he laid his cheek against the top of my head as he spoke. "We're really not so bad, Gavin and I."

"You're not," I said with fierce conviction into his lapel. "I believe that with all my heart."

His arms tightened around me. "You're shivering," he observed as if aware of my physical presence for the first time.

"I'm cold," I explained meekly, looking up into his face.

He was so near, so vulnerable.

I believe his initial intention was to kiss me lightly on the forehead in the reassuring, paternalistic manner of his kiss in the library, but this time he continued. He cradled my face in his hands and lightly kissed my cheeks, my hair, and my eyelids as I closed them. In a moment his mouth closed in upon mine.

As soon as our lips met the world began to ebb away. All thought of Rachel and Gavin Marshall was gone. *The*

Sentinel, my parents, Tully's Cove; it all melted away until only the gazebo and Jacob Collier remained.

There was urgency and hunger in his kiss.

Soon there was no thought at all, just ecstatic electricity moving between us and urging us on. My loneliness and longing welled up within me dissolving into a surge of desire for this mysterious, gentle man. My fingers moved through his thick hair and as we kissed I lightly caressed his face, his shoulders, his arms. I slipped my hands under his coat, tracing the contours of his broad back and moving willingly into his embrace.

The shivering continued but I was no longer cold.

Suddenly his kisses stopped. The sheer force of will he exerted upon himself was palpable. He smoothed my hair and held me literally at arm's length.

"Oh God, Martha, I'm sorry," he said with strength and sincerity. "Please forgive me. You must think me no better than Gavin to take advantage of you like this."

He moved away from me. "I don't want you to think of me like that."

He moved farther into the clearing. "We had better leave. If I think of anything that might help I'll contact you."

He spoke and moved quickly, leaving me little room for comment which was just as well. I was shaken both by his kisses and the abruptness of their cessation. I had nothing more to say.

He looked at me from across the clearing and smiled slightly. "I am sorry," he repeated rather sheepishly.

I made no reply.

He moved off into the woods and was gone.

V.

It was nearly time for dinner when I got back to the manse. I went to the kitchen door, avoiding the front entrance as it would take me past my father's study. Mother was working at the stove, the day's toll showing in the slope of her shoulders and the fact that she had set the kitchen table rather than the table in the dining room.

She mustered a smile as I came in, responding to my hug with a peck on the cheek.

"Were you able to find out anything," I asked.

"No," she replied simply and without further comment.

"I went to see Jacob Collier," I informed her, trying to sound matter-of-fact.

She stopped short, looking mildly horrified.

"I thought he might be able to help us discover where they might go."

"Did he know?"

"No..." I said too hastily. "No, I'm afraid not."

I was concerned that some trace of his kisses would remain in my demeanor, but if I seemed distracted or distant she apparently contributed it to the day's trauma.

"What did the police say?"

She took rolls out of the oven before replying. "We didn't go to the police."

"What? Why not? They have to find them and bring Rachel back!"

"Your father doesn't want them involved," she explained.

"Why not?"

She was silent.

"If you didn't go to the police this morning where did you go? You were both gone when I came downstairs."

"We went over to the church to meet with the deacons. Your father called an emergency meeting with them."

"You met with the *deacons*," I repeated. "What can they do?"

"We didn't ask them to do anything," she said flatly. "Your father explained the situation to them and offered to resign from the pulpit."

"He did what?"

"He offered to resign from the pulpit," she repeated slowly, continuing with her work.

I sat down heavily in my chair at the table. "I can't believe it."

"Well, he is justifiably concerned that people may feel he is no longer fit for the ministry because of what has happened. He rather feels that way himself at the moment."

"That's utterly ridiculous," I sputtered. "Apart from being incredibly thick-headed there's never been anyone more fit for the ministry!"

"It's good to hear you defend him," she noted with a wan smile.

"What did the deacons say?"

She sat down across from me, sighing deeply. "They discussed it at some length, read some Scripture, and spent some time in prayer..."

"And..." I prompted, more interested in the outcome than the process.

"And they told your father that they feel Rachel's actions are not grounds for his expulsion from the ministry."

"Well, hallelujah," I crowed, my voice more than slightly tinged with sarcasm.

Mother ignored both the eruption and the sarcasm. "They said that even though she is our daughter, ultimately we all make our own choices and decisions." She got up and checked on something in the oven. "Obviously Rachel has acted against her upbringing and our counsel and it was felt that she is responsible for her actions, not your father."

"Well," I admitted, regaining my composure, "I have to agree with them on that point. And I commend them for their decision. Is Father going to accept it?"

"I believe so; although he is terribly shaken."

"What about the congregation?"

"Well, they will have to be told."

"Why?" I challenged. "It's really none of their business!"

"No, now there you're wrong, Martha. It is very much their business. And there is no reason to hide it from them. Everyone can learn from our example. But the deacons did stress that it would be sufficient to just say Rachel has eloped and leave it at that."

"Well, that's something at least," I conceded. "But what are you going to do in the meantime? What are you going to do to get Rachel back?"

"Rachel won't be coming back," she said slowly, simply, and sadly. "Your father doesn't want her to. He says she has made her choices and must now live with the consequences."

I stared at her dumbfounded, feeling as if the wind had been knocked out of me.

"He'll change his mind," I finally managed to say.

"I don't know," she replied uncertainly. "We'll have to give him some time."

"But what about Rachel?"

"Rachel is gone. We have to let her go."

I couldn't believe my ears. Rachel was so special to them, the light of their lives. How could they possibly just "let her go" as my mother put it? Father would change his mind. He could be terribly stubborn but he'd change his mind. This was Rachel we were talking about after all. *Rachel*.

Dinner was a somber, silent affair. None of us said more than two or three words the entire time.

When Eli Thornton appeared at the back door we were all visibly grateful for the interruption. It was good to see someone who wasn't involved in our family crisis.

"Evening Pastor," he said, hat in hand, when Father went to the door. "Sorry to interrupt your supper – I could come back later…"

"No, Eli, that won't be necessary," Father assured him. "What can I do for you?"

"Well, sir, I'm afraid I really come to see Miss Martha. But it might be good if you and Mrs. Pendleton heard what I got to say, ah-yuh."

Mother and I rose from the table and joined my father at the door.

Certain that someone must have seen Jacob and me at the gazebo, my throat began to constrict and my heart was thudding so hard I was sure everyone would hear it pounding.

"I'm sorry, Miss Martha," Eli continued, "but I'm afraid we got bad news for you."

I could see Hannibal standing a few yards behind Eli. He was holding a large wooden crate.

Father touched my shoulder and followed as I led the way down the back steps. "What is it, Eli," he asked in my stead.

"Hannibal was off wandering in the woods today, like he's wont to do, and he found your dog, Miss Martha."

Although he was speaking to me, Eli kept his eyes firmly on the toes of his worn boots. He was silent for what seemed an eternity, punctuating the news he finally shared with long pauses and vigorous wringing of the hat he held firmly clutched in his hand.

"Hannibal found Bo... I'm sorry, Miss Martha... I'm afraid she's dead."

Behind me, Mother's breath snagged; she reached out and grasped my shoulder.

I shrugged her off, running the few steps remaining between Hannibal and me. With solemn reverence he lowered the crate to the ground so I could look in.

Bo lay on her side inside the crate, partially covered by Hannibal's jacket as if he had sought to warm her. Her eyes were closed and she appeared to be sleeping but there was no rhythmic rise and fall of her chest, no twitching of her legs as she dreamed of our woodland haunts; no sign of life. When I touched her she was stiff and cold.

I looked up at Hannibal and saw that he was crying.

"I'm sorry, Pastor," Eli said, breaking the silence. "I hate to hurt you, Miss Martha. But I thought you'd want to know."

He offered Hannibal his handkerchief before echoing, "Ah-yuh, thought you'd want to know."

"You're right, Eli," Father said, taking the man's hand and shaking it firmly. "Thank you. It's best to know... No matter how painful the knowing might be."

"Thank you, Hannibal," I managed to squeak out. "Thank you, Eli."

The two men slowly walked away and left us standing at three sides of the crate looking down at our beloved pet.

Silly dog. What adventure had she charged into with characteristic jubilant abandon – abandon that ultimately had claimed her life? She was still an impulsive, headstrong puppy.

She was so loyal.

She was such a good friend.

Mother put her arms around me and we began to cry. I noticed that Father was crying, too.

As much as we loved Bo, it wasn't only she for whom we wept.

Part Two:
Convergence
Spring, 1917

CHAPTER TWELVE

I.

In the spring of 1917 the United States teetered on the brink of world war. When the conflagration erupted in Europe three years earlier America had vowed to remain neutral and President Woodrow Wilson had committed himself to reconciling the belligerents without becoming actively involved in their disputes. Privately the president sided with the Allies against German aggression and atrocities but, fearing that taking sides would seriously damage the multiethnic tapestry of American society, he told the nation that "the United States must be neutral in fact as well as in name during these days that try men's souls." As a result of his convictions – and heeding public sentiment as reflected in the popular song "I Didn't Raise My Boy to Be a Soldier" – Wilson repeatedly attempted to bring the warring nations together to negotiate a "peace without victory." Every effort failed, however, and consequently America's neutral stance slowly eroded and more and more Americans began to acknowledge the seeming inevitability of ultimately joining the conflict.

The path to war had many significant milestones. Even early on, when optimism still ran high that the bloodshed could be contained, Germany had initiated an extensive campaign of espionage and sabotage in the United States. Attempting to thwart the European Allies' reliance on American industry, German agents bought up hundreds of tons of manufactured goods, worked tirelessly to stir up tensions between unions and management, and even successfully sabotaged ships heading to England and France with much needed supplies. In one particularly daring act of treachery, Black Tom Island across the harbor from New York City – where more than two million pounds of munitions were stored – went up in a colossal explosion, the concussion shattering windows in Jersey City and shrapnel being propelled with such velocity it actually dented the Statue of Liberty!

In July of 1915, the full intent of their planning came to light when a German diplomat in Washington inadvertently left his briefcase on a train. The unexpected windfall revealed espionage plans reflecting an investment by Germany of literally millions of dollars! Americans were appalled and many began to call for war.

The beginning of America's final descent into the morass of world war came in January of 1917 when, with only eight hours warning, Germany broke a pledge they had made the year before to restrict the activities of their submarines. In a note delivered to President Wilson, Germany boldly claimed the right to resume unrestricted submarine warfare in an area more expansive than the already controversial war zone they had delineated two years earlier. That earlier zone had led to the sinking of the British passenger ship Lusitania; a disaster that counted 128 Americans among the dead and nearly pushed the U.S. over the edge at that time. In response to the scope of their newest declaration, on February 3, 1917, President Wilson severed diplomatic relations with Germany and later in the month Congress passed a bill permitting U.S. merchant vessels to carry arms in order to protect themselves.

As February stretched into March new depredations by German submarines against neutral shipping continued to prime the pump of American public opinion. The ultimate blow, however, was the interception of a telegram in which Arthur Zimmermann, the Kaiser's foreign minister, approached Mexico about allying with them against America if the United States went to war against the Central Powers. In return for their cooperation, Germany promised to support Mexico's retaking of land in Texas, New Mexico, and Arizona. The contents of the Zimmermann telegram were explosive to say the least, finally pushing the United States over the brink and into the fray.

President Wilson's request for a declaration of war in order to "make the world safe for democracy" came on April 2, the day after Rachel disappeared. Although it was to profoundly impact my life, I was barely cognizant of the attendant implications. On April 6, 1917, while Congress passed a resolution declaring that a state of war existed between the United States and Germany, my father stood firm in his resolve that Rachel would have to live with the consequences of her choice to become involved with Gavin Marshall and grief seemed to color every facet of our existence.

II.

The manse was as quiet as a tomb. It hadn't been the place of refuge and comfort one associates with "home" for a long time but with Rachel's departure and Bo's death any vestige of normalcy was shattered. We all went about the business of living but no one's heart really was in it. Mother no longer sang around the house as she worked and Father was almost ghostly in his coming and going.

And both of them looked about ten years older.

In spite of everything Father's ministry didn't seem to suffer during those days. In fact, his personal tragedy actually seemed to make him far more sensitive to humanity's foibles. His sermons became more passionate and practical, and interactions between him and his flock seemed more caring and open. He always had been there for everyone who needed his counsel and spiritual guidance but now he seemed more accepting of their shortcomings, seemed to be growing in his ability to truly empathize with those around him.

I took this as a good sign. Although he said nothing to indicate a change of heart, I was sure he soon would recant his edict that Rachel was on her own. Surely it was simply a matter of time.

As hoped, Father even seemed to be more accepting of me. There was no dramatic reversal regarding his opinion of a woman's "place" but he finally seemed to acknowledge the fact that I merely challenged tradition rather than the higher moral standard against which he originally measured my actions. Or perhaps he simply didn't want to lose both his children. Whatever the case I was grateful – and, true to form, felt somewhat guilty to be benefitting inadvertently from Rachel's transgressions even while a barely audible voice deep within me said it served them all right.

The first evidence of Father's change toward me came the day after Bo died. When I was ready, he helped me bury her.

I stayed with Gazebo for a long time the night Eli and Hannibal brought her body to us and Mother even allowed me to keep her in the storage room off the kitchen over night. But by morning I was ready to let her go. Father helped me select a place for her interment, dug the hole for me, wrapped her body in some old linens, and gently lowered her into the ground while Mother and I looked on in silence.

The burial was cathartic. Bo's death gave all of us something concrete upon which to focus. Perhaps in a way we were transferring our disappointment and grief about Rachel to that small hole under Bo's favorite tree. I knew my parents well enough to know that the act of burying the dog was not symbolic of burying Rachel. She certainly was not dead to them and no matter what they said I knew they couldn't let her go so easily. But hopefully they would be able to release some of the pain they felt and leave it under the moist earth that now covered Gazebo, my best friend.

Losing Bo affected me as profoundly as if a member of the family had died. In a way one had. From the day Jacob Collier had sent her to us, Bo had been my constant companion. She had gone with me virtually everywhere. Just as I had come to be an accepted part of daily life in Tully's Cove as I went about my work for *The Sentinel*, so too had the dog who shadowed my every waking hour and waited patiently for me when duty took me somewhere she couldn't go. She was my friend, my confidant, my protector. She accepted me without reservation, was always there when I needed her, and gave me confidence when out and about by myself.

She would be sorely missed.

No one seemed to understand my feelings better than Andrew. I think he loved Bo nearly as much as I did and as a result shared my sense of loss. He had come to be a sounding board for me in other areas of my life and so I instinctively turned to him in my grief for my dog as well as for my little sister.

But as much as he was sensitive to my feelings and open to discussing them with me, I became increasingly aware of a subtle change in him. Ever since early February when President Wilson had severed diplomatic relations with Germany, Andrew had seemed distracted. Now that direct involvement in the war loomed large, he was as friendly toward me and as devoted to his work as ever but there just was something about him that was different. He was quieter – if that were possible – and there was an aura of resolve surrounding him that translated itself into a confidence and strength I hadn't really noticed before. He had always struck me as being the most grounded, stable person I had ever known but now there was something more, something even more decisive and purposeful.

After Congress declared war on Germany, Andrew became obsessed with what was going on abroad and was constantly updating himself. He was in contact with Mr. Carmichael's friend who worked for William Randolph Hearst's "International News Service" and it seemed that with every conversation between the two Andrew became progressively quiet and increasingly restless.

Perhaps because we had grown so close over the previous months, I realized what must be on his mind long before he shared his feelings with me; Andrew was going to leave Tully's Cove to get closer to the action.

One day in early May, as I was working with Mr. Quigley in the back room of the newspaper, Andrew burst in the front door and nearly tripped over several pieces of furniture in his haste to reach us.

"Martha, we've got to talk," he blurted out before any greetings could be exchanged.

Mr. Quigley raised a quizzical eyebrow but said nothing as Andrew took my arm and led me away.

The outer office was empty and he steered me over to his desk, almost pushing me into the adjacent chair as he plopped down onto his own.

"I'm moving to New York!" he exclaimed breathlessly.

"What?"

"I'm moving to New York," he repeated, as much for his own benefit as for mine.

He ran his fingers through his unkempt ginger-colored hair and adjusted his glasses. "I've been talking to Medford Potter, Layton's friend," he continued. "Now that we're in the war they're adding to their news staff... Layton called in a few markers Potter owes him and they're taking me on! Can you believe it?"

He didn't wait for a response but stood and began pacing around the cluttered office. "I've got to do this, Martha; I've just got to. It's been eating away at me for months and now that we're actually involved I just can't sit here and do nothing."

He stopped pacing long enough to adjust his glasses. "The army never would take me because of my eyesight and damnable flat feet... I've got to be more involved than just passing along second hand news to the good people of Tully's Cove. I've got to make some kind of contribution."

"I know you do," I assured him sincerely. "Anyone who knows you knows that."

He returned to his desk, looked at me and smiled.

"Even though I knew it was probably inevitable, it's still kind of hard to believe." For some reason it was difficult to meet his gaze and I averted my eyes. "When will you go?"

"I don't know yet..."

He adjusted his glasses, his voice gaining speed and intensity as he continued. "Potter says we'll be sending the first troops over within a month or two at the latest. General John Pershing will be leading them – he's the general who went after Pancho Villa last year. Martha, Potter may actually let me cover their departure! What a plum assignment!"

"That means you'll be leaving Tully's Cove quite soon, doesn't it?"

I felt sad – almost desolate – at the thought of losing him and was a little surprised by the depth of my emotion. "I don't quite know what to say. I'm really happy for you, Andrew. I know how much it means to you to know firsthand what's going on and I know you'll do a wonderful job reporting it."

He smiled broadly and I continued.

"You're on your way," I observed. "There'll be no more small-town newspapers for you!" The realization of what lay ahead of him began to sink in. "Wow, I can hardly believe someone I know will actually be covering the war as it happens. It's a terrific opportunity, Andrew!"

"Thank you, Martha. I knew you'd understand."

"I do understand – but I'll miss you," I said sincerely. "You've been such a good friend to me. Life just won't be the same without you... It'll be so hard to say goodbye."

"Martha," he began haltingly, adjusting his glasses. "Martha, we don't have to say goodbye..."

"I know," I replied. "I know we'll see each other again; you can come back to visit when the war is over. It's just that in the meantime nothing will be quite the same." I smiled teasingly. "Who will I dump all my troubles on when you're gone?"

"I don't feel dumped on," he insisted. "And seeing each other after the war isn't what I meant." He leaned forward in his chair and looked at me with a mixture of seriousness, embarrassment, and what I thought was actually a dash of fear. "Martha, we don't have to say goodbye at all... you could come with me."

I pulled back slightly and regarded him questioningly. "Me? Go to New York?"

He smiled somewhat sheepishly, pushing his glasses up his nose. "Martha, I'm asking you to marry me."

"*Marry* you?"

"Yes," he replied, beginning to look extremely unsure of himself and speaking deliberately. "I don't want to say goodbye to you, Martha, ever. I want you to come with me. I want us to work together. I want us to be together."

I listened without comment as he continued.

"I know you don't necessarily feel the same way I do. I'm a very practical person, Martha, and I realize you probably don't love me. But think about it. Isn't our friendship an ideal thing upon which to build a marriage? Think of all we've shared. Think of all we have in common. You've just said you don't want to lose me and I certainly don't want to lose you."

He leaned across the desk and took my hands. "Martha, think of what it would be like to go to New York together! On her own it would be highly unlikely that a female reporter would have access to the stories I'll be covering but with your husband it would be an entirely different thing. We could collaborate on all kinds of things. I've thought it all through. We could take rooms in the city and maybe Potter would take you on as a stringer. New York's much more progressive than Maine and you got a job here; I know Layton would give you a strong endorsement. We're quite a team, Martha. If we were married we'd be even better."

He paused just a moment but when I didn't speak he continued. "I know you love Tully's Cove – I do, too – but after all you've been through doesn't the thought of a fresh start sound appealing? This war is repulsive and tantalizing all at the same time. It's going to change the world forever, Martha. The United States can no longer deny her place as the vanguard of positive change in the world. I believe this is one of history's most decisive moments. Doesn't the prospect of reporting it as it happens sound enticing?"

I had to smile in spite of myself. He was once again the pitchman whose vivid word pictures months earlier had convinced the preacher's daughter she could actually flaunt tradition and take a "man's" job.

"You've always been a good salesman, Andrew," I told him sincerely. "Yes, it does sound enticing to view an historic moment as it unfolds. But we're talking about war, Andrew; I don't know if I would classify it as an appealing fresh start. This is not one of history's prettier moments. People are dying and New York isn't a quiet backwater like Tully's Cove where – quite frankly – one can sit out the conflict in benign ignorance. I don't know if I want to be that close to history in the making!"

I shifted nervously in my chair and tried in vain to withdraw my hand from his. "Andrew, I don't know if I'm who you think I am. You've always perceived me as more worldly and independent than I perceive myself."

He tightened his grip on my hand. "Martha, I don't think my perception of you is inaccurate. I think I see you more clearly than perhaps you see yourself. You've changed so much just in the short time I've known you. You've become more comfortable with your own abilities – and with your ambitions. You know that's true; why must I be the one to point out to you that women of your generation are different, Martha?"

His next words were spoken slowly and pointedly. "You aren't your mother."

"All right, I'll grant that most of what you say is true. I have interests with which my mother's generation could never identify. But dropping everything, getting married, moving to New York, and working for a news service is beyond any vision I have of myself. I'm not sure I'm up to it. And Andrew, I have to be very frank with you, what you're describing sounds more like a business proposition than a marriage proposal."

He smiled and released my hand. "And for that I apologize. I've never been much of one for romance. And circumstances being what they are, I guess maybe I felt my chances would be better with a sales pitch."

He adjusted his glasses, swallowed hard and met my eyes with an unwavering gaze. "It's not easy for me to say the words, but I do love you, Martha. I have almost since the day we met. And I promise I'll be a good husband. If you want me down on one knee," he offered, beginning to slide out of his chair, "I think I can manage it..."

"No," I assured him hastily, "that won't be necessary."

He looked relieved and we both had to smile.

"Don't answer right away, Martha. Think about all I've said. Sleep on it."

I stood and glanced back at Mr. Quigley who was still hard at work in the back room, oblivious to the momentous conversation taking place just a few yards away.

"I know we could have a wonderful life together," Andrew interjected tentatively.

I turned and hugged him impulsively. "Andrew, you are a wonderful person and I do care for you deeply. I'll think about everything you've said."

He returned my embrace enthusiastically and kissed me on the cheek. "Thank you, Martha. I ask for nothing more."

III.

It was nearing the end of the May and there still was no news of Rachel. For the first few weeks after her supposed elopement, I had firmly believed that Gavin Marshall's true intentions would become painfully clear to her, that she would find some way to contact us, and that Father would rush to her rescue out of sheer relief that she was all right.

But there was no word.

I continued to be terribly concerned for her – I know we all were – and intensely curious as to her whereabouts and whether Mr. Marshall had actually made an honest woman out of her. Every time I thought about it – which was often – I was staggered once again by the realization that this was my little sister I was talking about! It was my little sister who was going to have a bastard child. From what I knew of my family tree no one had ever gone so far outside the bounds of propriety. If there were skeletons in the family closet they were securely hidden within the folds of ancestral folklore. Ours was an extremely staid and proper lineage. Rachel's escapade – and to a lesser extent my own – must have rattled their bones!

Jacob Collier and I had communicated several times regarding Rachel and Gavin. He was actively following up any lead he could think of but so far had been unsuccessful in locating Mr. Marshall through channels they shared.

We exchanged telephone calls a couple of times and notes on an almost regular basis but neither of us had again suggested meeting face-to-face. It wasn't my reputation about which we were concerned. I knew he didn't want to see me again because of what had happened the last time we had been together. In my head I knew he was right and that it was safer to stay away but in my heart I wanted nothing more than to explore the feelings which had overcome us in the woods – especially now that Andrew had asked me to marry him.

I know it was rather disloyal of me in light of Andrew's proposal, but I savored and saved every note Jacob sent, tucking them behind the loose lining of my jewelry box. His penmanship and every nuance of his writing style became second nature to me, and I read as much between the lines as I did from the matter-of-fact words he committed to paper.

As a result, when he unexpectedly sent their carriage for me I was sure he must have important news about Rachel and went to him without question.

The note the driver handed me was type-written and surprisingly terse: *"Please come to me. I will meet you in the garden. J"*

It never occurred to me not to go, and I was relieved that the carriage had pulled up to the side of *The Sentinel* building as I approached; since I wouldn't cross in front of the windows Andrew wouldn't even accidentally know of my eager disloyalty.

It was after five o'clock and long shadows had begun to creep across the roadway as the carriage made its way out of town and on toward the seclusion of Patriot's Point. The air within the coach was stuffy and smelled of mildew and stale roses but I stayed well within the recesses of its black walls, safely tucked away from those who might be curious as to whom its passenger was. The Cove's attitude toward its "Remittance Men" had grown even chillier when news of Rachel's "elopement" spread; when war was declared and none of our fallen gentlemen made a move to sign up for military service it grew down-right icy! Even though virtually everyone knew of my friendship with Jocelyn Collier, the conventional part of my nature sought security from the town's prying eyes and undisguised disapproval of her cousin.

When the carriage began its climb up the circular drive leading to the Collier's house it struck me anew that Jacob must have significant news about Rachel for it was extremely impulsive to have us meet at his home. Even though our interests were entirely – or mostly – objective, it truly was a turnabout if he no longer cared whether people knew we were in contact.

I remembered that there was a decorative archway leading to the gardens from the midpoint of the drive and so called up to the coachman to stop and let me out there. He complied as if there was nothing unusual about discharging his passengers other than at the front door and didn't seem to notice that I kept my face turned from him and said nothing more before disappearing into the shadows of the darkening garden.

The wind had picked up but other than its persistent discourse with the shrubbery and trees there was virtually no noise apart from the crunch of my footsteps on the crushed gravel walkway. No one called my name and there was no indication of which way I should go.

I made my way toward the small replica of the city's band shell nestled in the middle of the Collier's horticultural map of Tully's Cove, the lush foliage and growing darkness making it easy to remain unseen from the house. Since no directions had been given I assumed that that was where Jacob would meet me, but I found it unoccupied and had about decided to leave when it occurred to me that Jacob must have assumed I would remember that his portion of the garden was beyond the well-manicured terrain of Jocelyn's showplace. That was where we had first met; beyond a rusted wrought iron gate, back toward the sea where the trees and shrubbery became one and the taste of salt in the air was as much a part of the aura of the place as were the untended plants flourishing there.

It was almost completely dark by the time I reached the gate, but I could see a dim light in the distance so knew that Jacob had indeed assumed I would know where to come.

The wind was now more an adversary than a mere inconvenience for it was stronger as I approached the sea, making it even more difficult to find my way through the overgrown plants standing between me and the light by which Jacob waited. Stray vines and branches of varying sizes continually blocked the path and when caught by the wind became whip-like as they lashed out toward me. I was becoming alarmingly disoriented and flailed my arms about me in an effort to ward off the vines and branches as they attacked.

I called out to Jacob but my voice was lost on the wind.

It was so dark and so windy that at first I thought the sudden tightness at my throat must be caused by yet another stray branch lashing out across the path and slapping my head and neck. But suddenly I could go no farther and as I began gasping for air and groping wildly about me in the dark I felt the crush of an attacker's hands as gloved fingers closed around my neck and cut off my breathing!

I struggled like a wild thing against an attacker whose presence I knew only from the strong hands that clenched my throat and the guttural sounds and broken sentences spat into my ear.

"Worthless whore..." I heard him croak out shrilly. "Just like all the rest; garbage just like your worthless sister, just like Celia..."

I was growing lightheaded and couldn't focus; was he talking to me or about me?

"No one to stop me this time," the attacker babbled on. "Where's your little dog this time, whore?"

The babbling continued in a shrill, sing-songy voice. "Over the wall... Over the wall... Throw the garbage into the sea!"

There was no point in trying to scream as I was dragged toward the low wall standing between me and eternity for whatever sounds I was able to make were swallowed up in the rushing wind.

I gasped and choked and pulled futilely at the gloved hands that held me like a vice. I had never felt such all-encompassing, gut-wrenching fear, and yet, in those moments, it seemed as if I had never known anything else.

After being grabbed by the throat, I was yanked backward so that my back was flat against my attacker's chest and his left forearm pressed tightly against my windpipe. Pulling fruitlessly at the unyielding arm that trapped me, my one rational thought was that I must leave evidence – my fingernails tore into exposed soft flesh above the gloved hand. He winced in response but the only lasting reaction was increased pressure against my windpipe.

My mind raced wildly – Who? Why?

There were no answers, only the darkness, the sound of the wind, and a hopeless, pitiful struggle.

In the midst of that sheer terror, I experienced a moment of clarity as frightening as the battle that consumed me. This, then, was my destiny; the threshold whose crossing I had sensed as synonymous with our move to Tully's Cove.

I was going to die here.

The cold simplicity of the thought caused an instantaneous parade of memories to flood my ebbing consciousness as the utter isolation of stark panic and terror yielded to a feeling of nothingness that I thought must surely be the prelude to death.

No more chances to make things right; with my father, with Rachel, with Jacob Collier...

There is no way of knowing exactly what transpired behind me as consciousness finally slipped away, but I distinctly remember hearing a loud, guttural screech and feeling a final, powerful tensing of muscle wrench through my assailant before everything went black and I began the disjointed freefall I numbly expected would deposit me at Heaven's gate.

IV.

I opened my eyes to a dazzling blur of whiteness, and bright light seemed to pour in on me from every direction. White-garbed beings floated in and out of my field of vision. They were talking softly. I could hear their voices but couldn't make out what they were saying. Someone was holding my hand; a gentle, light touch like gossamer.

At first I thought I must be experiencing the glory of God but as consciousness returned and the fog lifted from my brain, my focusing eyes revealed nothing more ethereal than the stark, antiseptic whiteness of a hospital ward flooded with sunlight from a bank of windows along one side.

I experienced a momentary flash of disappointment, closed my eyes, nestled back into my pillow, and drifted back into blissful nothingness.

I had survived. I was safe.

V.

It is virtually impossible to describe the almost-overwhelming confusion one feels when reviving from a period of unconsciousness. Your grasp on reality seems to return in stages, interrupted by spells of natural or medication-induced stupor. I would surface for a moment, go through the same scenario of from-heaven-to-hospital grogginess, and then drift back to sleep. I have no idea how many times my brain took me through that tedious regimen before my grasp on reality became firm enough to keep me awake and alertness began to replace my groggy fugue.

When I was finally back to stay, it was my mother's light touch I felt on my hand. "Here she is," she said softly over her shoulder.

In a moment my father, a nurse, and two men I didn't recognize were all looking down at me.

Andrew was there, too, standing off to one side looking concerned and frightened and slightly lost.

One of the men I didn't recognize stepped forward, peeled my eyelids back one at a time and pronounced me whole.

"We've been so worried, Martha," my mother cooed, arranging my hair on the pillow and cradling my face in her hands. "But the doctor says you're going to be just fine."

"Wh-what happened? I was at Patriot's Point..." My voice was terribly hoarse and talking made my head throb but I needed answers.

"Try not to think about it, dear," she urged. "You're all right now, that's all that matters."

A raspy male voice came from behind her. "I'm afraid she'll have to think about it, Mrs. Pendleton."

It was the other man who had come forward with my father and the doctor. "She's the only one who can really tell us what happened up there."

"It'll be all right," my father assured her. "She's strong. She can handle it."

He took mother gently by the arm and led her to the foot of the bed so the raspy-voiced man could sit on the chair next to me. I recognized him then as the oldest Eligible to whom Augusta Wilkes had introduced me during her short-lived stint as matchmaker.

Those days seemed a lifetime ago.

"Miss Pendleton," he began, "I don't know if you'll remember me. I'm Deputy Gilbert. We're going to need some information from you."

"All right..." I replied somewhat groggily, lifting myself up on my elbows as the nurse tucked another pillow in behind me so I could sit up.

"What were you doing up at Patriot's Point; why did you go up there?"

I glanced over at Andrew before reluctantly explaining that Mr. Collier had been helping me look for my sister and that he had sent a note asking me to meet him in the garden.

The deputy shook his head. "I'm afraid that's impossible, Miss Pendleton. Mr. Collier has been in New York for over a week and has witnesses to prove it."

"You mean he wasn't in the garden?"

"No, ma'am."

I don't know if I smiled, but with his words came a tidal wave of relief, and I realized that just as much as my mind had pushed the thought away I had, in fact, believed my attacker to be Jacob Collier. I was no better than the rest of the Cove; I, who fancied myself in love with the man! Just like them I judged him guilty on the basis of tainted suspicion, rumor and innuendo.

The doctor misinterpreted my dazed expression as renewed fatigue and stupor, pronounced the interview at an end, and escorted a frustrated Deputy Gilbert from the room.

In a few moments my parents left, too.

Andrew took over the chair by my bed. He said nothing but simply held my hand. I felt safe and warm and drifted off once again.

VI.

Over the next few days I learned that it was Hannibal who had found me, still unconscious, during one of his spells of aimless wandering. He had wrapped me in his coat and carried me all the way into town.

I was also to learn that, although it was not mine, there was, indeed, a body at the bottom of the cliffs at Patriot's Point! What everyone wanted from me was insight into exactly how it had gotten there.

The bruises on my throat and the evidence of a struggle around the garden's eastern ledge substantiated my account of the assault. The scratches I left on the arm of my assailant and my sketchy description of the coat and gloves they had worn provided proof that it was they who had ended up dead on the rocks below the Point.

But that was where the questions became very difficult to answer. For what mystified everyone was the fact that it was Jocelyn Collier who had died!

At first I refused to believe it. I thought there must be some mistake. But Deputy Gilbert assured me it was true.

Jocelyn Collier was dead.

Jocelyn Collier had tried to kill me!

And strangely enough the authorities seemed willing to leave it at that. Jocelyn Collier had attacked me and during the struggle it was she, rather than I, who had died. The town was undoubtedly aflame with rumor and speculation, but the official report was that a mentally unbalanced woman had died as the result of her own actions.

Case closed.

But I couldn't accept that conclusion. Despite what official reports said and what *The Sentinel* reported, I was certain I had not been able to overcome my assailant – I had been helpless and pitifully inept. The more I thought about it the more certain I became. I went over and over the sequence of events in my mind and ultimately came to only one logical and now obvious conclusion.

My recollection of that night ended with a distinct but unidentified sound nearby and with my attacker – that is, with Jocelyn – tensing dramatically in response. As I went over the same territory again and again, I realized that her stark momentary jolt was a reaction to something other than her struggle with me. That "something" had to have been Hannibal; he didn't just accidentally find me that night after it was all over. He once again had been following me and this time literally saved my life! It had to be. It was the only logical explanation.

Andrew followed my line of reasoning and agreed with my conclusion but Deputy Gilbert was skeptical, wondering why Hannibal would lie about what happened.

That, too, seemed clear to me. In his childlike mind, Hannibal was probably scared to death that he would get into trouble because Jocelyn had died. If I could convince him that that wasn't the case, I was sure he could shed more light on what actually had transpired that night.

Hannibal was more than willing to come visit me and accompanied Andrew the very next day. Deputy Gilbert was there, too, although he sat on an adjacent bed behind a privacy screen so as not to spook our reluctant hero.

Looking obviously relieved to see that I was still in the land of the living, Hannibal took the chair next to my bed when Andrew pulled up another for himself.

"How are you, Miss Martha," he asked shyly once we all were comfortable.

"I'm feeling much better, Hannibal," I began, "and I believe I have you to thank for that, don't I?"

"I dudn't do nuthin'," he replied quietly before lapsing into silence.

I smiled warmly at him and patted his hand. "What do you mean you didn't do anything? Why, without your help I would have died!"

He began to wring his hands, and I felt desperate to let him know he had done nothing wrong. "Hannibal," I plunged in. "I would have died if you hadn't helped me. You did a brave thing that night and you should know that. It wasn't your fault Miss Collier died. You were defending me, weren't you? When someone helps someone else he doesn't get in trouble for that."

"That's right, Hannibal," Andrew interjected. "People don't get in trouble for helping someone else. Why, we put their picture in the newspaper so everyone can know the good thing they did and thank them for it."

Hannibal glanced furtively toward the door. "I dudn't hurt that lady."

"Why, of course you didn't," I assured him. "But she was hurting me, wasn't she? And you couldn't let that happen, could you?"

He was silent and I was afraid we had lost him. Then, to my relief, he responded. "No, ma'am."

"Won't you please tell me what happened, Hannibal? After I got hurt, I was unconscious – I was asleep – and I don't remember what happened after that."

He looked first at Andrew, who smiled reassuringly, and then back at me. "That lady was hurtin' you... She was hurtin you... I made her stop."

"How did you make her stop, Hannibal?"

He hesitated again, looking frightened and ready to bolt. "I pulled her away," he said simply and once again was silent.

No one spoke for a moment or two. Both Andrew and I were reluctant to push him further.

Hannibal appeared to be lost in thought, his face taking on a confused, disbelieving expression. "I thought she was that man," he said at last. "Ah-yuh, I thought she was that man. She had men's clothes on – why'd she have men's clothes on, Miss Martha?"

Andrew explained for me. "She probably didn't want Miss Martha to know who she was."

He digested that for a moment, nodded his head slightly, and then continued. "When I pulled her away she laughed at me... She laughed an' cried an' hollered all at the same time. I put my coat on you an' when I looked back she was on the wall flappin' her arms like a bird and laughin' an' cryin' an' hollerin' all at the same time. I tol' her she couldn't fly, but she dudn't listen to me... Ah-yuh, she just dudn't listen."

He fell silent, his face contorted in a horrified, confused scowl at the memory, his mouth slightly open in the way of the simple-minded. There were tears in his eyes.

I reached over and took his hand.

"Augusta said she was sick," he began again. "Was she sick, Miss Martha?"

"Yes, Hannibal; I'm afraid she was very sick."

He shook his head and wiped the tears away with the back of his free hand. "She dudn't look sick," he observed. "She just looked mean."

"Her type of sickness makes people look mean, Hannibal, and makes them do mean things to others. Nobody really understands just what their sickness is or where it comes from..."

My voice trailed off and my throat constricted as I was catapulted back to the precipice at Patriot's Point and Jocelyn's hands once again were around my neck.

Andrew broke the silence. "You didn't do anything wrong, Hannibal. You helped Miss Martha and you didn't do anything to hurt Miss Collier. Would you be willing to tell Deputy Gilbert everything you've just told us? He needs to know what happened." He reached over and clasped Hannibal's shoulder reassuringly. "We'll go with you."

Hannibal looked at me. He seemed more coherent than I had ever seen him.

"Yes," he replied with simple dignity.

Andrew took him by the arm and led him from the room.

As the door closed Deputy Gilbert emerged from behind the privacy screen. "I got it all," he said, indicating a small notebook in his hand. "Just bring him down when you get out of here and he can put his mark on the formal version."

"I always admired Jocelyn's commitment to her cousin," I stated absently, as much to myself as to the somber policeman getting ready to leave my room. "She loved him so much; dedicated her life to him. She sacrificed everything for him."

"From what you've told us and from what I just heard, sounds to me like she loved him too much. Somewhere along the line devotion crossed over into obsession. Forgive my bluntness, Miss Pendleton, but everybody in the Cove knows how you've befriended both Colliers; looks to me as if she felt threatened by you – knew she couldn't have him the way she wanted and was going to make sure no one else did either."

I started to object but he put up a hand to stop me. "Now, I know I'm a policeman with a policeman's naturally suspicious nature but don't write off what I say too quickly. She probably would have killed you the night your dog died – your statement says she mentioned the dog and said something about no one to help you 'this time.' She killed your dog, Miss Pendleton; made sure you were unprotected up at the Point. Her's were not impulsive acts."

He opened the door as he made his final observation but looked as if he had more to say. Before speaking again, however, he quietly closed the door to ensure our privacy.

"I've looked into Collier's history a bit; finally got their lawyer here in the States to talk to me. You remember the 'Celia' you said Miss Collier rambled on about as 'garbage'? Well, that's the name of the woman Jacob Collier supposedly killed back in England. This town's been treating him like a leper for years; looks as if the wrong Collier was being shunned."

CHAPTER THIRTEEN

I.

Andrew and I were married on July 1, 1917 – three months after Rachel disappeared and a short two weeks after I was released from the hospital.

It was a small, intimate ceremony performed by my father in front of the fireplace in our parlor. My mother played the piano, her performance impeded slightly by eyes brimming with tears. Mr. Carmichael stood up with Andrew and Grace Whitley served as my matron of honor. The only other people in attendance were Eli Thornton and Augusta Wilkes, Grace's infant son, Winston, Mr. Quigley, and, of course, Hannibal.

Rachel and I had always dreamed of big church weddings in which we would serve as one another's honor attendant; that obviously was not to be. But it was a lovely wedding nonetheless. The day was beautiful, warm and fragrant, so the windows were open and birdsong filled the air. Mother and Augusta had trimmed the parlor doorway with a garland of flowers and bouquets of fresh flowers adorned the room. The pocket doors leading to the adjoining dining room were open wide revealing more flowers and a bountiful refreshment table crowned at the center by a two-tiered cake lovingly made by Augusta, spread with lush white icing and decorated with yellow daisies and blue bachelor's buttons.

I wore my mother's wedding dress, an intricately embroidered white shirtwaist and matching skirt that failed to reach my ankles since I stood nearly four inches taller than she. Hemlines had risen since her wedding day so it actually took on a fashionable look in spite of the fact that it had yellowed slightly with the years. It was a lovely garment and I was proud to wear it. We had bought a length of delicately rendered floral lace to serve as a veil and had affixed it to a wreath of yellow daisies and blue bachelor buttons that encircled the modest chignon into which I had twisted my hair. Daisies and bachelor's buttons also made up the simple bouquet I held in front of me as I appraised my reflection in the cheval mirror in my room. The effect actually was quite pleasing and I had to smile in satisfaction as I prepared to descend to the parlor when Mother began playing Bach's "Jesu, Joy of Man's Desiring."

Andrew waited for me in front of the fireplace looking handsome in a brand new pinstriped suit. Not once did he succumb to the self-conscious gesture of pushing his glasses up his nose, and he smiled with such happiness throughout the ceremony that I knew I had made the right decision. He was leaving for New York the following morning and there was no way I could stay in Tully's Cove without him.

Without both of them, that is.

Jocelyn Collier had been buried without fanfare or benefit of clergy in a remote plot of ground at the farthest edge of the church cemetery. There was strong opposition to her being buried on church property at all and, although he never admitted it, I would always believe that it actually was my father who interceded on the side of clemency. Her cousin had left town the same day having never even tried to contact me during the few days between his return from New York and his final departure from Tully's Cove. Jocelyn had been buried, Patriot's Point put on the market, and Jacob Collier was gone.

I couldn't believe he hadn't come to see me. I had been devastated, and then angry, and then desperate; desperate that both of the men I cherished wouldn't vanish from my life with no resolution of the feelings churning within me.

And so I turned to Andrew. His relieved heart welcomed me, his arms consoled me, and his kisses helped erase the longing I felt for a man I would never understand and probably would never see again. If I was feeling at all ambivalent over my decision I attributed it to wedding day jitters, kept my eyes on Andrew, and assured myself that I had made the best possible decision.

When the ceremony was over our small gathering moved on to the dining room where we shared a delicious meal and afterward enjoyed several leisurely hours singing, laughing, and talking about the war. Although neither a festive nor particularly suitable conversational topic for the typical wedding party the war was, of course, central to the marriage that had just taken place and it was inevitable that it would come up. No one seemed to mind.

The spring of 1917 had been a particularly dismal period as the European Allies experienced defeat and disappointment on almost every front. Desperately optimistic Allied offensives in France at Arras, Aisne, and Champagne were bloody, futile battles resulting in nothing but further inflation of the Kaiser's bravado. Germany truly seemed virtually indestructible as she easily repulsed all attacks; the loss of life and the carnage precipitating it being among the worst of the entire war. Decimated and demoralized – and clinging to the feeble hope that America could turn the tide – the Allies dug in and waited for U.S. troops.

Andrew's hopes of covering the initial departure of troops to Europe were dashed by what had happened to me. He chose to stay in Tully's Cove until I recovered and until we could be married. The "Teddies," as U.S. soldiers were called before the term "Yanks" became the norm, couldn't wait for him and, on July 4, 1917, advance troops of General Pershing's Allied Expeditionary Force paraded through Paris to ecstatic cheers. That same day Charles E. Stanton, an aide to Pershing, stood at the tomb of the Marquis de Lafayette – the French hero of our Revolutionary War – and gave war-weary France new hope when he boldly declared, "Lafayette, we are here!"

We might finally have been there, but we were hardly more than a shadow of what it would take to actually bring the Kaiser down.

When war was declared, the country was anything but prepared for the commitment of men and supplies it would take to effectively thwart the aggressions of the Central Powers. At the time of Congress's April 6 declaration, United States armed forces totaled a meager 378,000 men. Within a few weeks of our wedding, Secretary of War Newton D. Baker drew a lottery number from a large glass bowl and initiated the drafting of troops. Facing the daunting task of building and training a citizen army, Selective Service began conscripting men from age 21 through 30 and would eventually register those from 18 to 45 years of age. Almost 4,000,000 men were categorized in Class I and subject to the draft, but until the establishment of military convoys the movement of troops to Europe would be slow.

But on July 1, while the soldiers' fate was still in limbo, ours was being defined by the small festive group gathered in my parents' home, trying so valiantly to make our wedding day truly a celebration in spite of the painful shadow of loss and the bleak uncertainty of war.

Eventually it became time to leave. The guests had departed, except for Eli and Augusta who lingered under the pretense of helping to clean up but whose presence in reality was intended to lend continuing support to my grieving parents. Our offers of assistance were politely refused, and they all gathered at the front door to see us off with handshakes and hugs, wishes for happiness, and admonishments to write. Mother and I both succumbed to tears and when my father hugged me it was then that I realized for the first time that his sense of loss extended itself to me as well as to Rachel. His little girls had left him and there was so much left unsaid.

Andrew had surrendered his room at the boarding house he had called home for the past six years and, in celebration of our marriage, reserved a two room suite at the nicer of the two hotels in town. I had balked slightly at the expense but he said he wanted something special for our last night in Tully's Cove and our first night together as husband and wife. My pre-wedding butterflies had grown into hummingbirds at the thought of that first night together and continued to increase in wingspan as anticipation became reality.

Andrew and I were married.

My feelings for Andrew ran deep and true; I loved and respected him. I entered into marriage with confidence that we would make a success of it and enjoy many happy years together. But I also knew that what I felt for Andrew was different from the intensity of emotion I experienced around Jacob Collier. That emotion could only be what the novellas of the day delicately described as "passion" and characterized as virtually sinful and almost always self-destructive. Although not one to be overly influenced by fictional renderings, I had three true-life examples of passion's self-destructive nature that graphically supported the generalization – Grace Whitley, my own sister, and, most dramatically, Jocelyn Collier – so concluded that a marriage built around mutual respect and companionship was undoubtedly on more firm a foundation.

And anyway, Jacob Collier had left me; I knew Andrew never would.

II.

I awoke first the morning after our wedding. I lay still, wrapped in the comfortable grey of daybreak, watching Andrew sleep. He was nestled into the pillow beside my head, his ginger-colored hair disheveled, breaths coming in even rhythmic waves. I watched him for quite some time; a smile on my lips, the memory of our rather self-conscious love making fresh in my mind, and contentment welling up around me. Everything was going to be all right. I had done the right thing.

I slipped out of bed without waking him, washing and dressing in the semi-dark. It was two hours yet before we needed to be at the station, but I couldn't sleep any longer.

"Good morning, Mrs. Carlton," came a sleepy voice from behind me. "Have I overslept or are you just a little ahead of schedule this morning?"

I turned with a smile for the sweet, charming man in my bed.

"No man could ask for a more pleasant sight in the morning," he said in response to my smile. "Don't ever change your routine, Martha; always greet me with a smile."

"For someone who doesn't fancy himself very romantic," I teased, "you're doing a pretty good job."

"Must be love," he replied with a yawn, unfolding his lengthy frame as he climbed out of bed.

He came and stood behind me, folding his arms across me and drawing me to him so that we stood together looking out the window where I had been watching the first signs of life in the streets below.

"I do love you, Martha, and I'll do my very best to make you happy."

"I'm happy already, Andrew. I was just standing here feeling very blessed and very content. You've done so much for me; given me courage, strength, opportunity – and now even love. Being with you seems as natural as breathing and just as essential."

"Thank you, Marty," he whispered, using for the first time what would become his favorite pet name for me.

In a remarkably short time Andrew was washed, clean shaven and ready to go. I sat adjacent him while he shaved, both awestruck and mildly horrified by the interplay between razor and skin, realizing anew that very little of the time we had previously spent alone together could be even remotely classified as "intimate" and now we suddenly were privy to the most personal aspects of one another's life. Although being with Andrew felt very natural, there was a residual sense of embarrassment that I imagined would be with us both for quite some time to come.

Neither of us was particularly outgoing. There was always a certain degree of hesitation in our dealings with others. Andrew was far more focused than I – and downright assertive when it came to his work – but he approached interpersonal relationships with caution and more than a small dose of skepticism. It surprised me that it seemed so easy for him to make room for me in his small, decidedly masculine world. But then, it probably surprised him that the transition seemed so easy for me. I freely admit I had been a little surprised myself.

We went downstairs to the dining room, leaving word with the desk clerk that our bags were ready to be taken over to the station. We could easily have taken them ourselves but, once again, Andrew was insistent upon "sparing no expense" before resigning ourselves to the unavoidably austere lifestyle awaiting us in New York.

The dining room was virtually empty and we enjoyed a leisurely breakfast of ham and eggs, lingering over strong black coffee and speculating about the times that lay ahead. Andrew held my hand as we spoke, but the romantic gentlemen with whom I had shared my bed had been supplanted by the doggedly determined newspaperman.

"I can't wait to get there," he confessed. "There's so much that needs to be done; so much to be reported. And I can hardly believe we're going to see it all together. We'll make a great team, Marty, mark my words."

I smiled, realizing just how good it felt to do so. I was happy, and although my happiness was edged with sorrow –

for Rachel, for my parents, for Bo, and for Jacob – I no longer felt guilty about coming through the past months largely unscathed. I definitely was changed as a result of all that had happened – and still had bad dreams in which I was being pursued through wind-whipped trees that took on the exaggerated features of both my father and Jocelyn while the ground beneath my feet turned to sludge – but I had survived. In spite of everything – my parents' disapproval, Rachel's disappearance, Bo's death, Jocelyn's assault, and even Jacob's abrupt departure – in spite of it all I had recovered my sense of equilibrium and discovered in the process just how good it feels to stand on your own two feet. And in no small measure I had Andrew to thank for both my recovery and my discovery – my "emergence" as he referred to it, loathe to take any credit and likening it to a butterfly's emergence from a cocoon.

Mentor rather than Svengali, Andrew had made me admit my desires and ambitions while simultaneously helping me develop the skills I needed in order to make them a reality. And even though that "emergence" had become a "convergence" that led us to the altar, in no way did I feel I had surrendered any measure of my new found self-sufficiency for Andrew valued the person I had become; he wanted an equal, a partner, not a subordinate.

Arm in arm we walked from the hotel to the train station, taking a final look at Tully's Cove as we went. Our hearts would always be strongly connected to this small but complex community. For Andrew Tully's Cove was a cluttered desk, a printing press with a mind of its own, and a free-thinking, elfin man who was as much father as employer. For me it was a house at the crest of Church Street, a dilapidated gazebo in the woods, and a small grave under my favorite tree.

III.

    I had never been to New York City prior to moving there with Andrew, and the enlightenment offered by almost everyone in Tully's Cove who had ever had dealings there did little to prepare me for my inaugural visit. Quite frankly, I thought their descriptions and rambling pieces of advice had to be nothing short of colorful hyperbole; no city could be that grand, imposing, and labyrinthine. But as the train carrying us to our new home approached the city and periodic small towns and expanses of open terrain began to give way to a steadily growing number of increasingly tall buildings I found myself forced to reassess that original conclusion. By the time we began to slow for our approach into Grand Central Terminal I almost literally was hanging out of the window in order to gain a better vantage point, looking unapologetically like the small town hick I definitely was – agog at the drama of the city that was unfolding before me. As the train pulled into Grand Central I found myself perched precariously somewhere between transfixed and terrified.

    The terminal itself did nothing to help ground me, in truth I never had seen anything like it; and the mass of humanity clogging its arteries of arrivals and departures had me looking about in wide-eyed amazement, clutching my suitcase in a white-knuckled grasp and holding onto Andrew's hand with the other as we stepped down from the train.

    "Steady on, old girl," he said cheerfully, even while wincing a bit from the force of my grip. "You haven't seen anything yet!"

    We walked slowly along the platform that ran parallel to the train, merging into the ebb and flow of a seemingly endless stream of travelers. The human torrent coursed steadily in the direction of the main terminal up a gradually inclined passageway that made the long walk much less taxing than it might otherwise have been. As we moved along I was struck not only by the beautiful architectural details that surrounded me but also by the brilliant light that flooded virtually every corner of the immense structure. Built by the Vanderbilt family – America's preeminent railroad tycoons – Grand Central Terminal was a 70-acre compound comprised of 32 miles of track servicing 30 passenger platforms. But not only was the terminal the largest construction project in New York City's history, it also was one of the world's first all-electric buildings; everywhere one looked were chandeliers and light fixtures boasting exposed incandescent light bulbs. Giving into curiosity, I started counting bulbs as we walked but gave up the quest after reaching fifty-seven and growing concerned that I might not be able to blink away the ghostly glare that haunted my field of vision even after looking away from the glowing orbs. The thought of all that electricity crackling away in the walls brought Augusta Wilkes to mind – she was convinced that bringing electricity into a building was flirting with fire and death and surely would have run away in terror had she found herself marooned in the bowels of Grand Central as we now were.

Thoughts of Augusta led to thoughts of home; I clutched Andrew's hand even tighter as we walked.

When we emerged from the passageway the crowd dissipated a bit and we entered a room – although the word surely didn't do it justice – that was larger than any I ever would have imagined. Grand Central Terminal's main concourse stretched before us, a colossus of marble, metal, and glass measuring 275 feet long, 120 feet wide, and 125 feet tall. About fifty feet to our left was a length of ticket windows, at the end of which stood a dramatic double marble staircase leading up to street level. The expansive exit doorways along the wide walkway above the staircase – a dramatic statement of metal and glass themselves – were complimented by huge 75 foot high arched windows that graced the wall above them and showered the milling throngs with natural light.

We stepped off to one side in order to get our bearings and, while Andrew consulted a small guidebook he had purchased back in Tully's Cove, I looked about in awe; pure, dumbstruck awe.

"Wait here," Andrew said at last, sliding his suitcase tightly next to mine and indicating that I should sit atop both. "I want to check something out at the information booth." He gestured toward the center of the concourse where a circular kiosk stood, a small marble oasis for the disoriented traveler. Ever true to the opulent details that seemed to define the terminal, the booth was crowned by a magnificent four-sided brass clock whose internally-lit milk glass faces shone in opalescent splendor as their hands crept inexorably around the confines of their circular world.

I watched Andrew melt into the crowd and suddenly felt incredibly tired. It was warm and humid in the terminal despite the high ceilings and it felt good to rest for a moment atop the suitcases and fan myself with a lace-trimmed hanky.

Lifting the hair off my neck in order to fan myself to better effect, my eyes were drawn upward. I stopped short, hanky hanging limply in mid-air. I had been so enthralled by the crowds and the marble magnificence of the beautiful Beaux Arts building that one of its most glorious features had almost escaped me. The massive ceiling arching above the main concourse was a glory of cerulean blue adorned by more than two thousand effulgent gold leaf stars depicting the signs of the zodiac. It was dazzling and I couldn't take my eyes off it.

Andrew returned a moment later, looking very satisfied with himself.

"Have you seen the ceiling," I asked incredulously, gesturing toward the faux night sky. "I know you said this was no ordinary train station but I never would have believed you if you had tried to describe all this."

"It is amazing, isn't it," he replied, offering me his hand. "But come on, there's something else I want you to see."

We gathered up our belongings and once again joined the minimally organized chaos around us. But instead of heading toward the staircase leading to the street, Andrew altered our course and led me once again into the belly of the beast.

"Where are we going," I asked somewhat plaintively, feeling tired and increasingly hungry. If we weren't going to leave I wanted to just sit and drink in the ambiance a bit longer. "I'm hungry, Andrew. Can't we just get something to eat from one of the vendors outside and head for the apartment?"

"We are going to get something to eat," he assured me, "just not from a street vendor."

With our baggage and me firmly in tow, Andrew wove his way confidently through the crowds finally stopping in front of an expansive subterranean dining area defined by a succession of arches and vaulted ceilings covered in beautiful terracotta tile.

"Welcome to Grand Central Terminal's Oyster Bar," he announced triumphantly. "Let's eat!"

Nestled between the arches were long café bars in front of which stood swivel stools to facilitate the quick arrival and departure of patrons and behind which cooks labored efficiently over grills and stoves that filled the air with a delicious cacophony of smell. Andrew's eagle eye caught sight of three customers just leaving near the curved end of the bar and we quickly sidled up and took their place.

"What'll it be," a rather dour-looking waitress asked, handing Andrew a menu and tucking a stray stand of graying hair behind her ear.

"I'd like an order of raw oysters," Andrew said without hesitation, smiling in my direction upon noticing a look of chagrin. "But nothing raw for my wife, I'm afraid."

"That's for sure," I replied, quickly scanning the menu. "I think I'd like to try your oyster stew – is it any good?"

"Lady," the waitress smirked, "that's what we're famous for." She snatched up the menu and turned away, shaking her head in undisguised dismay at the ignorance of tourists.

She may have been rude but she also was right. The oyster stew was very good and I savored every spoonful, taking in the amazing variety of passersby while trying to avoid watching Andrew contentedly slurp his slimy-looking treat.

The constant presence of people milling about waiting to be seated definitely dissuaded one from lingering over their meal and so, once fortified, we hastily paid our tab, gathered our belongings, and surrendered our place at the bar to two men crowding in behind us. Obviously in a hurry, they barely gave us time to rise to our feet before swiveling the backrests in their direction and sliding onto the stools we were vacating, the one nearest me stepping on the hem of my skirt in his haste and causing me to stumble awkwardly. I tossed a scowl in his direction – which he missed entirely – and silently wished him luck with the curt waitress I anticipated would put him in his place.

In the seconds it had taken to stumble and scowl, Andrew was swallowed by the crowd and I found myself suddenly alone. Upon our arrival he had stressed that if we ever got separated we should head for the nearest main entrance so, fighting down a moment of panic, I decided to move toward the large arched entryway figuring Andrew also would head in that direction. Having nothing but a few pennies in my pocket I freely admit to feeling more than a little bit lost as I took up residence as close as possible to the entryway arch.

"Well, come on Marty, let's get going."

Andrew's voice was suddenly in my ear but when I swirled around in relief to greet him he was nowhere to be seen.

"What are you waiting for?"

I could hear him clearly but still he was nowhere in sight.

Looking about in utter bewilderment I finally caught sight of his tall, gangly frame at the opposite end of the long archway. He was smiling broadly and waving his arm in a sweeping arc in order to catch my eye.

"Wait right there, I'll be over in a second."

In spite of all the people between us I could hear him quite plainly and stood rooted to the spot totally perplexed.

"How did you do that," I demanded when he was again at my side.

"It's called the 'whispering gallery,'" he explained, gesturing to the long archway above us. "I read about it in the guidebook and wanted to check it out."

"Well, it certainly works –"

I stopped in mid-sentence as realization struck. "Hey," I accused, punching his shoulder. "You had this planned all along, didn't you? You intentionally abandoned me just to check out some architectural anomaly!"

He smiled sheepishly. "Sorry about that. But honestly, I never lost sight of you the entire time."

"But you almost scared the life out of me; being lost in New York is definitely not on my list of things I'd like to do."

Andrew took my hand in his and raised it to his lips. "I will never lose you, Martha; never."

It was one of those rare, perfectly romantic moments – regardless of the fact that it was taking place in the midst of countless strangers. I felt a ripple of chills dance down my spine and my cheeks heated in an uncharacteristic blush.

Andrew kept my hand in his and once again we made our way up one of the sloping walkways leading to the main concourse, finally leaving the terminal by way of the 42nd street exit.

Looking back as we walked away I once again stopped short. "This place just doesn't cease to amaze..."

Shielding my eyes from the searing July sun with my free hand, I looked up at the entrance façade behind us. Arching dramatically above the engraved stone announcing one's arrival at Grand Central Terminal were intricate sculptures of Minerva, Hercules, and Mercury. Hercules and Minerva sat on either side of a huge Tiffany glass clock while Mercury stood at its crest with arms outstretched toward the city. The sculptural group was stunning and, according to Andrew's guidebook, the largest in the world, measuring 48 feet high.

"I really thought people back in Tully's Cove were exaggerating when they described New York," I admitted, "but this place defies exaggeration!"

Andrew smiled somewhat stoically. "I have no doubt that the city will give us a wake-up call somewhere along the way but have to agree that it is pretty darned amazing." He gave my hand a little shake. "Are you ready to go home?"

Home.

Somehow I doubted whether I would feel like calling New York home for quite some time to come.

IV.

During World War I, New York City was a constant pageant of men and women in uniform as well as flags, banners, and parades of all descriptions. In point of fact, as well as being awed by Grand Central Terminal, our introduction to the city was further enhanced that day by a loud and enthusiastic "Liberty Loan" parade down Fifth Avenue.

President Wilson's Secretary of the Treasury, William McAdoo, believed that rather than following the usual procedure of issuing bonds to banks for subsequent resale to the public, the best "war chest" fund-raising strategy would be to market Liberty Loan bonds directly to the people without using the banks as go-betweens. Skeptics predicted complete failure of such an unorthodox approach but McAdoo persisted. As a result, Liberty Loan parades and rallies were held in virtually every corner of the nation and inspirational bond posters were as commonplace as other patriotic handbills. In larger cities, celebrities such as Mary Pickford, Douglas Fairbanks, Charlie Chaplin, and Irene Castle hawked Liberty Bonds to cheering crowds – and the majority of Americans bought them. The fact that the total sale of Liberty Loan bonds was only $3 billion less than the total cost of the war was proof that McAdoo definitely had the right idea and effectively silenced his detractors.

It hadn't been our intention to attend a parade – especially under the increasingly daunting sun of a July afternoon. Because of the heat we had decided to spend a little more of our precious store of cash to ride a streetcar at least some of the distance from the terminal to our final destination. As it trundled along we could hear a marching band nearby, and all around us people were hurriedly moving in that direction. The excitement was contagious and, when the streetcar lurched to a stop, we couldn't resist and soon found ourselves following, like the rats of Hamlin behind the Pied Piper.

With suitcases in tow, Andrew and I stood among literally thousands of onlookers as a parade of several hundred uniformed men and women marched enthusiastically down Fifth Avenue. The well-staged pageant moved slowly behind an open car from which none other than Charlie Chaplin and Douglas Fairbanks waved and called to the awestruck crowd. I stood in wide-eyed wonder as the film stars passed and nearly dropped one of the suitcases I carried when struck by the childish reflex to wave back as if they focused solely on me.

In addition to banners sporting inspirational bond-oriented slogans each group marching in support of the Liberty Loan campaign was identified by the signs and banners they carried; everything from groups of soldiers awaiting transport to Europe and the civilian-based Army Transport Service to the National American Woman Suffrage Association and an intriguing group of female clerical workers behind a banner which read "We are helping win the war with our rapid fire typewriting machines."

All around me people jostled one another as they competed for the best vantage point. I was enthralled and believe an uncharacteristic giggle may actually have escaped my delighted lips. The crowds here eclipsed even those enclosed by Grand Central Terminal. The city itself – with its countless buildings, humbling "skyscrapers," glorious Statue of Liberty, and tremendous number of automobiles – was enough to instill a healthy dose of awe and even a little fear but it was the number and variety of *people* that would always intrigue, delight, and inspire me.

As the last of the parade passed us we joined the throng of onlookers as they flowed in behind the participants and surged up the street toward a raised stage where the parade became a sales rally. For several minutes we moved helplessly along with the ebb and flow of the crowd, finally coming to a stop about a city block east of the stage. The wide avenue was literally packed with people. It was a hot day and standing cheek by jowl with such a great number meant that the smell of perspiration permeated the air and was made increasingly unpleasant by the cloying sweetness of perfume and hair tonic that also wafted upward from the onlookers. The dampness under my arms and the trickle of sweat down my back told me that I soon would be contributing to the crowd's malodorousness – if I wasn't already.

We wormed our way over to the curbing which distinguished the pedestrian walkway from the street,

Andrew placing the sturdiest of our suitcases flat on the sidewalk for me to stand on. From that slightly elevated vantage point I could look up the street across a seemingly endless ocean of felt hats and make out Mr. Chaplin and Mr. Fairbanks among the dignitaries on the stage. Mr. Chaplin was delighting the crowd with exaggerated comic antics as he portrayed an inept Kaiser Wilhelm "boxing" with Mr. Fairbanks, the latter of whose oversized boxing gloves were labeled "Victory" and "Liberty Bonds." After landing an overwhelmingly powerful "punch" on Mr. Chaplin's jaw, and the "Kaiser" subsequently going down for the count, Mr. Fairbanks took center stage and, exchanging boxing gloves for a megaphone, addressed the cheering throng.

"Ladies and gentlemen," he began, trying to quiet the delighted mayhem before him and helping Mr. Chaplin to his feet. "Ladies and gentlemen, Charlie and I are happy to be with you today and privileged to speak to you on behalf of the first national Liberty Loan Bond Campaign."

He put his arm around the shoulders of his colleague as they waited for the crowd to quiet. "You know, we make beating the Hun look awfully easy," he continued, playfully landing a punch on Chaplin's jaw. "But there's a lot more to it than that. This war is just as much our fight as the fellas' overseas so we've all got to pitch in and do our share! You and I have got to provide the supplies needed by the AEF and our allies. We've got to provide the uniforms, food, bandages, and medical supplies as well as the ships, planes, guns and ammunition needed to fight this war. Let's face facts, folks, it's going to take a lot of effort on all our parts if we're going to defeat the Central Powers and, as President Wilson says, 'make the world safe for democracy.'"

The crowd erupted into applause and cheers of agreement, and Mr. Fairbanks once again had to wait for the excitement to subside.

"In summary folks, those of us who can't go and fight have an equally important role to play in the righteous struggle before us. We must all do our part. So, if you can't fight, BUY LIBERTY BONDS! Our doughboys' lives depend on it – they're depending on us!"

Once again the crowd erupted into jubilant cheers and applause.

"Are you with me," he screamed through the megaphone, trying to be heard over the roar.

Thunderous applause swelled in response.

Taking their cue from Mr. Fairbanks, the band ensconced behind the dignitaries struck up a medley of patriotic tunes while a line of young women wearing Liberty Bond placards paraded across the stage and down into the crowd where they began distributing handbills describing the Liberty Loan campaign. As the women wove in and out of the throng I strained to read as many of their placards as I could and caught sight of several –

"*Every Liberty Bond is a shot at a U-boat – fire your shot today!*"

"*If you can't enlist – INVEST!*"

"*Beat back the Hun with Liberty Bonds!*"

Taking my arm to steady me as I stepped off the suitcase, Andrew shouted in my ear and pointed toward a streetcar about half a block away. "Come on; let's get out of here while we still can. Those cars are going to be packed in a few minutes."

We gathered up our suitcases and threaded our way through the crowd whose cheering was just beginning to subside and whose participants soon would be unfortunate castaways awash in the melee of a dispersing throng.

After ascertaining that the streetcar would, indeed, take us in the desired direction, we clambered aboard and took seats as close to the open door as we could get. Winning a brief and heated battled with the stubborn window next to him, Andrew managed to push the resistant frame most of the way down and, once settled, we allowed ourselves the luxury of loosening our collars and fanning ourselves with the Liberty Loan handbills that had been thrust into my hand as we made our escape.

We were hot, we were tired, but we were all smiles for we were having a wonderful time. Now all we had to do was find our way "home" through the crush and heat of midsummer in New York City.

Because of his long-term friendship with Mr. Carmichael, Andrew's new employer – Medford Potter – seemed to be taking special interest in him and had even gone so far as to put us in contact with an acquaintance of his who owned a brownstone and rented out the upper flat. Mr. Potter knew the apartment to be vacant because our new landlord was a German immigrant by the name of Franz Reichert who had confided in him that the flat had become suddenly undesirable because of the last name of its owner.

Mr. Potter had minced no words in his letter to Andrew conveying information about the flat. "I suppose there are bound to be jackasses who overreact and begin questioning everyone and everything of German extraction," he had written. "You can take my word for it that this family is as American as you and I – as American as any of us since, somewhere along our family tree, we all came from somewhere else! The Reicherts have worked like dogs ever since coming to this country and have earned the prosperity they're beginning to enjoy. If you have any objection to sharing their roof I'm afraid you're on your own to find something else and you should probably also find somewhere else more to your liking at which to work."

Andrew and I had neither reason nor right to question Mr. Reichert's loyalty to his new country and were thoroughly delighted to have our housing situation so easily reconciled, especially at the reduced rent he offered us. Andrew subsequently had contacted both gentlemen, reassuring the first and making arrangements with the second for us to take over the furnished apartment as soon as we arrived in New York.

The streetcar lumbered to a stop about three blocks from our new home. The ride hadn't brought much respite from what was proving itself to be a brutally hot July day and our enthusiasm was beginning to wane somewhat as the prospect of walking three more blocks carrying heavy suitcases loomed before us. My swollen feet told me in no uncertain terms that the last thing they wanted to do at the point was to take one more step while still within the confines of my uncompromisingly narrow dress shoes. Both of us were more than just a little damp around the edges, but Andrew still had a ready smile and gave me an encouraging wink as we mustered our determination and began the last leg of our journey "home."

About half a block west from the streetcar stop, we turned left and stood looking down a narrow residential street lined on both sides with virtually identical two and three story brick buildings. Facing the street like squat, angry sentinels, they either shared a common wall or had nothing more than a miniscule alleyway between them. Above us, opposing sides of the narrow street were drawn together at regular intervals by large curbside shade trees that created a leafy canopy overhead; in addition to providing welcome shade, they gave the long vista an almost tunnel-like feeling and broke the monotony of brick and stone. This was only one of hundreds of such streets in the city as identical layouts ran for blocks both east and west of the main streetcar route we had just traversed. We knew our final destination to be at least two and a half blocks farther west so after fortifying our resolve with a few moments rest in the shade of an obligingly nearby tree we forged ahead.

As we walked I was struck by the sameness of the buildings, one after another after another. The effect was claustrophobic but I tried to attribute the feeling to the stillness of the air and the heavy, humid heat. This was our new home and I was trying to remain optimistic but there was no denying that identical architectural designs, identical construction materials, and identical finish work had successfully robbed the brownstones of personality and created a sense of drabness that was almost as cloying as the hot and humid summer day. For someone raised in small towns where open spaces were the norm and no two houses were the same this was at best a curiosity and at worst a significant disappointment.

Because of the heat there were a lot of people out and about; sitting on the ubiquitous wide concrete steps leading upward to each brownstone's front door and even perched on windowsills in an effort to catch even a whisper of breeze. They all looked like week-old cut flowers; wilted, sad, and forlorn – hopefully an effect of the hot summer day and not the result of a contagion born of the cloying drabness of their environment. If such was the case I hoped my small town upbringing would prove sufficient inoculation.

The only thing that broke the spell of monotonous sameness and gave a semblance of personality to the neighborhoods through which we walked were the blends of sound and smell unique to the ethnic group dominating a particular area. Windows and doors were open wide and conversation as well as the smells of cooking wafted out onto the still summer air. I heard what I was sure must be Italian when we first turned into this residential area and smelled wonderful spiciness that made my mouth water. As we progressed, more English was being spoken but rich accents abounded and more interesting food smells I couldn't identify. In this brick and stone wasteland the senses of sound and smell might well be more reliable than that of sight when it came to finding one's way around. Most residents probably could find their way home blindfolded merely by following their ears and nose.

At last we came to our brownstone. Like its brothers, it was tall and narrow with the main entrance at the top of a brief flight of wide concrete steps framed by a broad, concrete railing that curved inward and upward in accommodation of the progressively shorter, higher steps. It was quite well-kept, like most of the other buildings and, in an obvious attempt to distinguish their home from those of their neighbors, there were flower boxes at all of the lower level windows and a small American flag suspended from an angled pole attached to the molding around the front door, drooping listlessly in the breathless July afternoon.

"This is it," Andrew said with no small measure of relief in his voice, looking up and down the street assessing the adults and children present – our new neighbors – who were likewise assessing us.

A young girl in her early teens sitting resolutely at the top of the steps stood as soon as we stopped and in a moment was trotting down the steps with outstretched hand.

"Hello," she chirped in a cheerful, businesslike voice. "Are you Mr. and Mrs. Carlton?"

Andrew and I smiled at each other.

"Yes, we are," he responded, taking her outstretched hand and shaking it firmly.

"Oh, wonderful," she exclaimed, the businesslike manner eroded by childish enthusiasm and rapid-fire chatter. "My mama told me to watch for you. I've been waiting for you for days! My mama said to bring you in just as soon as you got here. Papa and Grandpa are at the store right now but then they usually are. You'll meet them later. Oh, she'll be so pleased that you've finally arrived."

She paused hardly long enough to take a breath. "May I take one of your bags?"

Without waiting for a response she took the suitcase I willingly surrendered and continued chattering as we climbed the steps.

"Did you have a good trip? I think traveling by train is just the most wonderful thing. Isn't it terribly hot today? I think there's still some ice in the icebox so we can offer you a cool drink if you'd like. I hope you're going to be happy here. Is this your first time in the City? You're from Maine, right? I've never been out of the City myself. You're going to work for Mr. Potter's newspaper, isn't that right Mr. Carlton? I think that must just be the most exciting work there is in the entire world..."

She made me think of Rachel.

"Mama! They're here!"

She was leading us through the main entrance into a small vestibule area. Directly in front of us were two identical doors. The one on the left, being opened by our as yet unidentified hostess, led into the lower level apartment, the one on the right would presumably reveal stairs leading to the flat above.

There was no interior entryway and we found ourselves in the Reichert's sitting room. It was a high-ceilinged room with two large windows facing the street and a large fireplace dominating the opposite wall. The shades were drawn against the unrelenting summer heat and it was much cooler than the sun-baked concrete world outside. We took our hostess's lead and set our suitcases down and awaited the lady of the house.

The furniture was rather spartan and severe but the room was lovingly decorated and definitely reflected the family's rising economic status. The formal part of the sitting room was delineated by a thick rug in front of the fireplace flanked by a pair of matching overstuffed horsehair chairs and an elaborately curved, and equally uncomfortable looking, Victorian settee. There was a modest open archway to the left of the fireplace leading to a dining room and, presumably, a kitchen and perhaps other rooms beyond. From our correspondence we knew that the family's bedrooms were on the upper floor adjacent our flat, so there must also be an interior stairway somewhere beyond the two rooms we could see from the front door.

We didn't have long to wait for in almost immediate response to our guide's announcement of our arrival a large, matronly woman emerged from the back of the house followed by a much older, frail and birdlike woman leaning heavily on a walking stick.

Mrs. Reichert came forward, wiping her flour-covered hands on the enormous apron covering her ample bosom and cascading down the front of her skirt from her equally ample waistline.

"Oh, it is vunderful, you are at last here."

She spoke in a velvety, heavily-accented voice, turning to the older woman at her side and speaking quickly and quietly in German.

"You vill come and please sit down?"

She was indicating the uncomfortable looking Victorian settee – undoubtedly a place of honor – upon which we dutifully sat, its uncompromising cushions giving not an inch in response to the weight of our bodies.

"I am the mama," she explained, gesturing forward and then clasping her hands together and resting them above her bosom. "This is the greatmother," she continued, indicating the elderly woman who had seated herself in one of the horsehair chairs. "And Gerta you have met already."

Our guide, now identified as Gerta, spoke quickly as if slightly embarrassed. "'Grandmother,' mama, not 'greatmother.'" She directed her attention to us. "Mama's English is not what it might be. And my grandmother doesn't speak much English at all."

Gerta spoke with hardly a trace of an accent. Her voice was apologetic and I had the impression that she was at least mildly ashamed of her parents' first-generation immigrant status.

"We're happy to meet you, Mrs. Reichert," Andrew replied, ignoring Gerta's contribution to the conversation. "I'm Andrew Carlton and this is my wife, Martha."

"Ah, Mar-ta," she said, missing the "h" completely and smiling broadly at me. "Und you are married just, ist that correct?"

"Yes, ma'am," I replied, my face coloring in spite of my effort to sound and feel matter-of-fact.

Again the clasped hands rested above her bosom. "This ist vunderbar. We are so happy for you und vish you much blessings and long life together!"

She turned to the elder Mrs. Reichert and spoke again in German, presumably reminding the older woman of our newly rendered marital status. The elderly woman looked across at us with watery blue eyes, nodding and smiling her connubial benediction.

As we would learn over the days and weeks ahead, the Reicherts were a robust and enthusiastic family; the perfect embodiment of the Immigrant-American and the so-called American Dream. Mr. Reichert, lanky, fair-haired, and ruddy-complexioned was a quiet, determined, hard-working man who rarely spoke unless spoken to and whose intensity reminded me of my father. As a result I was, at time, intimidated by him. He and his father had worked tirelessly while in Germany, scrimping and saving in order to put aside enough money to transport their large family to the United States. Once here they shifted that determination to the establishment of their own general mercantile store and worked endless hours to make it a success and move the family from extremely modest accommodations in a less desirable part of the city to the comparative luxury of the more modern brownstone they now called home. Neither gentleman would say much about the process or their success but one could see the results in the lives of the family each man obviously cherished more than his own life.

Mrs. Reichert was both the physical and psychological opposite of her spouse, small of stature and rotund of form she was as gregarious as he was withdrawn. She loved to tell about the family's struggle to come to America and the hard work that was making them a success in their adopted homeland. I enjoyed listening to her vivid depiction of their family saga but often found myself lost in her rapid, heavily-accented speech and had to rely on one of the children for a translation. Mrs. Reichert also was something of a busybody, inclined to mother her tenants with the same lively devotion she gave her eight children and the elderly in-laws who lived with them. She insisted upon being called either "Mama" or by her Christian name, Katrina; both Andrew and I opted for her first name but as our relationship deepened there were times when I slipped into the comfortable familiarity of my own "Mama Katrina" hybrid.

Only three of the Reichert's eight children lived with them. A few weeks earlier, in the throes of patriotic fervor, two of the older boys, Otto and Manfred, had enlisted and were now at army camps in New Jersey awaiting transport to Europe. Anna, the oldest daughter, was married and would soon present Katrina and Franz with their first grandchild. Their own firstborn, a son named after his father, was also married and worked alongside his father and grandfather in the family's market. Three school-aged children remained at home, Gerta, whom we had met, and Libby and Freeman, twins named in tribute to the "liberty" and "freedom" found in America, who had been born two short months after the family's arrival in New York in 1907.

For quite some time after our introduction, one Reichert offspring was quietly unmentioned and unaccounted for. Franz Reichert's natural inclination toward introspection was intensified, I feel, by what we later discovered to be the family's personal tragedy. The Reichert's second oldest child, a son named Karl, was no longer a resident of the United States; a fact dramatically illustrating President Wilson's fear that U.S. involvement overseas would tear at the nation's multi-ethnic heart. Soon after war in Europe began, in 1915 while the U.S. was still pledged to neutrality, Karl had responded to compelling ties to his motherland and returned to Germany to serve the Kaiser. Now, three years later, the United States and Germany were at war and Karl's lot was cast on the wrong side. Even if he had wanted to – and no one could know which way his political convictions now leaned – there was no switching sides. As a result, the Reichert's faced the frightening reality that, in answering this nation's call to patriotic duty, their two sons serving with the Allies might actually encounter their older brother on the opposite side of the battlefield!

V.

Our "furnished" apartment turned out to be very sparsely furnished indeed – and very small. The entire flat was squeezed into the area directly above the Reichert's large sitting room on the ground floor. The stairs leading up from the building's main entryway led to a small landing and a narrow hallway to the left. There were two doors off the hallway, one on either side but not directly opposite each other. On the right hand side, near the landing, a large pair of pocket doors opened into a small parlor directly above the back half of its counterpart below. There was a worn settee in front of the fireplace, a single upholstered straight-backed chair, and a waist-high gate leg table with an oil lamp in the center. At the back of the room was a doorway leading to a small kitchen with all the amenities – a tiny icebox, a kerosene cook stove, a sink with running water via an antiquated-looking pump, two rows of empty shelves above the sink, and a round table and three chairs tucked into a barely accessible corner. Behind the kitchen lay the Reichert's bedrooms and a door opposite the table and chairs, at the other end of the small room, led to a common hallway and stairs leading down to the main level and a back door which opened onto a tiny back yard and the privy we all shared.

On the left hand side of the apartment's hallway, above the front half of the Reichert's sitting room, was the bedroom. Again, only the essential furniture was provided; a bed, a chiffonier, a table and oil lamp, and a straight-backed chair, the mate of the three in the kitchen. Two windows looked out over the street below but did little to either brighten the room or alleviate the stifling summer heat.

In hopes that a breeze might snake its way through the apartment and bring us some relief from the heat, we soon began leaving that back hallway door opened as well as the parlor's double doors and the bedroom door down the hall. Unfortunately, the only thing that consistently "snaked" its way around was a persistently curious neighborhood cat and, one time, a scrawny – and extremely agitated – squirrel I momentarily mistook for a rat.

The apartment was the tangible manifestation of the austerity we realized our tenuous economic status necessitated but it was spotlessly clean and Mrs. Reichert had done her best to make it homey; there were flowers in the parlor, a colorful quilted coverlet on the bed, and fresh-baked bread on the kitchen table.

We were home.

CHAPTER FOURTEEN

I.

For the first few weeks following our arrival in New York I was content to "play house" as Andrew put it. There was much to do and I really was enjoying myself. Mother had shipped us two crates of household items she and Augusta Wilkes thought we might find useful, everything from linens and doilies to dishes, pots, and pans. Despite the fact that most of the items were second hand, it truly was like Christmas in July and I had a wonderful time unpacking, washing, and arranging my treasures.

Such bounty definitely was unexpected but I was to be even more surprised and touched by their generosity when, at the bottom of the second crate, wrapped in several layers of newspaper, I found my mother's most prized piece of porcelain, a stately Victorian gentleman kneeling before and kissing the hand of an intricately rendered Victorian lady seated on a garden bench. I couldn't prevent the tears that began to flow and, knowing how much Mother loved that particular piece, had to fight the impulse to return it for I realized that sending it to me was the consummate gesture of reconciliation. I sent instead a long letter to both ladies profuse in gratitude and sharing every nuance I could muster of our experiences thus far – Grand Central Terminal, the parade which had introduced us to the city, a slightly-embellished description of the neighborhood and our apartment, and a detailed portrait of each member of the Reichert family.

In addition to making our tiny apartment a home, "playing house" in 1917 also included making the most out of increasingly scarce resources. When the United States came off the sidelines of the Great War and became directly involved in the struggle, President Wilson realized that "it is not only an army that we must shape and train for war, it is a nation!" Equipping and feeding an army of a million men required unprecedented planning, unity of purpose within the nation – and sacrifice on the part of an entire population.

To accomplish the first of those requirements – planning – Wilson established the War Industries Board, headed by millionaire Wall Street financier Bernard Baruch. The WIB was charged with the responsibility of creating a partnership between business, labor, and the military. Mr. Baruch took the reins with an autocratic zeal that led to a level of cooperation between government and industry that had never before been seen in the United States. Although often criticized for the level of government intrusion its programs generated, the WIB was seen by most as a necessary component of the war effort and Mr. Baruch's somewhat dictatorial reign as a temporary exigency.

Having stood in the wings of the international stage for three years before taking on a leading role, Washington also recognized war's effect on the average citizen and the vital supporting role in which they were cast. As a result, in order to facilitate the second goal – national unity – Wilson appointed newspaper editor and public relations expert George Creel as head of the Committee on Public Information which was, essentially, the government's primary propaganda machine. Mr. Creel had the dual task of stirring up national enthusiasm for the all-out war effort and unifying the public mind. Creel himself called his job "the world's greatest adventure in advertising" and "a vast enterprise in salesmanship." If George Creel's job was to sell the war he did it with aplomb! Within eighteen months of his appointment the CPI had distributed sixty million red-white-and-blue pamphlets extolling the righteousness of the Allied cause. And it wasn't just printed materials the CPI disseminated; approximately 75,000 CPI speakers criss-crossed the nation speaking at churches, clubs, movie theaters and anywhere else people gathered. Called "four-minute-men" because of the length of their prepared speeches, they stirred the patriotic spirit of the nation on topics such as "Why We Fight" and "Maintaining Morals and Morale." Also under the auspices of the CPI, patriotic movies like "Pershing's Crusaders" and "America's Answer" were commissioned and the skills of the nation's most talented artists were harnessed in order to produce colorful posters exhorting Americans to "Halt the Hun," and "Kill the Kaiser." Creel's work was extremely successful and, in the spirit of patriotism created by the CPI, musicians cranked out rousing tunes like Irving Berlin's "Oh, How I Hate To Get Up In The Morning," Al Dubin's "Hinky Dinky Parlay Voo," Young and Lewis's "How 'Ya Gonna Keep 'Em Down On The Farm?" and my personal favorite, George M. Cohen's "Over There." All combined, the CPI's efforts kindled the flames of patriotic fervor – and kept our toes tapping.

The final component of the war effort's triumvirate – sacrifice – was undoubtedly the one that impacted the average citizen most directly. In order to coordinate the myriad sacrifices soon to be required of every household in the nation, Herbert Hoover was selected to head the newly organized Food Administration. Under Hoover, the Food Administration successfully increased agricultural productivity as well as improving and streamlining distribution of farm products. Hoover also established price controls and initiated programs designed to drive home every citizen's duty to conserve, teaching the nation to "Hooverize" their meals with "Meatless Tuesdays," "Wheatless Wednesdays," and instituting the "gospel of the clean plate." Under Hoover's direction American housewives reduced food consumption and saved literally hundreds of thousands of pounds of meat, sugar, and flour; releasing food for shipment overseas and conserving the fats and oils necessary to manufacture munitions here at home. It was a unique time in which to make the transition from someone's child to someone's wife and my education progressed on multiple fronts – as did the more stark and brutal education taking place in Europe.

While I was busy learning the ways of the war-time housewife and putting our personal life in order Andrew was busy establishing his professional presence within the New York newspaper scene. He was, however, neither immediately successful with nor accepted by the entrenched and crusty "big city" reporters, many of whom seemed at least mildly jealous and distrustful of this young interloper receiving what they perceived to be preferential treatment from their editor. Not one to be easily daunted or dissuaded by being an outsider, Andrew took their skepticism and cold shoulder in stride, patiently waiting for both to subside. He unswervingly believed that he would prove himself to them and that time and experience eventually would forge the bond of camaraderie and finally gain him admittance to the inner circle of the New York newspaperman.

"It's like a boy's club," he explained one early September evening over dinner. "It may sound kind of childish but that's about the size of it. I'm the new kid on the block; I have to hang in there and wait to be accepted. In the meantime I'll just go about my business, doing my job the best I can and learning the ropes as I go along."

"Just as long as your so-called colleagues don't use one of those ropes to hang you along the way!"

"I don't think we need worry about that," he assured me as I began clearing the table. "They may not trust me yet and may even resent the breaks Med Potter is giving me, but I hardly think it'll boil over into anything more than that. Some of the fellows are already beginning to accept my presence among them and treat me less like an outsider every day."

"Well, that's a relief..." I paused before adding what else was on my mind. "Do you think there will ever be room for a girl in that 'boy's club' you speak of?"

The role of housewife had fit me more comfortably than first expected but I had begun to notice symptoms of intellectual claustrophobia recently as the walls of the apartment began to close in on me. It definitely was time to find more to do with my days than cooking, cleaning, and waiting for Andrew to come home.

Although I had accompanied him to the office and out on assignment a few times, as of yet there had been no appropriate project on which Andrew and I truly could collaborate. We had compiled a small portfolio of my best work to share with Mr. Potter, but Andrew had yet to approach his boss about the possibility of my serving as a part-time "stringer" with the newspaper.

His smile wasn't patronizing or indulgent but he appeared unsure of himself and adjusted his glasses before responding. "I have every confidence that there will eventually be room for both of us, Marty," he began, turning toward me from where he still sat at the table. "I'm sorry I haven't included you more before now; guess I've been preoccupied with my own initiation."

"And you're doing great," I assured him. "Your writing is better than ever. That's probably part of the problem with the other reporters – the quality of your work – but it's also undoubtedly what will finally win them over."

Andrew seemed embarrassed by my praise and turned to face the table again as I spoke. I put down the dishcloth I held, leaned forward and put my arms around his neck.

"I don't mean to pout. It's just that I've been feeling kind of restless lately. Maybe I should try to find a job somewhere; there are lots of things available with so many men overseas."

That was an understatement. By the time the war ended America would have nearly five million men serving in the military! The migration overseas of most of the country's able-bodied men caused severe labor shortages here at home as the nation became desperate to increase wartime production. The result was inevitable. Women were moving out of the house and into the labor force in unprecedented numbers, donning overalls and doing everything from factory work to working on railroad crews and serving as members of the "Women's Land Army of America," without whose help the record harvest of 1917 wouldn't have been possible. Men like my father may have grumbled and sputtered and sworn it was merely a wartime necessity, convinced that a woman could never replace a man, but the tide definitely was turning and it would never entirely return.

"You know I have nothing against you getting a job if you'd like," Andrew said in response to my suggestion. "But it would be a shame to commit to something and then not be able to move into some type of reporting when it became available."

"Don't you mean 'if' it became available? I guess I don't share your conviction that it's only a matter of time before I'm working for a newspaper again."

"Well, think about it, Marty; newspapers are experiencing labor shortages just like everyone else now that so many men are heading overseas. It seems only logical that there will be opportunities for women in that arena just like everywhere else, and you already have some experience in the field – that'll give you a terrific advantage when the time comes!"

I could almost see the wheels turning as he mulled things over in silence as we finished cleaning up the kitchen.

"You know," he said, picking up the conversation when we had moved into the parlor. "I suppose there's really no reason we shouldn't get the ball rolling as far as you writing for the paper is concerned. Mr. Potter is as much of a 'free thinker' as Layton Carmichael ever was so he should have no qualms about hiring women, especially right now when necessity has opened the door to so many previously all-male domains. You should come with me tomorrow and we can talk to him before I go out on assignment. How does that sound?"

"It sounds wonderful. I have to admit newspaper work is what I really want to do; you're to blame for that, you know. You got me addicted in Tully's Cove and now I'm going through withdrawal. And there just isn't much around this little place to distract me now that we're all settled."

I suddenly was choked up and had to fight back my emotions before continuing. "And I've been thinking about Rachel a lot again, too. The sooner I get acquainted with New York the sooner I can begin looking for her."

"I thought that might be part of it. Just remember, Marty," he stressed gently but firmly, drawing me closer to him on the settee. "She may not be here. Jacob Collier had no luck when he looked for them here."

"I realize that but I've just got to give it a try. Rachel always wanted to see New York, and this is supposedly Gavin Marshall's favorite city. I just can't believe they're not here someplace."

"They may have been here and gone long ago."

"That's true, of course, but I'll never know for sure until I try."

II.

I began working for the *New York World Gazette* the very next day. It was as easy as that. Medford Potter took one look at me, made a cursory examination of my modest portfolio, snorted his agreement that Layton Carmichael undoubtedly had gotten a hoot out of hiring the preacher's daughter, and promptly gave me my first assignment; all the while chewing voraciously on the end of a saliva-saturated cigar with the studiousness of a cow fixated on its cud. He was blunt to the point of being rude and had mildly disgusting personal habits but I liked him instantly – but then I probably would have liked Kaiser Wilhelm himself had he seen fit to give me a job!

In his quiet, low-key way Andrew shared my excitement, although he seemed more than a tad concerned about leaving me on my own. Not one for public displays, he nonetheless hugged me tightly before bidding me good luck as we went our separate ways to work on our respective assignments.

Appropriately, my first article for the *Gazette* was to be a feature on women joining the workforce. As Mr. Potter explained it he was looking for a fairly extensive examination of the subject and liked the idea of it being written by someone experiencing the phenomenon firsthand, seeming to think that that would give the article unique credibility. I was only too glad to agree with him and made no mention of the fact that I knew virtually nothing about the city and hadn't the slightest idea where to begin such a significant piece of work. I was out of his office and out on the street watching Andrew disappear into the ubiquitous New York City crowd scene before realizing that I was scared to death. My knees literally were knocking, my palms were sweating, my heart was pounding, and I was afraid I might actually humiliate myself by throwing up right there on the spot! There was nothing to do but start walking and hope that my heart would soon start beating normally and I would once again be able to breathe before it became critical and I collapsed in a heap on the sidewalk.

It was the sight of a small newsstand on the corner that began bringing me to my senses and helped me formulate a rudimentary plan of action. I had been just coherent enough upon leaving the newspaper office to snatch up a copy of that day's edition in order to peruse the business section so purchased a small map of the city, a pencil, and a pad of paper from the vendor, sat down at a nearby streetcar stop and began planning my route.

I would visit as many different types of businesses as possible, large and small alike, ascertaining how their work and workforce had changed since the declaration of war – specifically in terms of the number of women newly employed and the nature of the jobs at which they worked. Once I had that information and hopefully some useful quotes as well, I would draft the article itself and then ask Andrew to edit it for me that evening. Simple enough – or so I thought.

I set out with tenuously high spirits, a reasonably intact façade of confidence, and a definitely false sense of security.

By the end of the day I knew more about the city than I might otherwise have learned in a month – having been places that would have made by father spit nails of outraged disapproval – and also realized the sheer folly of my belief that the story would be drafted for Andrew's review yet that day. One could easily have researched the women-at-work phenomenon for weeks; I could perhaps take a few days before risking loss of the story to a more experienced and efficient male reporter. I was determined that that wasn't going to happen. This story was mine – and I believed it also was a stepping stone in my search for Rachel.

From uptown stores and offices to the railroad yards and nearby factories, I was determined to see it all – and learned two distinct lessons in the process. First, women definitely were being employed in record numbers for a remarkable variety of jobs and, second, New York City had an incredible number of businesses and there was no way my pennies for the streetcar – or my feet – could possibly hold out. I was going to have to be selective or my first article would also be my last!

I didn't want Andrew to know how naïve I had been in my approach to this first assignment and – hoping to get home first and have supper started by the time he arrived – I walked away from the streetcar stop and down the tree-darkened tunnel leading to our brownstone at a pace in direct defiance to the dictates of my sore feet. As luck would have it, however, the smell of pancakes greeted me as soon as I opened the stairwell door and Andrew was at the head of the stairs to greet me.

"Hail the conquering heroine," he said, smiling broadly and saluting me with the spatula he held aloft.

I almost collapsed on the bottom step, keeping my back to him so he wouldn't see me grimace as I unlaced and took off my shoes. Rising painfully to my feet, I put on a brave smile and, with feigned enthusiasm, began the long climb up the seemingly endless flight of stairs.

"I take it we need to get you a more sensible pair of shoes," he observed with a smirk, enjoying my plight rather more than he had a right to.

"It might not be a bad idea," I admitted, moving into his embrace and lifting my face to his kiss.

"Well, tell me all about it over supper," he suggested, "for I have prepared a truly lavish repast to celebrate your return from battle..."

"...Pancakes and bacon," I interjected, "which also happens to be the only thing you know how to cook!"

"Oh, you cut me to the quick, Mrs. Carlton," he said in mock humiliation, "for I have progressed from bacon to sliced ham; but if you tell me all about your day I shall surely forgive you for underestimating me."

We sat down to eat and I soon was giving him a detailed description of my first day on the job, including the naivete with which I had approached the project.

When I finished he ignored the foolishness of my original expectations, congratulated me on how much I had accomplished, but expressed concern regarding some of the places I had gone.

"I understand and appreciate your concern," I assured him, "and believe me I wouldn't have gone to some of those places except in broad daylight, but honestly those were some of the most pleasant and helpful businessmen with whom I spoke today. And you would have been fascinated by the stories of some of the women I met. In contrast, the most disagreeable and unfriendly encounter happened to be the most respectable place I went where I was told in no uncertain terms that they neither currently employ nor have any intention of ever employing females, not now or at any time in the future."

I began thumbing through the notebook I retrieved from the adjacent chair. "Let me give you a direct quote. 'To do so is to undermine the stability of society and flies in the face of God's plan of creation.'" Flipping the notebook shut and tossing it aside I added glumly, "My father would be proud."

"Oh, come on, Marty," Andrew's voice held a trace of rebuke as he liberally buttered a pancake, "there will always be people like that; good, decent people with whom we can still do business and be friends. You have to remind yourself that those folks are at the extreme end of the spectrum and that moving beyond tradition doesn't make you a radical or a communist; just as being conservative doesn't mean rejecting any and all social and political change. Quite frankly, I consider myself a conservative. I'm definitely a states-rights man, if not a down-right libertarian. The more liberal among us – the so-called 'Progressives' – see expansion of Washington's powers as essential; I'll oppose such proposals loud and long but at the same time have no problem embracing appropriate change like women's suffrage. Look at all these new government agencies that are meddling in everyday life; they may be acceptable in time of war – as are restrictive laws like the Trading With the Enemy Act and the Sedition Act – but as soon as an armistice is signed I'll be at the head of the line pulling the reins of government back in."

He wagged a buttery knife at me. "I believe there's a balance to be maintained somewhere between the total inflexibility you encountered today on one end and the government usurping our freedoms and autonomy in the name of taking care of us on the other. Wasn't it Thomas Jefferson who said a government big enough to give you everything you want is strong enough to take everything you have?"

My only response was a contemplative silence – and a tired smile.

"There I go again, huh," he said apologetically. "Seems I can't resist getting on my soapbox from time to time – even here at home. Feel free to knock me off if I get too obnoxious."

Momentarily energized, I gave him a shove and darted out of the room.

III.

Our landlords, the Reicherts, were a devout German Lutheran family who virtually never missed a Sunday service. Since Andrew wasn't a consistent church-goer I began joining them for their weekly sojourn to Holy Cross Lutheran Church and thoroughly enjoyed being included in their family traditions. Franz Reichert and his parents accepted me with polite deference but Katrina obviously was pleased to have her tenant come under her spiritual jurisdiction and the younger members of the Reichert contingent seemed to see me as a breath of fresh air in what was, to them, the more tedious part of their weekend rituals.

Just a few weeks earlier it would have been pointless for me to attend their church for they had only recently changed from German to English in their services;

undoubtedly an effort to dissociate themselves from the war-induced negative image of anything "foreign" – particularly anything German. So, instead of feeling out of place and being totally lost, I was able to follow the liturgy, join in the singing, and understand Pastor Koenig's sermons. Unfortunately, however, there was a downside to the English-only trend throughout the country during the Great War. As I looked around the church each Sunday I was struck by the fact that, in protecting themselves from the criticism of outsiders and striving to remove any question of their loyalty, they had turned their back on the older members of their congregation who understood little, if any, English. The senior Mr. and Mrs. Reichert, like thousands of loyal Americans across the country, now sat as foreigners in their own church, understanding the rhythm and flow of the service but hardly a word that was spoken.

Another casualty of the war.

In addition to joining the Reicherts for worship, whenever we wished we were also included in the family dinner that followed. And at the dinner table there was no attempt to deny the family's heritage. Katrina and her mother-in-law spread lavish and luscious German feasts, ably assisted by her daughter, Anna, and Franz junior's wife, Helen. Each week we were introduced to various German standards and delicacies; everything from "sauerbraten" (pickled beef) and "blutwurst" (blood pudding) to a wonderful fruity pastry called "stolen" which oozed buttery goodness all over your plate. And even though many German-Americans felt compelled to shun their heritage when it came to identifying the delicious food – sauerkraut was now "liberty cabbage" and hamburger had become "Salisbury steak" – all of us were more than willing to eat it!

Each week after dinner the pleasant limbo continued as there was time for relaxation in the Reichert sitting room, where good conversation, a game or two of cards, and impromptu recitals at the piano by Gerta and Libby made for a very relaxing afternoon.

It was after two such performances – a rather incongruous double-billing of Bach and Gilbert and Sullivan – when Andrew brought up a subject he had wanted to discuss with the Reicherts for some time.

"Franz, I'm interested in writing a story about how the war is affecting German-Americans and I'm hoping you can help." Not quite sure of the response he might get, he broached the subject with some caution. "We've all heard about German literature being pulled from library shelves, orchestras no longer playing Bach or Beethoven – and even that nonsense in Cincinnati where they've passed an ordinance forbidding the selling of pretzels..."

Some heads nodded in acknowledgement, some shook in understated sorrow.

"...but I want to know what the average German-American is experiencing. I know you had trouble renting our apartment and am wondering if you've had any other problems."

Mr. Reichert was silent for a moment.

"No," he replied quietly. "Everything is all right."

"Franz," Mrs. Reichert scolded, "tell the truth. Tell him."

Mr. Reichert silenced his wife with a glance but appeared more sad than irritated. He was a proud man and it undoubtedly was difficult for him to admit that there were troubles beyond his ability to solve.

Andrew didn't press the issue and for a long moment everyone seemed preoccupied with their coffee.

"Katrina is correct, of course," Franz said at last. "It is true that business is off and we are losing money. Many people who used to come in every week now walk past our door to do their marketing in an 'American' shop blocks away. For years their friend and neighbor I am, now suddenly I am the stranger not to be trusted."

The younger Franz looked as if he wanted to add something but remained silent.

"I'm sorry to hear that," Andrew said, "but frankly I'm not surprised. I know it's no consolation but you're certainly not alone."

He paused, judiciously. "Is there anything else?"

"No," Mr. Reichert replied, looking down at his hands.

"Papa," the younger Franz interjected. "Papa, why not tell him everything? We've done nothing wrong. There's no reason not to let people know just what's going on, just how far anti-German prejudice has gone."

The adults had grown very quiet and, as if reading his mind, Franz junior's wife silently ushered the children from the room.

His father didn't speak and so Franz continued. "We've had 'visits,' if you can call them that; visits from certain patriotic citizens who have taken it upon themselves to 'investigate' the activities of so-called foreigners. Foreigners. We, who have been here more than ten years and have become American citizens. We, who have family serving in the army. Don't we buy Liberty Bonds just like every other American? Don't our women roll bandages and save peach pits for gas masks just like every other American housewife? But no, we're different. We have to be watched; just because of our last name."

Andrew leaned forward in his chair. "The 'American Protective League'?"

Franz nodded.

"Vigilantism, pure and simple."

The elder Franz broke his silence. "Yah." There was bitterness in his voice. "Vigilantes. And not just watching they do. They assume we are not loyal. They accuse us of sympathizing with the enemy. And with the accusing comes more."

"They've threatened you?"

Mr. Reichert fell silent again; his son supplying what his father could not.

"Not in so many words. But they make comments as they loiter around the store; comments like 'there may be food shortages but there's no shortage of rope and lamp posts.'"

"Gott im Himmel," Katrina gasped, clasping her hands together and looking heavenward to invoke intercession from a Higher Power.

"I think we should change our name," Franz continued, ignoring his mother's invocation. "'Franz Reichert' the German would disappear nicely into the all-American crowd as 'Frank Richard,' and 'Richard's Market' sounds a lot better to a paranoid public than 'Reichert's Market' ever will."

"No," his father said without equivocation. "No, I vill not change my name. I am not like Heir Schmidt who becomes Mr. Smith the day he takes the oath of citizenship. I don't need a new name to prove that an American I am. This is my home now, this is my land. Und my children should be proud of where they came from just as much as where they now are."

"I agree with you, Mr. Reichert," Andrew said. "Spy fever has spread like wildfire in this country and changing your name isn't the answer. Vigilante groups like the American Protective League and, even worse, the Sedition Slammers, are harassing people all over the country; new Americans, pacifists – anyone they suspect of sympathizing with the enemy. Why, they've even gone after the First Lady herself, and isn't William Randolph Hearst supposedly using his New York townhouse lights to signal German U-boats skulking around out in the Hudson River? Good grief, I even read in the *Wall Street Journal* – the *Wall Street Journal*! – that pacifists should be hanged!"

"It's the fear," I interjected hesitantly. "It's all the fear that's been generated over the last few years, even before we joined the war. German espionage and sabotage are really at the heart of it all. Why, it's two years ago already that the munitions at Black Tom Island were blown up by German spies. And we've all read the stories about the sabotage of our ships and factories. It's an overreaction – and it's definitely unfair – but it's understandable. People are afraid."

Andrew nodded slightly. "Fear may explain it but that doesn't make it any more acceptable. And the people of this nation have got to wake up and realize just what's going on and what's at stake. My God, how can we claim to be the vanguard of freedom and equality in the world while at the same time turning a blind eye to this kind of victimization at home?"

He turned toward our host, his voice quiet with respect. "With your permission, Mr. Reichert, I'd like to tell your story in the newspaper. We can probably do it without using any names…"

"Aach, use my name; use it. Isn't that vhat this is all about? A name; an American name?"

IV.

It didn't take much salesmanship to get Mr. Potter to agree that there was quite a story lurking out there behind the prejudice and vigilantism being fed by what Andrew had called "spy fever." As a result, while I continued working on my story about women in the workforce and a sidebar article profiling one of the women I had met, Andrew began his investigation of the activities of groups like the American Protective League and the Sedition Slammers while simultaneously doing his share of covering the more routine news of the day.

Instead of representing himself to the so-called "patriot groups" as a newspaper reporter it was Andrew's plan to more or less infiltrate the ranks of some of the local "chapters" of the vigilantes. In this way he hoped to gain an insider's perspective on what they were all about and what fueled the fire of their anger and fear. It was, of course, a logical approach and, in light of the size of New York and his newcomer's anonymity, a relatively easy illusion to fabricate and maintain. It was also a source of extreme anxiety for me, forced to sit home and wait while he went about his journalistic intrigue.

The first meeting Andrew attended was a session of the American Protective League held in the backroom of a saloon near the shipyards. I spent the evening downstairs with the Reichert ladies, rolling bandages and trying to follow and join their aimless chatter all the while worrying that Andrew would be discovered and strung up from the nearest lamppost!

When at last I heard him going up the stairs nestled behind the wall against which I sat, I excused myself so abruptly that I dropped the rolls of bandages lying in my lap and left without retrieving them.

"Neuvermahlt," Katrina observed without looking up from her work, "newlyweds."

Andrew was pouring himself a cup of coffee when I reached him in the kitchen.

"Well," I demanded, "are you all right? How did it go? What did you find out?"

"Marty, relax," he replied, sitting down at the table and stirring sugar into the steaming liquid. "I'm back all in one piece. Everything went just fine."

He pushed the cup over to me and rose to get another. "It was a very interesting experience, that's for sure. Not exactly what I expected."

He took his time pouring out another cup, sitting down once again at the table, and stirring sugar into the strong brew. "They naturally were curious and a bit suspicious about any newcomer. But there were three or four of us attending for the first time so I didn't stand out too badly."

He took a long, slow drink before continuing. "There were about twenty men there. They all seemed to be working class people, although a few may have been businessmen. We had time to mill around quite a bit. They're really pretty average folks; afraid, like you suggested, and angry. One of them lost a son on Black Tom Island back in '15; he's obviously very motivated to fight saboteurs and was one of the more vocal of the group. There were a couple others motivated by firsthand experience in one way or another. One of them was injured during an explosion at the shipyards. But there were also lots of plain, ordinary men there and even a few members of the clergy."

"Members of the clergy," I asked in disbelief.

"Yes, that's right. I got the impression that the League is one of the less virulent of the vigilante groups. The Sedition Slammers are probably even less tolerant – and likewise more potent in their strategies. Anyway, one of the leaders is apparently more or less in charge of 'recruiting' and he drilled us pretty thoroughly about who we are, where we're from, what our backgrounds are and all that. It was easy enough to construct an identity for myself; mostly I just told the truth – with the exception of what I do for a living."

He directed his attention to his coffee once again. "The most tense moment," he observed, "was when I was asked point-blank why I'm not in the army. Most of them are well beyond military age and they definitely wanted to know why an apparently healthy young man hasn't signed up."

"What did you tell them? Didn't they believe you?"

"It wasn't tense in that way," he explained. "It was tense internally because it made me feel guilty for not serving."

I started to protest but he cut me off.

"I know, I know, I am serving. We've been through it all before and for the most part I believe it, or at least I've accepted my role in this thing. It's just that their patriotic fervor is sincere and pretty contagious." He took off his glasses and rubbed the bridge of his nose. "Anyway, back to my story. This basically was an organizational meeting; more a rallying session than anything else. You know; lots of flag waving and patriotic talk. Most of the meeting would have met with the approval of everyone."

"Then you didn't learn much of anything useful?"

"Well, it's all useful in terms of getting background information and gaining an understanding of what they're all about. But I said most of the meeting seemed harmless, not all. It took on a more ominous tone near the end when there were a few reports by some of the men regarding whom I gathered are their assigned 'suspects.' You should have heard some of the ridiculous things they take as evidence of disloyalty."

His voice took on mock horror as he continued. "One reported that a Hungarian man he's been watching was heard speaking Hungarian in public – that was the extent of his infraction; he dared to speak something other than English so he must have been plotting against the U.S.! If it weren't so tragic it would be laughable. He probably was talking to someone with a limited command of English – like when the Reicherts speak German to Franz's mother. Another reported following a German-American to the Post Office where he was seen mailing a package. That's all. Just mailing a package marked the guy as someone involved in espionage!"

He ran his hand through his hair and adjusted his glasses. "At the end of the meeting, when it came time to wrap things up, the man in charge spent at least twenty minutes lecturing us on reports of sabotage and espionage – the highly questionable being given equal credence with the few known to be true – and exhorting us to be vigilant and to report any questionable people or activities. That was worth the price of admission! And believe me, I paid very close attention right to the end."

"So what do you do now?"

"I'd like to attend another meeting or two, hopefully go along on one of their 'visits' like the ones paid to the Reicherts at their store. And I intend on doing the same thing with the Sedition Slammers, although joining their ranks may be a bit more difficult. They strike me as more secretive and close-knit..."

"And likewise more dangerous," I observed dryly.

"Yes, if these groups truly are dangerous at all then the Slammers probably are the more threatening. But quite frankly, Martha, I don't think any of these groups are all that dangerous. It's all smoke and mirrors; just a lot of talk. Hateful yes, but dangerous? I don't think so."

"Well, they make me think of the Ku Klux Klan so they seem very dangerous to me and I want you to promise you'll be careful. All right? Promise me you'll be careful and not take any unnecessary chances just to prove yourself to your colleagues at the paper?"

"I'll be careful," he assured me. "There's nothing to worry about."

V.

As Andrew set about infiltrating the Sedition Slammers, I put the finishing touches on my article on women in the workplace and used my new-found familiarity with the city to begin my search for Rachel in earnest.

I began to devote almost every waking hour to my quest to find my little sister. Like Don Quixote, I was obsessed with the challenge before me. I confided in Mrs. Reichert what I was doing, but refrained from telling her more than that Rachel had eloped and not contacted our family since. Coupled with my growing knowledge of the city, Mrs. Reichert's insights about inexpensive boarding houses and city missions supported by areas churches proved invaluable. Together we made a list of likely places to which a man and woman "on the run" might be forced to turn.

I began to work my way methodically through that list, but each stop brought either a dead end or false hope and another possibility to check out.

At one point I was certain that I was on the right track and that Rachel definitely was in New York. While inquiring at a modest but impeccably respectable boarding house suggested by Mrs. Reichert, my description of Rachel and Mr. Marshall was met with a confidently positive response. A couple matching their description, but calling themselves Mr. and Mrs. Jones, had boarded there for a couple of weeks but had moved out without leaving a forwarding address. Convinced that Mr. and Mrs. Jones were, in fact, Gavin Marshall and my sister, I was incredibly disappointed to have come so close but equally determined not to give up – especially since the landlady was able to provide a lead. She suggested that I check out a rooming house she had recommended to the wife when asked about accommodations in another part of the city.

Once again Don Quixote confronted the windmill.

That next stop – a less well-kept house in a less-pleasant part of town – led to another positive response to my description but, unfortunately, they no longer were among the tenants and, once again, had left no forwarding address.

No matter how much Andrew advised caution, I couldn't stem the tide of my excitement and believed Mr. and Mrs. Jones just had to be Rachel and Mr. Marshall. It was incredibly frustrating to be just a step or two behind them and this time have virtually no idea where they might turn next. Where could they have gone? It was fairly obvious that they were moving to increasingly modest living quarters – but New York literally crawled with cheap hotels and rooming houses. I reluctantly admitted that in a city this size the possibilities were virtually unlimited and that it was very much like looking for the proverbial needle in a haystack. I wasn't going to give up, but for the time being faced a dead end. I began to feel more like the long-suffering Sancho Panza than the obsessed don he served, and for the moment the windmills appeared to be winning.

Andrew was to meet with greater success in his quest to infiltrate the patriotic extremists, but he wasn't jousting with windmills and his éclat was to come at a cost.

As he believed, the Sedition Slammers were, indeed, the most secretive and virulent of the vigilante groups. As a result, they also were more suspicious of those expressing an interest in joining their ranks. The identity Andrew had fabricated for himself in his dealings with the American Protective League continued to hold, however, and, after two weeks of regular drinking at a factory-row saloon where he loudly spewed appropriate paranoid invectives, he was able to ingratiate himself into the confidence of an outspoken Slammer and earn an invitation to accompany his new-found friend to a rally.

When he returned home from that gathering bruised, bleeding, and covered with dirt, I feared the worst.

"Oh my God, Andrew," I exclaimed, darting pointlessly around him as he moved through the parlor to the sink in the kitchen. "What happened? Are you all right?"

He leaned over the sink, using a handkerchief to staunch his bleeding nose. "Yes, Martha, I'm all right. Well, reasonably so, anyway."

He ran cold water through the bloody cloth and mopped his dirty face with it before once again applying pressure to his nose.

"Got a little more than I bargained for," he explained with a feeble smile.

"I should say so! What happened?"

Still holding the handkerchief to his nose, he moved over to the table and lowered himself gingerly into a chair.

"Well, I certainly got a story," he began, holding up his hand when I once again would have interjected my concern. "I went to the meeting with the fellow from the saloon. As expected they weren't a particularly friendly group but since I was being 'sponsored' by an already established Slammer they were less suspicious of me than might otherwise have been the case. They aren't like the American Protective League that meets in a readily accessible public place. I wouldn't have known where to find them let alone have gotten through the door if I'd been on my own."

He paused to check the status of his nose and I was relieved to see that the bleeding had stopped. "The meeting was all hatred and vitriolic propaganda from beginning to end. They're really something – far more extreme than the Protective League."

He glanced over at the stove. "Could I have a cup of coffee?"

I poured us both a cup and brought along some pastry Mrs. Reichert had sent up earlier that day.

"The speaker, Will Bradley, was a real spellbinder," he continued, sipping his coffee carefully in order to accommodate a bruised and swollen lower lip. "He started out slow and quiet, talking about the blessings of democracy and what a great country the United States is. No problem there. But then he started to build up steam and really get rolling. He hit every ethnic group represented by the Central Powers – Germans, Hungarians, Austrians, Bulgarians, even the Turks, perhaps especially them since their culture is particularly foreign to our own. I've never heard such hatred and ridiculous generalizations. According to Bradley, everything about them is sinister and evil. And they don't want just Europe under their thumb; no sir, their voracious appetites – especially that of the Kaiser – will never be satisfied until the United States is vanquished as well. They want our land, our resources, our wealth... even our women."

He shook his head and threw up his hands. "And then Bradley turned his attention to the 'subversives' here at home. Politicians, teachers, writers, ministers – anyone who doesn't openly stand with them is seen as a potential traitor. And God help you if your last name reflects immigration from anywhere." He tapped his forehead with an index finger and smiled lopsidedly. "I've got enough here for a book..."

"Well maybe so, and all well and good," I interrupted, "but you still haven't told me what happened to you. How did you get hurt?"

"Now *that* I don't think I'll include in the article," he replied stoically with another wan smile.

"Stop being evasive," I insisted. "What happened?"

"Sorry, Marty," he replied, reaching across the table and patting my hand. "I don't mean to avoid your question. Guess I just wanted to set the stage. Believe me, I never was in any real danger..."

"...to which your bleeding nose and fat lip can attest. Oh yes, it's all 'smoke and mirrors' like you've contended all along!"

He cocked an eyebrow in response to my "smoke and mirrors" comment, but diplomatically ignored it – as well as my sarcasm – and continued his story.

"There was another apparent newcomer at the meeting." He shook his head in quizzical disbelief at the memory. "As soon as I noticed him I could see he was in for trouble; the fool was taking notes! He was trying to be inconspicuous, but in a setting like that – where everyone is a potential spy – you don't bring along pencil and paper! Well, throughout Bradley's diatribe the crowd is cheering and jeering and getting hotter by the minute. So when he's at a fever pitch, yelling about spies and traitors, someone in the audience – as if on cue – shouts back, 'There's one now!' indicating this fellow who's taking notes. Suddenly it's quiet as death and the whole group turns as one toward this man. He stuffs his notebook into his shirt and starts backing away toward the door so I start worming my way over to him..."

I started to protest but he cut me off.

"What else could I do, Martha? He was out-numbered 50 to 1 and they were really a mob by that point..."

"...but you never were in any real danger," I reminded him with undisguised sarcasm.

"What else could I do," he asked again.

When I didn't respond, he continued.

"Miraculously, I got to him about a split second before the seething mob cut loose. I grabbed his arm, hauled him out the door with me, and managed to latch it from the outside just as that mass of bodies converged on the other side. The latch didn't hold long against their weight, but it gave us a chance to take off down the alley. I tell you, I've never run so hard in all my life! We changed course half a dozen times but could tell from the sounds behind us that they weren't giving up and had split into several groups to track us down. We had a couple close calls..."

"'Close calls,'" I asked dubiously. "That's all? So just how did you come to be in your present condition?"

"I'm getting to that," he assured me. "We climbed into a woodbox next to an abandoned shed just in time to avoid a group catching up with us; I admit it was a tense moment, crouching there in the dark, hardly daring to breathe while they paused not ten feet away debating which way to go. At one point somebody kicked the door of the shed open. It was so dilapidated it fell off its hinges and landed almost on top of the box, splintering a couple of wood slats. We both lurched when it hit and I thought they'd hear us for sure but their own talking must have covered any noise we made. I could see the fellow who kicked the door peering inside the shed but he didn't bother to check the woodbox. If they had looked very closely they'd never have missed us –

there were gaps between the slats two or three inches wide in some places."

He took a long, slow drink of coffee and adjusted his glasses before continuing. "When it was quiet again we got out of the box – with what seemed like enough noise to wake the dead! – and stood for a moment straining to hear which direction the mob was taking. All of a sudden, a form emerges out the darkness and hollers at the top of its lungs 'They're over here!' The man lunges at us but we jump to either side and he goes sprawling on the ground between us spread-eagle. Without a second thought, I take off to the left just as the other fellow takes off to the right. I stopped and called out to him and thought about going after him but a group of men had just turned the corner toward me and I barely had time to dive into a shallow drainage ditch and hope the tall grass and shadows would conceal me. That's how I got all banged up. I didn't know just how shallow it was until I hit it – face first."

He gently and hesitantly touched his nose. "My nose got the worst of it, I'm afraid."

I tried to look sympathetic rather than afraid and angry.

"I don't know what happened to the other fellow. I'm assuming he made out okay. Heck, I don't even know his name," he confessed with an embarrassed smile. "I don't know who he was! And, unfortunately, helping him means there's no way I can go back to another meeting."

I bit back the retort that, as far as I was concerned, that was the most fortunate part of the entire experience!

CHAPTER FIFTEEN

I.

Andrew's expose on the self-described patriot groups was published in October. Although challenging their tactics, he wrote a thoughtful, balanced piece that didn't paint the vigilante groups as villains but rather depicted both them and their targets as victims of the perhaps inevitable hysteria surrounding full scale war. They, however, failed to see it that way and he was immediately branded everything from a pacifist to a communist or, worst of all, a spy.

The negative reaction to Andrew's article among certain quarters seemed to be fueled by additional fear and fury generated by the "October Revolution" going on in Russia at that time and apparently assuring a Communist take-over there.

Russia already had experienced near-cataclysmic change earlier in the year, but no one could predict what was to come. Czar Nicholas, a naïve and inept monarch, had been tragically blind to the needs and desires of his people, sharing his wife's aristocratic belief that they had been placed on the throne by God and thus shared in the archaic notion of the "Divine Right of Kings." Appalling defeats on the battlefield, staggering loss of life among both soldiers and civilians, and one of the worst winters in Russian history found the people starving, furious, and no longer loyal to the autocratic czarist regime. In Petrograd protesting mobs had sung "The Internationale" – the anthem of communist revolution – and still Nicholas failed to see the writing on the wall. In a lackluster and utterly futile attempt to bolster both his image and support for his regime, Nicholas took personal command of the troops at the front but was finally forced to abdicate in March of 1917. At that point, the reins of government were turned over to Alexander Kerensky, a socialist who called for moderate reforms and continued participation in the war. But the battle cry of the communists – Peace, Land and Bread – reflected that for which the Russian people yearned and the more radical Bolsheviks, led by Vladimir Lenin, Leon Trotsky, and Joseph Stalin, called for the overthrow of Kerensky's government and the end of Russia's contribution to the worldwide struggle – an interesting portent of their duplicity since they purportedly deplored tyranny. This second coup, the so-called October Revolution, brought the communists to power, and the new leaders soon ordered their troops to stop fighting and, to the horror of the Allies, subsequently opened peace talks with Germany.

American reaction to the end of what was perceived to be a tyrannical monarchy was initially favorable. President Wilson himself called it "wonderful and heartening." But America soon became alarmed by reports of communist brutalities, and when the Bolsheviks pulled out of the war and began negotiating with Germany there was an intensifying of fear and suspicion here at home. Once the Russo-German armistice was declared, Germany was able to reinforce its troops elsewhere; the world held its breath and waited for more carnage to come.

This was the atmosphere into which Andrew's article was published and from which the backlash sprang.

I discovered the first hate mail only two days after the article's publication when arriving home from checking out another in the seemingly endless list of rooming houses and cheap hotels where I hoped to find Rachel. The anonymous message had been shoved under the stairwell door. It was short and to the point:

> "Who the hell do you think you are? If you don't like this country then get the hell out of it. Go to Russia where you belong, you communist trash!"

Later in the week we received another, more vitriolic, note – this one brandishing crudely drawn skull and crossbones:

> "If you don't stand with us, then you stand with the communists who are trying to destroy this country. There's a word for people like you – TRAITOR... and we know what to do with traitors!"

"And I know what to do with this," Andrew said after reading it to me. He tore the unsigned sheet into several pieces and tossed it into the fire.

I tried to match his nonchalance. "Don't you think you should let the police see these notes?"

"No, Martha, I don't. I'm sorry if it frightens you but it's like I've said before – it's just smoke and mirrors with no substance. These people don't intend any real harm. They just need to vent their fear and frustration. All they do is point fingers and right now I happen to be the most readily available target. I wrote a fair and honest article and I'm willing to accept the consequences." He had moved to the window as he spoke, but came over to join me on the settee before continuing. "This letter-writing campaign won't last, you'll see. In a few days something or someone else will garner their attention and I'll be long forgotten as a potential menace."

I tried to share his optimistic attitude but couldn't quite shake the fear or the feeling that we, like the Reicherts and so many others, were now being watched.

The hate-mail continued to come, not a tidal wave but a persistent drizzle of bile and accusation. Some were brazenly shoved under the door of our apartment others came by way of the U.S. Post Office. It got to the point where I dreaded the mail's arrival and usually set it aside and waited for Andrew to do the honors.

On a chilly evening in early November my avoidance of the mail was to take an interesting turn.

I was putting the finishing touches on dinner, waiting for Andrew to get home. As had become my practice, I had put the small stack of letters beside his place at the table without even glancing through them.

Long before Andrew made his appearance at the kitchen door I knew he was home for the building itself heralded the comings and goings of the people within. There was the unmistakable sound of footsteps on the creaking stairs leading up to our flat. Some of them protested so loudly at being forced to bear their momentary burden that I knew exactly where Andrew was by virtue of the expression of annoyance unique to a particular stair. The protests persisted as he continued and I unconsciously charted his progress. In a moment he would be in the hallway, then crossing the parlor. I turned toward the kitchen doorway almost perfectly in sync with his arrival.

He leaned his lanky frame against the open door and sniffed appreciatively. "Smells great, Marty; when do we eat?"

"Just as soon as I can dish up the stew," I said with a smile. "Sit down and 'divest' yourself, as Gerta said to me today."

"I gather that was the word of the day," Andrew asked with a laugh. "That kid; seems like every day she has a new vocabulary word she wants to try out."

"Well, she's eager to learn. I think it's cute. She and the twins were up here most of the afternoon once I got home. Libby and Freeman were just looking for something to keep them from their homework but Gerta really wants to improve her English and I think she finds us a useful means to that end."

Andrew nodded and smiled before changing the subject. "Any luck today? You said the children came up after you got home. Where'd you go?"

"I tried several rescue missions on the lower East Side," I told him wearily, "but didn't have any luck."

"Sorry, honey." Andrew said simply while sorting through the mail. "Well, maybe this will cheer you up. Here's a letter for you."

"If it's not from my mother then I don't want to chance it; I've read enough hate mail to last a lifetime."

"It's from home," he observed slowly. "Hey, look at this. It's addressed to you as 'Miss Martha Pendleton,' and was sent to *The Sentinel*. Layton has corrected your name and sent it on."

He looked closely at the Post Office cancellation. "It was mailed right here in New York."

"Martha Pendleton? That doesn't make any sense; everyone in Tully's Cove knows we got married." I took the envelope from him and instantly was rocked by disbelief.

It was Rachel's childish scrawl staring up at me from the soiled and crumpled envelope!

II.

The human experience definitely is colored by the recurring theme of irony. I had nearly worn out my shoes in a futile attempt to track Rachel down and in the end all it took was a simple, one-page note:

> *"Dear Martha: I'm sorry to bother you but I don't know where else to turn. Gavin and I are living in New York but he is having trouble finding a job. I know I have no right to ask for help, but if you could see your way clear to send us a little money we would surely pay you back. Please send it to 'Mrs. Jones' in care of the Regent Hotel, 341 E.*

> Wilmington, New York, New York. Thank you, Martha. I hope to see you all again someday. Please tell Papa and Mama that I am all right.
> Sincerely, your sister, Rachel

Taking only enough time to assure that the stove was properly extinguished and to snatch our coats from their hooks at the top of the stairway, we were out the door and on our way to the nearest streetcar stop before the realities conferred by that single piece of paper had had a chance to hit us.

Rachel was safe.

Rachel was right here in New York.

Rachel was still with Gavin Marshall.

We climbed aboard the first streetcar that came along. I was still clutching Rachel's note in both hands, tears streaming down my face, and so Andrew took me by the elbow and ushered me to the nearest open seat. He then went up to the conductor to ascertain whether or not we were going remotely in the proper direction.

By the time he returned I had managed to stem the tide of emotion that had overwhelmed me and was searching my pockets in vain for a handkerchief. Why does it always seem that when you need them most they are never to be found?

"Here, honey," Andrew said, extracting a starched linen square from his own pocket and handing it to me.

I wiped my eyes and blew my nose. "Well? Are we on the right car?"

"We'll have to make several transfers," he explained, "but yes, we're heading in the right direction."

He put his arm around me and together we looked again at Rachel's note.

Other than her simple and straight-forward words there was no other information to be gleaned from that plain piece of paper. Neither of us knew where Wilmington

Avenue was. Neither of us had ever heard of the Regent Hotel. I didn't remember it being on my list of possibilities but drew the conclusion that it undoubtedly wasn't one of New York's finer hostelries.

That conclusion was confirmed as we made each of the necessary streetcar transfers. We traveled through a procession of run down neighborhoods, each a little more derelict than the one before, until finally being deposited at the corner of Wilmington and Darnell.

It was an area of saloons and mostly vacant storefronts; the smells and residue from nearby factories as oppressive as the darkness that oozed menacingly close to the respite afforded by an occasional street lamp and the oases of light spilling out from a few lit windows. These were our guides as we made our way toward 341 E. Wilmington and the Regent Hotel.

When we finally reached our destination, I was relieved to see that it wasn't as bad as the image conjured up in my mind's eye. The hotel was in a stretch of Wilmington where it appeared that most of the buildings were occupied – and occupied by something other than saloons at that. There was a faded striped awning over the front door and a threadbare rug with a faintly visible script rendering of "The Regent Hotel" greeted us at the front stoop. We stepped into a shabby but acceptably clean lobby area and walked over to the clerk's desk where a clean shaven elderly man stood waiting.

"Evenin' folks," he said with a smile. "Be needin' a place to stay?"

"No sir," Andrew began. "We're looking for someone."

"We're looking for my sister," I interjected impatiently. "She sent me a letter saying she was staying here. She said to ask for 'Mrs. Jones.'"

My heart was pounding so hard it made my ears throb; this just couldn't be another dead end.

The old gentleman smiled. "Well, of course. I can see the family resemblance now that you say it."

I thought the observation categorized him as a bit daft but didn't bother to take the time to contradict him.

"Is she here?" Andrew asked.

"Why yes, she's here. And I'm surely glad you've come. She ain't been feeling at all well since her husband got called away. I've been plumb worried about her, but she wouldn't let me call no doctor."

"Will you take us to her?" My voice was barely a whisper and for a moment I wasn't sure I had made myself heard.

The old man paused and plucked his lower lip with a gnarled index finger. "You goin' to take her with you?" he asked pensively. "I don't mean to be hard-hearted, but if you're goin' to take her home someone's got to settle her account. I been carryin' them for two weeks as it is."

Andrew nudged his way back into the conversation. "We understand, Mr..."

"Blanchard; Edwin Blanchard's my name."

"We understand, Mr. Blanchard. And don't worry; we'll make sure Mrs. Jones's bill is taken care of."

"I'd surely appreciate that. I been wonderin' what I was goin' to do if no one come for her. She's a real nice lady but I got expenses, you understand."

He had come around from behind the counter and was leading the way to the stairway beyond. Andrew held my hand tightly as we matched the extremely slow pace of our elderly host, his arthritic gait taking each stair as a separate obstacle to be painfully negotiated as he pulled himself upward using the handrail for leverage. Andrew told me later that I nearly squeezed the life out of his hand during that arduous trek, but I was only aware of the almost irresistible urge to literally push the old gentleman onward.

We came at last to Rachel's room and Mr. Blanchard knocked loudly on the chipped, brittle looking door.

"Missuz Jones," he called out. "Missuz Jones, you all right?"

There was no response from within and my heart sank at the thought that Rachel might have slipped out to avoid paying her bill.

"Missuz Jones?"

There was movement within the room and in a moment the door opened a crack.

It was Rachel.

Her hair was limp and held back from her face with a simple clip, her complexion pasty, and dark smudges of weariness lay under her eyes but she never had looked more wonderful to me.

I didn't even notice at first that she had reached the late stages of pregnancy.

"Martha," Rachel stammered in wide-eyed disbelief. "Martha, is it really you?"

"Yes, honey. Yes, it's really me."

She smiled weakly and then, as if on cue, slumped into my arms in a dead faint.

III.

Once we got Rachel home Andrew went out again almost immediately in order to send word to my parents that we had found her. Neither of us knew much about medical matters – and virtually nothing about pregnancy – so before leaving me on my own with Rachel he summoned Mrs. Reichert to my side. She bustled into the room the picture of efficiency and maternal concern. Already aware of my quest to find my little sister after her "elopement," we simply explained that Rachel's husband had been called away and that, in her current state, she hadn't yet been able to tell us how to contact him. Katrina accepted our words without question and Rachel immediately was absorbed into her capacious, loving heart.

Mrs. Reichert insisted that Rachel be moved to the room once occupied by the two Reichert sons now serving overseas. It was the only logical place for Andrew and I had no extra bed. Since the Reichert sleeping quarters were on the same floor as our flat, it was an easy matter for me to walk out our back door and across the hallway to Rachel's room, gaining access by way of an adjacent door used by the Reicherts when enroute to the privy out back.

I've never had much patience with those who are ill, not being blessed with what Mother called a good "bedside manner." Perhaps because of my father's impatience with weakness – and Rachel's infuriating tendency to turn a hangnail into a symptom of life-threatening illness – I never had been one to cosset or placate the weak and infirm. So great was my overwhelming relief that she was safe, however, that this time, once Rachel was securely tucked into bed in the Reichert's spare room and subject to the gentle ministrations of Katrina and her mother-in-law, I hovered, clucked, and coddled with the best of them. There was nothing I wouldn't do for my little sister. I made no demands, asked no questions, passed no judgments. She was safe and that was all that mattered.

Over the weeks that followed I was to spend most of my waking hours at Rachel's bedside, waiting, watching, and trying to keep up her spirits. She was lethargic and malnourished and, in spite of their attempts at optimism, I could tell that Mrs. Reichert and the doctor we consulted were concerned both for Rachel and for her unborn child.

The doctor's first order was that Rachel was to stay in bed until the baby came. She did so without complaint, which didn't exactly surprise me except for the fact that the old Rachel would have enjoyed it more. For the most part she laid still and blank-faced regardless of what went on around her, sometimes drifting off into restless sleep that found her twisting, turning, and plucking fearfully at the linens and quilts that covered her. All the females of the family gravitated toward her room in an effort to keep her company and an assortment of rocking chairs, sewing baskets, books, and the like were quickly strewn about. Whatever household tasks could be transplanted into a sick room were soon being done within sight of Rachel's bed and the room usually was full of cheerful chatter and contented domesticity.

But Rachel didn't seem to see or hear much of what went on around her and when she spoke the subject invariably was Gavin Marshall.

"Have you heard from Gavin yet," she asked one morning while picking at the breakfast tray I had just brought in.

"No, honey, not yet," I responded blandly, hoping her inquiry would go no further.

She looked up from the tray with more clarity than I had seen on her face for quite some time. Her voice was accusatory. "You never even left word for him, did you?"

"Now, honey, don't get upset..."

"Martha, you've got to send for him," she insisted with a vehemence that made a vein on her forehead bulge slightly. "He'll come looking for me and won't be able to find me! He's coming back... I know he's coming back."

She looked up at me in pathetic desperation.

"He'll come looking for me and won't be able to find me..." she repeated in a voice heavy with worry and doubt.

I set the tray aside, sat down on the bed and put my arm around her. She lay against me, trembling weakly.

"He'll come looking for me, Martha" she murmured listlessly into my shoulder.

"Don't worry, Rachel," I cooed, smoothing her hair and laying my cheek against the top of her head. "I'll go to the Regent and leave word with the landlord. Don't worry, honey. I'll do it today."

I would just as soon have ridden a horse naked down Fifth Avenue, Lady Godiva-style, making a public declaration of our private disgrace than go back to the Regent Hotel and leave word for Gavin Marshall! I had no doubt that he would never return. Whatever gentleness he may have harbored for Rachel – and I stress the word *may* – surely had been supplanted by his innate drive for conquest, freedom, and self-preservation. No, I was sure that as far as Gavin Marshall was concerned Rachel Pendleton was nothing more than an unfortunate incident and certainly not his responsibility. But I sequestered Lady Godiva and did as I had promised. And while I was out I sent another telegram to my parents – this time asking my mother to come as soon as possible.

Mother must have left almost the moment she received my request for in a little less than two days she was at Rachel's side. She said nothing about my father's reaction to the telegram and I didn't ask. I trusted that his resolve had softened sufficiently that her desire to rush to Rachel's bedside had been met with little, if any, resistance. Whatever the case, I was vastly relieved to have her with us. Mrs. Reichert, and all the Reichert ladies for that matter, had been wonderfully supportive and helpful but no words can adequately describe how it felt to see Mother sitting on Rachel's bed, holding her tightly and crying softly into her precious little girl's hair.

I heaved a long, cathartic sigh knowing that now no matter what lay ahead for Rachel, we would face it together as a family.

IV.

As is true of most newspapermen, Medford Potter loved to stir things up. As a result he was thrilled with the reaction to and attention afforded by Andrew's article on the patriot vigilante groups. In fact, he was down-right jubilant and gave Andrew several other high profile stories in order to capitalize on his potentially fleeting celebrity.

Even I was to reap the benefits of Andrew's good standing with his employer as his good fortune trickled down to me in the form of another assignment.

My maiden voyage on the sea of big city journalism had been reasonably successful. Mr. Potter had turned my article over to a seasoned veteran who had done some rather dramatic (and painful!) editing before the piece was published, along with the equally-edited sidebar article I had written about a young woman working in the rail yards. Both articles had carried my by-line, however, and had been preceded by a brief introduction – what I sardonically called a "disclaimer" – explaining that the author also was a new member of the wartime workforce.

I carefully cut all three out of the newspaper and added them to the scrapbook I had begun in Tully's Cove when my very first "Around the Town" was published on that fateful Sunday a year before.

Still relegated to feature stories, my second assignment was an interview with Elsie Janis, a tremendously popular singer of the day – if I could get an interview, that is. Like the dynamic Al Jolson, Miss Janis spent much of World War I entertaining the troops – quite literally while the war raged around her as she insisted on taking her entourage directly to the men doing the fighting. As a result of her tireless efforts on behalf of the troops overseas, Miss Janis was known as "The Sweetheart of the AEF" and one of her most famous songs, "Apres La Guerre" ("After the War"), became a standard for soldier and civilian alike, capturing the romanticized hope for life and love once peace was restored. She was an increasingly popular commodity, and a hot property for newspapers and magazines across the country.

Miss Janis was scheduled to depart from New York City aboard the USS Chesapeake for another tour abroad and, from what Andrew could ascertain for me, it was her practice to meet with selected members of the press just once prior to departures. The trick was going to be ranking among the select. Mr. Potter had given me a press pass but other than that I was on my own. I knew that if I was to get an interview with her I was going to have to be assertive and perhaps even a bit cunning.

I didn't hold out much hope.

The ship was an enormous monolith at least 700 feet long. Its massive hull was painted a leaden grey up to the point where portholes indicated the more public portion of the vessel. At that point it took on a rather jaunty appearance, coated in glossy white paint with equally-glossy red trim and decorated for departure with red-white-and-blue banners and bunting. The ship's smokestacks towered majestically above its moorings, and the multileveled, open-air structure designed to facilitate the loading of passengers, baggage, and cargo looked as inconsequential as twigs by comparison. Each successively lower tier extended from a parallel level of the adjacent brick building housing the shipping line offices and through which passengers, baggage, and cargo were processed and readied for departure.

The landward side of the building was busy enough as other businesses and shipping lines up and down the street went about their daily routine, but once you passed through the red brick structure and onto the appropriate level on the loading side, you crossed over into a dizzying maelstrom. The entire area was a crush of activity as passengers and well-wishers mingled, and workers of every description prepared to get underway.

This particular departure undoubtedly was even more hectic than usual for in addition to carrying a few miscellaneous passengers and the "Sweetheart of the AEF," the Chesapeake was being used as a troop ship for this particular Atlantic crossing. As a result, the pier was teeming with uniform-clad men moving inexorably toward the ship and family members vying for position in order to get one last glimpse of their beloved husband, sweetheart, son, or brother. I stood momentarily adrift in the midst of this emotional vortex as it eddied and swirled around me; the cacophony of sound washing over me so vibrant and alive it seemed almost physically tangible.

Since I was there on my own – and especially since I had never seen the likes before – it was a relief to finally catch sight of a cordoned off area plainly designated for the press. Pleased with this modicum of progress, I took my place among my fellows, drew in a slow, cleansing breath, and concentrated on finding my journalistic sea legs.

It wasn't long before the press area was full of reporters, all of whom undoubtedly shared my goal of getting on board to speak directly with Miss Janis. Several cast quizzical, if not outright brash, looks my way as I was the only female in the group. Their collective demeanor exuded maturity and confidence, a few being the perfect caricature of the big city reporter with slicked-back hair, slightly rumpled suit, dusty shoes, and crumpled hat. By contrast – although confidence was a commodity I definitely lacked – I thought I looked quite fresh and hoped that that might actually weigh in my favor when the time came to select representatives to go aboard.

As lines of servicemen continued to make their way up the gangplank, a man wearing the uniform and insignia of the ship's crew wormed his way down and, after straightening his hat and checking the ornate buttons at his throat, began making his way over to where we stood.

"Good morning," he said, his tone formal and extremely businesslike. "I have a list here of the reporters selected to come aboard to speak with Miss Janis."

My heart sank for I knew I couldn't possibly be on any list.

He began reading names. "Peter Maxwell, William Jeffers, Gideon Samuels..."

The people being called edged their way from among us and showed him their identification.

"C.J. Rosen, Jonathan Edwards..."

Just as I started to back away someone hooked arms with me and I was propelled deliberately and forcefully forward.

"I'm C.J. Rosen – Carlotta," the woman at my elbow shot into my ear, "and you're with me."

She stood at least a head taller than I, a striking woman of about forty, impeccably dressed, with a mass of jet-black hair twisted becomingly around her head topped by an equally becoming hat of the latest design. There was an air of flamboyance about her that was distinct and appealing.

We paused in front of the uniformed gentleman and she flashed him her press card. "This is Miss..."

"...Carlton..." I supplied quietly.

"Miss Carlton," she continued, hardly missing a beat. "She's with me."

She brushed past him without waiting for a response and we were soon making our way up the gangplank. If the officer had thought to object he obviously concluded it would be to no avail and surrendered without a fight.

"Thank you," I said in breathless disbelief as she released my arm and we made our way upward. "I can't believe I'm actually going on board."

She was smiling coyly at the uniformed men gallantly stepping aside for her. "You are most welcome, my dear," she began, "Quite frankly, I was amazed to see another feminine face in the all-male bastion we appropriately call the bull pen."

"Is that why you brought me with you?"

"Precisely," she replied with a broad smile. "Simply put, pet, we ladies of the press have to stick together."

Another uniformed officer waited at the top of the gangplank and as soon as the group of reporters was assembled he led the way up to the first class deck and into Miss Janis's state room. Ushered into a compact but comfortable sitting room, each of us took the seat indicated by the Purser.

"You're looking a little green," Miss Rosen observed tactfully. "I take it this is one of your first interviews?"

I nodded.

"Don't worry about it," she assured me quietly. "I guarantee it gets easier. This time around let the rest of us do the work and just jot down whatever sounds useful from the questions that come up. Your job this time is to sit there working at looking confident and just a little bit cocky."

She winked conspiratorially as Miss Janis came into the room and the interview began.

Carlotta was wonderful. She obviously was known to the popular singer and was allotted more than her share of questions. Miss Janis also took notice of me and Carlotta graciously introduced me as her colleague and protégé. It was a lively half hour conversation during which I rather frantically took notes and never once thought about looking confident, let alone "slightly cocky."

All too soon we had left the ship and were back on the pier.

"Well, what did you think," Carlotta asked, leaning gracefully against the railing and lighting a cigarette.

"That was fascinating," I replied with a cathartic sigh. "Thank you so much for taking me under your wing. I never would have gotten aboard if you hadn't said I was with you."

"It was my pleasure. As I said, we ladies of the press have to stick together."

Carlotta smirked around the long, leisurely draught she took on her cigarette. She didn't seem in a hurry to move on and so I turned back toward the ship for one final look at the unique mixture of patriotism and commerce about to head out to sea.

All along the ship's railings, at every passenger level, people were lined up three and four rows deep waving and calling futilely into the chaotic symphony of sound washing over us. It was bittersweet to survey the sea of faces both onboard and along the walkways on either side of me. Mixtures of sorrow, love, and anxiety along the pier looked upward into youthful faces full of excitement, patriotism, and only a trace of fear.

I searched the seemingly endless array of faces for that of Miss Janis and her entourage for I imagined that she certainly would be there along the upper deck joining in the celebratory farewell salute to the men going off to war.

After surveying the throng for several minutes my eyes did at last find something familiar upon which to rest but it wasn't Miss Janis to whom they seemed drawn like magnets to metal.

Standing among the civilians on the first class deck, obviously alone even while completely surrounded by people, was none other than Jacob Collier!

A sharp intake of breath caught in my throat and I stood rooted to the spot feeling as if I were about to hyperventilate. My eyes were riveted to Jacob's face as a rush of emotion threatened to knock me off my feet. I couldn't believe he was still in the United States. It had been months. Where had he been all this time? What had he been doing? Why had he never contacted me? The emotions I experienced while recovering from Jocelyn's assault surged up with startling clarity – anger, betrayal, loss, desolation. And he had been here the entire time! How fatuous it had been to believe that I was anything more to Jacob Collier than an amusing, childish distraction! Obviously my feelings had never been reciprocated – feelings I foolishly had believed to be love. If I had meant anything to him, anything at all, he wouldn't have let me pass from his life so easily.

This unexpected and alarming onslaught was almost instantaneously consumed by feelings of disloyalty to Andrew and a tidal wave of guilt – even as my heart cried out to Jacob to see me one last time, to return my gaze, to know that I was there.

But his eyes never wavered, were never drawn to mine, and the mournful face never changed expression.

Miss Rosen turned to leave.

"What is it," she asked, looking back at me when I didn't fall into step beside her.

"Nothing," I stammered, my face growing hot from a sudden flush of shame and embarrassment. "I just thought I saw someone I knew."

"One of the soldiers? Not surprising," she observed sardonically. "Men all look pretty much the same once you put them in uniform. It's a wonder the appeal isn't lessened as a result but somehow it isn't. The female of the species seems to lose all sense of proportion when a uniformed male is in the vicinity."

She took another long, leisurely drag on her cigarette. "If you want to stay that's fine, if not then we can share a cab back uptown if you'd like."

"I don't know," I replied vaguely, forcing my eyes to turn from Jacob's face and dragging my mind back to the present. "I suppose it's too late to do anything about it now."

She exhaled a cloud of smoke more gracefully feminine than I would have thought possible and lightly touched my arm. "Then shall we hail a cab? You and I have a lot to discuss. You know, it just struck me that it's about time I took on an apprentice."

We began walking just as the ship's triumphant horns bellowed out final notice of its departure. Like powerful hands taking me by the shoulders in order to shake some sense into me, the intense sound pinned me with an accusation of disloyalty that reverberated in my bones.

Feeling ashamed and humiliated by the faithless emotions rising like bile in my throat, I paused at the entrance to the building, fighting the urge to run back to the railing for one last look.

C.J. paused as well, dropping her cigarette.

The smoldering ash held me transfixed for a moment. I stepped toward C.J. and ground it beneath the sole of my shoe.

We turned and walked away.

ABOUT THE AUTHOR

Lorna Brockway Lieske is an award-winning educator who has taught American History and U.S. Government for more than 25 years. Although she'll tell you she found her calling in the classroom, Lorna has been a story-teller from childhood – spending summer evenings in Tucson, Arizona weaving tales with her sister for neighborhood adventures they billed as "Story-Come-True." Lorna's love of story-telling followed her into the classroom, where she has written educational short stories and plays for her students on topics ranging from the French and Indian War and Westward Expansion to the Bill of Rights, the U.S. legal system, and basic economics. This is her first full-length novel but – although historical themes are a natural fit – she currently has two other novels in the works, one in each of her other favorite genres, mystery and dystopian science fiction. Lorna lives in Michigan with the love of her life, her husband Richard, and their dog, an irrepressible Shiba Inu named Riley.

Made in the USA
Lexington, KY
11 November 2016